RULES OF BATTLE

"You have just made a grave tactical error, little one,"
Khamed said softly. "By entering his camp, you force
your enemy to act. He now has no choice but to engage
you in battle, a battle from which . . ." he drew her to
him, pressing her close ". . . he cannot—and will not—
retreat."

Eudora could feel the heat from his body through the
thin gown she wore. A tremor went through her at the
knowledge of his intent. She felt his hand at the back of
her neck.

He entwined his fingers in her hair and pulled her head
back, kissed the hollow of her throat, then claimed her
lips. His kiss was full of passion and need.

She felt the last of her will slipping away. Her body was
responding shamelessly, yet all she could do was stand
still and wait . . .

HEARTFIRE ROMANCES

SWEET TEXAS NIGHTS   (2610, $3.75)
by Vivian Vaughan

Meg Britton grew up on the railroads, working proudly at her father's side. Nothing was going to stop them from setting the rails clear to Silver Creek, Texas—certainly not some crazy prospector. As Meg set out to confront the old coot, she planned her strategy with cool precision. But soon she was speechless with shock. For instead of a harmless geezer, she found a boldly handsome stranger whose determination matched her own.

CAPTIVE DESIRE   (2612, $3.75)
by Jane Archer

Victoria Malone fancied herself a great adventuress, but being kidnapped was too much excitement for even Victoria! Especially when her arrogant kidnapper thought she was part of Red Duke's outlaw gang. Trying to convince the overbearing, handsome stranger that she had been an innocent bystander when the stagecoach was robbed, proved futile. But when he thought he could maker her confess by crushing her to his warm, broad chest, by caressing her with his strong, capable hands, Victoria was willing to admit to anything. . . .

LAWLESS ECSTASY   (2613, $3.75)
by Susan Sackett

Abra Beaumont could spot a thief a mile away. After all, her father was once one of the best. But he'd been on the right side of the law for years now, and she wasn't about to let a man like Dash Thorne lead him astray with some wild plan for stealing the Tear of Allah, the world's most fabulous ruby. Dash was just the sort of man she most distrusted—sophisticated, handsome, and altogether too sure of his considerable charm. Abra shivered at the devilish gleam in his blue eyes and swore he would need more than smooth kisses and skilled caresses to rob her of her virtue . . . and much more than sweet promises to steal her heart!

Available wherever paperbacks are sold, or order direct from the Publisher. Send cover price plus 50¢ per copy for mailing and handling to Zebra Books, Dept. 3327, 475 Park Avenue South, New York, N.Y. 10016. Residents of New York, New Jersey and Pennsylvania must include sales tax. DO NOT SEND CASH.

FIRES IN THE NIGHT

JUDITH HILL

ZEBRA BOOKS
KENSINGTON PUBLISHING CORP.

ZEBRA BOOKS

are published by

Kensington Publishing Corp.
475 Park Avenue South
New York, NY 10016

First printing: February, 1991

Printed in the United States of America

Chapter One

French Army Headquarters
Ghardaïa, Algeria, 1902

"I'm sorry, Mademoiselle. What you ask is impossible." Lieutenant Henri du Bois stepped away from his desk. He tugged at the hem of his khaki blouse to remove an unflattering bulge of cloth around his waist. As he'd hoped, the gesture drew his visitor's attention away from his face and down the length of his chest.

Eudora Morrel's green eyes skipped without interest over the polished brass buttons and rainbow-hued campaign ribbons dotting the uniform's front. She was not impressed. Not by the young officer's paradeground appearance—and not by his words.

"Surely, Lieutenant, there must be a way." She rose from her chair and smiled demurely.

Carefully du Bois scrutinized the woman standing before him. A trifle slim and petite for his own tastes, she was, however, well proportioned. Hers was not the fragile, porcelain-doll beauty prized by women. Her flawless complexion was unfashionably olive-skinned, her high cheekbones too exotic, and her lips too full. What Eudora Morrel possessed was the sensual type of beauty fully appreciated only by a man. Still, he shook his head firmly.

5

"My hands are tied. Army regulations are quite specific. The presence of a civilian on a military transport is forbidden. I cannot allow you to travel with the supply caravan I am leading to Ouargla. And if you are thinking of hiring a native guide, I must warn you . . . no caravan may leave Ghardaïa without travel papers signed by an officer of the Bureau des Affaires Indigènes. Neither I nor any other officer here will sign those papers for you." He stepped closer and reached for her gloved hand. "Please understand, Mademoiselle Morrel, the open desert is no place for a woman." He brought her hand to his lips. "Especially a woman such as yourself."

Undaunted by his refusal, Eudora purposely misunderstood the comment. "I assure you, Lieutenant, I am not as delicate as you seem to think." She withdrew her hand politely, wanting nothing in her actions to betray her annoyance. "Need I remind you, I have already survived a three-hundred-mile trek across the desert—by a means of transportation which defies the use of that word in its definition!" She shuddered at the vivid memory of the railroad journey from Algiers to Ghardaïa and arched her back to flex the still stiff muscles.

How the slight movement strained the taut linen fabric across her breasts was not a detail lost to Lieutenant du Bois. His eyes widened. "I assure you, Mademoiselle, my comment was not meant as a disparagement. Certainly your very presence in this office is a testament to your fortitude. But traveling in a closed railroad car is quite different from crossing the desert on camelback. Do you have any idea of the dangers you would face? Brutal heat, unbearable thirst, sunstroke . . ."

". . . Dust storms, snakes, and scorpions." Fighting to conceal her irritation, Eudora finished the sentence. "I have read all about your desert and its dangers, Lieutenant. I will *not* be intimidated."

"Did you also read then about the Reguibat?" Du Bois picked up a pencil from his desk and began to toy with it.

"Reguibat?" Eudora looked at him in confusion.

"Yes, Mademoiselle. Reguibat." He grimaced, pronouncing the word as if it were a vile taste in his mouth. "They are a fierce tribe of desert outlaws who have roamed the Sahara for centuries. Their sole purpose is to raid and terrorize any caravan which has the misfortune to cross their territory. In seventy years of occupation we have been unable to stop them. Their raids are long-range, well planned, and too well executed. These fiends possess a level of skill and endurance our soldiers are simply unable to match."

The pencil snapped in his fingers. Embarrassed by the display of emotion, he colored fiercely and turned to place the pieces on the desk top. With his composure regained, he continued. "Rest assured, Mademoiselle Morrel, there is no greater threat to a caravan than a Reguibat attack. And if a white woman were to fall into their hands . . ." His eyes darted from her face as he cleared his throat nervously. "Suffice it to say, death would be a most welcome alternative."

Sure that his words were designed to frighten her, Eudora looked at him calmly. "Even if these . . . outlaws . . . are the formidable threat you describe . . ." she coyly lowered her eyes, "surely, in *your* company a woman would have nothing to fear?"

She opened her purse and withdrew a lacy handkerchief. "And in regard to your regulations . . . I know for a fact that you have already made *one* exception—for a reporter from a Paris newspaper." She snapped the bag closed, smiling at the look of surprise which crossed his face. "I was told at the hotel that he would be traveling with you."

"I'd hardly call the sensationalistic tabloid he works for a newspaper, Mademoiselle." Du Bois snorted in disgust. "But you are correct. Monsieur Sabatin will be accompanying us to Ouargla. However . . ." He stroked his thin mustache in agitation. "The decision was not mine. The power wielded by the press and my superiors'

7

desire to create favorable public opinion made the exception—not I!"

Inwardly Eudora groaned. The reporter had been her ace in the hole. But at twenty-seven she was hardly a naive ingénue ignorant of the ways of men and women. Knowing she might have one option left, she brought the handkerchief up to her gown's décolletage. While fixing du Bois with a pleading look, she slipped her fingers through the opening of the gauzy chiffon overlay to dab delicately at the perspiration beading between her breasts.

"Lieutenant, please. It is imperative that I reach my father before he departs with the expedition." She held her breath and hoped fervently he wouldn't ask her why.

Through her dark lashes she watched as du Bois's eyes followed the scrap of lace. When they lingered on the site long after the ministration was completed, Eudora released the breath with a deep sigh. If she was to succeed in talking her father into resigning from Foureau's expedition, she had to reach Ouargla before he departed. She crushed the handkerchief into a tight ball and forced herself to finish what she had started. "I would be forever in your debt . . ."

Du Bois stood in silence, shifting his weight from one foot to the other.

Anxiously Eudora waited. Would he interpret her carefully chosen words as a willingness to trade favors? And if so, how could she later avoid honoring such a debasing agreement?

"If I may be allowed to intercede on the mademoiselle's behalf . . ."

Du Bois's head snapped toward the doorway.

Eudora followed suit, swiftly appraising the voice's owner—a tall, handsome man of perhaps twenty-five. Close-cropped brown hair topped the head now gallantly bowed toward her.

"Permit me to introduce myself. I am Pierre Sabatin from *L'Étoile*. And you are . . . ?"

8

Taken aback by the reporter's sudden intrusion into what had been a private conversation, she took a moment to answer. "Eudora. Eudora Morrel." She extended her hand. "My father is Louis Morrel—one of the civilians accompanying the Foureau/Lemy expedition."

"But of course!" Smiling charmingly, Sabatin took her hand and raised it to his lips. "It is indeed a pleasure!"

Out of the corner of her eye Eudora could see du Bois's face.

Again stroking his mustache, he now appeared to be chewing on the inside of his cheek.

She smiled a slow, secret smile of amusement. It would appear Monsieur Sabatin was being viewed as a rival! As her mind raced to find a way to put that realization to use, she heard du Bois speak.

"Monsieur . . ."

His cold, abrasive voice immediately drew Sabatin's attention.

"Lieutenant! Forgive me! My mind was elsewhere!"

"So I noticed!" Du Bois muttered. Saluting stiffly, he ignored the man's outstretched hand. "I am Lieutenant du Bois."

Embarrassed by his blatant rudeness, Eudora dropped her gaze to the stone floor. Du Bois was such a pompous fool!

Sabatin, however, seemed unaffected by the snub. Without a trace of self-consciousness, he lowered his hand and stuck it into his waistcoat pocket. "As I started to say, Lieutenant . . . though I have been assigned to report on the launching of the expedition in Ouargla— and while news of that noble effort *is* anxiously awaited back home—I can't help but think what a wonderful human interest story this would make!"

Eudora cocked her head. Where was the reporter headed with his roundabout, somewhat long-winded preface?

As if sensing her concern, Sabatin shot her a quick glance—accompanied by a conspiratorial wink. Without

9

hesitation he continued. "I ask you, Lieutenant, to consider for a moment the story as I see it. On one hand we have Mademoiselle Morrel, a lovely . . . if you will . . . damsel in distress."

As he turned and again bowed to her, Eudora caught sight of his eyes. She detected an unmistakable gleam of mischief in their tawny depths. He turned back to du Bois.

"Helpless and alone, she has come to *you*, Lieutenant, for comfort and aid. But on the other hand, we have the army's regulations, which forbid her to accompany you. I ask you—which scenario sheds the more favorable light on our gallant occupying forces, and on you? Will you abandon her in her hour of need? Or will you be her *preux chevalier*—the valiant knight who provides her protection and safe passage through this hostile and foreign land?"

Eudora looked at Sabatin speculatively. He was certainly articulate—but had he convinced the lieutenant?

Sabatin met her gaze confidently. He grinned and tilted his head toward du Bois.

Turning, she clasped her hand over her mouth to muffle a giggle.

Like a strutting peacock, du Bois puffed out his chest with self-importance. His face twisted in concentration, and he paced behind his desk, his gaze fixed on the floor.

Eudora looked back at Sabatin, who suddenly seemed to be fascinated with a map of Algeria hanging on the far wall. She returned her attention to du Bois and waited.

After several minutes—and an equal number of passes behind the desk—he finally stopped. His face smug with self-righteous importance, he squared his shoulders and stepped into the center of the room. Once again Eudora found her hand in his.

"What right do I have to thwart your efforts when you have already journeyed so far?" he asked, his voice ringing with condescension. "You shall see your father, Mademoiselle!" He lowered his head and kissed her hand.

10

Across the room Sabatin smiled. When he had received this assignment he had been less than happy. Fernand Foureau's plan to map out a railroad route across the Sahara to the Sudan did not enjoy popular support in France. The public refused to forget the earlier attempts which had ended in failure. The first attempt had merely been abandoned when supplies ran out. But the second had met with complete tragedy. The brutal murders of its commander, Paul François Flatters, and seventy-six of the eighty-eight men who had accompanied him, was a bitter defeat. Even after two decades, the rancor remained. Foureau's was a dead dream, and any story Sabatin wrote would be buried on a back page with the rest of the obituaries.

But now he could see the headlines, front page and under his byline: *Devoted Daughter Defies Desert to Bid Adieu.* It was just the type of romantic adventure his readers loved. And if there were two things in this world Pierre Sabatin knew, the first was what would sell newspapers. The second was beautiful women.

He glanced across the room. His initial impression was confirmed. Politely enduring du Bois's ingratiating fawning was one of the most entrancing women he had ever seen. Story or no, the chance to have Eudora Morrel's company on the week-long journey to Ouargla was worth the effort.

Suddenly a pair of smiling emerald eyes met his. Sabatin grinned. She knew where the credit for du Bois' *volte-face* truly lay. With a deep bow he acknowledged her unspoken gratitude.

Eudora brushed angrily at the swarm of flies buzzing about her head. Spending her last afternoon in Ghardaïa sitting in the hotel's open air café had not been her idea. It was hot. She was tired. And certainly the barrage of insects attracted by the glass of warm *limonade* on the rattan table before her was doing nothing to improve her

11

mood. Neither was her companion's choice of a topic for conversation.

"Your opinion is based on a limited exposure to the street Arab alone," Pierre Sabatin explained with a patient smile.

Eudora fought to stifle the unladylike sound erupting at the back of her throat. She had just spent the better part of two hours with Lieutenant du Bois's slovenly supply sergeant. Assigned the task of purchasing the camels and supplies she would need for the journey to Ouargla, the ferretlike man had insisted not only upon her accompanying him to the marketplace, but upon giving her a most thorough tour of it.

Street Arabs, indeed! Thanks to Sergeant Cheval's efforts she had seen enough hawking peddlers, veiled women, and black ragamuffin children to last her a lifetime. She could still smell the stench of unwashed bodies, of urine emanating from the ditch that served the city as a sewage system . . .

"Mademoiselle? Are you listening?" Sabatin's voice broke into her thoughts.

She nodded and forced an expression of polite interest.

"Now then, as I was saying . . ." Sabatin continued. "The nomad of the desert . . . he's an entirely different breed."

Though she was in no mood for his sermonizing, Eudora held her tongue. Secretly she even smiled.

Pierre Sabatin was unlike anyone she had ever known. From the moment she'd met him in du Bois's office, the lanky reporter had intrigued her. Obviously educated and well traveled, he nonetheless seemed to retain a childlike curiosity about life. Apparently, to his thinking, the simple act of living gave all men worth. She knew he found Algeria and its people fascinating and romantic. And because he did, he simply could not understand her disdain for her surroundings.

"I think I should warn you, Monsieur Sabatin. You are wasting your time. My opinion of this place and these

12

people will not be changed by words, no matter how eloquent."

"Please! Hear me out. The desert tribes are not like the rabble of the cities. They are a proud people with a different air about them—an air of superiority. They possess rare physical strength and courage. Theirs is a code of behavior which dates back to the age of chivalry."

"The noble savage!" Eudora rolled her eyes and reached for her fan. Snapping open the white silk blades, she awaited the inevitable monologue.

Sabatin grinned enthusiastically. He'd either missed her sarcasm or chosen to ignore it. "That's it exactly! Their way of life exists in defiance of both nature and the passage of time. They are governed by fundamental values and laws . . . 'an eye for an eye' . . . 'to the victor belong the spoils' . . . laws which have enabled them to survive and live in harmony with an ungodly hostile environment as no other people on earth do!"

Eudora slammed the fan closed against the palm of her hand. For the sake of politeness, and because she genuinely liked this young rake who had befriended her, she had listened without comment. But his last statement exhausted her patience.

"How can you sit there and extol their virtues? According to Lieutenant du Bois, these people are nothing more than murdering savages. Yet even he seems to describe them with grudging admiration. I don't understand it! What *is* it about these desert outlaws which seems to evoke such respect?"

Sabatin looked at her in amazement. The answer was obviously so clear to him he could not fathom her inability to see it as well. "Why . . . their passion, and their commitment to their way of life. Without these qualities living is nothing more than existing."

Eudora shook her head. "I don't understand."

Sabatin studied her carefully. A look almost of pity entered his eyes. "Perhaps you will . . . someday. It is one of those things one can't put into words unless one

13

experiences it." Suddenly his expression changed, and with it his voice. Smiling brightly, he raised his glass. "To the success of our journey."

Eudora moved to take up her own glass. She stopped short at the sight of the seething black mass on its rim. "To our journey," she echoed weakly, wrinkling her nose in disgust.

Sabatin grinned. Chinking his glass against hers on the table, he then drained it and set it down. "You know, Mademoiselle . . . I didn't hear the first part of your conversation with du Bois. Why is it you are so intent upon seeing your father? Or did you even provide our fearless leader with an explanation?"

Eudora laughed at the sobriquet he'd given to du Bois and smiled coyly. As charming as Sabatin was, she was not about to reveal her true purpose.

"Well, Mademoiselle? Are you going to satisfy my reporter's curiosity?" His eyes met and held hers with unrelenting persistence.

Realizing he would not be put off, Eudora acknowledged partial defeat. She would have to satisfy him with at least a semblance of truth. After all, without Sabatin's intervention, du Bois would never have changed his mind.

"I believe my father's taking part in this expedition is a grave mistake. A man of his age should be retiring and enjoying his last years—not traipsing across the desert on what he thinks is going to be some bold, romantic adventure!" She straightened in her chair and shaded her eyes with her hand in order to look him in the eye. "That is why I must reach Ouargla, Monsieur. I intend to convince my father to return to France with me."

Pierre Sabatin sat in surprised silence. Never would he have guessed that this was her reason for wanting to see her father. Had she really followed him across France, across the sea, and now across the desert, to fetch him home like a misbehaving schoolboy? In his mind a profoundly different story began to take form: *Daring*

Daughter Travels Desert to Denounce Father's Folly.

Sabatin's curiosity was piqued. It was incomprehensible that Louis Morrel, one of France's most respected engineers and a professor at Paris's prestigious École Polytechnique, should be the subject of his daughter's recriminations. What right could she possibly have to question his decisions? And what type of welcome could she expect when she did reach Ouargla?

After a long pause, he finally spoke. "What were your father's reasons for wanting to go? Surely he discussed his decision with you beforehand."

Eudora's response was a bitter laugh. *"Discussed?* My dear Monsieur Sabatin, he did not even *tell* me of his decision! In fact, he lied! When I asked him about his sudden interest in Algeria, he told me he was writing a paper on the Flatters expeditions—you know, the two fiascos of 1880?"

The resentment he heard in her voice was obvious. But as she sat back in her chair, he detected a flicker of hurt in her eyes as well.

"Knowing the fervor in the engineering community for Foureau's plans, I believed him. Like a fool, I even offered to help with the research! He accepted my help after insisting I not read anything about the current endeavor. He said it would compromise the objectivity of the research! But out of curiosity, I skimmed an article detailing the financing for Foureau's operation. That's how I discovered my father's deceit. His name was listed among the technical experts designated to join Foureau in Algeria!"

Now Sabatin understood her hurt and resentment—but not the logic of her actions. "Why didn't you try to talk him out of his decision while he was still in France?"

"I did! For three weeks I gathered facts enumerating the dangers—but it was like talking to a stone! He quoted me textbook justifications—telling me how important this expedition was. If successful it would not only help subjugate and tame the uncivilized desert tribes, it would

15

solidify France's claims to the entire Western Sahara, establishing a French monopoly on Trans-Saharan trade and demonstrating French enterprise and engineering skills to the entire world!"

She paused and took a shallow breath. "When I suggested that his decision might be an attempt to recapture his lost youth, it only made matters worse. He said I had no right to deprive him of the opportunity of a lifetime. He announced he would not be dictated to by a daughter who was wasting her own youth. He ordered me to get out, to get on with my life and to let him get on with his." Her voice broke. Nervously she played with the napkin in her lap, refusing to meet his eyes.

Sabatin guessed she had told him far more than she had intended.

"Eudora?"

She lifted her gaze slowly. "That's when I decided to follow him." She drew a deep breath and the strength returned to her voice. "I am convinced that once he experiences firsthand the dangers and discomforts, he will welcome any excuse to resign without loss of face. That is exactly what my appearance in Ouargla will provide! I know my father. Louis Morrel will not turn his back on his only daughter to pursue a foolhardy dream of glory. In spite of his stubborn pride, he will have to resign in order to escort me home."

Sabatin traced the woven pattern of the table's rattan top and considered a reply. When he spoke his voice was soft and gentle, his words carefully weighted. "Eudora, I think your father is right. He's a grown man, and you're a beautiful young woman. You *should* be making a life of your own, apart from your father. Let him pursue his dream."

Immediately her eyes grew cold, like reflections of green ice. She rose slowly.

"You do not understand, Monsieur Sabatin."

Her voice was as cold as her eyes. Flipping the train of her gown behind her, she whirled on her heel and headed for the open French doors that led to the hotel's lobby.

"Perhaps not, Mademoiselle Morrel," Sabatin murmured. Through the doorway he watched her lithe body ascend the staircase. As she took each step a trim ankle would peek momentarily from beneath the cloud of silken folds.

Several men milling about the registration desk paused to watch.

Head held high, eyes focused straight ahead, she was genuinely unaware of the appreciative glances her elegant beauty evoked.

Sabatin shook his head. It was strange indeed she had not yet married.

For a long while he remained alone at the table. In his mind he went over all she had told him and all that he knew of Louis Morrel. The man was a widower, had been for nearly twenty years. Suddenly the components came together like the pieces of a puzzle.

Fiercely dedicated to his work, the celebrated engineer would surely have had no time for the young daughter whose welfare had become his responsibility upon his wife's death. Eudora had probably been shuttled between relatives and boarding schools her entire childhood. Finally, as an adult, she had found a place in his life. No wonder she had then devoted herself to him and his career! Certainly it would explain both her dependence upon him and her inability to accept this decision of his. And if she believed he was abandoning her in order to join Foureau, it would most certainly explain her hatred for Algeria.

Sabatin pushed back his chair and stood. Tossing a few coins onto the table, he then stooped to pick up the napkin Eudora had dropped in her flight. He suddenly felt very sorry for his traveling companion. Doubting their journey would bring about the results she so fervently sought, he feared only bitter disappointment and heartache awaited her.

17

Chapter Two

"Up, over, around and under." With a final tuck, Eudora stepped back to gauge the success of her efforts. She groaned in frustration.

This result was no better than the last three. The precarious mound of loops atop her head was still lopsided. This time, however, she had managed to leave a loose end long enough to wrap across her nose and mouth, vital protection from both blowing dust and the sun's burning rays, according to Sergeant Cheval, who had provided her with the yards-long length of cloth she'd since learned was called a *shesh*.

Wondering if she looked as ridiculous as she felt, she took another step away from the full-length mirror. The stark contrast of the *shesh's* ecru color against her skin caused her to groan again. Already her complexion was two shades darker! She wrinkled her nose in disgust and reached for the second article of native dress Cheval had purchased for her—a shapeless robe of unbleached cotton.

She rolled her shoulders into the garment's voluminous folds and drew it closed over her shirt and riding skirt. She was as ready as she'd ever be.

She walked to the door, turning to cast a final look around the room. Her trunk had been picked up an hour earlier to be loaded with the rest of the caravan's supplies. Suddenly the twinge of uncertainty she'd been experiencing for weeks resurfaced. Was she doing the right thing by following her father? Sabatin's words echoed in her mind—"Let him pursue his dream." She pushed the nagging doubts aside and pulled the door shut behind her. The time for second thoughts had passed.

Sabatin stood at the bottom of the staircase, waiting. Outfitted in similar garb, his head topped in bright orange, his appearance answered her earlier question: she *did* look as ridiculous as she felt. Grinning his welcome, he pirouetted slowly for her inspection. Then, without a hint of the previous afternoon's unpleasantness, he offered her his arm.

"Shall we?"

Outside, the air was crisp. Still, Eudora knew it was not the temperature which caused the sudden shiver she felt ripple down her spine. Unconsciously she tightened her grip on Sabatin's arm.

As they neared the marketplace her apprehension subsided, giving way to excitement. Attracted by the assemblage of soldiers and camels, a large crowd of people had gathered. Eudora searched the sea of white robes and easily spotted the khaki uniforms of du Bois and Cheval.

Though busy supervising the transfer of supplies from wagons to pack camels, the lieutenant paused briefly to offer a smart salute.

In an attempt to look somewhat seductive in her acknowledgment, Eudora smiled and lowered her lashes. Only against his better judgment had du Bois allowed her to join the caravan. She would be a fool not to realize he could still change his mind. She needed to give him a reason not to want to. She had to let him believe she would show her gratitude more openly once they were under way. Besides, what harm could there be in satisfying the man's obvious need to demonstrate his masculinity?

An earsplitting howl shattered her calculations. She looked up in horror before realizing the sound had come from one of the camels being saddled. Bearing his teeth, the animal spewed a slick of green cud upon its handler's uniform. She watched in fascination as the native, undaunted, succeeded in couching and saddling his charge.

Standing at her side, Sabatin laughed. "I gather by your expression that you find this legendary 'ship of the desert' to be somewhat lacking?"

Her gaze remaining on the shaggy beast now contentedly chewing its cud, Eudora smiled halfheartedly. With its large body, ubiquitous hump, and serpentine neck, the animal seemed a tragic freak of nature. "'Somewhat lacking' would be an understatement, Monsieur. I've never seen a more imbecilic-looking creature."

"Don't judge the animal too hastily, Mademoiselle. To the Arab he is God's chosen. It is said that of God's hundred names only ninety-nine are known to man. The hundredth is known only to the camel. In fact, they have a proverb which states that after Nature erred in creating the desert, she repaired her mistake by creating the camel." He paused to smile at her. "Certainly, Mademoiselle, life in the desert would be impossible without them."

"Life in this place, Monsieur, is impossible even *with* them!"

To ignore any further discussion of the matter, she turned her attention to the natives saddling the riding camels. Working in pairs, they placed the triangular saddles forward across the animals' humps. The contraptions were then leveled with a cushion of blankets and cinched into place.

As the headropes were being attached and the camels couched, du Bois approached. "Mademoiselle—Monsieur—if you please . . ." He waved a hand toward the kneeling beasts.

Eudora looked at Sabatin hastily. Even he, the world traveler and champion of the desert tribes, seemed leery.

"Shall I demonstrate?" Du Bois smiled smugly. It was obvious he had guessed that neither had the vaguest notion of how to mount the creatures. "You pinch the

21

camel's nose with your left hand and jerk the head sideways." As he explained, he demonstrated. "Step into the crook of the neck with the left leg, swing the right over the pommel, and . . . *voilà!*"

Once he had mounted it, the demonstration camel heaved forward and rose, unceremoniously pitching the lieutenant backward and forward in his armchair saddle. Applying pressure to the camel's neck with his feet, du Bois regained both his control and his balance. "Well?" he concluded, somewhat impatiently.

"After you, Mademoiselle." Sabatin bowed graciously and grinned.

"Coward!" Eudora hissed. She approached the smaller of the two remaining camels. Mimicking du Bois's instructions she found herself suddenly lurching into the air, miraculously astride the shaggy animal.

"Très bien!" applauded Sabatin, stepping toward his own mount. He grasped the pommel and sprang up. Performing a half turn in the air, he landed—long legs astride the saddle.

In turn, Eudora applauded his successful, if somewhat unorthodox, technique.

As the native soldiers prodded the camels into place, she studied the line forming. Very few of the camels wore riding saddles. A peculiar sense of foreboding began to gnaw at her. She strove to keep her voice calm. "Lieutenant, how many of your men will escort us?"

"We will be accompanied by ten of the native soldiers and a native guide." Du Bois pointed to a large bearded man perched upon a snow-white camel. Seeing that his words had failed to reassure her, he added softly, "You must understand, Mademoiselle. A larger party, while safer, might also attract greater attention."

Eudora didn't have to ask from whom. The officer's previous explanation of the Reguibat threat needed no embellishment.

With a final, reassuring smile, du Bois rode to the head of the train, where he joined the native guide.

Suddenly the call for which all were waiting split the air: "*Nemchou Iallah*—Depart by the grace of God!"

The camels plodded slowly forward in single file.

Eudora felt a strange mixture of emotions—sadness, excitement, a sense of impending adventure—and danger. She resisted the urge to look back toward the marketplace, shifting her gaze instead to the seemingly boundless desert lying before them.

Once out of sight of the city, though, her initial interest in the open wasteland rapidly waned. The terrain remained unchanged—monotonous plains and dunes of unending sand covered by a burning sky. She found her eyes growing heavy and leaned back in the saddle. Lulled by the bouncy, rocking motion of the ride and the desert heat, she soon gave up the struggle to stay awake and allowed herself the luxury of a nap.

Hours later Eudora awoke to the same sounds she had fallen asleep to, the soft tread of the camels and the creaking of cargo. While across the vast, silent wasteland the horizon appeared no closer, in the distance she could see the small oasis which would be their midday rest stop.

Somehow able to bring down his own camel, Sabatin was the first in the group to dismount. Eudora noted his somewhat green pallor and smiled to herself. Apparently the world traveler suffered from motion sickness! Impatiently she waited as one of the natives couched her camel. Never had the thought of setting foot on solid ground seemed so wondrous! Lifting her canteen, she walked over to where Sabatin lay sprawled on his back, his eyes closed. Not wanting to disturb him, she sat quietly beside him. A moment later they were joined by du Bois.

"Our first day will be short," he explained. "Tomorrow we will alternate walking and riding at three- to four-hour intervals. At that pace we can cover twenty- to twenty-five miles a day. With a distance of better than a hundred and thirty miles to cover, we should arrive in Ouargla in less than a week's time."

Somewhat nervously his gaze darted toward an approaching camel and rider. "If you will excuse me, I must speak with Cheval. We've . . . ah . . . had some trouble with a loose pack saddle." Grasping the handle of the holstered revolver at his side, he bowed and withdrew.

Once more alone with Sabatin, Eudora watched as a blue-streaked lizard scurried across the rocks at his feet. The several grunts with which the reporter had responded to du Bois's detailing of their itinerary told her he was not asleep.

"I'm sorry about what happened between us yesterday," she began hesitantly.

"As am I." He sat up and offered her his hand. "Still friends?" Though his eyes were warm, there was a definite edge in his voice indicating a clear reluctance to address the subject further.

"Still friends." Taking his hand—and his lead—Eudora let the subject drop. She had wanted to say more, to offer a better explanation of her motives in the hope he might understand and see that she was right, but the effort was too great. The heat was causing her mind to become numb and her body listless. It suddenly didn't seem important whether the reporter agreed with her or not. She poured some water from her canteen onto the loose end of her *shesh*. Wrapping the cloth across her eyes, she lay back and tried to concentrate instead on green hills and cool lakes.

Pierre Sabatin sat and watched until her breathing attained a gentle rhythm. His desire not to discuss their argument stemmed from an uncomfortable sense of guilt he had been battling all morning—along with his nausea.

Whereas his presence and involvement had been the salvation of her mission, so too, he feared, would they be the cause for its failure. Once his interviews with Commanders Foureau and Lemy were completed, he would be returning to France.

Louis Morrel, therefore, would have no need to resign

in order to escort his errant daughter home—not with Sabatin available to play chaperon. Eudora's plan was doomed to fail—unless, of course, her father had indeed changed his mind. Considering all that he had heard about the esteemed engineer, Sabatin sincerely doubted that would be the case. Reputed to be a man of firm conviction and substantial backbone, Professor Morrel was not the type to have made a hasty and rash decision, nor to reverse it so quickly.

In an attempt to set his mind on other thoughts, Sabatin rose to wander about the small oasis. While his keen reporter's eye missed few details, it did not require shrewdness to see that the native soldiers were nervous. Rifles previously hung carelessly over the backs of the camels were being meticulously cleaned and reloaded.

He turned his attention to the edge of the oasis, where du Bois and Cheval stood with one of the natives. The man's voice, rising above the wind rustling through the palm fronds, seemed frantic, as did his repeated gestures toward the north. Curious as to the cause of his agitation, Sabatin walked down to the tree line.

Moving slowly to keep his approach undetected, he reached the palms just as du Bois and his men began to walk away. In spite of the distance, he was able to hear clearly the last part of du Bois's order to Cheval.

"Round up several of the men and we'll make a reconnaissance of the area. If we are being trailed, it could very well be by the advance scout of a raiding party."

Sabatin felt a sickening sense of immediate fear. He sank down in the sand and watched as the lieutenant and a handful of men rode to the rear of the caravan. When they returned twenty minutes later, his fear had evolved into anger. Rising to his feet, he stepped in front of the officer. "Du Bois! I demand to know what's going on!"

Du Bois hesitated for a moment. "One of my men thought he saw a rider on horseback following us. However, I have conducted a thorough reconnaissance of the area and have found no tracks made by a horse."

Sabatin was not satisfied. "Then what did the man see?"

Du Bois didn't bother to disguise his irritation. He stepped back, fists clenching at his sides. "The desert has its quirks, Monsieur! An overactive imagination easily finds substance. There is a malady—a slight form of madness induced by the heat and loneliness of the desert. *We* who are acquainted with the Sahara call it *le carfu*. I can assure you, whatever the man saw exists only within the confines of his own mind. Still, I see little point in mentioning any of this to Mademoiselle Morrel. I should not like to see her unduly alarmed."

"Nor would I." Sabatin bristled at the inference that *he* would be so thoughtless as to cause Eudora unnecessary worry.

"If you're through with your questions, Monsieur, I have work to do." Du Bois took a step back and waved a patronizing hand. "*You* might make yourself useful and wake her. We leave in ten minutes."

Eudora received the news of their departure with less than an enthusiastic response. She struggled to her feet, trying to ignore her muscles' aching protests.

Once under way she experienced a different sort of discomfort. For some reason du Bois had chosen to ride at her side. At first his company had provided a welcome diversion from the unchanging scenery and unrelenting heat. But now he was leering at her openly, boldly edging his camel closer to her own.

Eudora felt her cheeks grow warm. He was moving in faster than she had anticipated. Although they were still close enough to the city that he could send her back, she couldn't allow his growing familiarity to go unchecked. She eased her camel away from his. Feigning an interest in the piles of sun-bleached bones they had begun to pass with frightening regularity, she glanced over her shoulder.

As she did so her gaze fell upon a familiar form. Now

26

why should Sabatin have chosen to ride at the caravan's rear? Given the amount of dust kicked up by the train's more than forty camels, it had to be most unpleasant! Her curiosity increased when one of the native soldiers rode up to summon du Bois back to the same position.

"Mademoiselle, you're not eating?"

Eudora lifted her head to stare at the shadowy figure standing beside her. After the long day of travel she was exhausted, possessing the energy neither to eat nor to talk. Hoping to discourage du Bois from further conversation, she shrugged and fixed her gaze upon the small campfire before her. If she could have gathered the strength, she would have risen to her feet to avoid this unwelcome intrusion.

Du Bois appeared not to notice her coldness. He settled himself down beside her, gesturing to a small white tent erected a few yards away. "I hope your accommodations will prove adequate."

His words triggered an instant sense of guilt within Eudora. Though she would have never admitted it, the thought of sleeping on the cold ground in the company of snakes and scorpions had terrified her. Thanks, however, to du Bois's foresight and consideration, that would not be necessary. An expression of gratitude was certainly in order!

Before she could speak, however, Cheval emerged into the light of the fire from the shadows where he had been lurking. Moving quickly to du Bois's side, he whispered briefly into his ear. Du Bois nodded and the man withdrew.

Watching him disappear into the night, Eudora shuddered.

"Are you cold, Mademoiselle?" Du Bois moved to add more wood to the fire.

"No." She drew up her knees and rested her cheek upon them. When she'd first met Cheval, she'd not liked him. Accompanying him to the marketplace in Ghardaïa had not changed her opinion. He'd made her extremely uncomfortable, examining her in much the same way he had the camels he was considering buying. Even today, involved as he had been in the supervision of the pack camels, his eyes had never seemed to leave her.

"It's your sergeant," she finally stated quietly. "He makes me feel . . . oh, I don't know . . . uneasy, as if he shouldn't be trusted."

To her surprise, du Bois looked at her and laughed. "You have excellent instincts, Mademoiselle. Though an adequate soldier, Cheval is not one of the French Army's more illustrious recruits. Years ago he was given a choice: enlistment or imprisonment."

"What was his crime?" Sabatin, who had been lounging languidly against a bedroll several feet from the fire, leaned forward.

"*Crimes* would be more accurate," du Bois answered. "It's my understanding that he committed a myriad of offenses." He looked at Eudora, quickly averting his eyes as he realized she was returning his stare. Even in the fire's weak light, it was obvious his face had reddened several shades beyond the sunburn he sported.

Eudora felt her stomach lurch. She had no doubt that at least one of the sergeant's offenses had been sexual in nature. Her blood ran cold remembering the hours she had spent alone with him.

"Fear not, Mademoiselle!" du Bois hastened to assure her. He pulled a knife from his boot as if to give credence to his words with the physical proof of the blade. "I shall be stationed at your door. Should anyone or anything disturb you, you need only to call out. I will be at your side in an instant!"

She knew his words were intended to comfort her. But as she watched him clean his nails with the knife's tip, Eudora found anything but reassurance in his bravado. She doubted this peacock could take care of a hangnail— let alone a prowling desert marauder, be he Arab or Frenchman. Still, she smiled what she hoped was a

28

grateful smile and rose. "If you both will excuse me . . . it's been a long day."

Eudora was not sure what had awakened her, but something had—a noise, perhaps. Suddenly she had the uncanny sensation that she was being watched. She bolted upright in her narrow cot in time to see a shadow cut across the canvas wall of the tent. Frantically she blinked and tried to focus, but it was gone. Easing out of the cot, she stepped cautiously to the doorway and drew aside the flap.

True to his word, du Bois lay in front of the entrance. Seeing, however, how her protector snored in undisturbed, blissful slumber, she felt a twinge of annoyance. She looked out into the desert and saw only the huddled, cocoonlike forms of sleeping men and the couched lumps of dozing camels. There was nothing stirring, no hint of anything out of the ordinary. The shadow must have been her imagination, or some desert creature scurrying about to find warmth. She let the flap fall back into place and turned.

All of a sudden she was hit with the horrible realization of the meaning of her thought. Visions of snakes and scorpions inside the tent flashed into her mind. Immediately her flesh began to crawl. She jerked the hem of her robe from the sand floor. Clutching the folds tight to her body, she tiptoed to the crate beside the cot and lit the lantern. When the tent was flooded with its murky, yellow glow, she still could see nothing moving across the ground.

Oh God, could it have been in her bed? She reached out, gingerly grabbed a corner of the blanket, and tossed it violently back off the cot. Still no creatures appeared. A mixture of foolishness and relief caused her to laugh aloud. She bent to pick up the bedding. Straightening, her eyes focused on the wall of the tent behind the cot.

Eudora froze.

Halfway up the canvas wall was a small slit not more

than six inches in length. Obviously someone had slashed the canvas as she slept. The opening would be just at eye level for someone standing outside. Her teeth clenched in fury—Cheval! The noise that had disrupted her sleep had been the sound of cloth tearing, and the shadow she thought she had seen must have been his!

She threw the blanket onto the cot. Sleeping or not, du Bois was going to hear about this! She left the tent, stepping over the officer's still sleeping form in the process. She whirled to glare down at him. But now that she was outside the confines of the small tent, her anger seemed to abate. The graying sky told her it would soon be dawn. Her report could wait. She picked up a stick to stoke the embers of the campfire.

She was pouring the contents of her canteen into the enamel pot hanging from the tripod erected above the flames when she heard du Bois and Sabatin finally begin to stir.

"Mademoiselle!" Du Bois sat upright with a start. "Are you all right?"

Before she could tell him about her discovery—and her suspicions as to the culprit—a native soldier came running from the shadows.

He stopped and saluted nervously. "I beg the lieutenant's pardon, but one of the guards posted along the perimeter thinks he may have seen something moving out in the desert!"

Du Bois scrambled to his feet. Eudora could not miss the look of anxiety which clouded his features. Shouting for Cheval, he followed the soldier to the edge of the encampment.

Sabatin sat up and smoothed his sleep-tousled hair. As if having sensed her fear, he smiled gently. "I'm sure it's nothing. Probably just a hyena."

"Do you really believe so? In spite of what du Bois says, I think there's something he's not telling us. Did you notice yesterday how he kept watching . . . out there . . ." She gestured toward the horizon. "As if he expected to see something?"

"Eudora, your imagination is running wild. We are only a day's journey from Ghardaïa."

Eudora studied his face and eyes carefully. She saw nothing to indicate he felt anything other than the complacency he expressed. So why didn't she feel reassured? As she foraged for the tea, she realized she already knew the answer. Safe in Ghardaïa, she had scoffed at the idea of a Reguibat attack. It had seemed like such a remote possibility. But now, in the vulnerability of the open desert, the threat was very real, very near, and terrifying!

Several minutes later du Bois returned. "There is no sign of anything out of the ordinary," he stated calmly. He took the cup of tea she offered, casting her a tight smile. "I've even had the guide make an inspection to be doubly sure. He was unable to locate any tracks other than our own."

"But couldn't he have missed something? It's still rather dark, and there must be hundreds of tracks out there!" Eudora hated the way her voice sounded. Even to her own ears it was too shrill and loud.

"I have complete confidence in his ability, Mademoiselle. You must understand, these natives possess an uncanny gift for identifying tracks. By studying the imprints of a caravan of men and camels, they can tell not only the exact number of each in the party, but also whether the animals were loaded or unloaded, fresh or tired. If there were tracks to be found, believe me, he would have found them."

In spite of his words, however, Eudora noted that he remained standing as he drank his tea, his eyes constantly scanning the horizon.

He finished quickly and set the cup down beside the fire. "My men have begun loading the camels. It would behoove us to take advantage of the early morning's coolness, so we will not take time to cook, but will eat as we travel. Now, if you will excuse me . . ." With a curt nod he left to join his men.

Eudora edged closer to the fire and stretched her hands

31

out toward its warmth. It was a bitter irony that in a few hours' time she would be sweltering beneath the brutal sun. Retrieving a comb from a pocket, she began to pull it through her hair. Its normally rich auburn color was now dull and muddy. Her scalp itched from the crusty feel of sand and perspiration. She glanced at Sabatin and saw that he was watching her efforts in amusement. Every bit as grimy and sweat-stained as she, he appeared to be blissfully indifferent to his condition.

"How do you do it, Monsieur?" she asked, suddenly curious as to the key to his serenity. She was unable to recall a single disparaging word leaving his lips—nothing about the heat, the wind, the sand. . . .

"Do what, Mademoiselle?"

"Remain so calm, so unaffected by it all."

"That's because I long ago discovered the secret."

"The secret?"

"Yes, the secret." He smiled slyly—as if he were about to part with the wisdom of the ages. "The secret of adaptation."

"You're *not* going to tell me 'When in Rome,' are you?" Eudora struggled to contain her annoyance. She was in no mood for one of his lectures.

"That's part of it. But the real secret is in how one views one's circumstance. The mistake we Europeans make is in regarding any country or culture which is different as being inferior. There's a wonderful new word for it—'ethnocentrism'—the belief in the superiority of one's own way of life."

He paused as though struck by a new thought. "Instead of viewing the desert as human—possessing human characteristics such as hostility, harshness, and cruelty, and consequently treating it as an enemy to be beaten into submission until it conforms to our standards—we should simply view it as it is, not as it is not. We should accept it, respecting it for its differences."

"Respect it?" Eudora nearly choked. She was deeply disappointed by his empty words of wisdom. In Sabatin's platitudes she found no solution—in fact, within them she found not a shred of credibility. Careful to avoid his eyes, she rose to return to her tent to finish dressing.

Inside, his words continued to ring in her ears. She picked up her gloves and *shesh* from the crate. Perhaps it was a matter of gender, she thought. Even du Bois, hating the desert marauders, had seemed somehow taken with their way of life. And hadn't her own father been fascinated with the prospect of exploring the Sahara? Eudora decided Sabatin was wrong. The desert was human, all right—and female. She was a mesmerizing mistress able to seduce with her magical spell the men who entered her. Suddenly Eudora hated the desert all the more—for in her mind she now viewed her as a dangerous rival.

Her eyes closed, Eudora swayed in the armchair saddle in time to her camel's rocking stride. She tried to guess the hour. Late afternoon, she decided.

A shout forced her eyes open.

One of the native soldiers who had been stationed at the caravan's rear rode frantically back to the main body. Though his voice was raised in alarm, only one of his words reached her ears across the vast distance which separated them.

"Reguibat!"

She instantly felt as if a hand had closed about her throat. Frightful images of the desert savages du Bois had described loomed in her mind's eye. She looked to him to confirm or deny the heart-racing terror coursing through her.

His face proved the confirmation she feared.

The caravan was halted, the camels brought together to be couched.

A native moved to her camel to help her dismount. His eyes mirrored the fear pounding through her veins.

She stumbled to the ground and sank onto the sand. Biting her lower lip to keep it from trembling, she watched as the soldiers with rifles drawn dispersed themselves around the perimeter. Dimly, she realized Sabatin had dropped down beside her and taken her hand.

Sabatin knew Eudora was unaware that her nails were cutting into his palm—and he didn't tell her. Concentrating on the pain kept him from thinking about the revolver now resting in his pocket. Moments ago, du Bois had given it to him, asking if he knew how to use it. Sabatin had nodded in silence—with grim understanding of what the lieutenant was really asking. Eudora was not to be taken alive. In the event they were attacked and captured seemed imminent, her swift and merciful death would be his last act. The fear that he would have neither the courage nor the opportunity to fulfill his pledge to du Bois was one he could not put from his mind.

Huddled in the tight circle, they waited for almost an hour, but there was no further sighting of the dozen men the soldier had seen. Scouts were sent to the flanks and rear. Again no tracks were found.

Hearing the report, Eudora wanted to scream. What kind of a cruel cat-and-mouse game were these vicious savages playing? Why didn't they attack? Sitting under the cruel sun, her fear slowly turned to anger.

"Damn them!" she cried aloud. The caravan was so helpless—so completely at the raiders' mercy. She jerked her fingers from Sabatin's grasp—oblivious to the bloody halfmoons she had created. Standing, she began to pace.

But as the sun began its descent, her anger waned and her fear returned. She had overheard du Bois's whispered comments to Sabatin earlier and knew what the men had not wanted her to know.

The Reguibat's evil reputation included a penchant for attacking in the dark.

Chapter Three

The hours until sundown passed with maddening slowness. Even the camels seemed to jump at the slightest noise or unexpected movement. All eyes were fixed on the horizon. Eventually the sun dropped behind it, and the azure palette became a glorious collage of pinks and reds. But no one paid any attention or appreciated its beauty. Night fell and the darkness grew deeper. Still they waited.

Eudora sat by a small fire, hugging her knees to her. Though she was exhausted, sleep eluded her. Like a child she rocked back and forth, trying to force her jumbled thoughts into order.

Perhaps the marauders had been unimpressed with the small size of their group. Surely they would realize that a caravan transporting valuable cargo would have to be larger. Had they changed their minds, now intending to leave them alone? The hope sustained her through the long, interminable night.

Finally the first light of dawn crested the horizon. The camp seemed to sigh in collective relief. Exchanging furtive glances, the native soldiers rose from their cramped positions. Their strained faces relaxed into weary smiles.

Standing stiffly, Eudora brushed the sand from her robe and whispered a prayer of thanksgiving.

Suddenly a shout pierced the chilly air.

A soldier stood at the perimeter and pointed toward the west.

She followed the focus of his eyes and gasped. The forms of a score of mounted men appeared like black specks above the horizon. Instinctively she turned to look in the opposite direction. The same horrifying sight greeted her—and was duplicated north and south.

The men on horseback drew nearer, closing ranks until the individual specks formed into a solid line resembling a monstrous snake writhing around the camp. A broad white stripe ran down the center of its length. Above the stripe were small splashes of bright colors—reds, blues, oranges, and greens. Beneath it were larger, more somber blotches of black, browns, and grays. As it came closer still, the illusion disappeared and the solid line disintegrated, once again becoming individual horses and men.

Eudora realized it was the riders' brightly colored *sheshes* which had created the serpent's spotted splashes, their white robes the center stripe and their horses the darker tones below. Du Bois had told her the color of an Arab's *shesh* was an expression of the wearer's personality, a mark of his temperament and the key to his character. Her eyes were inextricably drawn to the lone black *shesh*. Riding slightly ahead of the others, mounted upon a magnificent black stallion, the man appeared to be their leader.

Suddenly Sabatin was at her side. He reached out for her and pulled her close, shielding her with his own body.

She clung to him as she watched the riders' approach. Their white robes billowing behind them, whipped about by the wind, they rolled across the sands like miniature clouds.

Crack! The sound of a single gunshot shattered the quiet. In unison the horsemen raised their rifles and fired. The thunderous volley left the native who had fired the first shot, a bullet-riddled heap upon the sand.

Eudora tore her eyes from the sight in time to see the leader of the Reguibat raise his arm. The horsemen followed his order and charged.

36

Almost simultaneously, gunfire erupted from both sides. Several more of the native soldiers and a handful of raiders fell, sprawled out in grotesque, lifeless shapes on the desert floor.

In a daze Eudora saw Sabatin pull a revolver from his pocket. He aimed at the approaching riders and fired repeatedly. Two of the Reguibat fell from their mounts. Strangely, their comrades did not return his fire, but continued to charge. Too late she saw a single rider approaching from behind. He leaned from his saddle to strike with the butt of his rifle. She heard a sickening thud and saw Sabatin's head fall to his chest. Instinctively she tried to catch him as he crumpled. His weight was too much, and she collapsed with him.

"Dear God! No!" Screaming, she rolled his limp body aside to scramble to her knees. "Pierre! Pierre!" Clutching his shoulders she shook him furiously. "You're not dead! You can't be. I won't let you. Damn you! Wake up!"

She tried to lift his head, and it slipped from her grasp, her fingers coming away warm and sticky. She stared at her blood-covered hands. The acrid taste of gunpowder burned in her lungs. Gasping for air, she pulled Sabatin's head into her lap and laid her cheek upon his. She could barely feel his breath. Out of the corner of her eye she saw the revolver still clutched in his hand. She hesitated for only an instant before reaching for it.

Suddenly, incredibly, in the midst of the thunderous gunfire around her, she heard the metallic click of a rifle bolt sliding into place. She looked up to see du Bois standing but an arm's length away.

He mouthed two words: forgive me—then leveled the muzzle of his rifle at her chest.

Eudora nodded in silent affirmation and understanding. The sounds of the battle seemed to grow distant as everything took on a dreamlike quality. She was going to die, yet she welcomed it! Gently she laid Sabatin's head on the ground and stood, giving her executioner clear aim.

Du Bois's finger moved to the trigger, but his second of hesitation was too much. A roarlike cry of rage exploded across the camp.

The Reguibat leader had seen the lieutenant's actions and had also realized his intent.

Eudora saw the man fiercely rein in his horse, the animal rising up on its haunches in response to the brutal pressure which had curbed its forward momentum. Lowering his rifle at du Bois, the Arab fired. The bullet struck the stock of du Bois's rifle, and the gun flew from his hands.

Eudora sank to her knees. It was over. The battle was lost. The dream was now a nightmare from which she couldn't wake. She watched in a daze as the Arabs dismounted to round up their captives. Like sheep, Cheval and three surviving native soldiers were herded in from the camp's perimeter and shoved into a line beside du Bois. Their hands were tied behind their backs before they were ordered to sit. Sabatin, still unconscious but alive, was rolled over, bound, and left lying with his face buried in the sand.

Finally she was approached. A small man squatted before her holding a length of rope. She realized her hands were to be bound as well, but in front, in apparent deference to her gender. After tying her wrists, the man moved away. Fear such as she had never known welled inside her. Terrifying visions of what the Reguibat might do to her filtered through her mind. She had read accounts of women taken captive in the desert. Sold into slavery or merely left to die once their captors had violated them in the most unspeakable way, few had ever survived.

A soft moan from Sabatin startled her out of the nightmare unfolding within her tortured imagination. She crawled to his side and rolled him over onto his back. Blood still flowed sluggishly from the deep gash behind his ear, staining the sand beneath him red. She rose unsteadily to her feet. An Arab standing guard gestured impatiently for her to sit. Her heart racing, she shook her head furiously and pointed to Sabatin. "This man will bleed to death if he isn't attended to!"

The Arab shrugged. Realizing he probably couldn't understand her, she whirled to kick the foot of the native soldier nearest her. The man stared up at her blankly. "You! Tell them Monsieur Sabatin requires immediate medical attention!" She was amazed by the sound of her voice. Though it was clear and firm, it seemed to come from far away.

Meekly the man did as she ordered, translating her words into Arabic. The guard only shrugged again and gestured once more for her to be seated. This time his finger moved to the trigger.

Extending her hands, she forced one foot in front of the other and began to walk toward him. Slowly she crossed the distance between them. Her throat ached from fighting the scream which tried to escape. When she did finally speak, her voice was a husky whisper. "Untie me and let me help my friend."

Backing away from her approach, the Arab leveled the gun at her and gestured with its barrel that she should sit.

"No! Damn it!" She stomped her foot. "I won't sit!" Suddenly she was past caring whether she lived or died. "I demand you untie me!" Lifting her hands to hold them but inches from the man's face, she ignored the rifle barrel now touching her shoulder. "Either shoot me or untie me!"

Several yards away a man on horseback sat watching as the combatants in the clash of wills stood toe-to-toe. Beneath his black *shesh* he smiled. He was quite sure he knew what his man was thinking—Allah be praised, what was he supposed to do now? The woman was crazy—or incredibly brave! In his low, deliberate voice the Reguibat leader growled an order in Arabic.

Upon hearing his voice, albeit not that of his Deity but one equally compelling, the guard pulled a knife from beneath his waistcloth and cut the woman's bonds.

She turned on her heel and returned to her friend's side.

39

With her thoughts only on Sabatin, Eudora did not dwell on her small victory of self assertiveness. She knelt at his side and turned his head to examine his wound. He was still unconscious, but his breathing seemed stronger. There was little she could do except try to stop the bleeding. She grabbed the hem of her robe to tear off a strip to bind the gash.

Suddenly a leather saddlebag plopped onto the sand beside her, seemingly dropped from the sky. She lifted her head and found herself lost in a cold, dark stare framed in black. With heart-stopping certainty she knew she was looking at the Reguibat leader.

His black *shesh,* worn low over his forehead down to the eyebrows and drawn tightly across his nose and mouth, completely concealed his face. Only his eyes were visible—orbs of onyx black which seemed to pierce her very soul.

Eudora forced herself to meet the icy gaze straight on.

He stared at her for a second longer, then turned his horse and rode away.

Eudora dropped her head into her hands. Her mind reeled in dismay. She had never seen such eyes! It was as if they had been probing, seeking to see something within her . . . but what?

Driving all thoughts of the man from her mind, she reached for the bag and untied its flap. Inside were rolls of bandages and gauze, several medicine bottles, a leather roll of surgical instruments, some syringes and vials. She opened the bottles and sniffed the contents of each until she found one that smelled like alcohol. Pressing a folded wad of gauze to the gash to stem the flow of blood, she gently cleaned the wound with another piece moistened with the alcohol.

Sabatin remained unconscious. She began to fear he might never awaken. Her hands shook as she quickly swathed his head in a thick layer of bandages before searching again in the bag. Finding a bottle of smelling salts, she opened it and waved it under his nose. After a moment he began to gasp and cough.

"Eudora," he whispered feebly. He opened his eyes and tried desperately to focus on her. "I'm so sorry . . ."

"Shh, you mustn't try to talk. You need to conserve your strength. All that matters now is that you're alive." Despite her best efforts to put on a brave front, her voice broke. Forbidding herself to cry, she turned her attention to the ropes binding his arms behind his back. A quick glance told her the guards' attentions were on du Bois and Cheval and the native soldiers. She loosened the knots as much as she dared.

For hours the captives sat under the hot sun, virtually ignored by their captors, who rested beneath the shade of their horses.

Eudora watched stonily as a few of the men went through the supply crates. Shouts of obvious delight and satisfaction erupted when the rifles and ammunition were discovered.

"So that's what they were after!" du Bois hissed.

"Guns?" Eudora looked at him in disbelief. The lieutenant's bitter observation was the first utterance he had made since their capture hours earlier. "What need have they for more guns? It appears they already possess plenty!"

"Those are not just any guns. Those are fifty-one-inch, nine-and-a-half-pound magazine-fed Lebel rifles and bolt-action carbines."

Eudora looked at him in confusion. The distinction was lost on her.

"They're modern weapons, Mademoiselle. More sophisticated than anything these bastards now possess. It's a sure bet they'll find their way into the hands of the interior tribes to be used in attacks on our remote outposts." Catching sight of an approaching guard, he clamped his mouth shut and lowered his eyes.

Prodding du Bois with his rifle, the Arab gestured for his captives to stand. Stepping behind the men, he then pulled a knife from his waist and cut their bonds. A curt

41

wave communicated to Eudora and Sabatin that they were to stay where they were.

"It would appear our men are expectd to aid them in the loading of their booty," Sabatin remarked dryly. He struggled to sit up in order to watch as du Bois, Cheval, and the three soldiers were led to a couched group of camels and waiting horses.

Once the camels were loaded, Eudora and Sabatin were ordered to join their companions.

Roughly, du Bois, Cheval, and Sabatin were bound and placed on horseback by their Arab guards, who then mounted their own horses before each took the reins of his respective captive's horse.

Eudora and the three native soldiers remained standing. An Arab guard arrived to lead away the soldiers, while most of his comrades mounted their horses.

Eudora looked about her in panic. It seemed the native soldiers were kept by the remaining Arabs to escort the caravan. But what was to happen to her?

Suddenly a red-*sheshed* Arab rode up, leading a gray mare. Indicating she was to mount, he leaned from his saddle to hand her the reins. The look of distrust in his eyes was clear. For some reason she was being allowed to guide her own horse, and the man didn't like it! She accepted the reins, mounting quickly. She took grim satisfaction in his look of surprise as she deftly maneuvered the mare into position alongside Sabatin. Meeting his gaze, she smiled bravely.

For hours they rode in close, disciplined formation, stopping only once to rest briefly. Remounting, they continued to ride even after sundown. Finally the order to make camp was given.

Eudora dismounted, then moved to help Sabatin. He leaned on her heavily before collapsing onto the sand. Sitting beside him, she watched as du Bois and Cheval were dismounted and untied. Only a small portion of the caravan's supplies had been transferred to the band of horsemen. She realized the added weight would only have slowed the horses. One item which had been included, however, was her small tent. The Frenchmen were now ordered to set it up.

As they worked, one of the guards approached and squatted beside Sabatin to untie his bonds. Though he could not have been more than sixteen years of age (for his unveiled face was as smooth as a girl's), Eudora felt herself recoil from his very presence.

As though sensing her fear, he worked quickly, casting her a shy, almost apologetic smile. With his task completed, he stood. Beckoning to Sabatin to stand also, he then hesitantly extended his hand to her.

"Take it, Eudora." Sabatin's soft voice jolted her to action.

She reached for the youth's hand and was pulled to her feet.

He led her to the tent's entrance and ushered her inside.

Sabatin, du Bois, and Cheval followed. Without speaking, the men settled themselves down upon the sand floor. Their silence prevailed until the tent flap parted and two bowls of rice and a cup of water were set inside.

"It looks like the bastards intend to starve us!" Du Bois crawled forward to reach for the bowls, handing one to Eudora.

"Are you serious?" She stared at the small wooden bowl in her hands. There wasn't enough food in it for one person, much less two. "Surely you don't intend to just sit here and meekly accept what little they dole out?"

"Eudora, please. There is no point." Sabatin reached out to lay his hand on her shoulder.

"Yes, Pierre, there is a point!" She twisted angrily from his grasp and rose to her feet. "You must have more than a few mouthfuls of rice. Look at you! You're so weak you can barely sit up!" She bent quickly to dump the contents of the bowl she held into du Bois's. Then gathering her robes to her, she exited the tent before the men could stop her.

Brushing past a startled guard, she walked determinedly toward a small group of men sitting around a fire. Though they ate with their fingers from a common bowl, it was clear the portion per man was no larger than what had been given to the prisoners. For a brief moment her anger wavered. Remembering what du Bois had told her about their phenomenal endurance, she realized the meager portions might not have been intentionally inhumane.

Struggling to keep her voice steady, she held out the bowl. "You may be used to such a diet, but my friend is not! He must have something to build his strength."

The Arabs looked up at her in mute astonishment.

At the far edge of the camp a tall man watched the fireside scene in amusement. His men didn't know how to react to the Frenchwoman. She was unlike any they had ever encountered, a diametric opposite to their own, who were taught from infancy to defer to men. This green-eyed vixen deferred to no man—at least, not yet! He laughed softly. "Give her what she demands," he ordered.

He continued to watch her for a moment longer. She had better be worth the effort, he thought with a sardonic smile. Because of her he'd lost two good men in the battle, killed by the one they called Sabatin. The Frenchman had held her so close, he'd been forced to order his men not to return his fire. Taking his eyes from her, he leaned back in the sand to stare at the night sky. By the grace of Allah, she had better be worth it!

Eudora looked in the direction from which the low, deliberate voice had come. Though its owner remained faceless, buried in the shadows, she knew it was the same voice that had ordered her bonds cut. A sudden vision of cold eyes framed in black sent an inexplicable shiver of fear up her spine. She took the now filled bowl and fled back to the tent.

Du Bois met her at the doorway, shaking his head in awe. "Mademoiselle, you are either a cat with nine lives or a witch, to have cast such a spell on these savages!

44

Knowing the subservient role they delegate to their own women, I am at a loss to explain the reverence they seem to have for you!"

"I can't explain it either, Lieutenant." Eudora fought a sarcastic smile. Obviously du Bois had not heard the order given from across the camp! Suddenly she felt drained and empty and too engulfed with despair to think further about the black-*sheshed* Arab or his motives. She handed the bowl to Sabatin and retreated to a corner to lie down.

Sabatin watched Eudora curl up on her side facing the canvas wall. He had a feeling the Arabs' 'reverence' for her was not reverence but tolerance. And he feared the point soon would be reached where it would end. Cradling his throbbing head in his hands, he listened for the change in her breathing which would tell him she was asleep. It was not long in coming.

Lifting his head to look at du Bois, he finally voiced the question which had hammered in his brain all day. "What are they going to do with us?"

"It's difficult to say." Nervously, du Bois shifted his position, casting a quick glance at Eudora. "My guess is they'll try to ransom us. They'll send a representative back to Ghardaïa offering the French officials our safe return—in exchange for a price."

"I thought the government's policy was refusal to concede to such demands. Buying back one hostage only opens the door to more kidnappings."

"That's true. But with you involved, your newspaper is likely to put pressure on the politicians. By arousing public support the press can force the government to negotiate with these bastards."

"It *would* make a great story," Sabatin noted wryly. Somehow the headline flashing in his mind: *Reporter Held for Ransom By Reguibat Raiders*—failed to fill him with exuberance. He turned his attention back to du Bois. "I imagine Eudora's presence casts a different light on the situation as well. With a woman involved, the government wouldn't dare ignore the situation."

45

"Yes, well . . . I'm not so sure about her."

"What do you mean?" Sabatin flinched at the ominous tone which had suddenly entered the lieutenant's voice.

"Let's just say that among the four of us, *you* have the best chance of returning to France alive. Cheval and I are soldiers. There's no love lost between the French military and the Reguibat. For more than fifty years they've resented and fought our intrusion into their territory. And the army won't bargain with them for our lives." He sighed and rubbed his eyes wearily. "A soldier spends his life hoping to die on a field of battle, bravely and heroically defending his homeland, and now . . ."

"My God, man! I'm not interested in your lost dream of death and glory in service to God and country! What do you mean, *return alive?* What about Eudora?"

"It's a matter of supply and demand." Cheval stretched his legs lazily and smirked. "Since I'm an expert on that subject—what with being a supply sergeant for ten years and all—let me explain it to you. Our lives—mine and the lieutenant's here—aren't worth spit! We're good as dead, because no one's going to be paying a *sou* to get us back—not the army and not the government. Now you . . . you be worth something to these heathens. Your newspaper will pay for your life. But the most valuable piece of merchandise these Arab savages have is her."

"Sergeant!" Du Bois glared at the man in silent warning.

"You know what I'm saying be the truth, Lieutenant!" Cheval jerked his head toward Eudora's sleeping form. "That bit of goods is going to fetch them a mighty nice sum—because there's a whole lot of demand for what she's got to offer!"

"That's enough, Cheval!" Du Bois began to rise to his knees.

"No! Let him talk!" With a burst of strength he hadn't known he possessed, Sabatin pulled the officer down. "Go on, Sergeant."

Cheval's pale eyes darted back to Eudora. "The government will be making an offer, all right. So will your newspaper. But my bet is she'll go to a much higher bidder."

Sabatin felt a wave of nausea wash over him. He knew what Cheval was going to say, but he needed his suspicions confirmed. "Who?"

"More than likely, some fat sultan with a yen to add a white woman to his harem—or brothel." Cheval smiled, perversely enjoying the shock he knew his words had wrought.

"They can't do that! The French government—"

"Wouldn't be able to do a damned thing! The government's got no power, no authority out here in the desert. Hell! They've got damned little in the cities! Why do you think *they* haven't touched her? I've seen them looking at her—especially their leader, that tall bastard in the black *shesh*. I've seen it in his eyes—black as Satan's heart they are! He be wanting her all right, wanting her for himself. But you know what? He won't take her— because she's too valuable to spoil before delivery!"

All too aware that du Bois's lack of contradiction only confirmed his sergeant's theory, Sabatin sat in stunned silence. Shutting his eyes in pain, he strove to block the man's lecherous face from his mind. He prayed Cheval was wrong.

With each jarring step her horse took, Eudora's hatred for her captors grew. Though it was only midday she was already exhausted, and based on the previous day's experience, she knew it would be hours before they stopped to rest. She had no idea how far they had already traveled. Pushing themselves and their horses to the limits of endurance, the Reguibat were covering great distances each day.

Unmercifully the sun continued to beat down. All that seemed to change was the terrain. With large, dramatic outcroppings of rock, it now reminded her of a postcard she had once seen of the American West. She sought out the black *shesh* at the column's head. Fixing her eyes upon it, she concentrated every ounce of loathing upon its wearer. Suddenly she saw him raise his arm to signal a halt. She wondered why, and then realized they were approaching a well.

The horses were reined in alongside a wooden framework erected on the desert floor. From the structure hung a bucket and rope.

Eudora dismounted and watched as several men began to lower the bucket—seemingly into the very depths of the earth. The water they hauled up from beneath the limestone bedrock was nearly clear.

The man who had originally tied her hands approached and handed her a cup. She ignored his gestures to drink slowly and gulped the cool water. His brown eyes smiled with amusement as he refilled the cup for her twice. In surprise she noted the order by which the water was being distributed by his fellow guards. First to their captives, then to the horses, and finally among themselves! At one bucket at time, it was going to be a laborious process. She lay back in the shade of a large boulder, grateful for the opportunity to rest.

She was almost asleep when a distant sound like dull thunder caused her to sit bolt–upright. Expecting to see storm clouds, she looked to the far horizons. Within seconds the serene juncture of heavens and earth became turbulent. The distant dunes looked as if they were on fire, the peaks melting away. The Reguibat jumped to their feet.

Du Bois's and Cheval's reactions were no less fervid. "Sandstorm!" shouted du Bois.

Hurriedly the guards helped their captives remount, leading them to cover amid the huge rock formations.

A foreboding darkness descended as a lurid yellow light burst from the horizon. The wind began to howl.

Dismounting, the men used their waistcloths to blindfold their horses, before rewinding the loose ends of their *sheshes* to cover their own eyes.

48

Mesmerized by the brown wall of sand skimming along the earth's surface toward them, Eudora had to be pushed into action by the guard who blindfolded her horse. Imitating the man, she crouched in the sand and wound the reins of her horse tightly around her hand. As she drew the end of her *shesh* across her face, she heard the guard's soft, singsong voice talking to their horses in an attempt to calm them.

The wind grew stronger and hotter. It found its way into even the smallest openings in her clothes, propelling minute particles of sand into her flesh with the sting of a needle. All around her she could hear the cries of men and animals.

Sharp cracks of thunder joined the howling wind. And still the sand and dirt rained down.

The cotton cloth could not filter out the fine dirt, and her mouth was soon full of the gritty matter. It worked its way into her lungs, filling them with a burning sensation until they felt as though they would explode.

Then, as quickly as it had begun, the sandstorm ended. The wind died, replaced by deafening calm.

Gasping, Eudora stood and removed her *shesh*. She drank in the fresh air and watched as the Reguibat rose like phantoms from their sandy graves, tearing off their sand- and dirt-saturated headcoverings. The still pale yellow light reflecting off their bronzed faces only added to the eerie effect of resurrected dead.

Daylight returned and Eudora gaped in wonder at the chaos and confusion left in the storm's wake. Hunched men coughed spasmodically to expel the dirt in their lungs, while others dug personal effects out of the sand. Still others tended their horses. Many of the animals were bleeding, cut by flying debris. Her heart began to race with hope. Not one of the guards was paying her heed!

Slowly she edged away from the group. Removing her horse's blindfold, she encircled its neck with her arms as though to calm it. Then, with a firm hold established, she placed her left foot in the stirrup, mounting and turning

49

the mare in the same movement. Kicking as hard as she could, she gave the horse free rein. The mare bolted toward the open desert.

She was only a few hundred feet away when Eudora heard a sharp cry echoing from behind. Flattening her body against the horse, she rode as if the devil himself were chasing her. Finally she summoned the courage to look back.

In pursuit was a lone rider—if not the Devil, then most certainly an angel from Hell. Like wings his white robes billowed behind him. Yet it was no halo of gold which topped his head, but a crown of black!

Burning, choking fear rose in her throat. She leaned even lower into the horse, kicking the animal savagely. Having overheard the previous night's conversation between Sabatin and Cheval, she was determined to run herself and the devil pursuing her into the ground.

She hadn't been asleep as the Frenchmen had thought. Lying in silence, she had heard their every word. But staring at the canvas wall had had a strange calming effect. Her initial terror had forged itself into her present state of steel determination. She would die before she accepted the fate Cheval was so certain would be hers.

Her slight head start and lighter weight were to her advantage. But the Arab's horse was quickly proving to be the swifter of the two. The powerful beast bore his master's greater weight easily, steadily gaining on the gray mare. Blinded by tears of fear and frustration and the hair whipped into them by the wind, it was too late by the time she saw the small boulders in her path. The mare swerved to avoid them and Eudora fell from the saddle, landing hard upon the sand. Her horse raced a hundred yards ahead and then slowed to a stop.

Eudora lay face down in the sand, the wind knocked from her. She was stunned but unharmed. Why couldn't she have broken her neck in the fall? Stiffly she rose to her knees. Clawing the hair out of her eyes, she watched furiously and fearfully as the black horse approached.

50

The Arab reined in beside her. Through the narrow slit of an opening in his *shesh*, he stared down at her. The now familiar onyx eyes were as cold as steel and void of any emotion, even anger.

"You would do well, Mademoiselle, to accept that which you cannot change."

"Go to Hell, Infidel!" So quick was her acid retort she didn't realize at first he had spoken in flawless though accented French. She stood and swept the sand from her knees.

He laughed a low, rich, throaty laugh which sent waves of terror through her very soul. "We are already there, little one."

The truth of his taunt rang in her ears. The fires of hell could burn no hotter than the Saharan sun, and surely no Lord of Darkness could be more terrifying than the black-*sheshed*, black-eyed lord of the desert who sat mounted above her!

The Arab spurred his horse forward to set out after hers, returning moments later with the mare in tow. Remaining mounted, the man simply tossed the reins down to her.

Wordlessly she stepped into the stirrup, fighting hard against the tears which threatened to fall. Wanting with all her heart to defy him—to prove she was immune to the fear he had planted within her—she could not. Something about him demanded complete and total obedience, and she suddenly didn't have the strength to fight it.

Returning to the others, they found them prepared to proceed.

One of the guards approached with a length of rope.

Eudora held out her hands wearily. After her escape attempt she could expect little else.

The black-*sheshed* Arab beside her checked his man's approach with a single, barely discernible shake of his head.

The guard withdrew.

In disbelief she turned to look at him. With it

51

impossible to read anything in his eyes, she found herself trying to imagine the face hidden beneath the blach *shesh*.

Soon it became evident why he had not ordered her bound. Taking hold of the mare's bridle, he led her to the column's head. Now riding at his side, she would be unable to get more than a few feet from him. At his single word of command, the riders moved forward.

As the afternoon wore on in a relentless trek toward the west, Eudora regained some of her earlier courage. Her contempt for the man riding at her side returned. Without looking at her, he seemed to know instinctively where she was, and if her horse slowed or picked up its pace, its stride was effortlessly matched by that of the black stallion.

To break the monotony and to deliberately annoy him, Eudora frequently altered her horse's pace and direction slightly.

The Reguibat leader stared straight ahead. If his captive had any hope of seeing a sign of irritation in his eyes, she was going to be greatly disappointed. He was, however, certain that were the green-eyed vixen able to see through the black cloth, she'd be horrified at the smile which parted his lips.

Chapter Four

Eudora had been watching the mere speck in the distance for some time. Moving toward them at a fast pace, it grew larger and larger, finally taking on the form of a man and a horse.

When he finally approached the main party, bringing up his mount beside the black-*sheshed* Arab, Eudora recognized him as the advance scout. He reported sighting an addax roaming in the desert a few miles from the main party. The possibility of fresh meat instilled an infectious excitement in the Reguibat. Their leader and half the band set out on the hunt, the others remaining behind to guard the prisoners and set up camp.

Under the watchful eye of an armed guard, Cheval and du Bois once again erected the tent. When they were finished, Eudora entered first. Her unsuccessful bid for freedom and the long hours spent silently sparring with the tall Arab on his black horse had exhausted her.

She flung off her heavy robes in disgust. Insulating layers be damned! Inside the small tent it was stifling. There wasn't the slightest movement of air. As the others entered she suppressed the urge to scream. Their canvas prison was hardly large enough for one person, much less four. Turning her back she opened several buttons of her shirt and mopped the perspiration from between her breasts.

The men's eyes, except for Cheval's, quickly and politely diverted to the floor.

"Ahem!"

At the sound of du Bois's cough, Cheval turned his head to look at his commanding officer.

Du Bois gestured for him to move back to allow the woman room to lie down.

Scowling, Cheval grudgingly obeyed, squatting beside Sabatin. Through lazily lowered lids he continued to watch her as she folded her robe as a pillow, then lay down on her side facing the canvas wall.

Her very presence was enough to arouse a man to stiffness, he thought. But it had been the previous night's speculations detailing her possible—and probable—abuse at the hands of their captors which had begun to erode his control. He licked his lips nervously. It was starting again—the throbbing erection he'd been unable to release the night before.

Outside the doorway he heard a sound. He glanced up just as one of the Arab guards parted the tent flap with the barrel of his rifle and gestured to the men.

"Another work detail!" Grumbling softly, du Bois shifted to his knees. Closest to the exit, he crawled out first.

Cheval eyed the woman and realized he would never have a better opportunity. As Sabatin began to rise to follow du Bois, Cheval grabbed at his arm. "Tell them I'm sick! Someone should stay with her!"

Sabatin apparently recognized the sergeant's request as good sense. In his own still weakened condition he would be little help should she be threatened. He nodded and exited the tent.

"The other man is ill," Cheval heard him explain. He leaned back and closed his eyes. Almost immediately he heard the impatient guard again part the opening. Through slits in his lids Cheval watched the man peer into the tent.

Seemingly satisfied with Sabatin and du Bois, the Arab

shrugged indifferently and let the flap fall.

Cheval sat up, continuing to leer at the woman as she rested. Her right leg was pulled up close to her waist, straining the fabric of her riding skirt tightly across the rounded curves of her buttocks. The left leg was outstretched, the skirt bunched above the knee revealing a white calf.

Feeling an itchy sting at his waist, he scratched. He plucked out the fat tick he found imbedded in his flesh and absentmindedly rolled it in his fingers. His thoughts remained on the woman.

From the moment he had first met her, she had preyed on his mind: So haughty, so proud, so high-born. She was the embodiment of everything he had resented his entire life and a symbol of all he could never obtain.

The material covering his crotch tightened uncomfortably. The time had come. He squashed the tick into the palm of his hand, breaking its hard shell with a dirty fingernail. He rubbed his palm nervously on his pants, then pulled out a small knife hidden in his boot. He crawled across the sand floor to her side, making sure to place a hand over her mouth before rolling her over onto her back.

Instantly her eyes flew open. Confusion, surprise, then fear flashed in the green spheres.

He leaned toward her. "Don't make a sound!"

Eudora gagged at the man's stench and fought the taste of bile rising in her throat. She nodded. She would have agreed to anything to get the man to remove his hand. "What's wrong? Where are the others?" she gasped the instant her mouth was uncovered.

"They've been taken on a work detail." His pale eyes, glassy and feverish looking, narrowed. "It's just me and you now." He reached out with his hand and ran it up her leg.

Immediate understanding exploded in Eudora's mind. Oh God, no! She opened her mouth to scream, and he clamped a filthy fist over it again. Straddling her, he

55

produced a knife and held it to her throat.

"I don't think you be understanding your position," he hissed, leaning his bristled face close to her ear. "These heathen bastards intend to offer you up to the highest bidder—probably an Arab pimp. I'd wager you're no virgin—a beauty like you has had men aplenty." He sneered. "So the price won't be as high. But you've never been touched by an Arab, and that makes you still very valuable. That's why they haven't taken you yet themselves."

Keeping the knife at her throat, he slid a hand down over her breasts. "They don't want to soil the merchandise!" He laughed. Clearly, he was enjoying her terror. "Now if I was to carve up that beautiful face of yours . . ." he ran the edge of the blade down her left cheek to emphasize his words ". . . you'd be completely worthless to them—damaged goods. They'd just go ahead and all take a turn with you. Then they would kill you. The way I see it, you can service me quietly and keep that pretty face—which might just get you ransomed intact. Or . . ."

He removed his hand to slide the knife's tip from the corner of her mouth to her ear. ". . . I cut you up real good and you can service a hundred of them . . . before they finish you."

Eudora's mind raced. She had to keep him talking to buy time. "They'll kill you!"

"I figure I'll be dying anyway. I might as well enjoy my last minutes on earth!" He lowered his mouth to hers.

Again she gagged. Violently she tried to twist away.

Cheval lifted his head. "Go ahead and struggle," he taunted. "I like it when you struggle!" He buried his face into the crook of her neck and shoulder and bit at the tender skin. An instant later his mouth was back covering hers. She felt his fingers fumble with the buttons of her shirt.

Helplessly she writhed beneath him, trying to push him off. He was small but wiry, and his strength was fueled by his demented lust. His mouth pressed to hers allowed her scarcely to breathe, much less cry out for help.

The knife reappeared at her throat and traveled down her chest, between her breasts. He caught the tip beneath the ribbon laces of her chemise and jerked the blade back toward her throat, slicing the ribbons. As his hand found and cupped a bare breast, she bucked and tried to scream. He only closed his mouth tighter over hers and muffled the sound, continuing to grope and fondle the soft mounds.

Fear blacked out the sounds outside the tent. She didn't realize the victorious hunting party had returned, nor did she hear the men gather to congratulate the hunters and view the kill.

Still mounted, the Reguibat leader instinctively scanned the camp. Seeing only two of the prisoners foraging the sandy dunes for scraps of wood, he dismounted quickly and summoned one of the guards. "Where is the third man and the woman?" he demanded.

"They are in the tent. He said he was ill and—"

Before he could finish his sentence, the tall man was running toward the small white tent.

Cheval sat up and pressed the tip of his knife into the hollow of Eudora's throat. Paralyzed with terror and revulsion, she lay limply beneath him. In agony she watched as he unbuckled his belt. "Please, please don't do this," she whispered.

Feeling his hand groping between her legs, she closed her eyes. Hampered by the seams of the split skirt, he could obtain no access. He began to work at the buttons which ran along the left side. She cried out and tried to pull away.

"Don't move! Don't make another sound or by God I'll slice your face to ribbons!"

He pressed the knife deeper into her skin and she felt a trickle of blood roll down her throat. Strangely, she had felt no pain. He was yanking at the waistband of her skirt when suddenly she heard the sound of the tent flap being ripped aside.

Cheval heard it too. He froze for a moment, then leaped off of her. Out of the corner of her eye she saw a white blur. Cheval lunged at it with the knife.

Eudora turned her head in time to see the Arab sidestep the blow. He grasped the wrist which held the knife, then, aided by the Frenchman's own forward momentum, he spun the smaller man around. Grabbing him across the neck with his forearm, he clasped the man's back to his own chest. He took hold of the side of Cheval's head and twisted. Under his brutal strength the neck snapped like a dry twig. He released his hold and the lifeless body dropped to the ground.

Eudora clutched at her torn clothing and sat up. A gasping sob she could not hold back drew the Arab's attention to her instantly.

He crouched down on his heels beside her and touched her shoulder gently. She recoiled from his touch as if struck. "I am sorry." He rose to his feet. "I had thought you would be safe with your own kind."

The tear-filled eyes the woman lifted to meet his gaze were blank. She stared at him and shook her head. He realized he had unwittingly spoken in Arabic. Switching to French, he did not, however, repeat his statement. "I will give orders that the others be kept elsewhere. You shall have the tent to yourself."

Eudora fought her way through the cloudy nightmare which was no dream but reality. She focused on his face, seeing only the onyx eyes. "No!" she managed to gasp. "Please! I want to see Sabatin!"

The Arab studied her face intently for a moment. Then nodding, he turned and left the tent. Almost instantly two guards appeared. Eudora forced herself to look away as they dragged Cheval's body from the tent. A few seconds later Sabatin burst through the opening.

"My God, Eudora!" He knelt by her side, his face pale, his eyes wide with shock. "What happened? Cheval is dead!"

"He . . . he tried to rape me!" She began to shake and clasped her arms about her breasts.

"That bastard!" Sabatin jumped to his feet and moved toward the doorway. "I'll kill him!"

"No!" she cried out, realizing his intent. "Not him! It was Cheval! He . . . the Arab . . . he stopped him! He killed him." Her voice broke. No longer able to hold back the pent-up terror, she began to sob uncontrollably.

Sabatin quickly moved to her side and gently gathered her into his arms. "Hush! It's all over. It's all right. I'm here now."

Eudora clung to him. "Why? Why did he do it?" She desperately needed to make sense of the horrid event. "Why?"

"The man was sick and evil, Eudora. It wasn't the first time—"

"No! I don't mean Cheval, Pierre. *Him!* The Arab. Why did he stop him? Was he afraid it would lower my price?" Again her voice broke. As the tears began to slide down her face, she buried her head in his chest.

Shocked, Sabatin realized she must have heard them talking the night before. It explained her frantic, senseless attempt to escape that afternoon. She knew what their captors intended to do with her.

But suddenly *he* was no longer so sure.

Like Cheval, he too had noticed their leader's interest in Eudora. But watching the tall Arab, he had seen in his cold, black eyes something more than simple desire. Sabatin was no fool. He knew the Reguibat had intentionally not returned his fire in the battle. Furthermore, du Bois had told him who had shot the rifle from his hands before he had been able to kill Eudora. And had the Arab not been the one to race madly after her when she tried to escape in the confusion after the sandstorm?

No. His every instinct was telling him the same thing. It simply wasn't conceivable that a man would go to such effort to keep a woman safe only to hand her over, even for a price, into the hands of another.

No, Eudora, he repeated silently to the woman in his arms, he'll not give you up that easily. Cheval had been wrong. The Arab *did* intend to take her for himself. But after he did, what would be her fate then?

Sabatin remained with Eudora the entire night, comforting her, cradling her, and reassuring her she was safe.

She finally slept, but fitfully. She tossed and turned, mumbled, and cried out in her sleep. "No, Constantin! No! It's over. I've had enough!"

As she whimpered in anguish, he held her gently and wondered: Who was Constantin? A former lover? Perhaps. But judging by her torment, whoever he had been, he had hurt her deeply. So, too, had he, Sabatin realized with a sudden, agonizing stab of conscience. For the sake of a story he had talked du Bois into allowing her to accompany them. It was his fault she was now facing an unknown future!

Wracked by guilt, Sabatin embraced her more tightly. Eudora's only hope was that the French officials in Algiers would act quickly, cutting through the bureaucratic protocol and bettering any offer made.

Clinging to that thought, he closed his eyes.

He dozed off only to be awakened a dozen times, if not by Eudora's nightmares, then by his own—a spectral vision of a black serpent crushing an emerald bird in his deadly embrace.

The next morning Sabatin awoke to a now familiar cry. "*I Allah! Noudou!* Everyone up!"

He struggled to sit up, ignoring the pounding ache in his head.

Eudora was awake. Sitting across the small tent from him, she was trying to hold her torn shirt closed as she attempted to straighten the unfastened skirt twisted

60

about her hips. Although her eyes were red and slightly puffy, she seemed to be her old self again. He smiled in relief.

Outside the tent they could hear the Reguibat already breaking camp. One of them appeared in the doorway dragging a trunk behind him. Keeping his eyes discreetly lowered, he bowed to Eudora and gestured toward the trunk.

Recognizing it instantly as Eudora's, Sabatin turned to look at her. "He seems to have thought of everything." He was painfully aware of the bitter sarcasm which had entered his voice.

"Who?" She glanced up and arched an eyebrow, obviously puzzled by both his comment and his rancor.

"Their leader. You don't think that man . . ." he gestured toward the departing Arab ". . . brought your trunk in of his own volition, do you?"

Before she could answer, he whirled and exited the tent. Seeing the Arab with the trunk, and knowing who had given him his orders, had brought back all his guilt and fear of the previous night. For some reason the Reguibats' leader was waiting to claim her. But when he was ready, he would. And there would be nothing Sabatin could do to stop him. The knowledge of that powerlessness was more painful than anything he had ever experienced.

He clenched his fists in helpless frustration. Ignoring a nearby guard who eyed him warily, he then turned his attention to the east. Awed, he watched as the transition from dark to light occurred and the dunes grew pink in color.

Moments later du Bois appeared, escorted by a guard. As they waited for Eudora, Sabatin informed the lieutenant of the past night's events.

Du Bois did not seem to be unduly distressed to learn of his sergeant's demise. "Is *she* all right?"

"For the moment." Before Sabatin could share his new theory regarding her future, however, the guards prodded him forward. Eudora had just exited the tent, and he and du Bois were now expected to strike the small canvas structure.

Eudora stood and watched as Sabatin and du Bois worked. Their task was nearly completed when suddenly she felt the hair on the back of her neck rise. She knew she was being watched. As she forced herself to turn slowly, her eyes froze on the familiar figure approaching her. As always, his face was hidden beneath the black *shesh*. Nervously she shifted her attention to the pair of horses he led. There was something very unsettling about being unable to see one's enemy!

Wordlessly he handed her her mare's reins and mounted his own horse. She was tempted to say something about the incident with Cheval, to thank him or at least to acknowledge what he had done. But try as she could, the words would not come. As he stared down in waiting silence, she swung into the saddle. Avoiding the gaze she still felt, she automatically guided the gray into place by his side at the head of the party. There would be no games today. She would keep her horse's pace steady, its path straight.

As they had the previous days, they rode hard. Eudora marveled at the pace he set. Yet his men and their horses responded, and by dusk they had reached their destination—the Reguibats' base camp.

Eudora stared in wonder. The huge oasis which stretched out before her was as large as a French village. A hundred tents of all sizes and colors were spread across the desert floor. Gay streamers drifted from their support poles in the wind. There were goat and sheep pens, horse corrals, and camels grazing in the distance. The now familiar white-robed men were in evidence, as were numerous women and children. But unlike the women in the cities, these were unveiled. Dressed in brightly colored skirts and blouses, their wrists and ankles encircled with silver, they looked more like European gypsies than desert nomads.

As the riders entered the camp, people streamed from its every corner to greet their loved ones. The largest crowd, however, seemed to be gathering around the black stallion.

Eudora ventured a sideways glare at its rider. *Hail the conquering hero!* she thought bitterly. Refusing to be a witness to his joyous and loving welcome, she dismounted and made her way through the throng to Sabatin.

Still bound, both he and du Bois stood in silence, their eyes anxiously scanning the growing crowd.

Eudora pressed closer to the safety of Sabatin's side. Unable to help herself, she glanced back at the black-*sheshed* figure surrounded by his admirers.

He turned, gesturing to the two guards on either side of Sabatin and du Bois. Responding instantly to his unspoken order, his men began to lead their prisoners away.

At the thought of being separated from Sabatin, Eudora felt her stomach knot with fear. Desperately she clung to him.

Suddenly two other men grabbed her arms and it became terrifyingly clear their orders were to lead her elsewhere. Icy panic welled up within her. She screamed and clawed at Sabatin's sleeve. "Pierre, please! Don't let them take me!"

"Leave her alone!" Furiously Sabatin fought against the ropes that bound him. He tried to put himself between her and the men. His own guards yanked him violently backward while hers pried open the tight-fisted grip she had on his robe.

Pulling her from Sabatin's side, they then led her to a large tent set apart from the others. None too gently she was pushed through its draped doorway.

Stumbling inside, she felt her eyes close automatically. The brightly lit interior was almost blinding. Slowly she opened her eyes to view her surroundings. Although the floor was sand, it was carpeted with thick, lush Persian rugs. Heavy tapestries hung from the walls.

One of the men pushed her forward again. She moved further into the tent, her eyes catching glimpses of furniture. There was a sofa strewn with bright pillows, a writing desk, a chest. She stopped at the thick drape at the far wall only to be shoved through it into another room.

Similarly carpeted and of comparable size, this room contained a large bed draped in netting, a tall dresser, a vanity, and an armoire.

Eudora glanced over her shoulder and found herself very much alone. She whirled about, trying to orient herself to her strange surroundings.

In the center of the room stood a massive metal bathtub. Looking once more around the room to assure herself she was still alone, she stepped forward and peered in. Surprised to find it filled, she tentatively dipped a finger into the water. It was warm!

Eudora stared, mesmerized by the pool of water beckoning her. How heavenly a bath would feel! But under the circumstances rendering herself so vulnerable would be insane—yet it was so tempting! Her fingertips, playing with the top button of her shirt, brushed against the skin beneath the fabric. The gritty feel wiped away all reservations. With a final glance around the room, she shed her clothing.

Savoring the moment, she settled down into the water. She couldn't recall anything ever feeling so good. She closed her eyes and leaned back, allowing the water to flow over her head. Sitting up, she then reached over the tub's side to grab a cake of soap from the floor.

Not wanting to relinquish the feeling of being clean and cool, Eudora lay in the tub long after the water had grown cold. Finally she stood and wrapped a towel around herself. Someone had thought of everything— the soap, the towels . . .

She gasped, realizing a shiver of panic. The words she had just formed in silent praise to that anonymous person rang hauntingly familiar: . . . to have thought of everything . . . *He seems to have thought of everything*. They were Sabatin's words, spoken that morning when her trunk was delivered!

Abruptly her surroundings took on a profoundly different appearance. There was a decidedly masculine air about the room. The vanity top was covered with brushes and combs, shaving paraphernalia . . . before she could firmly grasp a train of thought, she suddenly sensed she was no longer alone. She turned toward the doorway to find a young Arab girl staring at her.

Eudora met the wide-eyed gaze of fright with a sigh of relief. "Whose tent is this?" she demanded.

The girl backed away fearfully and shook her head. She held a bucket in each hand. Raising them, she gestured with one toward the tub.

Eudora realized the girl, no more than thirteen or fourteen, understood no French. Obviously there only to empty the bathwater, she would be of no help. She turned her back to her and began to pace the room. Remembering suddenly she was clad only in the towel, she moved to pick up her clothes from the heap on the floor.

The girl edged past her and ran from the room. Water sloshed from the full buckets in her haste, leaving a wet trail to the door.

Now again alone, Eudora shed the towel without hesitation. She pulled on her undergarments quickly. She was preparing to step into her riding skirt when a woman's voice stopped her.

"My lady . . ."

The words, spoken in French, caused her to spin around in surprise. Another, older Arab girl had entered and now stood hesitantly at the room's entrance. Eudora watched as her eyes darted in obvious concern to the wet carpet before rising to meet her own.

"My lord desires that you wear this." She stretched out an arm draped with a green silk gown of sorts.

My lord, Eudora's mind repeated. She had been right.

65

It *was* his tent to which she had been brought! She felt herself begin to tremble in response to the storm of emotion assailing her: confusion and anger, indignation and fear. She swallowed hard to dislodge the lump in her throat. "I shall wear my own clothes," she said at last. Stepping into the skirt, she found herself praying her knees would not buckle.

"My lord has given express instructions," the girl insisted, her voice soft, yet firm.

Strangely, the girl's dogged insistence seemed to unleash some reserve of strength. Feeling her trembling abate, Eudora fastened her skirt. "I don't give a damn what orders *your* lord has given! You can tell *him* to wear it for all I care!"

"My lady, please! My lord does not like—"

"I don't care what he likes or doesn't like! He is not *my* lord!" Eudora lifted her chin, squared her shoulders, and stared down at the girl. A haughty look and glassy tone had always worked on servants and underlings in the past. "The matter is settled. I should like to be taken to where my friends are."

To her surprise the girl returned not only her look, but her tone. "That is impossible. By his command you have been brought here. And here you will stay."

Eudora reeled in shock. Her nerves were already stretched taut, and the girl's continued references to the black-*sheshed* Arab's omnipotence drove her to an unreasoning fury. She took a single step toward the vanity, swiping furiously at the items lying upon it. "I demand you take me to my friends!"

As the vanity's contents crashed to the floor, the girl cried out in dismay. She clutched the green gown she still held to her breast. "I cannot! I do not possess the authority."

At once Eudora realized she had broken through the girl's veneer of control. She walked over to where she stood and calmly took the gown from her grasp. "Then perhaps you had better leave and find your lord. When you do, tell him I have no intention of remaining here or . . . of wearing this!" She flung the garment to the floor. "Now, go."

The girl did not move.

"Are you deaf? Go!" Eudora crossed over to the dresser. Lifting a vase, she whirled. "Go!" Menacingly she raised the vase over her head. She hesitated only a second before hurling it at the fleeing girl.

Chapter Five

The Reguibat leader entered the tent with his men. He passed a hand across his eyes in an attempt to ease their burning. He was tired, and his fatigue was compounded by impatience. Waiting in the next room was a far more pleasurable matter to be attended to. He had always hated the hours after returning from a raid. There seemed no end to the problems which had arisen in his absence—problems whose solutions only he could dictate. And then there were the dead and wounded . . . It would all take time, precious time. And all the while he knew she was waiting. . . .

Swearing softly, he turned to face his men. "I want no harm to come to the prisoners. They are far more valuable alive—"

A loud crash and a woman's shrill scream interrupted him. A moment later there was another crash just as a small dark-haired girl burst through the heavy curtains dividing the rooms.

She clasped her hands to her breast and bowed deeply. Fearfully she kept her eyes lowered. "I am sorry, my lord, but she is most . . . difficult. She refuses to wear the gown and insists upon joining her friends."

The man smiled—a slight smile which turned up the corners of his mouth but did not quite reach his eyes. Nodding that he understood, he dismissed the maid with a wave of his hand, then turned to the wall of curtains. For several minutes he stood in silence. He sensed rather than saw the knowing looks and sly grins being exchanged by his men. He chose to ignore them. The envy of his men was understandable.

What was not understandable was the conflict of desires raging within. He wanted the woman behind the panel, had wanted her from the moment he had first seen her. Yet the thought of merely taking her left him cold. Why? Certainly as sheik he was within his rights to claim her.

A discreet cough eased him out of his reverie. He would have to sort it later. Right now, as one of his men had tactfully pointed out, he had other matters to attend to. Still, it wouldn't hurt to give the woman in the next room something to think about in the meantime.

Nodding to his men, he excused himself.

He entered the room silently, catching her by surprise. A quick glance about the room explained the crashes. The vanity had been swept clean. Broken glass bottles lay on the carpet among the brushes and combs. A vase lay in pieces at his feet.

She turned to face him, her still damp hair swirling about her shoulders. Bright green eyes flashed as they stared at him. His own eyes swept over her, taking in every detail. Cheeks flushed from anger. Firm, round breasts heaving—straining the small pearl buttons of her white linen shirt. Her tight-fitting riding skirt, which hugged her curves before flaring at mid-thigh, was cinched in brown leather at an elegantly tapered waist. She was a prize indeed! He certainly could not begrudge his men their envy.

Eudora's breath caught in her throat. The black *shesh* was gone, as were the flowing white robes, but there was no doubt in her mind as to this man's identity.

"*You!*" she hissed. Slowly and never blinking, she walked up to him and raised her hand to slap him.

He grabbed it instantly, his eyes never wavering from

hers. When she raised the next, he captured it as well. Then, holding both of her wrists easily in one strong hand. He forced her to look up into his face. Bearing a week's worth of stubbled beard, it was handsome, yet cruel.

The now familiar cold onyx eyes bored into her. "I see you still have not learned to accept that which you cannot change."

"How dare you!" Eudora twisted away from his grasp. "Why have I been brought here? What do you want with me?"

A slow smile parted his lips. "I think you know."

Releasing her, he bent to retrieve the jade green gown from the floor. "You have caused me a great deal of trouble, little one. Now . . . before my patience is truly exhausted and I decide you are not worth it, I suggest you put this on." He thrust the gown into her grasp. Once again he cupped her chin, forcing her to look at him. "You would find me a poor lady's maid," he stated softly, his voice carrying an ominous tone. "However, as a lover . . ." he paused and watched for her reaction, "I think you will be pleased."

Her eyes widened. Her mouth gaped. Shock and understanding swept over Eudora in a single horrifying instant. As he released her, she took a staggering step backward. He had saved her from Cheval in order to take her for himself!

Numbly she heard his voice again. It was low and deliberate, accustomed to command and obedience. "You have twenty minutes."

Eudora stared at his broad back, now disappearing into the folds of the draped doorway, and began to tremble. She would rather die than endure the fate which awaited her. Could she beg him, plead with him to spare her? She knew the answer in her heart almost before her brain had formed the question. There had been no mercy in his piercing eyes, only desire. He would have her. If necessary, he would even take her by force—probably

71

enjoying it all the more if she did fight!

"I won't give him that satisfaction!" she vowed. She could not prevent the purely physical pleasure her body would give him, but she most assuredly could prevent him from feeling any emotional victory. No, she would not fight him. But neither would she respond to him in any way. Let him see how much pleasure he could take from a passive victim. With silent indifference she would endure all that he did to her.

Eudora's decision gave her courage and steeled her resolve. She tore impatiently at the pearl buttons and pulled off her shirt. After a struggle with the belt, the skirt followed, leaving her clad only in her underthings. Thin and filmy, they clung to every curve and concealed little. She stared at her reflection in the vanity's mirror. She tried to see what men saw. Round hips and buttocks that hinted at the pleasures to be found within? Full breasts which teased with their gentle curves?

Slipping out of the last of her clothing, she held the gown up to her and grudgingly admired its elegant beauty. With a daringly low décolletage in both front and back, it had short puffed sleeves too low on the shoulders to support the bodice, hence the need for its narrow satin shoulder bows. It was the perfect attire for a seduction, she thought, not a . . . She was unable to think the word. Tears welled in her eyes.

It had been more than a year since she had been with a man. She thought of the long and painful relationship—finally ended. It had made her wary of men. She had rebuked every attention, refused every offer, and denied all feelings—even her own. So careful and cautious she had been, not to allow herself to be hurt again by a man. Now here she was, in the span of twenty-four hours, almost raped by one man and about to be raped by another! An Arab! The tears spilled down her cheeks.

Suddenly the raucous sound of laughter coming from the next room cut through her thoughts. She could hear several voices—men's—speaking in Arabic. No doubt they were discussing her! She felt her cheeks burn with shame, and her anger fought back her fear.

"Damn you! I'll show you!" she cried aloud. Clenching her fists, she thought of the man who intended to take her. She pictured him lounging in the next room, laughing with his men about the white woman he would soon have. Her anger intensified. He would take her— but he would never have her! A plan began to take root in her mind. She would indeed show him.

She would taunt him with that which he could never have. Neither ignorant of nor unskilled in the ways by which a woman pleases a man, she would give him a taste—only an enticing sample of what she had to offer. Then she would retreat behind a wall of indifference, leaving him longing for that which she would never give.

She slipped the gown over her head and smoothed it down her hips, then moved to the mirror to study her reflection. The green of the gown brought out the green of her eyes, and they sparkled like emeralds. With each quick breath she drew, the swell of her breasts fought the silk's restaint. She knew she would have no trouble putting her plan into action. She sat at the vanity and reached for a brush from the floor. Picking shards of glass from its bristles, she awaited his return and planned her strategy.

The Reguibat leader was quickly growing tired of the good-natured teasing and reminiscing intentionally meant to delay him. He was anxious for his men to leave. He stripped off his heavy robes, feigning discomfort with the desert heat. Lighting a cigarette, he stood at the tent's entrance and gazed out into the compound. A cooling breeze ruffled the loose-fitting shirt. Dressed now in tight, white breeches and knee-high riding boots, he could have come from the riding stables of any European estate.

He was, in fact, not as dark in skin color as his

companions. And despite the black hair which waved past his shoulders, he had at times a decidely European air about him. Years of living on the continent while obtaining the education his father had demanded had set him apart from his childhood friends. At times he had been acutely aware of the differences. Now was such a time. He thought of ordering his men to leave. But that would have been an admission that his desires were stronger than his self-control. He could not make that admission, not even to himself.

He was sure they had heard him tell the woman twenty minutes, and twice that time had passed. He was equally sure that they, too, were growing weary of the game. Two of the three were married and had wives waiting. They had to be fighting desires of their own. He knew he was right when a few moments later they nodded in agreement to one another. Rising, they salaamed to him and finally left the tent.

Still seated at the vanity, Eudora seethed in silent rage. Did the bastard's arrogance know no bounds? How dare he keep her waiting for what seemed an eternity! Was this some method of torment by which he hoped to allow time for her fear and terror to reduce her to a sobbing heap—one he could easily subdue and humiliate?

A flash of white in the mirror caught her eye, and she spun around and looked up. Her gaze was met by the cold black eyes she now knew so well. In spite of herself, a gasping sob escaped her throat.

He grabbed her shoulders, pulled her up, and drew her close. "I have kept you waiting too long." It was not an apology, but a simple statement. Fatigue vanished as his desire surged. Slowly he lowered his head to caress her neck with his lips.

Eudora knew the time had come. She had to play the part. She forced the tension from her body and pressed closer to him. She shut her eyes and tried to detach

74

herself from what she was about to do. She could feel his hardness against her belly. Standing on tiptoe, she was able to put herself almost level with him. She ground her hips against him. At the same time she encircled his neck with one arm while with her free hand she unbuttoned his shirt to let her fingers rest on the bare, brown chest.

Hatred and her desire for revenge fueled her courage. She wanted with all her heart to strike the arrogant Arab bastard where it would hurt most—his pride. She forced herself to continue. She leaned against him, allowing her breasts to touch and tantalize his skin. She was rewarded with his sharp intake of breath.

She was not acting as he had expected at all. But he was not about to object. He eased his grip on her shoulders and leaned away from her to undo her gown.

Catching him off balance and off guard, she was easily able to shove him away from her. "Do you really think I could want you?" she spat. "The very thought of your touch sickens me! You are no less repugnant to me than the man you killed! I only meant to show you what you will *never* have!" Triumph shone in her eyes. "You can take only part of me—the other only I can give. And I will never give it to *you!*"

Eudora held her breath. Inwardly she trembled in anticipation of the fury she was sure would follow.

But instead of lunging forward, he stepped back. The same slow smile appeared on his lips. "As you wish."

She stared in disbelief as he moved to the doorway. Drawing aside the drape, he paused to look back at her. "The desert teaches a man patience. There will come a time when you will give me all you have to give—and beg me to give you more."

"You arrogant bastard!" Eudora grabbed blindly for the hairbrush on the vanity's top. Hurling it at his departing form, she vented her indignation in futile frustration. "All I have to give you is contempt!"

*　　　*　　　*

A sweet, pungent aroma wafting through the thick curtains drove Eudora to consciousness. She recognized the odor immediately. It was the same scent of Turkish tobacco as that which had clung to the black-eyed Arab. Like a raging torrent the memory of the previous night washed over her.

After he had left her she had paced the small room. Anticipating his return, she almost prayed for it—for a merciful end to the agonizing waiting. She had prepared herself for what he would do. Let him be done with it!

Hours passed and still he did not reappear. Finally she had lain down. But sleep would not take her. Throughout the night she tossed and turned, terrified by the knowledge he would be back and tormented by the fact he yet wasn't.

The seemingly interminable night had ended just before dawn. Exhaustion released her from her vigil and she slept. But now she was awake.

She struggled to sit up. Looking at the pillow beside her, she could almost imagine his head upon it. She flung the pillow across the room and it struck the dresser, toppling a lamp and sending it crashing to the floor.

In the next room the Reguibat sheik smiled. The sound of something breaking seemed to be a common occurence when his high-spirited captive was awake. He stood and lit another cigarette. Inhaling deeply, he walked over to part the curtains. Silently he entered the bedroom.

"Good morning, little one. I trust you slept well."

At the sound of his voice Eudora's eyes flew open. She sat upright and instinctively pulled the covers to her neck.

The action seemed to amuse him. "There will come a time when you will not be so modest."

The mocking laughter which followed sent a cold shiver up her spine. A cutting retort formed in her mind, but the pounding headache she'd awakened with was quickly draining the fight from her. The sarcastic words died on her lips. In their stead she heard a plaintive

76

whisper. "How long are you going to keep me here?"

He sat down on the edge of the bed. "For as long as I desire. I find your company a very pleasant diversion."

Not unaware of the fear that shadowed her eyes, he leaned over and brushed a wisp of hair from her face. "Why?" He grinned slyly. "Surely you are not so soon bored with me?"

His touch was almost a caress. Eudora felt her heart leap in her breast. She twisted her head away in sudden fear. The movement brought a stab of pain to her already throbbing head. She closed her eyes and pressed her fingers to her temples.

"A headache often accompanies a sleepless night. I will see that Dahr-la brings you something for it."

Feeling him then ease away from the bed, Eudora opened her eyes cautiously. He had walked to the armoire and was removing his robes. He turned toward her, and she immediately shut her eyes.

"I shall be gone for the rest of the day. You should rest."

Relief flowed through her body. She opened her eyes in time to see him disappear through the heavy folds. She sank back against the pillows.

She awoke hours later to a woman's soft whisper. "My lady?"

Eudora opened her eyes to find a young girl of seventeen or eighteen standing at the curtains. She carried a tray laden with a silver tea service. Keeping her eyes lowered, the girl cautiously approached the bed. Eudora recognized her as the one who had fled the room the night before.

"I am Dahr-la," she said hesitantly. "My lord . . . my Lord Khamed has ordered that I serve you. I have brought you tea and something for your headache." She set the tray down upon the bedside table, looking at Eudora shyly. There was a world of understanding in her soft

77

brown eyes.

Eudora flushed fiercely. No doubt the girl had assumed what all in the camp must be now thinking—that she had been bedded by their leader.

Seeing her discomfort, the girl hastened to reassure her. "My Lord Khamed is most discreet, my lady. He has promised to flay me alive if even one detail of what occurs in his tent ever becomes public knowledge."

The girl's words brought a mixture of feelings. She was at once relieved while even more furious. How ironic that a desert marauder who killed, raided, and threatened torture—all without conscience—should be so concerned with his privacy!

Dahr-la offered her a cup, explaining that the tea contained a powder which would relieve the headache. Promising water for a hot bath, she withdrew, leaving Eudora alone with her thoughts.

"*Khamed!*" she repeated to herself. So now she knew his name! Sipping her tea, she suddenly realized how hungry she was. Gratefully she eyed what the maid had brought—a plateful of small cakes stuffed with dates and glazed with honey.

Eudora had just popped the final bite of the last cake into her mouth when Dahr-la returned. True to her word, the maid was dragging the same massive metal bathtub behind her. Setting the tub in place, she disappeared. Returning a moment later with buckets of heated water, she continued carrying them back and forth until the tub was full. After setting out towels and a cake of jasmine-scented soap, she thoughtfully turned her back.

Eudora gingerly got out of bed. Limping to the bath, she eased her body into the water, grateful for its soothing warmth.

Dahr-la busied herself straightening the bed. Then, clucking to herself, she began to pick up the pieces of broken pottery and glass from the floor. "What is your name?" she asked, in shy curiosity.

"Eudora. Eudora Morrel." She welcomed the girl's

company, suddenly regretting her treatment of her the night before.

"You are French, no?"

"Yes."

Eudora studied the girl closely. Dahr-la acted as if her response had answered a myraid of unspoken questions—questions which suddenly began to loom in her own mind.

Could her nationality be a factor in Khamed's interest in her? By kidnapping a Frenchwoman, could he feel he was exacting revenge upon the encroachers of his desert territory? And if so, what ends would he go to to sate his need for vengeance?

"My lady?"

Dahr-la's voice startled her. She'd been so lost in her thoughts she'd forgotten the girl's presence. Looking at her, Eudora suddenly realized Dahr-la might have the answers to the questions swirling in her brain. "Dahr-la, why have I been brought here? Does he . . . Khamed, do this . . . take—I mean, does he . . ." Feeling the immediate rush of color to her cheeks, she knew she would never be able to ask outright what the Arab's motives and practices were. And did she really want to know?

Dahr-la looked at the woman, who had now grown silent. She was fairly sure she knew what her new mistress had been trying to ask. But how could she explain her lord's actions? Yes, he took women to his bed—women of the tribe who caught his fancy and then later whispered among themselves of their lord's skill in lovemaking. And as was the way of the desert, he had upon occasion singled out female prisoners for his personal pleasure. So, too, had he brought white women, met in the cities to his camp.

Still, she could not recall that any of them had ever fought his interest. This woman was a fool not to realize how lucky she was. Khamed was handsome and virile and more compassionate than most tribal lords. When finished with his women, he did not turn them over to his

79

men or to the slave auctioneer's block, as was the common practice. White or Arab, they were always returned safely to their homes, usually with a valuable piece of jewelry in hand as payment for services rendered.

"My lord sometimes entertains female guests." Dahr-la finally replied. "They are women who have caught his eye, who are pleased to have been singled out by him. It is not his usual practice to entertain unwilling guests." He had no need to, she wanted to add, for there were women aplenty who would share his bed willingly.

Eudora repeated the girl's words aloud. "It is not his habit to *entertain unwilling guests?*" She choked on the euphemism. "How fortunate for me he has made an exception!"

She realized how silly her comment must have sounded when Dahr-la began to giggle. She had to admit that looking upon her situation as an unfortunate digression from the desert outlaw's personal code of etiquette was an irony akin to lunacy. When she suddenly found herself beginning to giggle as well, she wondered what was in the powder she'd drunk in her tea. Or was she indeed losing her mind?

The sound of feminine laughter greeted Khamed as he stormed into his tent. His mood was as black as the *shesh* he tore from his head. The exchange of arms had not gone as planned. The renegade gun runners he was forced to deal with had failed to arrive at the prearranged site. The entire morning had been a waste of time. He strode across the room to the dividing drape and threw open the curtain.

He was unprepared for the sight which greeted him. His captive sat in the bathtub, tears of laughter streaming down her face. The maid, Dahr-la, lay flat on her back on the bed, apparently overcome with the same affliction. "Unless you plan to share my bed, Dahr-la, I suggest you get *out* of it!'"

Both women froze at the sound of his voice. Swiftly crawling off the bed, Dahr-la darted for the exit.

"Perhaps you should first finish attending to . . . ah . . ." Realizing he didn't know her name, he looked at the Frenchwoman.

"Eudora," Dahr-la whispered, hurrying toward the dresser. She fetched a dressing gown from the bottom drawer and held it for the woman. Standing between them, she effectively blocked his view.

Eudora stood with her back to him and stepped from the tub. Silently she thanked the maid for her thoughtful discretion. Hastily she slipped into the gown. To her horror she realized the lilac garment was a negligée—soft and loose, with ruffled elbow sleeves and a lace bertha designed to reveal more than it concealed. A single hook at the waist provided the only closure. Clutching a fistful of fine Valenciennes lace in her left hand, she held the folds closed across her hips. She turned to face him, nodding to Dahr-la.

Relieved to have been excused, the maid rushed to the curtains, throwing her a sympathetic look over her shoulder.

Khamed could not take his eyes off his captive. In spite of her efforts, a sumptuous amount of soft flesh remained uncovered. And below her waist the dampness of her body was causing the lilac fabric to cling to every luscious curve.

Eudora moved very slowly away from him toward the vanity. She could feel his eyes on her, burning through the lace.

"Well, little one, would you care to explain what that was all about?"

"I doubt *you* would understand!" Despite her growing fear, she glared at him, refusing to let her eyes drop. When he finally looked away, she felt a victory had been won. She sank down into the chair, her knees suddenly weak. Feigning an indifference she did not feel, she picked up a brush from the vanity and began brushing her hair. Cautiously she watched Khamed in the mirror.

He shrugged off his sand-laden robes and then sat on the bed. After removing his boots, he stood up and pulled off his shirt. When he started to unfasten the drawstring belt at his waist, she whirled to face him. "What are you doing?" she gasped.

"Relax, little one." He smiled, his eyes lighting up with a golden cast. "I only want a bath." He bent to strip off the pants, and she immediately turned her head away.

She heard his laughter and a splash. She risked a peek at the mirror. He was already in the tub and had begun to rub the cake of soap across his muscular chest. She watched as the lather slid down to his belly. Even as he sat it was taut, rippled with muscle. The same sensation she had felt that morning at his touch happened again. Ignoring it, she began to yank the brush furiously through her hair.

The seconds passed as hours.

She couldn't bear it any longer. If she had to sit there another minute she'd go mad.

"Am I permitted to go into the next room?" She glared at his reflection in the mirror.

"Do you not care for my company?"

"No!"

"I do not believe you, but I shall let it pass. You may go. I would suggest, however, that you dress first. My men often enter that room unannounced."

From the look of anticipation on his face, she knew he was thinking that she would first have to undress. She quickly decided she was, at least for the moment, safer attired in the negligée than she would be changing in front of him. "When are you going to let me go?"

As if purposely delaying his response to heighten her fear, he returned to his bathing, bringing up several handfuls of rinse water to his chest before answering. "I told you this morning, when I am tired of you."

"But Dahr-la said . . ." she turned to face him. "She

82

said you do not keep women against their will!"

"Dahr-la talks too much! Especially about matters which do not concern her!"

Eudora flushed, realizing she could have brought harm to the girl. "She didn't mean anything . . . she only . . . I asked her—"

"Enough!" He stood and wrapped a towel around his waist. "I have no intention of explaining my actions . . . to you or to your maid."

He stepped from the tub, and she found herself mesmerized by the small drops of water beading together on his bronzed skin. Like the tributaries of a river, they converged to run down his broad chest. His black hair curled around his forehead and neck in wet ringlets. She realized his face was now smooth-shaven. Had he shaved while she slept that morning?

He picked up another towel from the bed and began to dry himself.

Confident that he was too preoccupied to notice, she continued to watch him. His movements were fluid and graceful, like those of a jungle cat. And like a wild beast, the grace did not mask but only emphasized his underlying power and strength.

God, he is a handsome man! she thought suddenly. Women at home would swoon with just one look from those piercing dark eyes. She knew she would never forget his eyes. For days they were all that she had been able to see of him as he peered out from the slit of the black *shesh*. She'd been certain his eyes were black, but, strangely, in the light they now looked golden.

"Are you finished?"

The soft, even voice cut through her thoughts like a knife, bringing her abruptly back to the present. She felt her face grow hot and quickly lowered her eyes. Had he been aware of her staring at him the entire time?

"What?" she finally murmured, still unable to look at him.

"I asked if you were finished examining me."

83

She glanced up at him, hesitantly.

His face had lost much of its hardness. The menacing fierceness which had so frightened her was gone. His eyes were indeed a soft golden color, and the smile he gave her was gentle and teasing, without its usual sarcasm.

Unnerved by his awareness of her silent appraisal and confused by the change in his eyes, she was unable even feebly to deny the charge. She lowered her head once again in embarrassment.

"Eudora."

The sound of her name coming from him startled her. It was the first time he had ever addressed her as such, and his accented pronunciation made it sound like a caress. She lifted her head to meet his eyes. He was sitting on the bed, lighting a cigarette. The sharp edge had crept back into his voice. "Come here."

He tossed the spent match to the floor and exhaled slowly. The blue smoke drifted lazily upward, past eyes which were now black and cold.

She gripped the back of the chair, hoping against hope she might miraculously become rooted to it.

"I am accustomed to having my orders obeyed," he said, as if giving her a final warning.

Eudora was physically unable to move. Her legs felt as if they had turned to water. Her stomach was knotted, her chest tight. She blinked repeatedly, but her eyes would not focus.

The room reeled and time suddenly stood still.

She choked back a cry of fear. She saw him rise, slowly, as if in a dream. Her breath came in labored sobs. He neared her and she opened her mouth to scream. No sound would come, save a hoarse rasping for air.

He reached for her and she felt herself being lifted. She stood, supported only by the brown hands which gripped her arms. Her head rolled back and her eyes met his. The twin black coals burned brightly, consuming his face and leaving the room in total darkness.

Chapter Six

Khamed sat in the main room and contemplated his captive's behavior. He considered, then dismissed the possibility that her swoon had been contrived. He was certain she was not the sort of woman to resort to such a consummately feminine wile. Were she, he reasoned, she would have done so long before this. And were she such a woman, he would have had no interest in her at all.

Women who so easily succumbed to that uniquely European anomaly "the vapors" had always filled him with disgust. It was strength which he admired in a woman—strength of spirit demonstrated by a display of singularly unfeminine behavior. That was the single factor which had generated his interest in her long before he had ever seen her.

Khamed rose from the sofa and began to pace. He remembered how his spies in Ghardaïa had first informed him of the proposed military supply caravan. An attack had been planned upon it. He had summoned men from the outlying camps and assembled a raiding party. A week before the caravan's scheduled departure, he'd dispatched several men to Ghardaïa to follow its progress and to report any change in plans. Finally, Khamed and a hand-picked following of a hundred men had left to rendezvous with his advance spies, at a site several days' journey from the city.

On the day scheduled for the caravan's departure, one of his spies had intercepted his raiding party. The scout reported having seen a white woman in the marketplace with the French supply sergeant. He was certain they had been purchasing camels and provisions for her to accompany the caravan.

Khamed had been immediately intrigued with this information. The French rarely brought their womenfolk to the interior, and no woman had ever accompanied a military transport. Could she be the wife of a high-ranking official in Ouargla? If so, her worth was far greater than that of the guns and ammunition they sought.

His man hadn't known her identity. But as the scout had described her, Khamed's interest was piqued. She was young, perhaps in her late twenties, and exquisite. Deciding to see the woman for himself, Khamed had left the main party to join his scouts trailing the caravan. Stealing into the French camp that first night out, he had slashed the wall of the small canvas tent to view her as she slept.

His man had not lied or exaggerated. The narrow shaft of moonlight penetrating the tent's dark interior had illuminated a face of exceptional beauty. For a reason Khamed himself could not explain, seeing her those few seconds had ignited his desires, and sealed her fate. He wanted her, and what he wanted, he took. The guns and ammunition became a secondary consideration. Not wanting to risk endangering her life in the darkness of a night assault, he had decided to attack at dawn.

Memories of the attack now brought his thoughts to the one called Sabatin. What was the lanky Frenchman's relationship to the woman in the next room? Instinctively, Khamed knew she did not belong to him. If she had, Sabatin would have shot her as soon as the Reguibat had charged. No man would have hesitated and left the task to another, if the woman were truly his.

Silently Khamed again thanked Allah for his own unerring aim and Sabatin's indecisiveness.

He paused in his pacing to stop at the desk. Lighting a cigarette, he cast a glance at the room's dividing drape. His fascination with the woman beyond the curtain was quickly becoming an obsession. More than physical, it was almost spiritual. Her courage and pride seemed to touch his deepest instincts. Never had he desired a woman more than when he had come to her the previous night.

Vividly, he recalled the sensuous curves of her body outlined and enhanced by the silk gown, the burning touch of her fingertips, which had scorched his very soul. It had not been easy to walk away, then or now, yet he had. He had because he wanted a willing woman in his bed—or rather, he wanted *this* woman willing. She was different, unique. As much as he wanted her, he knew he would want her tomorrow. Therefore he could walk away. But the thought did not please him. The desire to have her still burned in his loins like fire.

Angrily he grabbed for the shirt he had brought with him after leaving the bedroom. He strode across the tent and ripped open the outside flap. A white figure instantly appeared in his field of vision.

"My lord."

Khamed glowered at the man standing before him. His lieutenant had been given orders that he was not to be disturbed. "What is it, Kahlil?"

Kahlil gestured across the compound toward a small tent set off from the others. "The prisoners have been demanding all morning to speak with you." As he spoke, his gaze went to Khamed's bare torso. "If you are . . . ah . . . otherwise occupied, I can act on your behalf."

Noting the man's suppressed grin, Khamed scowled. Turning his attention to the shirt in his hands, he slid an arm into a sleeve. "I will take care of it." He stabbed his other arm into the sleeve behind his back. He needed to take his mind off the woman in his tent. A confrontation with her countrymen might just accomplish that. Besides, Kahlil was scheduled to lead a relief patrol out into the desert to rendezvous with the men who had been left behind to escort the captured French supply train.

He yanked on the shirt, not bothering to button it. "Go and assemble your men. I want you under way within the hour."

As Kahlil bowed and withdrew, Khamed cast a final glance back toward his tent. What was it about her which so intrigued him? Resolving to put her from his thoughts, he turned and headed for the edge of the compound.

As he walked, he scanned the camp. To his eye it was clean and orderly. He smiled, watching the children and dogs chasing one another in the dirt. The sounds of the barking and laughter floated in the air, mixing with the chatter of women's voices. Their colorful forms scurried about the camp, hauling water and gathering wood. Khamed felt the tension leave his body.

He approached the small camel's-hair tent with its posted guard. Nodding in response to his man's greeting, he drew back the flap and entered.

The Frenchmen rose immediately to their feet.

Khamed touched his forehead, lips, and breast lightly with the fingers of his right hand and bowed slightly. "*Salaam al laikum*—peace be upon you." He watched the lieutenant return the ritual gesture that signified neither captor nor captive would think, speak, or harbor evil in his heart for the other.

With Sabatin standing stiffly at his side, du Bois then responded in halting Arabic. "*Al laikum el Salaam*—and upon you peace."

Khamed's jaw tightened. It was a ridiculous statement in view of their circumstances. They both knew neither would hesitate to kill the other if they were anywhere but in the Reguibat camp. Yet Moslem hospitality was a peculiar, twisted paradox. A guest, even an enemy, was treated well, and with respect. As long as he remained, he was fiercely protected against all—even members of the host's own tribe.

Khamed rose to his full height. "*Ach tehabb*—what do you want?" he demanded. He lit a cigarette and waited for the lieutenant's answer.

Flushing furiously, du Bois swallowed hard. "*Sidi*— Lord—ah . . ."

"Khamed."

"*Sidi* Khamed, do you speak French?"

Khamed nodded curtly.

"I am Lieutenant Henri du Bois." Turning, he gestured to Sabatin. "This is Pierre Sabatin. Monsieur Sabatin is a civilian, a reporter for a newspaper in Paris. We humbly request to know, *Sidi,* just why it is we were attacked and taken prisoner."

Suddenly Sabatin stepped boldly forward. "This is an outrage! You cannot hold us here. We are French citizens! I demand that we be allowed to speak to your sheik."

Khamed raised an eyebrow and withheld a smile. Apparently Sabatin had not yet realized just whom he was addressing. "You are in no position to demand anything, Monsieur," he replied calmly. He dragged on his cigarette and studied the younger man.

The lieutenant's nauseatingly solicitous demeanor was an offense to his own warrior code—no Reguibat would behave in such a self-defacing manner in the presence of his enemy. However, Sabatin's display of nerve amused him, and earned the man a degree of his respect. "Your government shall be informed of your . . . situation. Until an exchange can be arranged, you both shall remain here—as my guests."

Khamed smiled, waiting for the meaning of his words to become clear to the Frenchman. "As long as there are no attempts to . . . refuse my hospitality, your safety is assured."

Sabatin stared at the man in dismay. He and du Bois

had requested an audience with the marauders' sheik, yet this Arab who now stood before them was but six or eight years older than himself. Logic told him he was far too young to be the tribe's chieftain. Still, he had called himself "Lord" Khamed, and there was no mistaking the arrogance and demeanor of authority with which he carried himself.

Choking back his pride, he forced himself to address the Arab civilly, introducing the topic which was the real motive for this requested audience. He and du Bois hoped to persuade the tribe's sheik to grant Eudora protection from abuse by his men—specifically from one man, the black-*sheshed* leader of the raiding party. "Lord Khamed, there was a woman in our party. Last night she was separated from us and taken to another tent. I want your assurance that she, too, will not be harmed . . . in *any* manner."

Khamed looked at him coldly. "The woman is no longer your concern." He dropped his cigarette on the dirt floor and ground it out with the heel of his boot. Suddenly a sinister smile distorted his handsome face. "She is mine."

Sabatin felt as if he had been struck. In a flash of recognition and understanding he realized the man's identity. Khamed and the black-*sheshed* leader of the raiding party were one and the same! The hope he'd had, that the tribal lord might intervene and protect Eudora from their captor, died. Fighting for control, he glared at the Arab. The man's ruffled hair and partial state of undress now took on an alarming significance. "What have you done to her?" he gasped.

"Nothing she did not want done."

"You bastard! I'll kill you!" Sabatin hurled himself at the man in a blind rage.

Khamed easily sidestepped the lunge. He had anticipated the Frenchman's reaction and for that reason had discarded the cigarette. Using the same tactic he had used with the sergeant, he grabbed Sabatin across the neck, choking him with his forearm. "Don't be a fool, Monsieur!" He held the iron grip for a moment longer, then released it, tossing his hapless opponent from him.

Sabatin clutched at his throat, gasping for air. "If you have harmed her," he wheezed, "I swear, I'll kill you!"

Khamed laughed at the emotional, irrational threat. "As I stated before, Monsieur . . . you are in no position." Turning, he exited the tent, still smiling. It would appear his captive instilled fierce passion—of all kinds—in the men who encountered her.

Walking across the camp he spotted a group of riders gathered outside his tent. As he approached, he put aside further thoughts of Eudora and her countryman.

Eudora fought to remain within the comforting black fog which embraced her. She didn't want to wake up. Consciousness would only deliver her back into the hell she could not escape. She knew she was lying in the Arab's bed. The knowledge that it was he who had placed her there, like a sacrifical lamb upon an altar, filled her with outrage and fear. Was he merely waiting for her to regain consciousness?

For several minutes she lay there. Suddenly she knew he was not coming back. As on the previous night, he had walked away. But why? It was almost as if he were toying with her, deliberately arousing her fear to taunt her with her position. He was the one in power, in control. It was obvious he intended to keep her for some purpose, and the what, when and where were all at his discretion.

Suddenly his words came back to haunt her. *There will come a time. . . .* Dear God! Could he really believe that she would someday willingly surrender? No . . . the thought was just too unfathomable. It had to be the other. The arrogant bastard was merely playing a game of manipulation and control.

91

Well let him, she thought. It certainly was a game he would never win.

With the matter resolved, she rose and looked about the room. The negligée she wore was unsuitable. She had to find something to wear. Dahr-la had taken the clothes she'd arrived in, and she didn't know what had become of her trunk. Perhaps she could find something in the drawer from which the girl had taken the gown.

She knelt before the dresser and pulled out the bottom drawer. Her eyes widened at the sight of its contents. The assortment of lace, silks, and satins it contained was breathtaking. She fingered the delicate lingerie, all exquisitely made and wonderfully feminine. She had seen nothing finer in the best shops in Paris. It appeared Khamed kept his "guests" well clothed!

Setting aside her indignation, she rifled through the drawer. She was torn between a rich green silk dressing gown and an ivory-colored one embroidered with gold threads on its satin lapels and deep cuffs. No, she decided, the intricate motif of flowers and vines made it much too fancy for her taste.

"I would prefer the green one—on you. It matches your eyes."

The sound of Khamed's voice drew a gasp from her. She had not heard him enter. How long had he been standing behind her, watching her? With a shaking hand she reached for the ivory gown. "I would prefer my own clothes!" she managed to snap. "But since my trunk seems to have vanished, this one will have to do." She was pleased her voice held firm, without betraying the trembling she felt within. She clutched the gown and stared at him.

If he felt any irritation at her small gesture of defiance, Khamed did not show it. His expression remained unchanged as he walked to the armoire and withdrew the familiar white robes.

Eudora glared at him. "I said I would like to have my

own clothes! Surely that's not too much to ask? Or have they been stolen along with the rest of the caravan's supplies?"

She felt her anger rising as he continued to ignore her. He buttoned the shirt across his broad chest and fastened the waistcloth in place. Then he began to wrap a long length of black cloth around his head.

Intrigued, Eudora momentarily forgot her anger as she watched the deft movements of his hands. Completing his task, he pulled on his robe and walked to the dresser. From the top drawer he removed a revolver. Flipping open the cylinder, he seemed to be checking to verify that it was still loaded. As he tucked the gun into his waistcloth, he walked toward her.

"I will not be back until tomorrow. You are to remain inside the tent."

Eudora stared at the gun. Her thoughts were not on what he was saying. If only she had known it was there sooner. . . .

"Eudora."

She looked up and met a fierce glare.

"I want you to remain inside the tent."

Refusing to acknowledge his order, Eudora averted her eyes. She felt his fingers dig into her upper arm and jerked her head up.

"Inside this tent, little one," he repeated. His head bent swiftly. He kissed her, neither roughly nor gently, but in a taunting demonstration of possession, then put her from him.

Eudora stumbled backward. As she watched him disappear through the dividing drape, she wiped her mouth with the back of her hand. The effort proved futile. She could still feel the touch of his scorching lips branding her as his own. She could feel something else as well—a twinge of a sensation she refused to acknowledge: desire.

Turning from the wall of fabric, she closed her eyes

and pressed her fingertips to her temples. Khamed would be gone for an entire day and night. The knowledge of her temporary reprieve filled her with hope, and a curious sense of panic. She clenched her hands in anguish. She had to think rationally; she needed a plan. She had to find Sabatin and du Bois. They would help her. They would know what to do.

Eudora opened her eyes and started to move toward the bed. The sight of it brought her up short. No doubt before her arrival he had slept upon those same sheets! There was no way she would sleep another night where he had lain. She ran to the bed and began to tear the white silk coverings from it.

"My lady!"

Dahr-la's gasp of dismay from the room's entrance served only to spur Eudora on. Ignoring the girl, she tossed the wadded linens to the floor and went to the armoire. Throwing open the doors, she quickly eyed the neatly folded stacks of towels and sheets before reaching for a cream-colored cotton set.

"My lady . . ." Again Dahr-la spoke up from the doorway. "My lord prefers silk."

"Well, *I* prefer cotton!" Eudora whirled to face her. She could feel herself shaking with anger, but lashing out at a girl who was not the source of it was pointless. "I'm sorry. I didn't mean to snap at you. Will you help me?"

Dahr-la hesitated. It was obvious she was reluctant to do anything that might incur Khamed's displeasure.

"You can tell him I insisted. Surely that will absolve you from responsibility."

Seemingly satisfied with that option, Dahr-la stepped forward. Wordlessly she held out her arms to accept the cotton sheets from Eudora's hands.

Eudora acknowledged the mute obedience with a slight smile. As the girl began to make the bed, she turned her thoughts back to her earlier deliberations. Before she could make use of Khamed's absence, she needed to be sure he had in fact left the camp. Somehow she felt certain it was not beyond the realm of possibility for him to have lied to her, tricking her into a false sense of security. "Dahr-la, where did Khamed go?"

"To one of the outlying camps." Dahr-la bent to tuck in a corner. "The headman, who was quite old and in failing health, has died. A successor must be appointed."

Eudora forced a response. "Oh." The tribal affairs of her captor held no interest for her other than to instill gratitude that they had taken him from the camp. With her first question answered, she broached a second. "Dahr-la . . . the two other men who arrived with me, where are they?"

The girl hesitated. "They are safe, my lady. I assure you."

"Where are they?"

"They are being kept in a guarded tent at the edge of the camp."

Hope flared in Eudora's heart. She had feared that Sabatin and du Bois might have been moved to another camp. "Can you help me? I want to see them."

Dahr-la shook her head. "That is impossible! My lord has ordered that you remain here—inside the tent."

Eudora's earlier anger returned instantly. "I don't care *what* he has ordered!" She spat out the words contemptuously. "I do not follow his orders. He is not *my* lord."

"You are wrong, my lady." Avoiding direct eye contact, Dahr-la looked up from her task. "By taking you for his own, Khamed has made himself your lord. You are now as much subject to his word and will as I . . . perhaps even more."

The soft-spoken words were like a sobering blow. Eudora felt her breath catch in her throat. She turned away and swallowed hard.

Suddenly the sound of a man's voice outside the room drifted through the curtain. Though it was not *his* voice, she tensed.

Dahr-la heard it, too. She darted from the bed and disappeared through the drape. A moment later she returned. "Would you like your trunk, my lady?"

Eudora looked at her astonished. Khamed *had* heard her! Masking her pleasure, she nodded.

Dahr-la parted the curtain and a white-robed man entered, dragging the trunk behind him. Eudora watched as he set his burden down in the center of the room. As had all of Khamed's men, he kept his eyes lowered, bowing respectfully to her as he withdrew.

She moved toward the trunk. Kneeling before it, she noticed instantly that its heavy brass lock had been broken. She seethed in mounting rage. There was no doubt in her mind that the trunk and its contents had been searched. She felt violated. "Did he think he might find a weapon hidden in a corset or rolled up in a petticoat?"

Her sarcastic comment, unwittingly muttered aloud, brought Dahr-la to her side. "My lady?"

"It's nothing, Dahr-la. I was talking to myself." Eudora looked up at the girl and forced a reassuring smile. Returning her attention to the trunk, she began to unfasten the heavy leather straps that bound it. Expecting the worst, she raised the lid. To her surprise not a single chemise or silk stocking appeared out of place. She stared at the neatly folded articles of clothing. Upon closer examination it became clear the items had been removed, but carefully replaced.

Eudora slammed the lid shut and stood. Nothing the man did made any sense.

Dahr-la looked at her in wide-eyed confusion. "Shall I put your things away?" She gestured helplessly toward the trunk.

Eudora knew her own actions were making no sense to the girl. She had to admit they were making precious little sense to herself. She nodded numbly in response to

Dahr-la's question, then turned away. She could not understand him, and it was tearing at her. Somehow he was able to anticipate her thoughts—then do the opposite, chipping away at her perception of reality.

Suddenly, for the first time, she began to fear his threat. *There will come a time*. . . . Well before that could happen, she would be gone! First thing in the morning, before the camp had risen, she was going to find Sabatin. Together with du Bois, they would devise a plan of escape.

Chapter Seven

Eudora arose the next morning before dawn. Physically and mentally exhausted, she had slept deeply, her mind refusing to focus on the fate that awaited her upon Khamed's return. She prayed this morning's contact with Sabatin and du Bois would somehow deliver her from his hands.

She dressed quickly in chemise and petticoats before moving to the large armoire where Dahr-la had hung her dresses. Opening the doors, she clenched her teeth. The sight of her gowns closeted alongside her captor's robes filled her with outrage. The allusion to an intimacy between them seemed vulgar.

She crushed the offensive white garments to one side and selected a simple shirtwaist of yellow silk organdy. Donning the dress, she sat at the vanity. She needed a few moments to gather her courage. Seeing her toiletries laid out before her, she reached for a gilt-backed brush. Brushing her hair seemed to have a calming effect. She twisted the smooth auburn waves into a knot atop her head, securing the arrangement with tortoiseshell combs. Rising, she shivered slightly . . . from the chill of the early morning air, she told herself.

She returned to the armoire and withdrew a red and black challis shawl. Its deep colors clashed horribly with the pale yellow of her gown. Her concern, however, was warmth, not fashion. She tossed the shawl over her shoulders and walked to the curtained doorway. Drawing a deep breath, she hesitantly stepped through the folds.

Instantly Eudora recognized the larger room's curious blend of Arab and European furnishings: the small sofa of midnight blue damask, with its cushions of red and purple silk, the low black lacquer table before it, inlaid with mother-of-pearl and abalone shell, the bookcases along the tapestried walls. . . .

She shivered again and wrapped the shawl more tightly about her. Forcing aside the vivid memory of her arrival at the tent two nights earlier, she quickly crossed the room to the doorway and unbuttoned the flaplike covering to peer out.

The camp appeared still asleep. All was dark and quiet. She drew the flap aside. Slipping through the opening, she ventured a few steps forward—and promptly froze. Her heart jumped in her chest.

Somehow she had missed seeing the blanketed form of a man propped against the awning's support pole! Afraid to move, for fear he would detect her presence, she stood, her eyes closed, her pulse racing. She would have to go back. Suddenly above the sound of her own shallow breathing she heard a deep and rhythmic snoring. Her eyes flew open. He was fast asleep! Quickly she stepped back. Keeping close to the wall of the tent she began to edge away from him. At the corner, she paused to collect her thoughts.

She had no idea where Sabatin and du Bois were being held, other than what Dahr-la had told her: *a guarded tent at the edge of the camp.* How many guarded tents could there be, she wondered—and in what direction? Hoping fervently there would be but one, with a guard no more vigilant than her own, she stepped away from the tent. Turning, she gasped in terror.

Her eyes were filled with the sight of white blocking her path. Instinctively she stumbled backward, but her flight was halted by a tight grip on her arm which yanked her forward.

She lifted her head. Though her vision was blurred with panic and fear, she instantly recognized the bearded face before her. The man was one who had accompanied the raiding party. He'd appeared to be a sort of lieutenant to Khamed and had been the one who had handed her her horse's reins with such obvious reservation.

"Let me go!" she demanded, a surge of anger lending her false courage.

Eudora felt the grip on her arm tighten as the *sheshed* head slowly shook back and forth. He began to pull her toward the tent's entrance. Icy fear twisted inside her. Could it be that in Khamed's absence she was to be given over to his men? Suddenly the hold on her arm was released.

Spotting the still sleeping guard, her captor let forth a scathing stream of Arabic. The guard jumped to his feet, terror filling his eyes. Eudora watched as he cowered before the man at her side, seemingly begging forgiveness.

Ignoring him, the bearded Arab returned his attention to her. Keeping one hand at the small of her back, he reached out with the other to draw aside the tent's flap. A firm push toward the opening followed. "Our lord has instructed you to remain inside the tent. Do not attempt to leave again."

Relief flowed through her. Weakly she stepped forward. Suddenly she stopped. He had spoken to her in French! "Wait! I wasn't trying to escape. I only want to see my friends. Please, would you take me to them?"

Eudora shrank from the cold stare he leveled at her— cold not like Khamed's dark gazes, which were devoid of emotion, but cold as in lack of warmth. Khamed's lieutenant did not approve of her. More aptly, he did not approve of his lord's indulgence of her.

He shook his head. "I am sorry, madame. I have my orders."

Though his words were respectful, somehow she knew

if the bearded Arab were to have his way, she'd be bound and gagged. Unwilling to raise his ire, she turned and entered the tent. As the flap fell into place behind her, she stared at the room, now suddenly so familiar. She moved to the sofa and numbly sat down. How would she face that which she had no choice but to endure?

Eudora paced the main room. Several hours had passed since her thwarted attempt to see Sabatin and du Bois. Dawn had broken, and with its arrival the sleeping camp had sprung to life. All morning the sounds of the Reguibats activities had drifted through the heavy tent walls. She'd heard children crying, women scolding, the canter of horses entering and departing the oasis.

Dahr-la, who had arrived sleepy-eyed and yawning only minutes after the confrontation with Khamed's lieutenant, now scurried about the tent tending her own duties.

Eudora suspected the man had awakened her, ordering the maid to the tent to remain with her mistress until Khamed's return. Certainly the disapproving frowns the girl leveled at her each time she entered the tent lent credence to that theory.

Ignoring yet another reproachful look, she crossed the room to the bookcases along the far wall. Bored, she scanned the titles. Although most were in Arabic, many were in French. A few were even in English. Her curiosity was aroused. "Dahr-la, does Khamed speak English as well as French?"

Dahr-la nodded. "My lord's mother was an English-woman, the daughter of a British colonel stationed in Cairo."

While the girl's words surprised her, intuitively Eudora had suspected as much. She had thought him too tall and light-skinned to be a full-blooded Arab. And without question his demeanor was oddly different from his men at times—decidedly European.

"Oh?" Hoping to disguise her growing curiosity as polite interest, she reached for a French novel. "Did his parents meet in Egypt?" she asked casually, opening the book.

"No, in Algeria."

"Indeed?" Eudora looked up from the book in surprise.

"She was on holiday with her father in Algiers. At the time Khamed's father, *Sidi* Haisim, was also in Algiers, attending a meeting to settle a boundary dispute between the desert tribes. The French Ambassador invited all the tribal leaders to a soirée. The colonel and his daughter were also invited, and it was there that she and Haisim met. According to the lieutenants who were with him, it was love at first sight. Her father, of course, was outraged at the very thought of their involvement. Even though Haisim's intentions were clearly honorable, a mixed marriage was inconceivable to him. He ordered her back to England immediately. But before his orders could be carried out, she eloped with Haisim and returned with him to the desert."

Dahr-la paused.

Eudora was sure the girl expected some reaction from her upon hearing that a white woman had freely fallen in love with a Reguibat, choosing to live with him in his desert world. She forced her expression to remain unchanged.

"Khamed was born a year later," Dahr-la finally continued. "But the childbirth was difficult. She nearly died and never regained her strength. Life in the desert proved too harsh for her, and after two more years she returned to England, taking Khamed with her. She and Haisim agreed that she would keep their son only until he was seven. Then he would have to be returned to his father."

"Seven?" Eudora stared at her in disbelief. "He was but a small boy! Why would a permanent separation from his mother be forced at such a young age?"

"It is the age of circumcision," Dahr-la explained matter-of-factly, "the age at which a boy passes from the parental control of his mother to that of his father. The men of the tribe then school him in the art of riding and the use of arms. In Khamed's case, he was also Haisim's sole heir. His place was with his people. The decision proved to be most wise, for in the following year his mother died."

Eudora was unconscious of her sharp intake of breath as she relived the pain of her own mother's death. "How hard that must have been for him!"

"Such is the will of Allah. Khamed remained here, in the desert, until he was sixteen. Then, *Sidi* Haisim insisted he return to Europe to be educated. When Khamed refused to go back to England, he was sent instead to Paris. He remained in France for five years until his education was completed. At age twenty-one he returned to take his place at his father's side. When Haisim died three years later, he became sheik."

"Your 'sheik' is like a king, then? It is the custom that upon his death his son becomes his successor?"

"Not always. Heredity is oftentimes not enough. The direct heir can be removed by a more powerful kinsman whose claim is less direct—a cousin or an uncle or such. According to our law, supreme authority is vested in he who is strongest and most capable."

In spite of herself, Eudora felt a grudging respect for the man who had obviously earned and maintained the loyalty of the desert tribe when so young. She was unable to prevent herself from voicing the thought aloud. "Was twenty-four not a young age to have possessed those qualities?"

"We believe in divine favor, my lady, and Khamed displayed all of its manifest signs: the ability to rule, wealth, physical strength, and prowess tried and proven on the battlefield. In the ten years he has been sheik, there has been no other man near his equal."

Eudora stiffened. Dahr-la's words of heartfelt admiration had caused an instant, bitter taste in her mouth. Respect was one thing—but outright adoration was another! She had heard enough. Determined to put an end to the conversation, she slammed the book closed. Turning to replace it in the bookcase, she caught sight of Dahr-la's face. The girl was trying hard to suppress a smile.

Angered that her thoughts and emotions were so transparent, Eudora quickly diverted her attention. She fingered the rich leather spines of the books whose titles indicated subjects ranging from medicine to travel, philosophy to history. Along with the novels, there were a couple of books of poetry. Silently she scoffed at the idea of the desert warlord being moved by verse. A European education may have furnished him the pretense of civilization, but underneath the veneer her arrogant captor was no different from the savage tribesmen he ruled.

Eudora selected another novel. Brushing wordlessly past Dahr-la, she moved to the sofa and sat down. The book remained unopened in her lap. Try as she might, she could not stop thinking about what the maid had told her of Khamed's childhood. How could a seven-year-old child have possibly understood the reasons he could no longer stay with his mother? He had to have felt abandoned and no longer wanted. The pain stemming from such a feeling was one she had known well. After her mother's death she had been but an unwelcome intrusion in her father's life.

Suddenly she felt a strange sense of kinship with the boy, Khamed had been. Immediately she forced the feelings aside. How could she feel anything but loathing for the cruel Arab who now held her captive?

At that moment Dahr-la entered from the bedroom. With her housekeeping tasks apparently completed, she settled herself upon a cushion on the floor.

Eudora watched as she removed a length of soft, white cotton cloth from the basket she had brought with her that morning. A needle and fine silken thread appeared next. Intrigued, she followed the deft movements of the girl's fingers as she began to embroider the fabric. "What is it to be?" she asked finally.

"A wrap for my sister's baby." Dahr-la smiled broadly. "He shall be born soon."

"He?"

"Or she." Dahr-la laughed. "Of course, Kahlil prays daily that Allah will see fit to bless him with a son."

"Kahlil? He is your sister's husband?"

Almost sheepishly, Dahr-la smiled. "Yes. In fact, he is the man you spoke with this morning. His position in the tribe is second only to my lord's. They have been friends since boyhood."

Anxious to keep the conversation from again turning to Khamed, Eudora quickly changed the subject. "How long have he and your sister been married?"

"Nearly a year. However, Kiri is not his first wife. Because his first was barren, he took another, younger wife."

"He divorced his first wife merely because she could give him no children?" Eudora looked at the girl aghast.

"No heirs," Dahr-la corrected solemnly. Then she smiled. "Kahlil did not divorce Elon. Though he would have been within his rights to do so, there was no need. You see, our laws permit a man to take up to four wives. Most often, however, a man keeps his first wife always. Then, if he desires, he takes one or more secondary wives—one after the other."

"What a barbaric and vile custom!"

Dahr-la seemed unaffected by her outburst. "Without such laws, my lady, a woman such as Elon would be forced to return to her father in shame and disgrace. No man will take himself a wife who cannot bear him heirs."

"Is that all a woman is? Nothing more than a brood mare to bear a man's seed to fruition, thereby assuring him a measure of immortality!" Eudora shook with outrage. Du Bois had been right. The station relegated to

106

a woman in Arab society was one of total subservience. First as a child to her father, then as a woman to her husband—provided she was fertile and hence able to attract and hold one. "And how many wives does Khamed have?" she asked sarcastically, thinking suddenly of her arrogant captor.

As soon as she had spoken, she regretted the question. What possible difference should it make to her how many wives Khamed had? And why did the thought of his making love to a score of veiled, dark-eyed women disturb her?

Dahr-la looked at her quizzically. "He has none," she answered softly. "Why do you ask?"

Eudora shrugged, searching for an answer which would make sense to the girl—and to herself. "I thought if he did have a wife or harem somewhere, he would not . . . I mean chances are . . . he wouldn't be . . . I'd just hoped he might be spending his nights elsewhere," she finished weakly.

It was clear Dahr-la did not believe a word of her feeble logic. "The only bed Khamed sleeps in is his own," she replied, "the bed you now share."

Eudora jumped to her feet. She did not share his bed—at least, not in the manner Dahr-la believed. But what point was there in refuting the girl's charge? She was still his captive, to do with as he pleased. Cheeks burning, eyes stinging with tears, she fled into the bedroom and threw herself across the bed.

"His bed!" she sobbed. With Dahr-la's words ringing in her ears, she pounded the silken coverlet with her fists. "Curse him! Curse him and his bed!"

Exhausting herself with tears, she fell asleep. It was late afternoon when she woke. The air was hot and still, enveloping her like a heavy blanket. Anxious to escape the small room, she stumbled from the bed. After splashing water on her face to wash away the traces of her tears, she entered the main room.

Dahr-la stood at the tent's entrance. She had drawn

107

aside the flap and was looking out with obvious interest to the compound beyond.

"What is it?" Coming up beside her, Eudora peered over her shoulder, relishing the faint breeze she felt against her face.

Startled, Dahr-la stepped back, letting the flap fall. "My lady! I did not hear you enter!" She placed her hand on Eudora's arm and began to lead her toward the room's center. "Come and sit down. I'll bring your tea."

Eudora yanked her arm from the maid's grasp. Her eyes narrowed in suspicion. "What is happening out there that you don't want me to see, Dahr-la?"

"It is nothing. Nothing that concerns you. Please, my lady. Come away from the doorway."

The pleading tone in the girl's voice only firmed her resolve. Eudora pushed past her and opened the flap.

In the center of the camp a crowd was gathered about a solitary figure. There was no doubt as to his identity given the black-*sheshed* head rising above the ring of onlookers.

Khamed had returned.

Instinctively she stepped back. Suddenly an opening broke in the mass of bodies. Eudora stared in horror: at Khamed's feet lay a limp and bloodstained heap. She tore her gaze from the huddled form, instantly nauseated. Her hands groped at her throat as she watched Khamed toss the whip in his hands to one of the men in the crowd. Without a second glance at the motionless body on the ground, he turned and strode unconcerned toward his tent. One by one the witnesses to his monstrous act walked away.

"My lady, please. Come away from the doorway." Dahr-la reached out to pull the tent flap from her grasp.

Eudora's fingers clenched the heavy fabric. Struggling to control her revulsion, she turned to face the girl. "Why was that man beaten like an animal?"

"He was negligent in his duty. He must be made an example to the others."

Eudora recoiled in shock at the indifferent, almost casual tone of the girl's voice. What manner of savages were these desert people to condone such an atrocity? She lashed out in outrage. "How can you stand there in approval of what your lord has just done? What could that poor man have possibly done to warrant such an inhuman punishment?"

Dahr-la stared at her coldly. "He was the guard Kahlil found sleeping this morning outside your door."

Eudora winced in pain. Dahr-la's answer sickened her. She was responsible for the man's flogging! Had she not ventured outside the tent, his infraction might never have been discovered. She uncurled her fingers, and the tent flap fell back into place.

Dahr-la looked at her for a moment longer. Seemingly satisfied with the reaction her words had wrought, she turned and walked away.

Numb, Eudora watched as the girl disappeared into the back room. Suddenly she heard Khamed's voice and realized he was just outside the tent. Her instinct was to flee; every muscle in her body tensed. She fought the urge and stood fast. She would not hide or cower from him!

He swept into the tent, his flowing robes trailing majestically behind him.

Fists clenched, she lifted her eyes boldly.

Khamed noted his captive's silent defiance with a look of undisguised approval. She was even more beautiful than he had realized. The proud carriage of her head seemed emphasized by the upswept arrangement of her hair. Gleaming with deep auburn highlights he'd not noticed before, it was the color of rich earth kissed by a radiant sunset. His gaze traveled downward over the swell of her breasts, past her slim waist. Mentally he stripped away the bell-shaped skirt which seductively outlined the curves of her hips.

Eudora wavered inwardly. His unbroken stare scorched her with shame, and she could feel the color rising in her cheeks. She bit her lower lip to keep it from trembling, yet her eyes held fast. She refused to lower them under his fiery gaze of undeniable raw passion. But as his dark eyes continued to stare at her with nerve-racking steadiness, she felt her courage slipping further and further away.

Suddenly, without a word, he tore his gaze from her. Brushing by her, he crossed the room and entered the bedroom.

Eudora staggered to the sofa, sinking into its plush softness. After what he had done to the hapless guard, he had to be furious with her as well. Yet he had said nothing. Surely he did not intend to let her deliberate disobedience go unpunished? Or was the punishment he intended for her a private one? The thought left her weak and trembling, filled with fear.

The minutes ticked by slowly. It seemed an eternity had passed when he finally returned. He had washed and shaved and changed his clothes. Now wearing a loose white shirt and the baggy trousers called *sirwel*, which were tight fitting only below the knee, he carried in his hand the revolver he had removed from the dresser that morning.

Eudora froze, her eyes darting to the gun in terror. Did he intend to kill her for her disobedience?

Laughing softly, Khamed walked over to the carved chest. Her reaction to the sight of the gun had not gone unnoticed. It amused him to think she credited him with such savagery. He took a key from his pocket and unlocked the chest. After placing the revolver inside, he relocked it, returning the key to his pocket. He slowly approached her, noting how her eyes widened in alarm. In their emerald depths he could see everything she had been feeling—fear, then relief, and finally confusion.

He reached out to run his index finger lightly down her cheek. "To kill you for your disobedience would be too easy, little one. It would mean abandoning the battle before it is waged—and for a warrior, that is an admission of defeat." He moved aside and lit a cigarette. Then, tossing one of the cushions from the sofa to the floor, he settled himself across the inlaid table from her. He smiled and absently flicked an ash into the ashtray upon it. "You will soon learn that I am not a man who accepts defeat easily." He paused to drag on the cigarette. "Nor am I one who is easily defeated."

Exhaling slowly, he studied the green orbs glaring at him. While the fear was still present, the relief and confusion had vanished. He now saw disgust and contempt. To her he was a savage. And as long as she viewed him as such, she would fight him. Yet if she could look at him, truly look at him, stripped of the prejudices and prejudgments of her upbringing, she might like what she saw. She might even allow herself to feel what he felt: desire.

He rubbed his jaw, deep in thought. By separating her from her countrymen he had hoped to foster a need within her—if only for his companionship initially. The isolation had not brought about the desired results. In her mind she still clung to the Frenchmen for support. Her attempt that morning to see them proved that. But if she believed they had abandoned her, forsaken her. . . . Perhaps a meeting with du Bois and Sabatin might be in order after all.

His decision made, he stubbed out his cigarette. "After dinner you shall see your friends. Then you will believe me when I say they are being well treated."

Instantly Eudora became alert. Obviously both Kahlil and Dahr-la had relayed to him their conversations with her. Khamed knew she'd not been trying to escape. Could that explain why he seemed no more than amused by her disobedience in leaving the tent?

She stared at the bronzed face before her in renewed confusion. Yet why was he now so suddenly willing to grant her her wish? Unable to decipher a clue as to his thoughts behind the emotionless mask he wore, her inner voice cried out that she should not trust him. Still, if she

111

wanted to see Sabatin and du Bois, what other choice did she have?

She forced a terse reply. "Thank you."

Khamed inclined his head in acknowledgment. "We will eat now."

As if on cue, Dahr-la appeared, bearing a tray laden with exotic-smelling dishes. These she placed on the table between them before quickly disappearing again.

Eudora stared at the numerous bowls. Seeing neither plates nor forks, she realized they would be eating Arab-style. Each would have but one spoon for the entire meal. They would eat the various courses from a common dish, taking food from the section of the dish nearest them. The mere idea of sharing a meal with him robbed her of what little appetite she'd had. Like a bizarre play in which he would act out the role of gracious host, her part was to be that of a polite guest.

However, she knew she would have to play her part to advance the action to the next scene— her meeting with Sabatin and du Bois. She prayed at least for the solace of silence.

But Khamed denied her even that.

He spoke of his day's activities as a man would to an intimate and tried to force her to carry on a dialog. It was a bitter, painful irony that under different circumstances she knew she would have enjoyed his company. He was obviously intelligent. The titles of the books in the room attested to that. And as hard as she tried, she could find no fault with his appearance. The high cheekbones, straight profile and chiseled jaw, the firm, well-muscled body—all were physically appealing to her.

She grew increasingly uncomfortable. It took every ounce of control she could muster to remain indifferent to his presence.

Suddenly it seemed that Khamed had grown tired of trying to draw her into a conversation. He asked her a question that required her to respond. "Are you related to Louis Morrel?"

Eudora stared at him. She was tempted not to answer. She quickly thought better of it when she noticed the shadow of annoyance darkening his features. "He is my father," she replied. Silently she wondered how it was he had known the name.

"He is accompanying the Foureau/Lemy expedition, is he not?"

"Yes." Again she was surprised.

Abruptly he changed the subject. "You do not care for my country, do you, little one?"

From lowered lids she shot him an icy glare. Each time he used it, his maddeningly mocking term of endearment grated on her even more. She could bear it no longer. "My name is Eudora." Ignoring caution, she raised her eyes defiantly. "And to answer your question, I have found nothing about it which could possibly warrant any emotion other than complete loathing! The climate is unbearable, the terrain unlivable, and the people savage and cruel!"

Though the affable smile on his lips remained unchanged, she saw a distinct hardening of his eyes.

"Our behavior . . . our code of morality and sense of right and wrong may not mesh with that of your world's—but then ours is a harsh life, fraught with the struggle for survival in a fierce and unmerciful land."

Eudora met his stare. "Your struggle for survival has nothing to do with what you are doing now! Why are you doing *this*?" She waved a hand at the room. "Why have you made me your prisoner?" Furiously she brushed aside the tears welling in her eyes.

"Because one night I saw you asleep in your tent and I wanted you. And what I want, I take."

For an instant the brutal candor of his words overshadowed their meaning. She shook with outrage. Did the man's omnipotence deny him nothing? Suddenly the significance of what he'd said became clear. She gasped in immediate understanding. "It was you! You slashed the tent!"

113

Khamed nodded.

His arrogant smile dried her tears instantly. "The raid . . . the attack . . ." Disbelief caused her voice to quiver, her words to falter. "It was all done because of me?"

"Do not give yourself *too* much credit, little one!" Amused, he laughed. "You are indeed a prize, but the raid on the caravan was planned because of the guns and ammunition it was transporting. Any other cargo found to be of value simply sweetened the fruits of our victory."

Eudora felt as if she had been struck. Somehow being taken not by design but by default seemed even more humiliating. With every breath she drew, her rage increased. More than anything, she wanted to reach out and slap the handsome face before her. She forced herself to control the urge, but only the thought of seeing Sabatin at the meal's conclusion kept her sitting at the table.

Finally Dahr-la reappeared to clear the dishes. Khamed rose, uttering a few words in Arabic to her. As the girl withdrew, he returned his attention to her. "Eudora, would you like to get a wrap from the bedroom?"

Nodding, Eudora stood. She waited until he leaned forward to stub out his cigarette in the ashtray on the table before darting past him.

When she returned a moment later, he was waiting by the room's entrance. Taking the challis shawl from her, he stepped behind her to drape it over her shoulder. His nearness unsettled her. Still, she lowered her gaze to the floor and passively endured his touch. If she had learned anything of him this evening, it was that he was a man of changing moods. The chance that she could forfeit the opportunity to see Sabatin by angering Khamed with an exhibition of contempt was one she was not willing to risk.

As his hands came to rest upon her shoulders, she

heard the tent flap part. Sabatin and du Bois entered, followed by a guard who immediately took up a watchful position behind them.

"Pierre! Lieutenant!" Eudora greeted the men with relief and joy. But when she tried to move toward them, the long brown fingers on her shoulders tightened like talons, digging into her flesh. She flushed with anger. Afraid Khamed might end the audience, she did not try to pull away.

Sabatin and du Bois remained speechless, their eyes locked upon the sight of her with their captor.

The guard prompted du Bois with his rifle.

"Mademoiselle Morrel." The lieutenant bowed stiffly.

Eudora flinched. There was no mistaking the coldness in his voice—or the look of revulsion on his face.

"Eudora." Sabatin gave her a weak smile.

"You see, little one . . ." Khamed leaned closer to whisper into her ear—loud enough for all to hear. "It is as I told you. Your friends are safe."

Sabatin clenched his fists. What he was seeing tore at his insides. His last memory of Eudora was one of a terror-stricken woman, clawing and pleading at him to save her from the hands of the very man who now held her in his embrace. The conversation he'd had with Khamed flashed through his mind. *What have you done to her?—Nothing she did not want done.*

Sabatin felt sick. He now understood the reason behind the Arab's mysterious summons to his tent. The arrogant bastard was presenting indisputable proof of his boast!

Suddenly Khamed took his hands from her. "Go and greet your friends properly, Eudora." He gave her a gentle push and a warm smile.

As she stepped forward, Sabatin heard du Bois emit a choking cry of disgust. He turned in time to see the man whirl on his heel and leave the tent. Their guard was but a few steps behind.

"My God, Pierre! Why is he acting this way?"

Eudora's voice was full of confusion.

Sabatin forced himself to look at her. How could he answer her? It wasn't that he didn't know what du Bois was feeling. He was feeling the same emotions himself—outrage and abhorrence. No decent white woman would have allowed herself to be bedded by an Arab. It was an affront to God and nature. Again Khamed's words returned to haunt him: *Nothing she did not want done.* Unable to help himself, he drew back from her. "You must understand . . . as a Frenchman it is difficult for him to accept what has happened."

"Accept what?" Eudora looked at him. Clearly feeling his discomfort and distance, she stepped back. "Pierre, what's wrong? What have they done to you?"

He looked at her sadly and shook his head. "It is not what they have done to us, Eudora. It is what *he* has done—to you. Or rather, what you have *let* him do."

Eudora stiffened. "What *I* have let him do?" Suddenly, as if a cloud had moved away from the sun, everything was bright and clear. Du Bois's exit, Sabatin's coldness—it all made sense! She reeled in shock. The Frenchmen actually believed she had given herself to Khamed!

Standing by the desk, Khamed smiled in secret satisfaction. Leisurely he lit a cigarette. The Frenchmen, especially the lieutenant, had reacted exactly as he had suspected they would. They were revolted by the thought that the woman had willingly given herself to him, a savage of a different race. And she . . . she was close to the edge. Just one more slight push . . .

"Monsieur, if you would like to see Eudora tomorrow, it can be arranged. But now . . . if you will excuse us . . . it *is* late. We were about to retire for the evening."

Eudora's eyes widened. She spun around to face Khamed. It had all been staged! He had had the men purposely brought to his tent—the one she obviously shared with him—to vividly illustrate her position to

116

them. How could there be any doubt in their minds that this was where she belonged? Even the ruse about fetching a wrap had been carefully planned and timed so that at the moment they entered they would see her in his arms! And then his last comment: *We were about to retire.* . . . Given the evidence, a blind man would have known exactly where she would be sleeping! It was a *coup de maître,* an action worthy of a master, but it was not going to work.

She turned again. "Pierre, you don't understand! I—"

"Eudora."

Though Khamed's low voice at her back sounded like a caress, the grip she immediately felt on her arm was anything but.

The pressure increased. He was forbidding her to continue.

"Go to bed. I will join you shortly." He then turned to Sabatin. "Monsieur, permit me to escort you to your tent." He gestured to the doorway.

Wordlessly Sabatin turned. As he did so, he caught sight of Eudora as she disappeared white-faced behind the drape into the next room. She was clearly upset. Yet how could she have thought her actions would be condoned?

Khamed followed him out, stopping him under the awning. "Are you satisfied, Monsieur? Or would you have preferred to see her bound, gagged, and beaten?"

Sabatin's head jerked up. Khamed's point was valid. Eudora had obviously made her choice to be with him willingly, and she was being well treated. Instinctively, too, Sabatin knew the man would keep her only for himself. Her fate could have been much worse. Was it fair for him to judge her so harshly based upon his own racial prejudice and morality? Did he have the right to judge her at all?

"Well, Monsieur?" Khamed's low voice demanded a response.

Sabatin lowered his eyes beneath the persistent dark

117

stare. "It is as you stated earlier, *Sidi*. She is no longer my concern." Out of the corner of his eye, he saw Khamed smile.

Beckoning to one of the men who had been waiting a few feet from the tent, Khamed turned to re-enter. "Good night, Monsieur."

Chapter Eight

Eudora sat at the vanity and yanked the combs from her hair. Tears of rage and shame burned her throat. In bringing Sabatin and du Bois to his tent Khamed had shown her what she had become in their eyes. She was no better than a common whore—a harlot who would give herself to any man, even to a savage. Never mind that she was innocent! He had planned it too well for them to believe otherwise. And because of what they now perceived as truth, she no longer had anyone to turn to, no one to help her escape this place.

She heard the curtain rustle and turned. The sight of Khamed's tall form entering renewed her outrage. "How dare you!" she hissed. Forgetting she was dressed only in chemise and petticoat, she jumped to her feet. "You planned that entire disgusting scene!"

"Are you asking me, little one? Or merely telling me something I already know?" He stepped up to the vanity and reached over her shoulder to extinguish his cigarette in the ashtray behind her. "It did go rather well, I must admit. Your friends behaved in a most predictable manner."

His scent was now in her nostrils; his very nearness threatened to shatter her composure. She forced herself to ignore his mocking smile. He wanted to unnerve her, to arouse her fear. She would not let him. "I want to see

119

Sabatin tomorrow . . . alone," she stated flatly.

His gloating smile became a sarcastic grin. "After what he saw this evening, do you really think you can persuade him that you and I are *not* lovers?"

Without waiting for her reply, he continued, "I think not."

Indignant, Eudora tried to walk away, but he reached out to hold her fast.

She looked up and found her gaze locked with an onyx stare that was almost hypnotic. She was powerless to move. As his other hand traveled lightly down her neck, she shut her eyes. It served only to partially break his spellbinding hold. She still could not resist, not even when she felt his fingers working the laces of her chemise and parting the garment.

"You have a body made for a man's pleasure."

The sound of his voice, husky with passion, shot needles of icy fear through her. Yet in its wake there was something else—a warmth centered deep within her.

Khamed looked down at her. He ached with longing. He hungered to feel her arms embrace him, to feel her body rise to meet his, to know she sought from him the pleasure he could give, if only she would allow him. He traced the dark circle around her nipple, encouraged as the bud hardened in response to his touch. "Your body does not lie, little one. It yearns for a man's touch. Let me make love to you. Give to me what you have denied us both."

When she did not answer, he continued. "What is to be served by your refusal? If it is pride . . . your friends already believe you have given yourself to me. Did their reaction this evening not prove that?"

Eudora squeezed her eyes shut. Feeling his lips suddenly following the path of his fingertips, she cried out. Her skin burned each place his moist breath touched it. "Please, don't," she whispered weakly, opening her eyes.

Ignoring her request, his lips met hers. Her pleas

120

melted beneath the kiss. "Let me make love to you," he repeated.

"No. *No.*" Eudora sobbed aloud. The warmth within her had intensified to a hot ache. The knowledge that her body was actually responding to him filled her with confusion and shame. What was wrong with her? But her body, too long denied a man, would not be controlled by reason. Her dormant sexuality was being awakened, and her appeal for respite was hollow.

His fingertips lightly touched her lips as though to silence her. Gently he wiped a tear from her cheek and kissed her. "Listen to your passion, Eudora, not your pride."

She felt his hands move intimately down her thighs and knew she had to make him stop. She forced all emotion from her voice. "There is no passion to listen to. The only feeling I have for you is loathing—a captive's loathing for her savage captor!"

Khamed's body stiffened. He had never begged a woman to submit to him, nor would he start with this one. He fought back his anger, dropped his hands, and stepped back. "This is becoming a habit, little one . . . a habit I am quickly growing tired of. For now the field is yours." He reached out to brush a stray tendril of hair from her tear-stained cheek. "But I warn you . . . next time I may not walk away."

When he felt her body recoil, he pulled her close to stare down into her eyes.

They were open and unwavering, and a silent storm raged within their depths. In that moment he knew: it was not her physical beauty that compelled his need. Even her obvious uniqueness in comparison to the other women he had known did not explain the depth of his desire. It was her indomitability, her complexity—her spirit which drew his.

He stepped back and walked toward the doorway. Out of the corner of his eye he saw her turn her head to watch him. He was unable to resist a single last barb. "One more thing . . . as it is still *my* bed you sleep in . . . tomorrow I want *my* sheets back on it."

When Eudora awoke the next morning the scent of burning tobacco wafting through the drapes told her Khamed was back. She dressed quickly, slipping a shell-pink tea gown over her head. Not wanting to take the time to arrange her hair, she left it down. She was anxious to confront him before he left—and before her courage waned.

Most of the night she had lain awake, tortured by the events of the previous evening. Slowly her shame gave way to anger—anger first at Khamed, then at herself. She was angry at her failure to insist on telling Sabatin the truth no matter what the consequences. She was even more furious with her reaction to Khamed's kisses and caresses. She was determined now, in the bright light of day, to vindicate herself in her own eyes as well as in the Frenchman's.

Drawing a deep breath, she pulled the heavy cloth panel aside.

"Good morning."

Khamed's greeting startled her. She had hoped to have a moment to compose herself. She stared at him dumbly. Seated upon the sofa, he was pouring his morning tea in purely Arab fashion—from a ridiculous height unerringly into a tall glass.

"Tea?"

His casual question put her even more off balance, yet she was determined not to let him crack the calm facade she'd so desperately wanted to convey.

"I shall assume by your silence that you are still angry about last night." He smiled and the mocking laugh she had grown to detest followed. "The question is . . . are you angry at me—or at yourself?"

Eudora's control slipped. His gloating was intolerable! He was so sure of her, of himself, of his possession of her!

"You bastard! You arrogant Arab bastard!"

"Actually . . ." He yawned. "I am not an Arab." Leaning his head back against the cushions, he clasped his hands behind it and extended his legs in an indolent pose.

Shaking with rage, she found herself speechlessly staring at his long legs, encased in black leather from the knee down and stretched out before him. Their strength was obvious even in the manner in which he half lay, half sat. She forced herself to look up at his face. The black eyes were almost yellow, shining in amusement. His jovial mood, achieved at the price of her chagrin, infuriated her all the more.

Determined to touch a nerve, she plunged recklessly ahead. "Of course. Forgive me." Her voice dripped acid sarcasm. "I had forgotten. You arrogant *half-breed* Arab bastard!"

To her utter surprise he burst out in laughter. And as the deep, resonant tones filled the room, he reached out for her, pulling her down beside him on the sofa. She twisted her body from his, presenting him her back. She heard another glass of the hot, strong, minty-sweet tea being poured. Out of the corner of her eye she saw him place it on the table before her.

"I am not a half-Arab either, little one. I am a Reguibat."

His low, even voice was still weighted with amusement.

She reached for the glass. "Is it not one and the same?" she muttered disdainfully, almost to herself.

"No. I am a Moor. In fact, my ancestors were white Berbers from North Africa who were conquered by the Arabs over a thousand years ago."

Eudora turned her head slightly. Though she was interested, she kept her expression blank.

"It is a common misconception," Khamed continued, "for we Moors have borrowed from the Arabs their language, religion, and some customs. But the Arabic we speak contains various Berber expressions and in the area of religion we follow the *Koran* only to the extent that fits into the framework of our tribal law. We are, I am ashamed to say, rather lukewarm Moslems."

The sly smile he offered mocked his words, and he laughed softly. "It seems most ironic when one considers that our original ancestor was supposedly a fourteenth-century saint. His name was Sidi Ahmed-er-Rguibi. He is said to have been a pious man who came from Barbary as a Moslem missionary to the valley of the Draa. There he married an Arab woman who bore him two sons. After his death, disputes between them split the tribe into two factions: the Sahel and the Lagouacem. To this day all noble Reguibat clans claim direct descent from their sons."

Sipping at her tea, Eudora almost choked. "*Noble!*" she gasped, turning to face him. "You're nothing more than a pack of outlaws—a tribe of thieves!"

"We *were* peaceful herders—for centuries. But the growth of our herds made us a target for constant attack by our neighbors: the Tuareg, who are also of Berber origin, and the Chaamba, who *are* Arab. We became warriors to defend ourselves, and in the process we became raiders as well. The Sahel moved into the Spanish Sahara and the Mauritanian Adrar. The Lagouacem went west, as far as the Adrar des Iforas and Aïr."

With no knowledge of the geography of the country, the foreign names which so easily rolled off his tongue meant nothing to her. Eudora's mind spun with confusion. She looked at him quizzically.

As if reading her thoughts, he smiled. "I will find you a map."

It was the first genuine smile she had ever received from him. Warm and engaging, it lit up his handsome face, making him even more attractive. Embarrassed by the traitorous thought, she averted her eyes. What was it about this man which enabled him to utterly disarm her with a simple smile?

"Only in the last century did the two confederations unite, taking the name *Reguibat*. Agriculture and trade are important to our livelihood, but you are correct. Raiding has become the driving force in our lives. Even clans of the same tribe sometimes steal from each other. When envoys are sent to confront the culprits, however, most of what was taken is returned." He laughed.

Without looking at him, Eudora knew he was smiling that same smile. She set down her glass. He was clearly in a good mood. It seemed the perfect time to restate her request. She shifted her position to face him. "I still want to see Sabatin. Perhaps we . . . ah . . . could reach some agreement—a compromise or a truce?"

Immediately Khamed's smile widened into his usual taunting grin. "What I want you are not yet ready to give, little one."

Eudora saw the burning passion in his eyes an instant before she felt his mouth hungrily claim hers. She put her hands flat against the hard chest and pushed herself away. Standing quickly, she stepped back. It was, however, a shallow victory. She knew if he had wanted to use force she would still be in his arms.

Forcing herself to meet his gaze, she blurted out the first thing that came to mind. "I don't know what you want."

Instantly the heavy, black scowl she was quickly learning to dread, descended across the bronzed brow. His eyes narrowed. "Yes, you do."

Moving with the lithe grace of a wildcat, he reached for her and pulled her swiftly back down into his lap. "What I want is a woman in my bed who responds with the heat of a lover's passion. I do not want a mere receptacle who yields in cold indifference. Nor a woman who denies and fights her own desires."

Trying to escape his piercing eyes, she looked away. The man saw too much—and wanted too much! He wanted to possess her very soul! He wanted . . . no, he expected: he expected her to respond to his desire in kind—with desire of her own!

"Look at me, Eudora. Why do you not let yourself respond to me? I want an answer."

"I do not know how to pretend out what I do not feel." Knowing she was inviting the return of his ire, she spoke slowly. She could feel her cheeks burning with shame. "In spite of what you have made of me in the eyes of others, I am *not* a whore who can perform at will in a man's bed."

"Then you had better learn to before you come to me again with an offer of a 'truce.'" Roughly he put her from him. "For those are my terms, and they are unconditional and unnegotiable!"

Eudora stood slowly. Nervously she smoothed her wrinkled skirts. "May I go now?"

"Yes. Go and change your clothes. I want to go riding." His voice was again even.

"But I don't want . . ." She stopped in mid-sentence as the black head snapped upward. Immediately she realized her mistake. He tolerated no interference with his wishes, no boundaries on his will. To even his slightest whim he demanded tacit obedience.

"I did not ask," he said icily, with the unconscious tyranny of one who had been born to rule. "Now go. Put on your riding clothes. A robe will not be necessary. We are not going far."

Khamed watched as she fled into the bedroom. Hearing a discreet cough outside the tent, he turned his attention to the entrance.

Dahr-la stood hesitantly in the doorway. "Shall I clear the table, my lord?" She gestured to the teapot and glasses before him.

At his nod she moved forward.

"Dahr-la."

The girl's eyes rose questioningly to meet his.

Pulling a small black leather pouch from his pocket, he held it out to her. "Watch your mistress closely. When her monthly time comes, begin giving her this. You know

126

the amounts and time intervals?"

Wordlessly she nodded, taking the pouch.

Khamed watched as she tucked it beneath her waistband. It contained an herbal concoction which prevented pregnancy. With their lives too harsh and their country too poor to support large families, the desert tribes had been using it for hundreds of years. It was his usual practice to give it to his mistresses. He had no desire to father a bastard child and did not trust the women he bedded to attend to the matter themselves. Having Dahr-la add it to their food without their knowledge had been a very effective method of birth control. The only problem was the timing: the administration of the herb had to begin precisely on the seventh day of the woman's cycle.

Dahr-la would have to wait until Eudora began her flux before she could begin giving it to her. Even though he had not yet gained the objective which would necessitate the precaution, his instincts and impatience told him she would soon be his.

Confident the maid would comply with his wishes, Khamed dismissed the matter from his mind. He lit another cigarette and stood to wait for Eudora at the tent's entrance.

She emerged from the bedroom a few minutes later. His eyes raked over her, noting every detail. Dressed in a beige riding skirt and a cream-colored blouse, she was tying a long white scarf about her head as she hesitantly approached him.

Under his close scrutiny Eudora lowered her eyes nervously. She wished she'd been able to don the form-concealing robes she'd worn in the open desert.

Wordlessly Khamed parted the tent flap, waving her ahead of him. Then with a firm hand at her elbow he led her from the tent and across the compound.

Men and women alike bowed as they passed, greeting him respectfully. It was obvious his people adored him, and for some reason that observation irritated her. Yet as

127

they walked toward the horse corrals, interest and curiosity in her uncommon surroundings seemed to push thoughts of him aside. Everything was so very different from that to which she was accustomed. Even the camp dogs, running free, were of a breed she had never seen.

Suddenly one of the stocky white mongrels approached.

Alarmed, Eudora stopped. She drew back, looking up at Khamed questioningly.

"He is only curious. Unless one is a stranger wandering the camp at night, he is quite harmless." Smiling, he reached out to scratch the dog behind its erect ears.

The veiled meaning of the words was not lost on her. As the dog wagged its bushy tail, seemingly in agreement with his master, Eudora glared at them both before turning her gaze to the scrawny, nondescript chickens scavenging in the camp refuse. She eyed the small creatures warily.

"They are not eaten." Khamed's low voice intruded into her thoughts. "Domestic fowl and eggs are foods forbidden to us. The chickens are kept to kill scorpions."

Concealing a shudder of revulsion, she allowed him to urge her forward. Futilely she tried to ignore the fact that his hand, which had been at her elbow, had moved to the small of her back. She focused on the horse corrals just ahead and found herself awestruck at the sight of the magnificent animals there. Her first sight of the Arabians had been during the attack—hardly a condition conducive to an appreciation of their power and beauty.

"They are impressive, are they not?" Khamed's voice, filled with pride, echoed her own thoughts.

She nodded and he continued.

"Horses have been present in the desert for at least two thousand years. But they are costly, not only in terms of money, but in water. Unlike camels, they must have it every day. Over the centuries they have become an increasingly expensive luxury and have been disappear-

ing. Yet we Reguibat have stubbornly held on to them—
too attached to the romanticism and chivalry of a past
age."

Mockery crept into the black eyes as he placed a hand
lightly over his breast and bowed. "We desert brigands
have very romantic souls, little one."

Eudora bristled instantly at the barb. Ignoring his soft
laughter, she brushed past him, walking swiftly toward a
pair of saddled and waiting horses some distance ahead. A
young boy of fourteen or fifteen stood between the
animals, holding a set of reins in each hand.

At her approach, the boy dipped his head in the
direction of the horse on his right, a chestnut mare. Were
it not for the earnest expression on his face, she would
have laughed out loud. The other horse, a black stallion,
did not have to be pointed out as Khamed's. She would
have recognized the huge beast anywhere. Obviously
impatient to be ridden, he fought the boy's tenuous
control, snorting and pawing at the dirt.

Suddenly Khamed was at her side. Acknowledging the
boy's greeting with a warm smile, he patted each animal's
neck, speaking softly to them in a language which did not
sound like Arabic.

Eudora watched in amazement as the stallion calmed
noticeably. Even the damned horse obeys him, she
thought furiously. She walked to the mare's side and put
her foot in the stirrup. Before she could protest,
Khamed's strong hands were encircling her waist,
hoisting her unceremoniously into the saddle.

Taking the reins from the boy, he held them out to her.
"No tricks today, eh, little one?"

Eudora now knew the man well enough to realize his
warning, though spoken lightly, was to be taken quite
seriously. Smiling down at him sweetly, she accepted the
reins from his hand. Then, in a burst of spite, as soon as
his back was turned, she spurred her horse forward.
Though he caught up to her almost immediately, she
knew she had scored a small victory. As he reined in the

129

big black beside the mare, she heard him swear softly under his breath. Eudora laughed silently.

From beneath the awning of his prison tent, Sabatin watched the pair. The distance aside, there was no mistaking the identity of the couple crossing the compound. The Reguibat's tall form could belong to only one man. Everything about him—his demeanor, his mannerisms—bespoke power and authority. And even without the European clothing, there was no doubt as to the woman at his side. She walked with her head held high, with a proud and purposeful grace Sabatin had found absent in Moslem women.

Du Bois, who had been standing at his side, suddenly hunkered down. Sitting on his haunches, he began to draw circles in the dirt with his forefinger. All the while he muttered to himself.

Sabatin looked at him in alarm. With each day that passed, the man's animosity for their captors seemed to eat away a little bit more of his soul. He rarely spoke. When he did, it was only to vent the hatred which had become his impetus for living. "Lieutenant?"

Ignoring him, du Bois stared stonily past him, out into the compound. His unshaven face twisted into an ugly sneer.

Curious, Sabatin turned to see what had caught his attention. As he watched Khamed lift Eudora onto her horse, he heard du Bois grunt out a single word.

"*Whore!*"

Sabatin whirled to face him. In spite of what they had both witnessed the previous evening, something about the meeting with Eudora continued to gnaw at him. The pieces had fit almost too neatly together.

Du Bois began to rise. Still bent at the waist, brushing the sand from his knees, he repeated his aspersion, but this time he expounded on the slur to include her paramour. "*Arab whore!*"

In a blinding fury Sabatin lashed out. Before the man could straighten his back, he was lying flat in the dirt. Choking back his rage, Sabatin rubbed the knuckles of his right hand. He was dimly aware they were throbbing. "If I were you, du Bois, I would watch my tongue! I won't tolerate you maligning her. If I hear anything that even remotely sounds like a denigration, I swear . . . I'll break your jaw!" Stepping over the man's prone body to enter the tent, a very real possibility exploded in his mind.

He turned to voice a final warning. "And if *he* hears it . . . he will very likely kill you!"

Chapter Nine

As she rode at Khamed's side beyond the palm-lined fringe of the oasis, Eudora was struck with the sudden quiet. In sharp contrast to the noisy activity of the camp, not a sound could be heard. Not a breath of air ruffled the sand. Overhead, only the dark specks of swooping desert larks marred the flawless calm of the perfect blue sky. Strangely moved by the bleak, grandiose beauty, she lowered her eyes to conceal their tears.

They had ridden for only a few miles when suddenly a green field appeared before them. Upon closer inspection, she realized it was not a field per se, but a wide, sinuous river of grasslike plants. A dozen or so men, naked from the waist up, tended the crop she guessed to be a food grain.

Khamed reined in the black stallion, gesturing for her to do the same.

"Where does the water come from to farm out in the desert?" she asked, unable to disguise her amazement.

He laughed. "What you see is normally a dry riverbed. But when the rains come it is transformed into a raging torrent. We build small temporary dams to keep the accumulated rain water from running off, and then plant barley, millet—even watermelons."

"I thought it was considered degrading for a nomad to cultivate the soil." Silently she wondered if anything she had read of the desert tribes was accurate.

"It is, except out at pasture when it is necessary for survival. As long as we do not settle down and devote ourselves primarily to gardening . . ." he grinned and dismounted "we retain our honorable nomad status."

Narrowing her eyes, more in response to his mocking arrogance than the bright sunlight, she watched as he walked over to speak with several of the men. She couldn't help but note the commanding manner of his stance, the proud, noble poise of his head. As he spoke, he moved his hands with quick gestures, pointing toward something in the distance. Eudora looked up to see the object of his attention, but saw only the crude iron-shod plows and the men working. There were no women. Apparently his tribe's primitive, quasi-agriculture was the business only of its men.

When Khamed returned a few minutes later, she avoided his eyes and pretended to be concentrating on a puzzling question. "Where is the harvest stored?" Her question was in fact legitimate. She hadn't been able to imagine a logical solution, but the thought she'd actually given it had been minimal.

He smiled up at her, as though pleased with the intelligence of the question. "In subterranean silos. They are shaped like huge bottles, lined with straw and covered with sand or stones. The grain they hold is owned collectively by the members of the tribe."

He mounted his horse before continuing with his explanation. "When the tribe moves on, it is watched over by a guardian—usually a shepherd. You see, we follow the same routes season to season, moving west toward the seacoast in the spring and autumn, north in the summer and south in the winter, returning always to the same encampments." He urged the black stallion forward. "Come. It is time we returned."

They rode slowly, at first in silence. Again Eudora was impressed with the quiet solitude and peacefulness.

"It is said that Allah removed all human and animal

134

life from the desert so that there might be one place for Him to walk in peace. That is why the Great Sahara is called 'The Garden of Allah.'"

She looked at him in wonder. It was uncanny and unnerving how he seemed so able to read her thoughts and emotions. Silently she compared what he had said to the proverb relayed by Sabatin. Clearly even the desert dwellers had mixed emotions about their environment. She slowed her horse's pace to match the stallion's. Khamed seemed to be in a mood to talk.

"The Sahara is estimated to be three and one half million square miles. It stretches from the Atlantic Ocean to the Red Sea, from the Atlas Mountains in the north to the Niger River in the south. The western desert, north to the region you know as Spanish Rio de Oro, and the French Saharan territory which adjoins it on the east and south are the exclusive domain of the Reguibat."

Eudora raised an eyebrow. "*I* was under the impression that the Spanish and French governments controlled those lands."

He laughed and smiled, but the smile did not reach his eyes. "In theory, perhaps, little one, but not in practice. We recognize neither the colonial administrations' authority over us nor their political boundaries. The politicians in the anterooms of the *Palais Bourbon* are devoted, first and foremost, to their own survival. They have compromised their principles in the face of practicality. Your foreign ministers are unwilling to commit the resources of men and supplies necessary to enforce that authority. They know their troops are no match for us. We enjoy the advantages of mobility and surprise, and possess a far superior knowledge of the terrain. Our Prophet has condoned the sword and we will fight to keep what is ours!"

The dark eyes were blazing—for once he had not taken the trouble to mask his emotions. She marveled at the depth of the resentment and hatred he bore the foreign

135

usurpers of his country.

After a moment he continued, once again calm and detached. "And so the Sahara remains 'occupied' . . . but in name only, by a force too small and weak to allow for either further conquest or effective control."

Eudora knew what he was telling her was accurate. Before leaving France she had read a newspaper account of a remote French army post that had remained under constant attack by natives in retaliation against the foreign penetration into their territory.

Forgotten by the colonial administration and without supplies, the post had had to be abandoned by the few who remained alive. Even the military outposts that managed to maintain a shaky foothold fared little better. The colonial troops considered such assignments the worst kind of punishment. Fits of madness and mutiny were common. In fact, du Bois had told her he was himself nearing the end of his tour, the general staff having recommended that officers be stationed no more than two years in Saharan Africa because of the bleakness of the duty.

She wondered why France coveted the desert wilderness. The lure of wealth was minimal, and its geographic location had no significant strategic importance. Life in the harsh land, with its vast distances, brutal terrain, and pitiless weather, was simply existence in defiance of nature. She actually felt a grudging respect for the courage, hardiness, and love of independence which so characterized the Reguibat.

Startled, she realized she was not only beginning to understand du Bois' and Sabatin's earlier expressions of admiration for them—she was beginning to share it! The disconcerting thought instantly cooled her interest in further conversation.

Khamed seemed to sense her mood change and did not speak again until they had returned to the camp. Turning slightly in his saddle to look at her, he appeared to be weighing a decision. "Come," he ordered at last.

He changed the stallion's course and she followed his lead, riding behind him through the maze of tents to a small one set apart from the others. A guard stood at its entrance, salaaming as he spotted his lord's approach.

Khamed dismounted. Moving to the mare, he lifted her off the horse. "Go and see your friends."

Eudora looked up at him in unconcealed surprise. As usual, his handsome face was an emotionless mask. Her anger surged. He was so sure of himself! She could talk to Sabatin for as long as she wanted. And even if she were able to erase with the truth the impression Khamed had manufactured, nothing would change. She would still be his captive. But at least Sabatin would know she'd not surrendered to him!

The need to redeem herself in the reporter's eyes compelled her forward. She stepped past Khamed to the tent's entrance.

The guard drew aside the flap, allowing her to enter.

Sabatin and du Bois, both lying on woven mats of esparto grass, jumped to their feet. Du Bois stared at her. His outrage and contempt filled the small space like a thick, dark cloud.

She quickly glanced at Sabatin. At least he looked to be more surprised than disgusted by her presence. "Pierre, could we talk . . . in private? Will you walk with me?"

Sabatin nodded and followed her out. Seeing Khamed standing with the horses, he stopped. He looked to her for an explanation.

"We have his permission," she said dryly.

With the guard following at a discreet distance, they headed toward the date palms at the oasis' edge.

Eudora tried to forget the black eyes she knew were watching them. "Pierre, I want to talk to you about last night . . . about what you saw—or rather what you *think* you saw." Looking at the man covertly from beneath her lashes, she saw his cheeks stain.

"Eudora, this isn't necessary. I'm sure you have your reasons for what you've done. You don't owe me an explanation." In spite of his words, his voice retained a harsh, distant edge.

"But I do, Pierre!" she cried in exasperation. She placed her hand on his arm, forcing him to stop and face her. "What you saw last night was a carefully staged scene. Khamed planned the entire thing. Don't you see? He wanted you to think I was . . . that I am his mistress!"

"And you're not? Eudora, you can't expect me to believe you've not slept with him. My God, woman, I have eyes! He has wanted you from the beginning. Yet now I am to believe that you have been sharing his tent for three days—and nights—but not his bed? That he hasn't touched you?" His voice rose with anger and disbelief.

Out of the corner of her eye she saw the guard step forward. Realizing he was concerned for her safety, Eudora waved him back. She then turned her eyes to the man before her. "He hasn't, Pierre. He really hasn't. I know you don't believe me. And after what you saw, I don't blame you. But I swear . . ." Her voice began to waver and she took a deep breath to steady it. "It's the truth." She searched his face, desperately looking for a sign of belief.

"And for three nights he's been sleeping . . . where?" Sabatin's voice had softened somewhat, as though he wanted to believe her, but still couldn't.

"I don't know. One night he was gone from the camp entirely, though. Pierre, he's waiting for me to accept him willingly. He thinks I will come to . . . to want him." She stopped abruptly, not sure if she wanted to confess the thoughts and emotions tormenting her. "The . . . the terrifying part is that I don't know how to fight him. I don't understand him. He can be kind, then cold; tyrannical and tender. He knows what I think, how I think. . . ." She shut her eyes to stop the tears about to fall.

Suddenly warm, comforting arms enveloped her. Sabatin's gentle voice whispered in her ear. "It's all right, Eudora. I'm here."

She buried her head in his chest. Her control finally broken, she began to weep.

Sabatin knew he was defeated. His hand moved to stroke her hair. "It's all right. Cry. Shed your tears. God knows, you're entitled."

His words seemed to be all the encouragement she needed. Great sobs wracked the slender body in his embrace.

"Please don't turn away from me!" she begged. "I need your friendship."

Her plea twisted in his chest like a knife. "I'm not turning away, Eudora." To prove his words, he tightened his embrace. Then, feeling that he was being watched, he looked over the top of her head back toward his tent. Khamed was impatiently grinding out a half-smoked cigarette beneath the heel of his boot into the sand. Reluctantly Sabatin lifted Eudora's head from his chest. "Come. We'd better go back. He is getting impatient." He put her from him gently and took her arm to lead her back to the small tent. "Come."

At their approach, Khamed nodded curtly. "Monsieur." He stretched out his hand. "Eudora."

Without a word she left Sabatin's side.

As Eudora watched Sabatin disappear behind the flap, she felt Khamed take her arm. She pulled away from him and set out for her own prison tent. She knew he would follow her across the compound.

He entered his tent only a moment later.

Expecting a confrontation, she stood, still stubbornly avoiding his gaze. To her dismay, he wordlessly walked past her to the desk. Sitting, he opened a thick leatherbound ledger and began to write in its pages. She stared at his broad back. The words she had spoken to Sabatin just moments ago returned to haunt her. She could not understand him! She passed him to go into the next room, and his head never lifted.

Once in the bedroom, she stared back at the drape in

139

dazed confusion. Suddenly she heard the sound of the ledger being slammed shut. In fear she backed away from the doorway. But the heavy folds did not part to yield his powerful form. She was now more confused than ever. Why was he now choosing to ignore her? A warm glow of hope spread through her. Was the novelty of his possession of her losing its allure? Or was he beginning to doubt he could win this game? She waited a moment longer before venturing back into the outer room.

As she suspected, Khamed had left the tent.

Dahr-la arrived minutes later with an offer of food and tea. When Eudora declined both she withdrew to the bedroom. She returned almost instantly, carrying a cream-colored bundle.

Eudora did not need to ask its contents. As Khamed had ordered, his bed had been returned to its former state. And lest she forget her position in his absence, he'd made sure she would be blatantly reminded of it—by witnessing Dahr-la's removal of the cotton sheets.

Dismissing the girl with a curt wave, she sat on the sofa to await his return. As the hours passed, her vexation grew. When he finally returned it was late evening.

Still ignoring her, he briskly entered the bedroom to wash and change before Dahr-la served the evening meal.

As on the night before, they ate Arab style. But unlike their previous meal together, this one passed in near total silence. Khamed spoke only to Dahr-la, in short, terse commands.

His uncommunicativeness was so unnerving, Eudora wondered if it was not a new form of torment. She grew increasingly nervous, tensing when he suddenly rose to his feet.

Warily, she watched as he went to the tent's entrance. Drawing back the flap, he unconsciously jerked an ash from the cigarette in his hand.

Khamed stared out into the night. Though the sky was brilliant, an inky canopy ablaze with a thousand stars and a startling white moon, he saw nothing of its beauty. He was aware only that she was watching him.

Mechanically he brought the cigarette to his lips. Finding no pleasure in its taste he tossed it aside, swearing silently. No woman had ever affected him so profoundly. Agitated more than he'd wanted to admit by her afternoon encounter with the Frenchman, he had retreated behind a wall of silence. He'd wanted to punish her for inciting within him the imbalance of emotions which was so foreign to his nature. But ignoring her had only forced his smoldering desire to the surface. Wanting her more than ever, he had left the tent in a cold rage. Even after spending the remainder of the day away from her, the feelings had not abated.

Dinner had been a tortured exercise in self-control and now, like a youth experiencing his first arousal, he was standing in the doorway, hoping the night air would cool his hot blood and clear his head. Merciful Allah! Was he no longer master of his own desires? He wanted her. But did he want her enough to take her?

"Eudora . . . come here."

She rose hesitantly from the sofa and walked slowly toward him.

He placed an arm around her waist to guide her through the doorway.

Suddenly the blood-curdling howls of a pack of hunting jackals shattered the stillness. Startled, she jumped in fear, clinging to him for a brief instant. The feel of her body against his sent the blood racing through his veins. Clasping her tightly, he capitulated to the passion he could no longer control.

"*Hamdullah!* Do you know how beautiful you are?" he whispered thickly.

Immediately her body stiffened and he felt her grow rigid, cold and unyielding in his arms. His mouth claimed hers, but the fire which coursed through his veins could not thaw the ice which flowed through hers. Frustration and anger surged, kindling his unrepentant temper. He pushed her roughly from him. "Damn you! It is not me

141

that you fight, but yourself!"

Eudora shrank from the black eyes flashing with rage. Turning, she fled to the bedroom gasping in fear. Knowing she had awakened not only his displeasure but his passion, she looked about the room in a panic.

On the vanity, partially concealed beneath Khamed's discarded waistcloth, a glint of something shiny caught her eye. Knowing what it was, she pulled back the cloth without hesitation. She touched the ornate hilt of the dagger she had seen Khamed wearing a dozen times. But before she was able to grasp the knife firmly, a strong brown hand closed over her own.

"I did not dismiss you."

The voice at her back was as hard and cold as the steel lying beneath her hand.

Her heart skipped a beat. In desperation her fingers curled about the weapon.

The fingers which clasped her hand moved to her wrist, tightening in a savage exhibition of force until she cried out in pain. "Release it," he growled.

She opened her fist and the dagger slipped from her grasp. Jerking her head around, she glared at him in utter hatred.

Ignoring her, he leaned over and picked up the knife. Upon standing, he turned her hand over, laying the hilt in her palm. He then stepped back and ripped open his shirt.

She stared at the bronzed chest.

"Go on. Your eyes tell me you want to." He tapped the smooth skin over his heart. "Here is your target."

As though paralyzed, she stood mute before him. Her vision began to blur. Blinking back the blinding tears, she turned and laid the dagger on the vanity.

Immediately she felt his hands upon her shoulders.

"Do not ever take up a weapon unless you have the stomach to use it, little one. For if your enemy sees your weakness, he will use it against you."

"As you have?"

With a rueful smile, Khamed turned her to face him. "Yes." Crooking his forefinger beneath her chin, he forced her to look up at him. His thumb arced across her cheek to carry away a lingering tear. *And as you have without knowing it,* he thought silently, lowering his mouth to hers. He kissed her gently and then released her.

"I will wait . . . a little longer." Without another word he walked away.

Dismayed, Eudora watched him leave. For just an instant she had seen him stripped of his arrogance. She shook her head in confusion. There was no relief in her heart at his departure. For the first time she wasn't sure if that was truly what she wished. "Dear God!" she whispered to the swaying panel. "What are you doing to me?"

After undressing, she paced the room for the better part of an hour. Though her gaze went repeatedly to the curtain, she knew its folds would not part. Once he left, he did not return.

Where, she wondered silently . . . where did he go on these nights he left her to lie alone in his bed? She'd always assumed he'd left the tent. Could it be that he did not? Dahr-la said he slept in no bed other than his own. . . .

She whirled to look at the drape. Was he behind it, waiting? She resumed her pacing. Each pass brought her closer to the doorway until finally she was standing before it. Telling herself this was merely to satisfy her curiosity, she took a deep breath and snatched the fabric aside.

The outer room was unlit, and it took a moment for her eyes to grow accustomed to the darkness. Still, she knew: she was not alone. Across the room the sofa contained a recumbent form. What she did not know, however, was if it was him, or a guard he had posted.

She lifted the hem of her nightgown. Now poised to retreat the instant she heard any sound that might

143

indicate the man was awake, she stepped forward cautiously.

With the honed instincts of a warrior, Khamed awoke. He could feel her presence. She had come to him. Never moving, never changing his breathing, he waited.

Eudora stopped a few feet from the sofa. From her position she could not see the face clearly. She was sure though, that he slept. His breathing was deep and even. She took a step closer. A strange feeling unfolded within her. If it was Khamed, was this where he had spent those other nights, waiting, as he had said, for her? She still could not see his face. Slipping between the sofa and the lacquered table, she leaned over, extending a hand to the sofa's edge for balance.

Her hand never reached its destination. Like a striking snake, his own intercepted hers.

"You have just made a grave tactical error, little one." Retaining his hold on her wrist, Khamed slowly stood. "By entering his camp, you force your enemy to act. He now has no choice but to engage you in battle, a battle from which . . ." he drew her to him, pressing her close until she was aware of his entire length ". . . he cannot—and will not—retreat."

Eudora could feel the heat from his body through the thin gown she wore. A tremor went through her at the knowledge of his intent, and yet she could not move. She felt his hand go to the back of her neck.

He entwined his fingers in her hair and pulled her head back. He kissed the hollow of her throat, then claimed her lips. His kiss was full of passion and need, insisting on an answer. The pressure of his lips against hers increased. She knew what he wanted and the desire inside her suddenly came alive. She hesitated only for an instant. She opened her mouth. His tongue darted inside to explore all of it.

A moment later the hand which had been at her back was at her breast. Slipping beneath the silk of her gown, his fingertips brushed over her nipples, which firmed instantly in response to his caress. A moan escaped her lips. She felt the last of her will slipping away. Her body was responding shamelessly, yet all she could do was stand still—until he began to lead her into the bedroom.

The inevitability of what was going to happen was suddenly too much. While part of her wanted him, another part demanded she resist. She stopped and drew back. "No . . . I can't do this."

Khamed heard but refused to acknowledge her words. His arousal was beyond the point of control. He was tired of games. In his mind, only one fact was clear: *she* had come to him. "I warned you, little one. This time there can be no retreat." He swept her up into his arms and carried her into the bedroom. He positioned her on the bed, then stood back.

Lost between reason and desire, she watched as he stripped off his clothing. She tried to look away. His voice stopped her.

"Look at me. Tell me what you see, Eudora . . . do you still see a savage?"

She squeezed her eyes shut. She saw not the cruel barbarian she had once feared but a virile man—one her body yearned for. She shook her head and mouthed a single word: no.

"Then why do you resist me?"

She couldn't answer. It was as if she were in a trance, or a dream. She heard him move toward the bed, then felt his weight as he straddled her. His lips seared her mouth, her throat, the soft swell of her breasts. At the same time his hands slid her gown up over her thighs.

Skillfully he waged his assault, his fingertips enticing, coaxing, urging her to full arousal. And still the trancelike state continued. She couldn't move—not even when he parted her legs with his knee.

Khamed knew he could take her. He could feel her need. Wet with desire, she was physically ready for him. But while her body was willing, her spirit was not. Simply possessing the one without the other would not extinguish the fires burning within him. He needed her to respond totally, to give herself to him, to greet his passion with her own.

He reached over her, deftly opened the drawer of the bedside table, and removed a small vial. It contained a clear liquid the vapors of which he knew would heighten her sexual desire. Preferring his own natural instincts, he had never used the aphrodisiac himself. But some of the women who had shared his bed had enjoyed the feeling it evoked.

"You still listen to your pride, little one." There was no anger in his voice, only command. "It is too strong to allow you to hear your passion. Therefore we must make your passion louder, stronger." He twisted off the cap and held the vial under her nose. "Breathe in and you will feel the truth."

Eudora smelled the slightly flowery scent and was confused. Suddenly she began to feel strange, light-headed and dizzy. She closed her eyes. Every nerve seemed to be on fire. Through the blood pounding in her head she heard his voice guiding her.

"Let your desire take you. Do not fight it."

Heat spread through her, building to an aching need concentrated between her thighs. She realized in shock that she wanted him inside her. But he did not move to take her.

Khamed remained still. Though his own body ached with the need for release, his need to break down her resistance was stronger. He waited as she struggled with her conscience and with her desires.

"Please," she whispered, as if remembering his first night's vow to her. "Please make love to me."

"Love has nothing to do with this, little one." He let a hand roam sensually over the soft firmness of her breasts.

"Damn you!" she gasped. "What do you want from me?"

"I want you to want me as I want you."

"I can't! I don't!"

"You will . . . very soon now." He smiled as her treacherous body became faithless to her former resolve, now trying to lure him with undulating movements. He only drew back further.

The hands lying at her sides clenched. Her lips trembled. Slowly the words he'd demanded to hear passed through them. "I want you."

He plunged himself deep within her and she cried out from the sheer pleasure of his possession. Welcoming each thrust, she met them with those of her own. The tide of desire, pent up for years, began to flood through her. Without being aware that she had reached for him, she found her hands behind his head, her fingers entwined in his long hair.

Feeling her embrace, Khamed knew the stimulant had worked. She was completely awash in her body's natural passion and would do anything to obtain the release it now craved, even beg as he once vowed she would. He no longer wished to humiliate her in that way, but in order for her surrender to him to be complete—both physical and mental—she would have to acknowledge her need. "Do you want me to continue?"

"Yes." She whispered the word, so low he barely heard it.

But he did hear it, and it was all he needed. He cupped her buttocks, lifting her so that his possession of her was total, his claim true.

With each deepening thrust she trembled and arched her back, understanding his rhythm and moving with him. Expertly he took her past desire and need to the spiraling heights of ecstasy, then joined her. As she tumbled over the edge to fulfillment, his own release tore a cry from his throat.

Eudora clung to him, quivering helplessly as the aftershocks of her climax washed over her. But once her breathing returned to normal and he withdrew from her, she rolled away instantly. The sweet aftermath of her

147

pleasure was gone. Now came the bitter recriminations of her pride.

She felt him leave the bed, then heard him replace the vial in the drawer and walk to the dresser. The familiar sound of a striking match followed. Feeling she was safe because of his distance, she struggled to sit up. The wetness she immediately felt between her legs, the proof of his possession, seared her soul. She had not only admitted she wanted him, she had asked him to take her!

"Damn you!" she whispered.

When his head lifted she realized he had heard her. "Your rage is with yourself," he stated flatly. "It shames you to think you gave in to your desire."

"I did not 'give in' to desire!" she retorted. "I gave in to a drug! You drugged me!" She sat up and tugged the sheet to her chin. Her eyes narrowed in fury. Despite what she had just done, she could not let him think she had found pleasure in his heinous act. "I would have preferred your giving me to your men," she countered, her voice ripe with loathing.

"I doubt that."

"*What?*" She cried, frustrated by his even reply.

"I doubt you would have preferred my men." He walked over to the bed and sat beside her. "Of course . . . we could always test your theory. . . ."

Eudora trembled at the sinister inflection which had crept into his voice. The tight line of his jaw told her how near his control was to breaking. Had she gone too far?

He reached out and took hold of her chin, forcing her to face him. "I will give you that choice. Decide now, little one—while the choice is still yours to make."

Unable to turn away, but refusing to look at him, she closed her eyes. She was completely at his mercy. If she hesitated, even for a moment, he might very well carry out his threat.

"Decide." His steely voice cut through her. "Me or my men."

"You," she whispered, hating the very sound of the

word and the message it carried.

"A wise choice."

Khamed dropped his hand and she immediately turned her head. Half angry, half amused at her continued struggle and denial, he pulled her into his embrace. She tried to push away, but he held her fast. He had to make her see the truth. He lowered his head and kissed her tenderly. Her eyes flew open in surprise. "Eudora, listen to me. I did not drug you. What I gave you was merely an aphrodisiac. Its only power is one of enhancement."

He spoke slowly and gently. "It cannot force you to feel what you do not already feel. Nor can it force you to do what you do not want to do. But I will make a bargain with you. I will not use it again—if you will accept the reality of your situation."

Eudora knew she had no choice. If she refused, he needed only to use the drug to obtain what he wanted. At least if she agreed to his terms, she could still maintain a measure of dignity even in submission. She nodded in concession and he freed her. She slid down under the covers. Feeling him lie down beside her, she tensed.

He laughed softly. "You will not have to honor your part of the bargain so soon. I will not take you again . . . tonight."

Arrogant bastard! her mind screamed. Under the coverlet her hand clenched into a fist. She was considering striking him when she felt his fingers close around her wrist.

"Consider first who it is you are *really* angry with. You wanted me, Eudora—as much as I wanted you. Admit that to yourself, and then see if you still feel the need to strike out." He released his hold.

A moment later her fingers uncurled. He was right. She *had* wanted him—and had found physical pleasure in what they had shared. It was herself she was furious at.

"There, you see, little one? It is as I said it would be."

She turned to look at him in disbelief. She couldn't be hearing him correctly. He couldn't possibly be gloating!

"What?" she gasped.

"It is as I said it would be," he repeated. "You have felt the truth—both painful and pleasurable. And now that you have . . ." He reached out and stroked her cheek. "We will enjoy one another. I will give you not only what you need, but what I know you want."

"You bastard!" She twisted her face from his caress and scrambled to her knees. Unmindful of the sheet which fell from her heaving breasts, she glared at him. "How dare you presume to know what I need and want? I agreed to this bargain only because I have no other choice. Do not, do not *ever* think that I want, need, or enjoy you!"

He shook his head and smiled. "Passion. Such passion."

His softly uttered comment hurled her past reason. "Get out. Get out!" she screamed, stabbing a shaking finger at the room's exit.

He raised an eyebrow. "It is *my* tent, little one."

Suddenly Eudora realized her fury was only feeding his amusement. The harder she'd tried to express her outrage, the wider his smile had grown. She forced herself to rein in her raging emotions. "In that case . . ." She jerked the sheet to her. "I will leave." She got off the bed and wrapped the sheet around her.

"You are acting like a spoiled child."

His voice, cool and complacent, knifed her more deeply than had his self-righteous arrogance. And yet she showed no emotion. She was done showing emotion. From now on all he would see in her would be cold indifference and passive resignation to her fate.

"Very well." Unexpectedly Khamed rose.

But as he moved to the doorway, Eudora was helplessly aware of the question running through her mind: Why, if it was he who was retreating, did she feel it was she who had lost?

Chapter Ten

"My lord?"

Khamed looked up from the letter he was writing.

Across the room, framed in the doorway, Kahlil bowed. "You sent for me?"

His lieutenant's question elicited a mute nod. Gesturing for the man to enter, Khamed returned his attention to the paper before him. He had put this off long enough. His ransom demands should have been put into writing right after the raid on the French caravan two weeks ago. . . .

With that thought he leaned back in his chair, shook his head, and silently frowned. Had it really only been two weeks that he had been battling his green-eyed captive? It seemed much longer . . . and still they were as enemies.

Perhaps he was to blame. If he had not insisted upon a verbal affirmation of his victory after making love to her, they might not be embroiled in this seemingly unending contest of wills.

Before he could continue with his train of thought, he heard Kahlil's voice.

"Should I come back, my lord?"

Khamed glanced up. "No. I am nearly finished." He sat forward and picked up the paper on the desk. Carefully he read what he had written. Satisfied, he then folded the sheet and returned his gaze to Kahlil.

"I have written the French, informing them of the seizure of the caravan. My terms for the release of the Frenchmen are detailed in this letter."

"Shall I dispatch a rider to deliver it to Ghardaïa?"

"No. A messenger would enable them too easily to trace the letter's source. And while I doubt the French army would retaliate with an attack against me, or attempt a rescue, I see no point taking that risk. The customary method will suffice." Thinking of the desert's system of mail delivery which could take weeks instead of days, he smiled. Time was his ally. "The next time a traveler arrives in camp headed east, give it to him—with the instructions that he is to pass it on to someone traveling north."

Kahlil stepped forward to take the letter, now sealed in an envelope, from Khamed's hand.

Khamed watched as his lieutenant's eyes went to the address scrawled across the envelope's front.

"The *chargé d'affaires?*"

"Yes. With the reporter involved, it becomes a civilian matter."

Kahlil opened his mouth as if to speak, then quickly shut it.

The action did not escape Khamed's note. He smiled. Kahlil knew better than to question his judgment without invitation. "What is it, Kahlil? Do you disapprove?"

"No, my lord . . . but . . ." Again he hesitated.

"If there is something you want to say, then say it."

"Very well." Kahlil squared his shoulders. "You did not mention the woman. Does this mean you have decided not to ransom her with her companions?"

Khamed leaned back and lit a cigarette. "At this time I see no reason to do so. One of the men overheard the Frenchmen talking. Apparently her presence with the caravan was a fact known neither to the French Army officials nor to her father. Over the last two weeks I have had discreet inquiries made in Ouargla. Louis Morrel, who is now well under way with the Foureau/Lemy expedition, has no other living relatives. Therefore her disappearance will not immediately be noticed. It may take months for her friends and acquaintances in France to question her continued absence—if they do at all. As long as the French do not know of her involvement, she shall remain a . . . personal matter."

The look which crossed Kahlil's face was unmistakable. "Do you think that is wise?"

"Do you question my will, Kahlil?" Despite his efforts to the contrary, Khamed was unable to keep the hard edge from his voice.

"No, my lord. I question your judgment." Kahlil lowered his eyes. "From the moment you first saw her, this woman has consumed your thoughts and colored that judgment. I know the ways of the West are different from our own. Their women are accorded many of the rights of a man." He grimaced, making no effort to conceal his personal abhorrence for the very thought. "Because you have lived in their world, you have been influenced by their customs. Therefore her disobedience goes unpunished, her defiance unchecked. But the men see that as weakness."

Nervously, Kahlil raised his gaze. "And in our world a man who appears unable to rule his woman will not long rule his men. I caution you not to allow your indulgence of her to give your men cause to question who is captive, and who is captor."

Once again, he looked to the floor. "Forgive me if I have spoken out of turn, my lord. But our friendship, and my loyalty to you do not accord me the luxury of apathy."

Smiling, Khamed extinguished his cigarette. "I would be a poor friend, and an even poorer sheik if I did not recognize and value such honesty. Your words of caution are noted. Now, in that letter . . ." He gestured toward the envelope still clutched in Kahlil's hand. "I have

153

requested that a third party act as go-between, one who is acceptable to both the French and to myself. Does a name come to mind?"

Obviously relieved that his words had not incurred his lord's wrath, Kahlil rubbed his bearded chin, answering after a moment of deliberation. "Doctor Gerard. He is well known and well respected by the French, and trusted by the tribes."

"My thoughts exactly." Laughing, Khamed stood. "At least in this we agree." He clapped Kahlil affectionately on the back. "Go, my friend. It grows late, and your wives no doubt are wondering as to your whereabouts."

Kahlil bowed. "My lord."

With Kahlil's exit, Khamed moved to light the lantern above the desk. Deliberately he chose not to think about the conversation that had just transpired and let his thoughts wander to the past.

He had first met René Gerard more than twenty-five years before, when the Belgian missionary had been a guest in his father's camp. After a decade of living among the Saharan tribes, Gerard had abandoned his quest for their immortal souls. The desert Moslems made poor converts. Instead, he traveled between encampments, tending to their medical needs and interceding with the colonial administration on their behalf.

For a reason Khamed had never understood, but had always been grateful for, Gerard had taken an immediate liking to him . . . and he to Gerard. He seemed to understand Khamed's moody, glowering sullenness, recognizing it for what it was—so much armor concealing his insecurity.

Lighting another cigarette, Khamed crossed the room to the sofa. He did not often think of his childhood. He found the memories painful. They were memories of living in two worlds and belonging to neither.

As a child living with his mother in England, he had known he was different. His very name, along with his black hair and eyes and a dark complexion, had set him apart from his milk-faced, fair-haired playmates—all of whom had fathers. One of his earliest memories was of asking his mother what a "heathen savage" was. Having overheard another child's nanny refer to his father that way, he hadn't known what the words meant—but he had understood the prejudice they carried.

With a child's logic, he had decided he belonged in his father's world. He escaped into romantic dreams of riding at his father's side across the sands of the faraway desert kingdom he ruled. But when his mother returned him to his father, the strange sights and sounds that assaulted his senses on the dock of Algiers had filled him with fear. His mother had had to pry his hand from her own in order to push him forward to meet the fierce-looking white-robed stranger who was his father.

Khamed spoke no Arabic, and in his terror he forgot the carefully rehearsed, polite greeting in French. He had clung to his mother, begging her not to leave him. But she had only gently scolded him and admonished him to act like the prince he was, insisting he not cry anymore. He kept his promise to her. He never cried again—not even at the news of her death a year later.

Eventually he adjusted to his life in the desert, coming to love it. His years in England were nearly forgotten. The sullen little boy grew into a self-assured youth who had finally found his place. A source of great pride and joy not only to his father, but to the entire tribe, he was denied nothing. His every whim was fulfilled—until he turned sixteen and his world once again came crashing down. His father insisted he return to England to be educated.

René Gerard alone had understood his refusal to return to his mother's homeland. It had been he who had suggested Paris. Khamed had not wanted to go to Paris either. He'd argued bitterly with his father in a futile attempt to change his mind. Yet in the end he obeyed— for Haisim was not only his father, but his sheik.

Once more thrust into a world to which he did not

155

belong, his sullen, dark side returned. Though his physical strength and prowess earned him the respect and admiration of his classmates, and his uncommon dark good looks brought him more than enough attention and interest from the fairer sex, civilization held no appeal for him. He lived only to return each summer to his father and tribe, yet in the autumn he dutifully went back to Paris. He did not disguise or make a secret of his displeasure, but neither did he ever ask to be allowed to remain. His sense of honor and duty, to his father and to his people, was too strong and deeply inbred.

Hearing Eudora moving about in the next room, he set his thoughts of the past aside. It was the future that needed to be considered now. He was confident Gerard would agree to act as intermediary. He could release the Frenchmen into his hands knowing the man who had befriended him as a boy would not betray him.

Eudora listened as the voices in the next room grew silent. Though she was sure Kahlil had left, she did not venture beyond the drape. A week ago she had made the mistake of entering the outer room while Khamed was having an audience with several of his men. He'd not uttered a word, but the scathing look he'd leveled at her had sent her dashing back into the bedroom. It was not until days later that she had learned the cause for his displeasure.

Khamed had decided to accord her limited freedom of movement within the camp. Delighted to have the opportunity to escape her prison tent, if only for a short while, Eudora had gratefully accepted Dahr-la's invitation to accompany her on a visit to her sister, Kahlil's very pregnant young wife.

Eudora was not so naive as not to have realized Khamed's position would provide him certain luxuries. Still, the sight of Kahlil's goat-hair-and-wool tent had taken her aback. Furnished with only the barest of necessities, it was substantially smaller than Khamed's, appearing even more so because of the dividing curtain that ran front to back.

Dahr-la had explained that the Arab style tent, called a *kaima*, was partitioned for a reason. The two sides provided separate quarters for its occupants, the men to the right, the women and children to the left. The men's side served as the sleeping quarters, living room, dining room, and parlor for receiving guests. And while the Reguibat did not adhere strictly to the Moslem practice of secluding their women, it was on the left that a woman remained whenever a male not of her kin was in the tent.

Eudora had first bristled, then cringed in understanding. She was to be subject not only to the whims and moods of her captor, but to the misogynistic practices of his heritage as well! In spite of her outrage, however, she did not repeat her mistake. If she heard male voices coming from "his" side of the curtain, she remained in the bedroom, pacing—as she did now.

"You are going to wear a hole in my carpet, little one."

Spinning, Eudora found her gaze locked into one of Khamed's golden stares. Damn his uncanny ability to creep up behind her without warning! She was sure he did it deliberately just to unnerve her. "I . . . I was restless," she offered by way of a feeble response.

A slow, lazy grin slipped across his face. "In that case, might I suggest a physical activity which would leave the nap of the carpet intact?"

Though he made no move toward her, her guard was instantly raised. She instinctively tensed and stepped back, closing her eyes in fear. He had not attempted to make love to her again after that first time. Still, she did not trust him.

The sound of his soft laughter caused her to open her eyes.

He had not moved from the doorway. "I was referring to a walk, little one. I was about to check in with one of the returning patrols. Will you accompany me?" His gaze, rife with promise, slid down the length of her. "I am afraid anything else you had in mind will have to wait until later."

Eudora felt her cheeks burn. "It's like an oven in here," she snapped.

"Then it is settled." He bowed. "A walk will do you good." Without waiting for her response, he turned.

Eudora hesitated for only an instant and then followed. Her desire to leave the confines of the small room was far stronger than her need to rebuff his invitation for pride's sake.

They walked across the compound in silence. Eudora watched as Khamed's eyes periodically darted to specific sites along the camp's perimeter. Each time a white-robed figure emerged from the darkness to make his presence known.

"Do you always live like this?" She gestured to an armed man in the distance. He was the fifth sentry they had seen since leaving the tent. "As if you were at war?"

"In a manner of speaking, we are at war. Jealousy, ancient feuds, and competition between the various tribes necessitate a need for constant reconnaissance and security."

"He who lives by the sword . . ." Eudora stopped short.

"Shall die by it?" Khamed laughed. "If I am to understand your analogy, little one . . . because we raid, we are raided?"

"Something like that. You have admitted it is the driving force in your lives."

The grunt she heard might have been affirmation or denial. She wasn't sure, and it was too dark to see his face. She decided not to press the issue further. For the moment she was weary of sparring with him.

The days that followed soon stretched into weeks. Each night Khamed came to her, slipping into bed beside her. Never did he touch her. It was as if he knew of her silent resolve to yield to him only in passive indifference and had decided to wait until such time as she was willing to respond. The tension that existed between them grew as a result . . . so much so that a release of it was inevitable.

Eudora had been in the Reguibat camp a month when Khamed returned one evening after a three-day absence. She had been sitting on the sofa, reading.

As he entered, she glanced up and immediately noticed how tired he looked. He exhibited all the signs of hard riding. The white robes were sand-laden, and his face, lined with fatigue, was shadowed with days' worth of black stubble and a dark scowl.

He stared at her for a moment. Then, without speaking, he went into the next room.

At once her guard was raised. She remained seated, thumbing the pages of her book disinterestedly. Her thoughts had already turned to the conversation she'd had with Dahr-la the day Khamed had left.

Out of curiosity she had asked the girl the reason for his frequent and sometimes extended trips from camp. Some she knew were undertaken for the purpose of settling tribal business. His permission was needed before a couple could even marry. He also mediated clashes between clansmen and decided all manner of petty disputes, and was responsible for the overseeing of the farming and herding and day-to-day routines necessary for survival.

Still, these duties and responsibilities seemed too few to foster the ceaseless, demanding routine she witnessed. That thought aside, she had too often seen him ride from camp in the company of large, fully armed parties of men.

Never one to shy from an opportunity to sit and chat, Dahr-la had eagerly revealed that side of her lord he had chosen to keep from his captive.

Eudora learned that the Reguibat were paid tribute by the caravans that crossed their territory—thereby ensuring them safety from attack. For a price, Khamed also provided armed escorts to safeguard the caravans of smaller, weaker tribes from the Chaamba and Tuareg—traditional enemies of the Reguibat. Only those caravans which did not pay tribute, or those which belonged to their enemies were raided. The Reguibat also ran caravans of their own, for the tribe was active in arms trading.

That fact did not come as a surprise to Eudora. Had her own caravan not been attacked because of the guns it was carrying? What did surprise her, however, was to learn that in as much as Khamed despised the French presence in the Sahara, he did not engage them directly. Because his enemy had no army posts located within the borders of his own territory, his retaliation against them consisted of supplying the tribes who were fighting encroachment.

It was this trade in arms, conducted with the gun runners in Rio de Oro who had abandoned their peaceful salt trade in favor of one far more lucrative, which had taken him from the camp this latest time. Judging by his appearance and mood, Eudora could only guess the trip had proved to be less than successful. She braced herself for an unpleasant evening.

Yet when he returned from the bedroom his scowl was gone, as were his beard, his robes, and his shirt. His damp hair clung to his forehead, and he unconsciously ran his long fingers through its black waves. A white towel, contrasting vividly against the bronzed skin, was draped around his neck. With one end he was wiping the last bit of shaving soap from his chin.

His casual manner infuriated her. Had they been man and wife for years, his actions could not have been more nonchalant. He stopped at the writing desk to light a cigarette. She watched him, noting how the smooth muscles in his back rippled with his movements—so masculine, yet so graceful in their practiced ease and deftness. Irritated with herself—with her thoughts, which could be deemed admiring—she threw the book toward the floor.

It landed instead on the small table in front of the sofa, smashing the ceramic ashtray which lay upon it.

Khamed did not turn or even flinch in response to the sudden crash. "I grow weary of your temper tantrums, little one," he said dryly. "If they persist you shall find yourself over my knee. Clean it up."

Eudora stood slowly. She could not see his face, but there was no mistaking the patronizing inflection of his voice. "I will not be spoken to or treated as a child!" she retorted.

Without turning, he seemed to know she had not moved to comply with his order. "You will be treated as you act. And you *will* do as you are told. I repeat, clean it up."

"Clean it up yourself!" The instant the words left her lips she knew she had made a grave mistake.

He whirled with an oath. Unknown to her, her defiance had struck a nerve—Kahlil's warning of weeks past. He stabbed his cigarette into an ashtray and threw the towel to the floor.

As he moved toward her, she tried to run. As always, she was too slow and he too quick. He grabbed her wrist and pulled her to him. "Be careful, Eudora," he stated at last, very slowly. "I will indulge you only to the point that it amuses me to do so."

As swiftly as he had seized her, he then released her and stepped to the sofa.

Trembling in a release of the fear which had clutched her, Eudora watched as he settled himself down upon the plush cushions. He picked up the book from the table and began to flip through its pages. That he now intended to ignore her was clear.

"You bastard," she whispered. Her vow to show no emotion was forgotten.

He remained motionless.

"I hate you. Do you hear me? *I hate you!*"

"Then hate me," he answered sarcastically, "as long as you do so passionately—for I have grown tired of your icy presence in my bed. Now leave me. Your presence bores me."

With a choking cry, she fled from him.

His voice stopped her at the heavy drapes. "You have forgotten something, little one."

She whirled to look at him. His head was still lowered.

Suddenly, with the point of his boot he kicked over the table.

The pieces of the broken ashtray scattered across the carpet.

Tossing her head with as much dignity as she could muster, Eudora ripped the curtain aside. Nothing he could do could torment her any further. She was wrong.

As the sound of his deep laughter floated through the thick folds, she went rigid with fury. Fists clenched, she awaited his appearance.

But Khamed did not follow her into the bedroom.

Relief washed over her like a calm tide. Yet when he still had not come to her an hour later, the waters of her emotions began to churn anew.

His rejection of her was what she had been praying for. But why, lying now in his bed alone, did she feel no joy? What she felt was a sense of loss. It was madness! What had she lost but the interest of a man whose passion she had feared and fought? Was it possible she had been so long in his control that her powers of reason had been perverted?

Indeed, she had begun to feel strangely at ease with him. At times she even regretted her decision to yield in indifference should he try again to take her. But he had not. And that confused her—until she remembered his conditions for a truce between them. He wanted a willing lover. Yet he had honored his part of their bargain and had not used the aphrodisiac again.

Eudora struggled to comprehend the thoughts and emotions teeming within her. Her complete and utter

162

dependency upon Khamed had eroded her sense of self. Was *that* why he no longer had need of the small vial and its contents? Was he using a different method of seduction—time? Would her condition seem the more right the longer it prevailed? Would she forget who she was and become what he would make of her?

With no clear answers to her questions, she had no solutions. Wondering if he would come to her, she drifted into a troubled sleep.

When Dahr-la woke her the next morning, she was still alone. According to the girl, Khamed had spent the night on the sofa, leaving before dawn to ride out with the morning patrol.

Eudora's mind began to race. She had thought of going to Sabatin. Seeing him would remind her of what she was, serving to rescue and restore her lost sense of self. Khamed's timely absence now seemed an omen. She would never have a better opportunity.

Her decision made, she bathed and dressed quickly. As she pulled aside the dividing curtain to enter the outer room, her eyes were drawn to the far side of the tent.

The table still lay on its side, the pieces of the shattered ashtray strewn about it. Like a tangible testimonial to the war of wills being waged between her and Khamed, its presence overwhelmed the room.

"He will *not* win this time!" Her spoken declaration seemed immediately neutralized by the shiver that raced up her spine. She wrapped her shawl closer around her. Tearing her eyes from the table, she left the tent.

As she made her way across the compound to du Bois's and Sabatin's small goat hair prison, she thought of how differently the two men were reacting to the same set of circumstances. Du Bois regarded his confinement in the Reguibat camp as internment in enemy hands. As a soldier, he had suffered a fate far worse than death. Not only had he been defeated on a field of battle, he had become a prisoner of war. Sabatin, on the other hand, seemed to consider the Reguibat a subject for study,

163

almost viewing his imposed stay in their camp as an opportunity for education.

When she reached the isolated tent, its lone guard bowed, greeting her respectfully in Arabic. Eudora was still very uneasy around Khamed's tribesmen. The entire encampment knew who and what she was. She felt certain that as their lord's white mistress she was an object of their private ridicule.

Dipping her head in nervous response to the man's bemused stare, she cried out, "Pierre?"

Sabatin called out for her to enter, and the guard stepped aside. As she entered the small tent, du Bois immediately averted his gaze.

"Lieutenant."

He turned away, ignoring her greeting.

Sabatin, who had been sitting with his back to her on a small wooden crate, stood. "Eudora! I wasn't expecting you. What a pleasant surprise!" He reached out and took her hand in his, raising it to his lips in a poignant gesture of chivalry.

Eudora's eyes watered instantly. His kindness and acceptance touched her deeply. She was sure he had guessed at the truth. But the knowledge that she had been intimate with their captor had not caused him to break his promise to her. He had remained her friend. She looked away lest he see her tears. Her gaze came to rest upon a large crate in front of the one he had been sitting on. A dozen or so sheets of paper lay strewn across its slatted top.

"Have I interrupted something?" She gestured toward the papers upon the makeshift desk.

Grinning sheepishly, he nervously began to gather the pages into a pile. "I've decided to keep a diary during my stay here. You know, I've never been very serious about anything . . . my writing . . . my job. I think you've always suspected that about me. My journalistic endeavors have been at worst cheap exploitation and at best only mediocre sensationalism. All I've ever accomplished with my writing is to pay the bills."

He paused, raking his fingers through his hair. "But a study of these people . . . a firsthand look at their lives just might open the eyes of those armchair colonialists in Paris. After all, if a government is going to occupy a country, some attempt should be made to learn about the people who have been occupying it for centuries!"

The sincerity in his voice caused her to smile. "May I?" She stretched out a hand.

Sabatin hesitated for a moment before giving her the stack of poor-grade paper.

His penciled scrawl was difficult to read. To make better use of the weak light, she stepped away from him to stand closer to the doorway.

After several minutes she looked up from the pages to meet his anxious eyes. "This is wonderful!" she whispered softly. "Truly it is!"

Flushing a deep crimson, Sabatin sat down on the small crate. Normally self-assured and even cocky, he seemed embarrassed by her words of praise.

Eudora was amused to see him so flustered. Her purpose in coming to the tent was forgotten. "Your insight into their lives, their struggle for survival, is amazingly accurate. I have heard Khamed voice many of these same thoughts. I have learned a lot from him—"

"I'm sure you have!" du Bois snarled from the doorway.

Eudora's back stiffened, but she pretended not to have heard the crude remark. ". . . about the Reguibat's history and—"

Suddenly she felt herself being grabbed by the arm and spun around. The pages in her hand fell unnoticed to the ground as du Bois's face, bearing a contemptuous smirk, materialized before her.

"And just where does your Arab lover teach you this *history*, Mademoiselle? Is it in or out of his bed? Before or after he defiles you?" As he taunted her, his face seemed to twist and contort in a mirror image of the hateful

165

vileness he spewed. "Or perhaps it is during? When he mounts you to plant himself within you, does he whisper these tidbits of knowledge in your ear?"

Eudora stood numb, unable to move or speak. No response to his vulgar unprovoked attack would come.

"See here, du Bois!" Sabatin shouted in outrage.

But just as he pushed the large crate aside to rise, Eudora's wits returned. "How dare you!" she hissed. "Take your hands off me!"

"Forgive me, Mademoiselle." Du Bois released his hold, stepping back with a deep, mocking bow. "I had forgotten you prefer the hands of a filthy savage!"

"Lieutenant, it is *you* who are the savage!" As if from far away she heard her own voice, even and calm. "And had I the choice of being 'mounted' by him or you, I would prefer *him*."

Du Bois's upper lip twitched and his fingers closed slowly into tight fists. Before she could react, he took a single step forward. Grabbing her arm with one hand, he raised the other. "You little whore!"

A deep, resonant voice rang out at the tent's entrance. "*That* would be the last move you would ever make, Lieutenant."

Eudora whirled. Khamed stood in the doorway, his powerful form so filled the narrow opening that no sunlight had entered the tent to give away his presence. Though his bronzed face was a dispassionate vizard, the black eyes burned with deadly intensity.

Du Bois released his hold and slowly lowered his fist.

"Eudora." Khamed stepped forward and extended his hand.

Wordlessly she took it.

Roughly he pulled her toward the tent's entrance. His eyes never left du Bois's terror-stricken face. But it was not until she was safely behind him that he again addressed the man. "If you ever touch her again, I will kill you."

Eudora turned and ran. Her lungs burned from the

166

sobs she fought to hold back. It was too late to stop her tears; they stung her eyes, blinding her as she fled across the compound.

What had she done to warrant du Bois's hatred and violence? He would have struck her had it not been for Khamed. *Khamed!* The name tore through her. Dear God, what she had said to du Bois. . . . Could she have *meant* it? Could she have really meant to defend him?

Eudora entered her tent and collapsed on the sofa. Any moment Khamed would arrive. She had to compose herself. She had to forget what had just happened. The desire to strike back at du Bois had put the words in her mouth. They meant nothing. Nothing, she told herself. Brushing the tears from her face, she stared at the overturned table at her feet.

Suddenly Khamed was standing before her. "Are you all right?"

"Yes." Startled more by the gentleness she heard in his voice, than his appearance, she lifted her gaze. "I . . . I don't know what came over him . . . it was like he was possessed."

Khamed sat down beside her. His expression was so strange, Eudora wondered how much of the argument he had overheard. Had he heard her defend him? He continued to stare at her until she finally turned away.

"You are not to go to the Frenchmen's tent again," he said suddenly. As she started to object he held up his hand. "You may see the reporter here, if you so desire, but you are not to go anywhere near the lieutenant. Do you understand?"

She nodded silently. It was one order from him she would gladly obey.

Apparently satisfied with her answer, he stood to leave.

"Wait!" Before she fully realized what she was doing, she had reached out to touch his arm. "I . . . I want to thank you . . . for what you did."

Leaning toward her, Khamed smiled cryptically. His

knuckle grazed her cheek. "As I told you before, little one, a Reguibat fights to keep what is his . . . and will protect it at any cost." With that he straightened and walked to the tent's entrance.

She watched as he left. Her gaze returned to the table and the broken pieces of the ashtray.

When Khamed returned hours later, Eudora was napping in the bedroom. He sat down on the sofa and immediately noticed that the shattered ashtray had been removed. The table, however, still lay on its side.

He began to laugh. So this was how this particular battle in their war of wills was to end—in a stalemate! She had broken the ashtray and, in partial condescension to his will, had picked up the pieces. But *he* had tipped over the table and *Hamdullah*—Praise be to Allah—no power on earth would make her pick *it* up!

He leaned back and smiled. Her pride was dying hard. Yet even in her steady defiance, Eudora Morrel was more intoxicating than any woman he had ever known.

"Touché," little one," he whispered aloud. Leaning forward, he reached out, setting the table on its legs. *"Touché."*

Chapter Eleven

Eudora parted the drape. Slipping through the folds, she entered the main room cautiously. Almost at once she noticed the righted table. Her gaze flew to Khamed.

With his back to her, he was standing by the doorway, looking out into the compound.

Was the impasse broken? His stance told her nothing. Face me, she cried silently.

As if he had heard her, he turned. "Kahlil thinks he may become a father tonight."

His words barely registered. She was too busy searching his face. He looked to be in a good mood, smiling as he let the flap fall. Had he finally tired of the game between them?

"Eudora?" Khamed stepped forward and grasped her arm gently. "Are you all right?"

"Yes. Yes, I'm fine." She moved away from him to the sofa. She had lied. She wasn't all right. Her legs had suddenly grown wobbly. She sank down onto the cushions.

Willing it away had not made it disappear, nor had ignoring it. The crushing feeling of confusion she could not shake persisted. She stared at her hands clasped in her lap, and as she felt him sit down beside her, she crumbled. She couldn't bear it any longer. She had to have answers.

"Why . . ." She turned to look at him. "Why would a man want and protect a woman who does not want him?" Intentionally she posed the question hypothetically, forcing a casual, detached quality to her voice she did not feel.

Khamed raised an eyebrow. Her charade of phrasing her question in the third person had not escaped him. "Perhaps the man is not convinced," he replied, keeping up the pretense.

"Not convinced of what?"

Silently Khamed laughed. The calm and neutral tone present in her voice a moment earlier had vanished. "That the statement is true," he answered evenly.

Eudora stared at him in disbelief. "*What?*"

Khamed chose to purposely misunderstand her exclamation. "Perhaps the man in question is not convinced," he repeated. He spoke slowly, as one would to a child when explaining a complex thought. "He may not truly believe that the woman does *not* want him." He paused a moment to study her reaction. "After all, she *did* defend him." He reveled in the look of horror which exploded across her face.

Eudora lowered her head immediately. So he had heard her! Fervently she fought to regain her composure. "It was merely an unconscious response to du Bois's hateful prejudice," she explained coolly. "I would have done the same for anyone."

Khamed laughed out loud as she abandoned the third person pretense. "Really?" He stood and reached for her, pulling her easily to her feet and drawing her close. Her head was tilted back, her eyes staring blankly past him. "You have wounded me deeply, little one." Pressing a hand to his chest, he moaned in feigned exasperation and pain. "And here I thought you were actually beginning to succumb to my charms!" Seeing her head snap forward, he smiled. Releasing her, he turned away.

Once more presented with his back, Eudora sputtered in outrage. "Why, you . . . you . . . arrogant bastard!

Your *charms* may have worked on your other *guests* . . ." She choked on the euphemisms. "But I assure you, *this* woman does *not* want you! I loathe you with a passion every bit as strong as it was the first night you came to me—if not more! You are the cruelest, most arrogant, despicable man it has ever been my misfortune to know!"

He turned to face her, his eyes blazing, whether with passion or anger she wasn't sure. "I am curious, little one. Just what *is* my distinction? Are we speaking in the Biblical sense? Am I the most despicable man you have ever met?" His lips parted in a mocking smile. "Or merely the most despicable one who has ever bedded you?"

Eudora went numb. He had never mentioned her lack of virginity before, nor had he ever questioned her about her past. She'd been grateful for his silence, sensing respect for her privacy. But now his taunting remark was like a slap in the face. She shrieked and hurled herself at him in a blinding rage.

Khamed was delighted at her response. His taunting had been deliberate, a calculated attempt to arouse and inflame a passionate reaction of some kind in his lovely captive. Even if it was impassioned loathing that his words evoked, the spark and fire it brought to her eyes served the same purpose: igniting his very soul and consuming him with burning desire.

He deftly captured the hand she raised, wrestling it to her side. But its mate evaded his grasp. He clenched his teeth as he felt her nails rake the smooth plane below his cheekbone. Snatching her wrist, he twisted her arm behind her back. The other followed. Now holding both wrists with one hand, he clutched a fistful of hair and dragged her to him. His mouth descended upon hers.

Eudora fought to catch her breath. Her lips parted and he thrust his tongue deep into her mouth. She moaned softly. Melting into his embrace, she surrendered to the authority of his touch.

Probing and teasing, he ravished her hungrily before

171

permitting himself a different enjoyment. He nipped at her bottom lip then moved his mouth from hers. Down her throat to the tops of her full breasts, he delivered his assault. Through the fabric of her gown he teased the erect nipples before returning to her throat, where he nibbled and sucked. He knew he was bruising the tender flesh, marking her as she had marked him. "I am still not convinced, little one," he whispered roughly against her ear.

Eudora felt the blood pounding in her head with the same throbbing intensity she had endured under the influence of the aphrodisiac. But there had been no stimulant forced upon her this time. He had administered only the mind-numbing, will-stealing power of his desire.

"No!" she cried out, struggling to break his hold, to divorce herself from her body's need. But the moist fire she felt where his own hard, pulsating need touched her had taken on a will of its own. It demanded to be extinguished and defied her control.

His mouth found hers again. Instead of the hard, crushing force he had rained upon her before, he was now gentle in his insistence. The tenderness of his soft kisses was matched by the touch of his skillful fingers as they left her hair to trace a caressing line down her body—one which began at her breasts and ended at the apex of her desire. He slipped one knee between her legs, parting them easily.

She groaned in helpless ecstasy, grinding herself against the heel of his palm, lost in the spell he had cast over her. This was no resignation to fate!

"My lord?"

Eudora plummeted back to reality. The sound of a woman's voice outside the tent had shattered the spell. Reason surfaced and she recoiled from his embrace.

Khamed stormed to the doorway. His face was a glowering mask of rage as he ripped open the flap.

Eudora caught a glimpse of a middle-aged woman cowering before him. She whispered a few sentences in

172

Arabic and then quickly fled.

"Kahlil's wife is in labor," he informed her coolly, walking past her to enter the bedroom.

Eudora watched him disappear behind the thick folds only to return a moment later pulling on his heavy robes.

"I am going to find him. The midwife told him the child would not come until morning. The fool was unable to bear the waiting and rode out into the desert. Now his heir threatens to enter this world within the hour."

"Can't someone else go?" She immediately realized the implication of her words. She felt her cheeks, already flushed with passion, flame even hotter. "I . . . I just thought it odd you would not send someone else to find Kahlil."

Khamed raised an eyebrow. His sly grin told her any explanation she offered would be futile. "I have a good idea where he is—a place we found as children. We swore we would never reveal its location to another living soul. I must be the one to ride out after him. He would never forgive me if I did not bring him back in time for the birth of his heir."

He went to the carved chest and unlocked it, withdrawing a black saddlebag she recognized instantly. It contained the medical supplies he had dropped to her when she had attended to Sabatin after the raid.

He thrust it into her startled grasp. "Take this to the midwife. If Kiri has any difficulty it will be needed." He smiled wanly. "Hopefully the stubborn old witch will admit it if her superstitious incantations and charms are not enough, and accept the aid of modern medicines."

A strange look crossed his face, and Eudora wondered what thoughts were going through his mind. Was he thinking of the difficulty his own mother had encountered during his birth?

With a start Khamed realized she was watching him. There was no way for her to know that the midwife he had spoken of had been the same one who had brought him into the world more than thirty years ago. Nor could she

173

know that he loved the old woman like a grandmother. Still, he forced a stoic expression and turned. At the doorway he stopped. "Tell Kiri she will have to answer to me if the child is born before I return with its father."

Eudora stared at him blankly—as if she thought he might be jesting. "Are you serious?"

"You tell her exactly that!" He snapped at her impatiently, unable to disguise the irritation he felt at her questioning of his order.

Grateful to be able to escape his anger, Eudora hurried into the bedroom to fetch her shawl. When she returned, he was gone. Tossing the wrap around her head and shoulders, she walked to the doorway, stepping outside in uncertainty. She had never been farther than the awning at night before, and the air of unfamiliarity wrapped around the camp by the cloak of darkness alarmed her. In spite of the small cooking fires burning at almost every tent, and the torches and lanterns that added their own flickering light to that of the fires, the inky darkness was overwhelming.

Carefully, she made her way from tent to tent. Would she even recognize the one she sought? They all looked so much alike. As she rounded the corner of a small tent, her worries became groundless. Kahlil's tent stood before her, illuminated in bright light from the dozens of torches held by the people gathered outside. Clearly the birth of a child was an important event to the close-knit tribe.

As she approached, the crowd grew silent, parting to allow her to pass. Intending to hand the saddlebag to a burly man who seemed to be in charge of keeping order in the gathering of well-wishers and curious onlookers, she walked to the tent's entrance.

Surely he would recognize it and be able to guess Khamed's instructions, she thought. She held out the bag. But instead of taking it, he wordlessly drew aside the flap, gesturing for her to enter. Hesitantly she stepped inside.

Two women sitting upon cushions on the parlor side of the small tent looked up in mutual surprise. Eudora recognized the mother of Dahr-la and Kiri immediately. The much plumper, older version of Dahr-la nudged her companion and murmured a few words of Arabic. As the woman rose, her face became visible in the dim light.

Recognizing Kahlil's first wife, Elon, Eudora realized it was she who had come to the tent to summon Khamed. Anticipating her acceptance of the saddlebag, Eudora held it out to her. Shaking her head, Elon slipped past her to enter the next room.

"My lady!"

Eudora turned to see Dahr-la rushing toward her.

"Dahr-la!" She released a sigh of relief. "Khamed has gone to find Kahlil." She held out the saddlebag. "He told me to give this to the midwife."

The same look which had crossed Khamed's face earlier now appeared in Dahr-la's.

Eudora felt a knotting of fear in her stomach. "Is Kiri all right?"

"She is doing fine." Dahr-la smiled and the apprehension in her eyes disappeared. "Come. See for yourself." She stepped back toward the drape just as Elon exited.

"Oh, no, I don't think so. It wouldn't be proper. Shouldn't your mother be with her?" Eudora looked to the older woman who was now talking softly with Elon. It did seem strange she wasn't at her daughter's side. Shrugging the thought aside, she returned her attention to Dahr-la. "Just tell Kiri . . . tell her that I wish her well and . . . oh! I almost forgot. Khamed gave me a message for her. Tell her—"

Dahr-la raised her hand. "If my lord gave you the message, then he intended you to deliver it. Come." She drew back the curtain with one hand while reaching for the saddlebag with the other. "And to answer your question, my lady . . ." She cast a glance back to her mother. "My mother has what you call a weak stomach.

175

She is unable to bear the sight of blood."

Eudora had to swallow hard to stop the taste of bile rising instantly in her throat. Not sure she was going to fare any better than Kiri's mother, she followed Dahr-la.

In the small room, Kiri, supported by a tiny brown-faced woman, walked slowly in a tight circle. Her round face glistened with the perspiration which had already dampened her hair so that it clung to her forehead in wet strands. She offered a weak smile. *"Grib*—soon."

Out of the corner of her eye, Eudora watched the midwife. Her eyes narrowed in disdain as she caught sight of the saddlebag Dahr-la was trying to unobtrusively place in a corner. Spitting a few words of Arabic to herself, she returned her attention to Kiri.

Eudora grimaced. A knowledge of Arabic was not needed for one to know the old woman was not pleased with Khamed's interference.

Dahr-la nudged her at her back. "Tell her," she whispered.

Eudora frowned. The message she'd been ordered to give was so absurdly dictatorial she was embarrassed to relay it. She cleared her throat. "Khamed asked me to tell you . . . he said . . ." She glanced at Dahr-la, who was waving her hand impatiently. "He said that you will have to answer to him if the child is born before he returns with its father."

To her surprise a wide smile broke out across Kiri's face. Nodding in obvious understanding, she actually seemed to draw strength from the ridiculous words. Eudora turned to face Dahr-la. Was the loyalty and blind faith his people had in him so powerful and compelling?

Dahr-la smiled and shrugged. "If our lord gives an order, it is to be obeyed," she explained easily.

Eudora looked at her in shock. "You don't actually expect her to delay giving birth because *he* has ordered it, do you?"

Laughing, the girl gently pulled her to a corner. "Of course not, my lady. But the mind is a powerful force. In

176

his way, Khamed was reassuring Kiri that she has the strength to endure. And if she is strong, he will bring Kahlil back in time."

Eudora shook her head. Unable to think of a reply, she turned to look at Kiri.

She had stopped walking and was hunched over, clutching her swollen belly. Tears flowed down her cheeks. As the midwife placed her arms around her waist, a sharp cry of pain escaped her lips.

Cooing soft sounds of comfort, the woman helped her to the center of the room, where a thick layer of fine, clean sand had been spread. Slowly she lowered the girl to a kneeling position. With her knees spread wide, her hips resting on her heels, Kiri reached for a cord attached to the roof pole of the tent.

Eudora watched her as she clung to the rope to keep her body upright. Then, without warning this time, Kiri cried out again as yet another contraction raked her body.

Eudora felt the color leave her face. If she had to stay and watch a second longer she would surely faint. Turning, she fled into the main room.

The grandmother-to-be looked up at her in sympathetic understanding.

For her sake Eudora tried to force a reassuring smile.

The screams from the next room were coming closer now. Eudora was sure of it. Each cry, lasting longer than the one which had preceded it, set her teeth to grinding. Her jaws ached from clenching back her own screams.

She stood and began to pace. How many minutes had passed? Thirty-five? Forty? A noise outside the tent distracted her, and she turned toward the entrance just as Kahlil entered. Ashen-faced and very nervous, he was followed by a familiar form.

At that instant everything faded into the background. As her pulse raced, she watched Khamed take up a

177

position by the doorway.

Lighting a cigarette, he nonchalantly took in his surroundings before allowing his gaze to rest upon her. In apparent approval of her presence, he nodded.

Nervously Eudora met his eyes. The memory of the passion that had passed between them not an hour ago was still vivid in her mind—as vivid as the red lines that ran down his right cheek.

Without breaking his stare, Khamed flicked an ash from his cigarette. Slowly the fingers of his free hand rose to trace the scratches on his face.

Eudora's breath caught in her throat as she realized what he was telling her. He was not yet ready to forget the incident. What had been interrupted would be resumed.

Suddenly the piercing, undeniable wail of a baby broke the tension-laden silence. Eudora heard the crowd outside the tent burst into cheers and applause. Inside the tent all eyes were riveted on the curtained wall.

The drape parted and the midwife appeared.

Eudora stared at the tiny, blood-covered infant she cradled in her arms. A sensation she had never felt before bubbled up inside her, warm and enveloping. Blinking back tears, she looked to Kahlil.

As if in shock, he started to stumble forward.

Khamed's hand on his arm held him back. "Patience, my friend," he murmured softly in French. "She must present the child *to you*."

Oblivious to the presence of everyone except the new father, the old woman walked to Kahlil. Bowing, she held out her precious burden to him. "A son," she proclaimed proudly.

At her announcement squeals of excitement erupted from the women still seated at Eudora's feet.

Kahlil's bearded face split into a grin. Hands shaking, he took the baby from the midwife. Squaring her shoulders in triumph, she turned to look at Khamed.

With a tender smile tipping the corners of his mouth, he took a single step forward and bowed.

A wide, toothless grin of pure delight and sheer satisfaction instantly lit the old woman's face.

A victory scored for superstitious incantations and charms, Eudora thought, watching as the midwife re-entered the bedroom. She was immediately followed by Elon and Kiri's mother. Though Eudora would have liked to congratulate Kiri as well, she hesitated. Not knowing their customs, she looked to Khamed.

But Khamed's attention was occupied. With an ear-to-ear grin, Kahlil was presenting his infant son to his lord for his inspection.

Watching the two men, seeing and hearing their joy, Eudora suddenly felt out of place. A feeling of overwhelming sadness descended upon her, accompanied by a painful realization. She was an outsider and did not belong.

As Khamed and Kahlil left the tent to present the newborn to the anxious crowd outside, she wiped away her tears. Casting a final glance over her shoulder to the curtained room alive with feminine voices, she slipped out of the tent. Unnoticed, she skirted the crowd and walked into the night.

Sabatin stood outside his small tent. Listening to du Bois's snoring within, he stared at the crowd of people assembled in the center of the camp. Awakened by their applause only minutes earlier, he had exited the tent curious as to the reason for the jubilation. The people gathered in front of the tent appeared to be waiting for someone or something.

Shrugging, he turned his attention to the thoughts that had occupied his mind since the incident with Eudora that morning. While du Bois's attack had been both unprovoked and incredibly cruel, he still could not fathom her defense of Khamed. An outsider witnessing the scene with no knowledge of the circumstances would have thought she cared for the black-eyed Arab. Why, if

179

he didn't know better himself, he would have thought the same thing.

But he didn't know better. And that was what was gnawing at him. Whether willing or not, Eudora had become the man's mistress. It was not beyond reason to suspect that an emotional bond had formed between them. Certainly there was no doubt in his mind Khamed would have killed du Bois had he laid a hand on her. And whatever her motivation had been, either conscious or unconscious, she had made her feelings—and her preference—known.

He heard a new outburst of applause accompanied by additional cheers. Now even more curious, he stepped from beneath the tent's awning and saw a solitary figure approaching. With no other tents around it was obvious whoever it was was headed toward him. Keeping his gaze fixed on the lone figure, he tried to identify it.

When he did, he couldn't believe it. *"Eudora?"*

She stepped from the darkness into the dancing light of the torches mounted at the tent's entrance. Seeing her face glistening with tears, he quickly moved to her side. As his mind filled with possibilities, he encircled her shoulders, drawing her close. "What's wrong?"

Without replying, she laid her head on his chest.

He could feel her heart pounding, and in an attempt to console her, he tightened his hold. Careful to keep the tension from his voice lest he upset her further, he repeated his request. "Eudora, tell me what's wrong."

"I just can't make sense of it anymore." She twisted from his embrace, releasing a sigh of hopeless despair. "I don't understand what I'm feeling, or why I'm feeling it. Everything used to be so clear. Right or wrong, black or white. But now . . ."

"But now what? What are you trying to say?"

She shook her head. "I don't know. I should hate them for what they've done—for what they are. They're cruel savages with a barbaric view of life, killing and stealing, kidnapping—all without conscience. Yet I feel . . . I feel something for them."

Silently Sabatin wondered if her confusion were as general as her description. He had a haunting feeling the conflict in her emotions did not pertain to the Reguibat *en masse,* but involved one man and one man only. And after what he had seen and heard that morning, no other explanation made sense. Before he could dwell on the implications of his thought, a new one hit him. "Eudora, does Khamed know where you are?"

She shook her head.

"Mon Dieu . . . I don't think this wise at all. Come." He reached for her arm. "I'm going to take you back before he discovers your absence."

But the moment he stepped beyond some intangible boundary a guard appeared. Raising his rifle, he gestured impatiently toward the tent. Sabatin glared at him in frustration. Usually the restrictions placed on his freedom by his captors did not bother him. This time it was different and he felt his temper rise. "My God, man! I'm just going to take her back to her own tent."

By way of a response the guard leveled his rifle at him.

"Look, if it will make you feel better, you can come along." Sabatin took a tentative step. He instantly heard the sound of a rifle bolt being slid into place. His frustration mounting, he threw up his hands. "Fine! Then *you* take her back."

The guard stood firm.

It was too much. His composure was lost. Grabbing Eudora roughly, Sabatin thrust her in front of him for the guard's inspection. "Listen, you dim-witted fool! I know you can understand me. This is *your* lord's woman and if anything happens to her, he will have your head!"

"You are quite right, Monsieur." Khamed emerged from the shadows. His mouth curved up in a tight smile. "On both counts." He barked a few words of rapid Arabic and the guard withdrew.

At the sound of Khamed's voice Sabatin had felt Eudora's body grow rigid. Now she sprang to life, angrily jerking her arm from his grasp.

"I am *not* his!" she spat at him. Then, whirling to face Khamed, she delivered a second salvo. "And *you* do not own me!"

Khamed leapt at her. Entwining his fingers in her hair, he jerked her head to the side, exposing to the torchlight a dark bruise on her long, graceful neck.

"That is my mark you bear, little one," he hissed. "And unless you prefer that I brand you like a horse, you would do well to consider this . . ." his finger stabbed at the bruise ". . . proof of my possession."

At once taken aback and intrigued, Sabatin was unsure how to respond to what was clearly a private battle. His first instinct was to remain in the background. He had the feeling Eudora could handle the Reguibat without any help from him.

As if having heard his thoughts, Eudora twisted out of Khamed's hold and proudly drew herself up to her full height. "You bear *my* mark as well, Arab! And *you* would do well to consider this . . ." her fingers flicked at his lean cheek ". . . proof of my freedom—for your possession of me is physical only!"

Secretly Sabatin was delighted at Eudora's display of mettle. He doubted, however, that Khamed would be equally appreciative. He stepped forward, hoping to dissolve the tension between them. "Ahh, I don't think that—"

Khamed shot him a scathing look that silenced him instantly. But then, as the man returned his attention to Eudora, Sabatin saw the dark scowl soften. He stared in disbelief. Khamed should have been furious with her. Instead, he smiled slowly and grabbed her wrist, holding it firmly to his chest.

"I told you before, little one, that I would indulge you only to a point. You have reached that point. Your defiance has just crossed over to disobedience. Now . . . I have been very patient with you. *C'est à dire*— that is to say . . ." he grinned slyly ". . . patient for me.

182

But my patience is nearly exhausted. You were ordered to stay away from this tent. The next time you disobey me, I promise—you *will* regret it."

Eudora stared up at him. For a second it seemed as if she had lost her earlier courage. Suddenly she yanked her wrist free. Without a word, she turned on her heel and walked away.

Khamed motioned to the guard who had mysteriously reappeared. Dipping his head in acknowledgment, the man set off to follow Eudora across the compound. As Khamed watched them, he pulled a package of cigarettes from his pocket.

Sabatin stared at his face. The eyes above the match poised to light the cigarette in his mouth were yellow, as if mirroring the glow of the flame.

Once Eudora had disappeared from his sight, Khamed tossed the match to the ground. One eyebrow rose slightly as he dragged on the cigarette. Upon exhaling, Sabatin heard him emit a soft moan.

"Hamdullah!"

Dahr-la looked at the brilliant orange sun hanging high above the horizon. She could feel its warmth already radiating up from the sand beneath her bare feet. Picking up her skirts, she ran across the compound, her silver ankle bracelets chinking softly with each step.

She was late. But *insh'allah*—God willing—her mistress might still be sleeping. At least Khamed would not know of her tardiness. Still asleep in Kahlil's tent where he had spent the night celebrating with his friend, he had not even stirred as she'd slipped past him. Hers having been a night spent in sleepless slumber, she'd looked at him in envy. The birth of Kahlil's son had set her to thinking, and her deliberations had given rise to a horrifying possibility.

Eudora had been in the Reguibat camp for over a month, yet Dahr-la had seen no signs of the woman's flux. Khamed had not mentioned the matter since the morning he'd

183

given her the pouch containing the herb. Gone as often as he was, he had no doubt assumed Eudora's time had come in his absence and that his orders had been followed. Only Dahr-la knew differently, and she was worried.

Her lord would not be pleased to learn the herb had not yet been administered. And should what she now feared come to pass, he would be furious. But before she approached him and raised the question hammering within her mind, she was going to talk to Eudora.

Arriving at her destination, Dahr-la paused under the tent's huge awning to straighten her head scarf. She opened the flap and entered. Finding the main room empty, she quickly crossed it to enter the next.

Already dressed in chemise and petticoat, Eudora sat at the vanity. As Dahr-la entered, she turned and smiled. "How are Kiri and the baby?"

Dahr-la looked at her. How was she going to bring up the subject? To ask the woman outright would most assuredly raise questions. She couldn't very well tell her the reason for her interest. She forced a smile. "They are doing well. Kiri has already gotten up and walked a bit."

The woman's emerald eyes widened. "Gotten up?"

It was Dahr-la's turn to be surprised. "Why, yes. Always within twenty-four hours of the birth the mother is made to stand and walk. It speeds the recovery. Is it not so where you come from?"

Shaking her head, Eudora laughed softly. "In my world, after giving birth, a new mother remains in bed for weeks, pampered and waited on."

Dahr-la realized she had found a way to question the woman without raising suspicion. She moved to straighten the bed. Keeping her voice even, she offered a comment she was sure would lead to the topic. "Perhaps it is because European women are different."

"Different?" Eudora turned in her chair to look at her. "In what way?"

Shrugging, Dahr-la smoothed the silken coverlet. "I was thinking of you, my lady. You have been here for over

184

a month, yet I have seen no evidence of your monthly time. I had therefore naturally assumed that a European woman's cycle was longer than an Arab woman's."

"That is ludicrous," Eudora replied stiffly, her cheeks reddening. "All women are the same."

"Then why have you not—"

"Dahr-la," she interrupted with a sharp look. "The only difference between us is that where I come from this is not a topic that is discussed."

"But why not? It is a part of life."

"Yes, I suppose it is. But there are some things which are considered . . . private."

"I see." Dahr-la moved around to the other side of the bed. With her back now to Eudora she did not have to worry about concealing her disappointment. Given the woman's ridiculous embarrassment, it would appear she wasn't going to learn anything of value.

"Dahr-la?"

"Yes, my lady?" Dahr-la turned, questioningly.

Eudora stood slowly. "I apologize for my childish reaction. You're right. It doesn't make much sense to be uncomfortable discussing what is a perfectly natural aspect of life. To answer your question . . . I have never been what you might call 'regular.' I am often late and can even skip months. At times of stress and change, I . . . it . . . can be even more unpredictable. For me it is quite normal and not a cause for concern."

In spite of her words, she appeared eager to put an end to the conversation. "Does that answer your question?" she asked quietly.

"Yes, my lady." Dahr-la returned her attention to the bed. The woman would know her own body, she reasoned silently, smiling in satisfaction and relief. Certainly the last thing she had wanted to do was to confront her lord with the possibility that his mistress might be carrying his child.

Chapter Twelve

Khamed looked at the man riding at his side and smiled. In the days which had passed since the birth of his son, Kahlil had become a different man, his earlier surly personality and brooding frowns having all but disappeared.

"Fatherhood must agree with you, my friend," he noted, his voice warm with affection.

At the mention of his infant son, Kahlil's face burst into a broad grin. "There is no other feeling to rival it," he confessed. "The pride and pleasure of beholding one's heir has no equal. It gives a man a sense of immortality." Looking at Khamed from the corner of his eye, he grinned slyly. "You know . . . you are of an age when *you* should be considering such things."

Khamed laughed. He found it amusing that Kahlil's fatherhood should suddenly give the young man an old man's cognizance of mortality. "I am but a year older than you, Kahlil, and hardly ready for the grave."

His friend looked at him, puzzled. "I did not mean to imply that you were. I only meant to point out your responsibility to your people to produce an heir."

Khamed was unable to stop a cynical smile from parting his lips. "You know me, Kahlil. No woman can hold my interest for longer than a few weeks. In such a relationship there is hardly a foundation for marriage."

"Still, you have an obligation to the tribe."

Khamed's smile twisted into a frown. This was a subject that had been broached before by his own father, with disastrous results. Haisim had wanted grandchildren, heirs to ensure future generations. To that end he had sought to arrange a marriage for his son the year Khamed had returned from France.

For the only time in his life Khamed had refused obedience to his sheik. He'd wanted no part of commitment or entanglement with a woman on any level, for any purpose. The ensuing battle of wills between father and son had nearly driven Khamed out of the tribe. Finally Haisim had relented. But the rift between them had never been completely mended, the matter never resolved. Until Haisim's death the question was repeatedly raised with the same results—hot tempers, harsh words, and Khamed's violent refusal.

Turning a cold gaze to the man at his side, he spat out a reply. "I will not marry for the sole purpose of siring an heir."

Kahlil shrugged. "Then perhaps you should consider begetting a son outside of marriage. Legitimacy is not a requisite."

Khamed's temper exploded. "I will not sire a bastard!" He saw Kahlil wince.

"Forgive me, my lord. My foolish rantings are but a new father's clumsy expression of joy. Besides . . ." he offered a weak smile ". . . were you to follow my poor advice at this time, we would have a future sheik who was but a quarter Reguibat and . . ." he paused, arching an eyebrow, ". . . half wildcat."

Unamused at Kahlil's attempted humor, Khamed glared at him. The man's words had not only aroused his ire, they had raised a question in his mind. Unconsciously he traced the scratches on his cheek. Had the one and only time he'd been with Eudora been before or after Dahr-la had followed his orders? He had never questioned the girl to verify *when* she had begun giving

Eudora the herb.

Shouts from the scouts riding ahead forced that thought aside as a burst of sudden rifle shots sent the black stallion beneath him bounding forward. Instinctively Khamed gripped the horse tightly between his knees and reached for his rifle.

Urging his own mount forward, Kahlil followed suit. He drew his rifle, leveling it at the small herd of gazelle leaping into view.

Khamed sighted the lead animal, a large buck, and pulled the trigger. He saw the shot ricochet harmlessly off a boulder at the animal's feet. Before he could aim again, a second shot rang out and the buck wheeled. Veering from the herd, the animal set out across the open desert with Kahlil's gray mare in pursuit.

Khamed reined in his horse. His poor markmanship was proof enough his mind was no longer on the hunt. He slammed the rifle back into the scabbard at his knee. Mechanically his fingers searched for a cigarette as he watched with half-hearted interest Kahlil's steady gain on his wounded prey. He knew the outcome. Kahlil would pursue the animal until it collapsed exhausted in the sand. To end its suffering he would then slit its throat, having first twisted its head toward Mecca.

Khamed tossed the unsmoked cigarette to the ground. With a silent oath, he turned the stallion.

"What do you mean her time has not yet come?" Khamed glared at the girl cowering before him. Remembering suddenly that Eudora was napping in the next room, he lowered his voice. "She has been here for over a month."

Dahr-la tugged at the end of her waist sash for a moment before lifting her gaze. "I know, my lord. But she assures me it is quite normal for her. With all the confusion of her . . . uh . . . coming here . . ."

Khamed felt his control slipping. "Girl," he growled

189

softly, "I am not interested in any 'confusion' which may or may not have influenced the timing of her cycle. I want this matter resolved. Begin giving her the herb today."

"But my lord, the herb does not work unless it is begun at the right time. And if . . ." She lowered her gaze nervously.

"If what?" he demanded. His impatience was growing by the minute.

"If she is already with child, it could harm the child."

Khamed felt as if he had been struck. He took a step forward and grabbed Dahr-la's arm, forcing her to look up at him. "Are you telling me there is a chance?"

"There is always a chance, my lord," she whispered, wincing from the pain of his iron grasp. "Whenever a man and a woman . . . join together there is a chance a child may be conceived. But I am sure there is nothing to worry about. She has shown none of the other signs."

Khamed looked down at her in stony silence. He had no idea to what other signs she was referring, and yet he was reluctant to question her more fully. He released her arm. "GO."

He watched her flee through the drape and numbly lit a cigarette. His own expertise with the female body involved the achievement of pleasure, not procreation. What he needed was a man with intimate knowledge of a pregnant woman. He stabbed out his cigarette . . . *insh'allah!* God willing, an expert on that very subject should have already returned to camp.

He found Kahlil in the horse corral, bent over, examining the right foreleg of his horse.

Hearing his approach, Kahlil looked up. "She stumbled while pursuing the gazelle." He lifted the mare's leg. "What do you think?"

Khamed leaned over the man's shoulder to get a closer look. The leg appeared to be only slightly swollen. "Wrap it," he suggested. Standing upright, he nervously ran his fingers through his hair. "Kahlil, how would a man know if a woman was with child?"

Kahlil set the mare's hoof on the ground and stood slowly. Wisely his face reflected none of the surprise he must have been feeling. "Before it is physically evident, the most obvious sign is the absence of her monthly time."

"I know that!" Khamed exclaimed impatiently. "I am not so naive. What are the other signs?"

"Well . . ." Kahlil paused and thought for a moment. "Kiri became ill . . . nauseated . . . almost at once. Especially in the morning. She had no appetite, and whatever little she did eat, she could not hold down. Her breasts became tender and gradually became larger. Her waist thickened. She also complained of feeling dizzy and weak."

Though Kahlil continued to speak, Khamed was no longer listening. The words now inconsequential, the man's voice had become a distant hum: "But not all signs appear in all women. Nor do they appear in any particular order."

Khamed sighed in relief. Dahr-la had been convinced there was no cause for concern. Now that he too knew what the signs were, he was also convinced. Eudora's appetite had been fine, and she was not sick in the morning—or at any other time, for that matter. It must be as Dahr-la had said: Eudora was simply late. Besides, he reassured himself, he *had* been with her only once. Dismissing the matter from his mind, he turned his attention back to Kahlil. "Let me look at that leg again."

Thundering hooves and the shouts of riders jolted Eudora awake. She cursed the sudden mayhem which shattered the stillness of inactivity brought to the camp by the late afternoon heat. Untangling her legs from the folds of her dress, she rose and went to the doorway. Curious as to the cause of the noise, she pushed aside the flap.

191

In the center of the compound she saw a group of no less than thirty riders. Travel-weary, their horses lathered, none of the men looked familiar. As she studied the party, its apparent leader parted from his companions and guided his horse to the corrals where Khamed was examining the foreleg of a white mare.

Stooped, intent at his task, it was only when the shadow of the rider eclipsed his vision that he appeared to note the man's presence.

Eudora watched as he rose slowly, almost indifferently. Then, like a coiled snake, he suddenly attacked, pulling the rider from his horse and wrestling him to the ground. Both shocked and intrigued, she stepped from the doorway to get a clearer view.

Now rolling in the dust, each man fought to pin the other. It was Khamed who finally triumphed. Straddling his opponent, he pressed a forearm across his neck to hold the man immobile. From across the compound Eudora heard his cry of victory as he drew his knife. A scream of horror rose in her throat.

But instead of plunging the blade into the man's chest, Khamed suddenly rocked back on his heels and stood. Extending his hand, he pulled his vanquished foe to his feet and embraced him warmly.

The stranger's rich laughter floated across the oasis. Breaking free from Khamed, he pointed toward the group of mounted men.

Eudora squinted and focused on the object of his attention. From the crowd of *sheshed* and robed men a single rider was guiding his horse forward. As he reined in beside Khamed and the stranger, he pulled the *shesh* from his head and tossed it to the ground. Eudora stared in shock. The rider was a woman.

She threw open her robe and swung her leg over the saddle. Sliding down into Khamed's waiting arms, she appeared utterly oblivious to the way her full red skirts bunched about her hips, seductively baring her long legs. Once on the ground she tossed back her head as though

4 FREE BOOKS

TO GET YOUR 4 FREE BOOKS WORTH $18.00 — MAIL IN THE FREE BOOK CERTIFICATE TODAY

Fill in the Free Book Certificate below, and we'll send your FREE BOOKS to you as soon as we receive it.

If the certificate is missing below, write to: Zebra Home Subscription Service, Inc., P.O. Box 5214, 120 Brighton Road, Clifton, New Jersey 07015-5214.

GET
FOUR
FREE
BOOKS
(AN $18.00 VALUE)

to drink in the sight of the man who held her. Her lips parted in a warm smile an instant before they suddenly and hungrily rose to meet Khamed's.

Eudora bristled. An inexplicable feeling of anger at the woman and her companions washed over her. She had no desire to see more. She whirled on her heel.

Once inside the cool sanctuary of the tent she plopped herself down on the sofa. She was trying hard to ignore a sudden churning sensation in her stomach when she heard the tent flap part.

Dahr-la entered, out of breath and clearly agitated. "My lady, you must go into the bedroom."

"Why?"

Dahr-la glanced anxiously over her shoulder. "Please, my lady. You must remain out of sight. It is Khamed's order."

That was all the license she needed. In a burst of stubborn spite, Eudora leaned back against the cushions and crossed her arms. "I am not a pet to be summoned or dismissed at its master's will, Dahr-la."

Dahr-la rolled her eyes upward, as though seeking divine intervention. "My lady, please. I'm sure that was not his intent. It just would be awkward at this time for my lord to explain your presence to his guests. Please . . . won't you come into the next room . . . if not for your sake, then for mine?"

The realization that Dahr-la might be punished for her mistress's obstinacy melted Eudora's resolve. She stood but made no effort to hide her displeasure as she retreated to the smaller room.

Dahr-la followed, carefully drawing the curtain closed.

Eudora yanked the chair from the vanity and sat down. She could hear voices and footsteps entering the tent. "Who are they? These guests of Khamed's?"

Dahr-la stepped forward, bringing her index finger to her lips. "The man is called Montar. He and Khamed were childhood friends. Each year Montar leaves his home near Rio de Oro to visit my lord." She cautiously looked back at the drape. "I don't believe Khamed expected him this early, though. Otherwise he would surely have made arrangements for your . . . ah . . . transfer to another camp."

It occurred to Eudora to ask why her removal from Khamed's camp would have been necessary. But instead she asked the question uppermost in her mind. "And the woman?" She winced, hearing the tightness in her voice.

"She is Saleena. Montar's sister."

Something in Dahr-la's tone told Eudora there was more. "Is she also a childhood friend?"

Dahr-la hesitated. "Not exactly. She was but an infant then. Last year she accompanied Montar on his visit. She and Khamed were . . . er . . . together for a while."

Dahr-la's words did not surprise Eudora. Instinctively she had known as much the moment she'd seen Saleena. She smiled in secret satisfaction. In Khamed's predicament she found a peculiar sense of pleasure. It was not to his guests that he was reluctant to explain her presence, but to his former mistress. "And her brother . . . Montar, he approves of his sister's mores? I thought Moslem men were fanatical about protecting the virginity of their women."

"You confuse us with Arabs, my lady. Among the Reguibat a girl is free to engage in sexual liaisons with unattached men of her choosing from the age of fifteen until she is married."

"Really?" Eudora looked at the girl's face, which had suddenly reddened. It wasn't like Dahr-la to be embarrassed about discussing the ways of men and women. Was it perhaps because she too had availed herself of the tribe's unique practices? It certainly would explain the wisdom she possessed. The thought of Dahr-la with one of the camp's young men brought a touch of a smile to Eudora's lips.

As the minutes dragged by, however, her amusement quickly waned. The small room grew hotter. The sounds of voices rising and falling in conversation reminded her

194

too much of that first night she'd been brought to the tent. She remembered the hour of agonizing waiting she'd been forced to endure before Khamed had finally come to her. He'd been entertaining guests then, too.

The memory continued to gnaw at her until she was sure she could stand it no longer. She stood and began to pace.

With every outburst of laughter she heard, she froze. And still the minutes dragged by, until more than an hour had passed. It was now so stifling hot in the room, she couldn't breath. "Enough!" She whirled toward the doorway. "I can't bear any more!"

Dahr-la rushed to her side. She clasped her hands together in a pleading gesture. "Please, my lady. Just a little longer!"

Deaf to Dahr-la's plea, Eudora pushed past her.

Khamed alone heard the rustle of the curtain. Looking up, he saw Eudora emerge haughtily from the folds. Then, as if she were contemplating her next move, she hesitated. Her eyes met his, and he could see the defiance blazing within their depths. With an almost exaggerated aplomb she scooped up the train of her gown.

"I must have some air."

Silence spread through the room like an electric shock. Without looking, Khamed knew every head had jerked up at the sound of her voice.

Eudora stepped away from the drape. Unmindful of the eyes following her, she carefully picked her way through the maze of reposing bodies. At the doorway she paused dramatically to drop her train. Then, in a pale green and lilac wake, she left the tent.

All eyes now turned to Khamed. He kept his face blank of all emotion.

"*Hamdullah!* Who is that?" His eyes still riveted on the tent's exit, Montar choked out the question.

"One of the French prisoners captured in a raid last month," Khamed replied, without the barest trace of expression in his voice.

195

"Their ransom has not yet been arranged."

For some reason this volunteering of information by one of his lieutenants angered Khamed. He shot the man a silencing scowl.

"A *prisoner* shares your tent?"

The question drew Khamed's attention to the woman sitting across from him. Eyebrows arched, Saleena was staring at him in disbelief.

"And my bed." His low voice rang with an ominous quality that dared any—especially her—to address the subject further. Out of the corner of his eye he saw Montar gesture to his men.

They stood immediately, as did his own men, who had been given their signal by Kahlil. The men salaamed and filed out.

When only Montar and Saleena remained, Khamed stood. Deliberately he avoided his friend's eyes. Any encouragement on his part would lead to questions he was not prepared to answer.

Without a word Montar took Saleena's arm and led her to the doorway.

Unconcerned further with their departure, Khamed returned his gaze to the curtain. He could still see Eudora standing there, facing him in bold defiance. He clenched and unclenched his fists. He knew Dahr-la had relayed his order that she remain hidden. In spite of his warning the night Kahlil's son had been born, she had chosen to disobey him again!

Kahlil's words returned to haunt him: *a man who cannot rule his woman will not long rule his men.* Damn her. Verbal threats had done nothing to curb her impudent behavior. This time she had shamed him not only in front of his men, but in front of Montar's as well! He kicked at a cushion lying in his path. He had to act; she had left him no other choice. She would pay a dear price for her pride.

He stormed out of the tent and quickly caught sight of her near the goat pens. As he strode toward her, children and dogs alike seemed to sense his fury, and hastened to get out of his way. Less astute, or perhaps just more curious, the adults knotted in small numbers to watch as their lord crossed the compound toward the lone figure.

She was watching a herdsboy leading a small flock of goats to the pens. With her hair and skirts blowing gently in the wind, she was the picture of serenity. At first he thought she might be unaware of his approach. But as he neared, she looked straight at him and then turned on her heel.

A scalding fury rose up within him. With deadly calm he walked over to the herdsboy, his gaze locked on the whip the youth wielded over his charges. Without a word he held out his hand.

The boy's eyes grew round in mute and immediate understanding. He bounded forward and placed the handle in Khamed's hand.

Without looking at it, Khamed closed his fingers around the smooth wood. He turned and slowly walked back.

She had not moved.

"Eudora." He waited to see if she would turn and acknowledge him.

She did not.

He let out his breath in a growl of disbelief. Planting his feet firmly apart, he issued a final warning. "Eudora, turn around. Now."

She flinched at the sound of his voice but made no move to obey. Carelessly she brushed at a fly buzzing around her head.

With that one simple gesture the fragile hold he had on his control was lost. In his mind she was shooing away his own presence with the same disdain she had given the insect.

His arm snapped out and the whip cracked in the air. She whirled.

"Your hearing has returned," he noted sarcastically.

She lifted her chin and glared at him.

He retracted the lash with a deft jerk. This time when

the leather descended, it encountered more than air. A long slash appeared in the folds of her dress.

"How dare you," she hissed.

In one stride he was at her side. He seized her arm and dragged her to him with such force that their bodies slapped together. "I dare because I am master!" His fingers tightened until she cried out in pain. "It is time, little one, that you learn that fact. And unless you are prepared to be taught it, along with submission and obedience, as women are taught in my world, you will return to your quarters now."

He watched her eyes widen in stark, vivid realization and imagined more than heard her exclamation.

"You wouldn't—"

"I would. Make no mistake, Eudora. You are to turn around and walk back to that tent. You are to hold your tongue and you are to keep your eyes lowered. Utter one word, one sound, and I will forget every European value I ever learned which tells me it is wrong to whip a woman." Knowing his every move was being watched, he tossed her from him with enough force to send her sprawling onto the sand at his feet. He held his breath. If she raised her eyes, was he prepared to carry out his threat? He had never beaten a woman. The mere thought brought a taste of bile to his mouth. He spat in disgust.

The action effectively concealed his relief as Eudora rose to her knees.

Eyes lowered, head bowed, she extracted herself from the encumbrance of her twisted skirts, and stood.

From the doorway of a tent across the compound, a bearded man watched in interest as the Frenchwoman retreated across the camp.

Montar knew his friend as he knew himself. Khamed's fiendish temper was capable of overriding all self-control and reason. Still, what the man had just done was something Montar had thought he'd never see. Khamed had allowed his captive to impair his honor. In front of witnesses she had blackened his face, yet he was now meting her a most merciful punishment.

Montar smiled. The proud spitfire would doubtlessly look upon her public humiliation as anything but merciful. But faced with the alternative of the lash . . . indeed, Khamed had been generous.

Khamed watched Eudora until she had disappeared inside his tent. Realizing he still held the whip, he tossed it to the ground and headed toward the corrals. Not a single person dared to cross his path. Even the young boys who normally lingered near the horses, in the hope they might win a ride to the oasis' edge, behind one of the men riding out on patrol, were conspicuously absent.

Without bothering to saddle Hasaad, Khamed jumped on the stallion's back and urged him toward the open desert.

He returned hours later, his emotions under control. Sitting across from Montar in the tent provided for his guest, he finally felt ready to discuss Eudora.

He lit a cigarette, flicking the spent match to the floor. "Say it, Montar. I can practically see the words fighting to escape your lips."

Montar met his gaze straight on. "No, my friend. It is not my place to pass judgment. Your relationship with this woman is your concern. I am, however, curious: is it not a contradiction to seek to alter that which most intrigues you?"

Khamed exhaled and stared at the cloud of blue smoke. Montar knew him well, almost too well. "Let us say it poses a most unique challenge."

Montar watched as an odd smile flitted across Khamed's face. His friend's eyes were shining like deep topaz with a look he'd been sure he would never see in their depths. "Then I am most eager to meet this 'challenge' of yours."

Careful to keep her eyes discreetly lowered, Saleena stared at the man sitting across from her brother. In an hour's time she had been unable to draw even a single glance from Khamed. Still, her heart raced as her gaze

199

traveled the length of him. If it were possible, Khamed was even more handsome than she remembered.

She recalled the passion of his kiss that very afternoon as her fingertips traced the gentle swelling his lips had caused. He still wanted her, she was sure of it. In spite of the white woman now housed in his tent, his desire for her was strong—as strong as the powerful arms she longed to lie in.

A male voice cut through her thoughts, and she lifted her eyes to glare at its owner. Montar had relegated her to a far corner of the tent the instant Khamed had arrived. Forbidden by custom to speak unless spoken to, she could now only sit in silence.

She returned her gaze to Khamed and watched as he tossed several cushions behind him. Leaning back, he laid his sleek head upon one and lit yet another cigarette. He seemed to be in no hurry to leave. That thought sent her heart soaring. She smiled and closed her eyes. His white whore could not hold much fascination for him. When Saleena had been the one in his bed, he'd not wasted his time elsewhere.

Wrapped in joy and lulled by the sound of Khamed's voice, she drifted into sleep.

Saleena awoke the next morning to the same thought to which she had fallen asleep: the sweet ecstasy of being crushed within Khamed's embrace. She rose up on one elbow and looked to the room's center. Montar's pallet was empty. As was his habit, her brother had already left for his morning prayers. Pulses racing, she searched the room's dark corners at yet untouched by the dawn's gray light.

She knew Khamed would be there even before her gaze fell upon him. Lying on his back, he was motionless except for the rise and fall of his chest. She listened for a moment to his breathing. It was still sleep's deep rhythm. Her own breathing quickened.

Like a cat she crept across the space between them. Lying by his side, she curled her body into the curve of his. Her fingers trembled as she opened her blouse and reached for his hand.

Khamed slid his hand across a silken belly, seeking the breasts he knew would be swollen with desire.

The green-eyed woman in his dreams moaned in pleasure. She pressed her body closer and opened her legs.

Khamed took her hand, guiding her to the source of his own need. His passion surged at her touch. He pulled her into his embrace, indulging himself in the soft yielding flesh at his fingertips. Finally, intent upon complete fulfillment, he rolled on top of her and stripped off his shirt.

Not yet fully awake and anxious for release, he fumbled with the belt at his waist.

"Hurry, my love."

The soft plea in Arabic resounded in his head like a gunshot. His body instantly went rigid. His eyes flew open. "Saleena!"

Though uttered in shock, the sound of her name seemed to please the woman beneath him. Her passion-glazed eyes smiled up at him. Then, with an impatient wriggle she reminded him of his position as her arms encircled his neck to draw him back down.

Khamed knew he could take her. But she was not the woman who had stirred his passion. Pushing her callously from him, he stood and swore silently.

Kissing her yesterday had been a mistake. He didn't even know why he had done it. Perhaps he'd been too long without a woman. To suddenly have one of such unbridled passion draped in his arms had stirred his innate urges. Her warm mouth open to his had demanded a response. But now, looking down at her, he suddenly felt nothing.

Eudora stared at the patch of gray light staining the carpet beneath the tent's flap. The sun was rising. She tossed the blanket wrapped around her to the floor and sprang to her feet. She walked restlessly around the room, pausing to retie the belt of her dressing gown.

That Khamed had not returned to his tent confused her. He never stayed away the entire night unless he was gone from the camp. Curled on the sofa, awaiting his arrival in dread, she had formulated dozens of vicious verbal attacks. But she knew none would ever be voiced. She had finally accepted the truth.

She had pitted her will against one stronger than her own, and she had lost. The memory of what had taken place at the goat pens would burn eternally in her mind.

By deliberately goading him she'd finally pushed him too far, and she had been with him too long not to know he did not threaten idly. Instinctively her woman's weakness had capitulated. In retaliation for her defiance, and as reparation for the battle waged and lost, he had then demanded the greatest price: her humiliation.

God, how she wanted to hate him for it! Yet she could not. Like the lash he would have raised against her body, it was that realization which slashed her spirit. She fought back a sob of despair.

Suddenly the walls of the large room seemed to close in. She couldn't breathe. She spun around, half ill, and ran to the doorway. Ripping aside the flap, she drank in the cool air. Gradually she felt the wave of nausea recede. Wrapping her arms around herself, she stared out into the compound, deserted save the figure of a lone man which she now spotted racing madly across it.

Beneath his robe he appeared to be carrying some kind of bundle. Its weight affected his balance, and he stumbled on the slight incline that elevated Khamed's tent above and behind the others. To right himself he had to reposition his burden, and she was able to make out what looked like a small, dark head pressed into the crook of his neck and shoulder.

With a start Eudora realized that the object he carried was a child. Instantly the frenzy of the man's actions took on a fearful import. Rooted where she stood, she watched as he ran straight toward her, shouting in Arabic. His voice, weighted with urgency, filled her with a sense of helplessness. All she could understand of his cries was Khamed's name.

He repeated it over and over until he finally halted in front of her. Gasping, fighting to catch his breath, he looked at her. His eyes were glazed with panic. "I must see *Sidi* Khamed."

Without waiting for a reply, he pushed past her.

"Wait!" Eudora hurried after him into the tent. "Khamed is not here."

He stopped and spun around. His head whipped from side to side, his eyes searching the large room as though he didn't believe her.

"Khamed is not here," Eudora repeated. She stepped forward cautiously. He had a look of almost wild determination about him and for a moment she was afraid.

"I must see him, *imra'ati*. Please. *Ya walad . . .*" He opened his robe to display the boy in his arms. "My son has been bitten by a snake."

Snake.

The word hit Eudora like a fist. Her breath escaped in a gasp. She reached out to touch the child, then stopped. Slowly she drew back her trembling hand, a horrible, numbing panic welling within her. "I don't know what to do," she whispered, not realizing her thoughts were being voiced. "I don't know where he is."

"Do you know where the medicines are?"

The man's desperate question seemed to spark her dulled senses. Her mind and body reacted almost simultaneously. She thought of the black saddlebag with its collection of vials and bottles and pointed toward it. "There, in that chest. You will have to force it open. It's locked. Give me the child."

The man nodded in understanding. Quickly surrendering his son to her, he drew the knife at his waist

203

and went to the carved chest by the entrance to the bedroom.

She watched him prepare to gouge at the wood which held the heavy brass lock, then turned her attention to the boy in her arms.

He was scarcely more than a baby, not more than two years of age. Protectively cradling him to her, she reached out to the slowly beating pulse in his throat. His skin was cold to the touch, and moist.

Her thin silk wrap quickly became damp, cleaving to her wherever the boy's body touched hers. She carried him to the sofa, reaching for the blanket she had tossed to the floor.

As she tucked the blanket around the tiny limbs lying so terribly still, she glanced back over her shoulder.

In spite of his furious efforts, the child's father had managed little more than to remove a few splinters.

Her panic rose anew. She looked back at the child. His chest was heaving. The poison had already affected his breathing. Her own lungs constricted with fear. His father would never open the chest in time—not without the key.

The key, she repeated silently, the key Khamed always kept with him!

Quite suddenly she knew what she had to do. She whirled and ran from the tent. She could not let the child die. She had to find Khamed. But where? The compound was still deserted. She looked to the perimeters. Almost at once she saw what she was searching for. Above the palm line a wispy trailing of white smoke rose in the gray sky.

She headed for the smoke, and the sentry's fire she knew she would find beneath it. As she ran, the folds of her wrap whipped back to trail behind her. She clawed at the silk to keep it closed and kept running.

At her approach the two shadowy figures squatting beside the fire stood.

At their stares of shock Eudora remembered her state

of dress. A hot flush rose up her neck and she clutched at her gown's lace bertha. "Please, I must find Khamed. Do you know where he is?" She looked from one bearded face to the other and saw only bewilderment. "Please, you have to help me. A child has been bitten by a snake. He will die if I don't find Khamed!"

She stood in agonized silence, waiting for a response. The men turned to one another and began to argue. She could hear Khamed's name being repeated, and knew they had at least understood what she wanted. One of the men, the shorter of the two, seemed, however, to want to take her back to her tent. With angry jabs he pointed repeatedly toward the compound and Khamed's tent.

"No! You don't understand. I must find Khamed." Eudora grasped the arm of the taller man, the one who appeared to be on her side. "Please, help me." She saw his eyes soften.

He looked to his companion and whatever he said seemed to pacify the man. Gesturing for her to follow, he started back across the compound.

Eudora looked up questioningly at the man whose arm she still held.

He smiled in reassurance and gently removed her hand. Nudging her forward, he pointed out their destination—a small tent with a striped awning. The man running ahead was nearly at its entrance.

Eudora quickened her pace.

She needn't have bothered.

As soon as they reached the tent, the man at her side took her arm and swiftly pulled her out of sight of its door. Shaking his head, he indicated that on no uncertain terms was she to walk up to the entrance unannounced.

With more than a twinge of annoyance Eudora guessed at both his reasoning and the cause for the men's argument. If Khamed was there it was possible he would choose not to see her. Neither man was about to incur his wrath by presenting her without warning or approval.

As Eudora watched, the man at the doorway squared

his shoulders and called out.

Hurry, she cried silently. So much time had already been wasted. Every second was precious. Feeling the earlier waves of nausea returning, she closed her eyes.

"What are you doing here?"

Khamed's sharp demand ripped through her. She opened her eyes, shrinking instinctively from the powerful form which had suddenly materialized before her. Naked from the waist up, he was towering over her, displeasure at her presence patent in every tense muscle. He reached for her arm, jerking her from his man. "I asked you your purpose for being here." His cold onyx stare impaled her, waiting for a reply.

Suddenly the image of the child in his tent loomed in her mind. "A . . . a child . . ." At first she could manage only a stammering whisper. "A child has been bitten by a snake. I need the key to—"

Khamed did not wait for her to finish. With a speed one would have thought impossible for a man of his size, he pushed past her. His shouted orders in Arabic sent both men racing at his heels.

Eudora watched as they crossed the compound. Whether from relief or exhaustion, her knees suddenly felt weak. She leaned against the tent wall.

Suddenly from the other side she heard sounds of movement. Someone was still inside.

She had barely formed the thought when she saw the tent flap lift and a woman appear. Eudora recognized her at once. Up close Montar's sister was breathtakingly beautiful. But it was not the woman's beauty that caused her to gape.

Saleena's yellow blouse hung open to her waist, revealing almost in their entirety her full breasts. Making no move to cover herself, she stood and watched Khamed's flight, a henna-tipped hand rising to her mouth to stifle a sleepy yawn.

Eudora's stomach churned. Now she knew why Khamed had not returned to his tent. The woman's appearance left no doubt as to what had been interrupted between them.

Fine. Let him, she thought furiously. Let him take his pleasure elsewhere.

Hurrying across the compound, it did not occur to her to wonder why she felt no relief in her heart for the words her mind had so readily spoken.

Chapter Thirteen

Eudora entered the tent silently. Unnoticed she slipped into a corner where she had a complete view of the room.

Khamed was kneeling over the child, his back partially to her. She could see little of his face. But the line of his jaw was very tense. In his hands he held a small vial from which he filled a syringe.

Eudora marveled at his composure, his strength. She was not the only one who felt it. She looked at the men standing with the child's father, then at Dahr-la, who hovered at Khamed's side, awaiting instruction. In their faces she saw the same calm faith. She shook her head in awe. He was their lord, and the trust they placed in him was unshakable.

Khamed handed the vial to Dahr-la. Eudora felt as if she was watching a scene from a play. She saw him push the plunger to expel the air from the filled syringe, then pinch the boy's stomach to inject him with the first shot.

The next one he administered to the outside of the tiny thigh, and the final one just above the bite on the child's left calf. As if on cue he stood. "It is in the hands of Allah now."

Eudora was stunned by the look of compassion and sorrow she saw on his face. She was seeing depths of tenderness in the stoic desert warlord she had never before glimpsed.

But almost at once the look was gone—unseen, she realized, by anyone in the room save her. His face now devoid of any emotion, he handed the syringe to Dahr-la. Walking over to the father, he clasped the man's shoulder.

The man nodded at his lord's private words of comfort and moved to kneel by his son.

Khamed gestured to his men.

Wordlessly they exited to stand guard outside the doorway.

Dahr-la, too, moved away from the sofa. Picking up the black saddlebag from the table, she left the father to his private vigil.

"Eudora."

Khamed's sudden presence at her side startled her more than the sound of his voice. Eudora lifted her gaze from the father, now hunched over the still body of his son. "No." She shook her head. "I want to stay."

Khamed grasped her elbow and propelled her aside. "Allow him the dignity of private prayer, Eudora. You have done all you can. Dahr-la will call us when there is news."

His softly spoken words contained a message of subtle praise. Unsettled by it, she lowered her eyes and allowed him to lead her into the bedroom.

Once beyond the folds he released her arm and walked over to the bed. Sitting wearily, he lit a cigarette.

She sat in the chair at the vanity. But in seconds she was on her feet, pacing, her attention riveted on the curtain.

Khamed kept his head bent, lifting only his eyes to watch her. Each pass became more frantic. Suddenly she wheeled and walked over to the night table. As her hand snaked out, reaching for the package of cigarettes he had placed upon it, he became instantly confused.

European women did not smoke. True enough, he had known a few who did. But they had been women who moved in circles far removed from the drawing rooms of refined society. To quell her nerves, a refined society woman turned to a crystal decanter of sherry. But one of his few adherences to his faith was an abstinence from alcohol. Was Eudora therefore attempting to seek solace in the only means available?

Eudora lit the cigarette, fiercely avoiding Khamed's bemused gaze. She inhaled slowly and grimaced at once. But she could not hold in the choking cough her body reflexively generated to expel the acrid smoke.

Khamed's soft laugh brought an instant warmth to her face. How was she to have known it would taste so horrible and burn her throat? She crushed out the cigarette.

"Turkish tobacco is not known for its mildness, little one."

She shot him a hostile glare and resumed her pacing. Deliberately she moved in a pattern which kept her back to him.

"Come here."

Eudora froze. She could feel his eyes on her. But her inherent obstinancy roused her to courage. She would not go to him at his call.

"Eudora, please come here."

The command which had crept into his voice was unmistakable, yet the addition of the word "please" caused her resolve to falter. She clenched her fists at her sides as if to hold on to it.

Suddenly he was behind her, his hands resting on her shoulders. "I know you are still angry about yesterday. Eudora, look at me." With uncharacteristic gentleness, he turned her to face him. "That you continue to defy me privately is one thing," he stated softly. "But I cannot— and will not—tolerate your public disobedience. The next time, I will not hesitate to do what is necessary. Do you understand?"

"Damn you!" she whispered in tearful frustration.

Without warning the hands on her shoulders released

211

their grasp. Khamed stepped back. "Why? Why do you continue to fight me, to thwart my efforts?"

As she stood in shock, attempting to comprehend his words, he reached out. His finger traveled the curve of her cheek and then lifted her chin so that her eyes might meet his. "Do you hate me so very much?"

The tender sadness in his voice unsettled her completely. But when she felt a familiar warmth seeping from within, she stepped back and leveled an icy gaze. She could not let him know the effect he had upon her. "Go back to your Arab whore!"

He reached for her with one of the catlike moves she could never evade, dragging her hard against him. Slowly he drew her hands together up to his chest and pressed her close. "I think not. Not while I have a *French* one."

The stinging insult of his taunt gave her the strength to break his hold. Wrenching a hand free, she slapped him furiously.

The sound of the blow resounded sharply. Her palm burned, and as her eyes focused on his face, she saw the imprint she'd left on his cheek.

Dark fury filled the black eyes staring down at her. He grabbed her wrist, still in mid-air, in a viselike grip.

"My lord?" Dahr-la's voice sliced the air.

Immediately Khamed flung her from him and hurried toward the drape.

Eudora stood trembling. The wild heartbeat in her ears was drowning out any sounds from the next room. She stumbled forward to follow him.

She entered just as the father lifted the child from the sofa. Cradling the tiny, obviously lifeless body of his son to his breast, he bowed to Khamed.

Eudora buried her face in her hands. She wanted to run, to escape and hide. She couldn't endure the arbitrary savagery which touched and ruled every aspect of these people's lives any longer. But there was no place to go, no place where she could be protected from it.

Through her sobbing she heard the father's departure

and Khamed's dismissal of his men and Dahr-la. And then he was at her side, touching her shoulder gently.

Eudora turned and fell into the refuge his arms offered.

Khamed held her tightly. When her sobbing had abated, he led her to the sofa. She sat mutely, watching as he crossed the room to the desk. He removed a package of cigarettes from a drawer and returned to her.

He lit one wordlessly and held it out. "Take it," he urged her softly.

Willing now to suffer the horrible acrid taste if it could help quiet her nerves, she took it.

Khamed smiled at the look of surprise which leaped across her face. After lighting a cigarette for himself, he tossed the package into her lap.

She glanced down, then back up at him.

He read her question in her eyes. "While living among your people, I acquired a taste for two of their vices."

Eudora picked up the package and placed it on the table. She wanted desperately to be able to concentrate on anything other than the memory of the dead child. "French cigarettes and . . . ?"

"French women," he answered evenly. He sat down beside her, propped his feet up on the table and dragged on his cigarette. Then, exhaling slowly, he reached out and gathered her into his arms. "Unfortunately, neither is easily obtained in the desert, and so I have learned to savor them all the more."

Eudora stiffened at his candid reply. But when his arms tightened about her, she found herself welcoming their embrace. She curled up beside him and allowed her head to rest on his bare chest, just over his heart. She could feel the regular beat against her cheek, hypnotic and soothing. Coupled with the warmth of his body, she realized a curious sense of calm.

Attributing it to her first taste of nicotine, she handed him her cigarette and closed her eyes. But even with them closed she could still see the man who held her. She knew him through every sense.

The feel of his smooth skin, stretched taut over hard muscle, was as recognizable to her as her own body. Each breath she drew was filled with his scent—a faint mingling of leather, horses, and tobacco. In her dreams she constantly heard his deep, melodious voice with its slightly singsong intonation unique to the desert tribes. Even the taste of him when he devoured her with his passionate kisses was his and his alone.

In scarcely more than a month she had grown to know this man more intimately than she would ever have thought possible. She knew his moods and his scowls, his smiles and his laughter. Sometimes they seemed cruel, mocking, or arrogant. But lately it had been the times when he was tender and kind that she had been most frightened and confused. On more than one occasion she had felt her defenses loosen and her fear and distrust of him melt away. Each time she was painfully aware of the one feeling which remained: a dull aching in her heart.

God, she was feeling it now . . . but more powerfully than she had ever felt it before. She didn't understand it, nor did she want to try to any longer. The effort of thinking made her head pound.

Unknowingly, she moaned softly.

"Eudora?" Khamed shifted his weight, putting her gently from him. "Are you all right?"

She opened her eyes and nodded.

"Go to bed. You are exhausted."

She shook her head, more in an attempt to clear her mind, than to respond to him. "I can't sleep."

"You need to rest, and I have to go." He leaned forward to extinguish his cigarette in the ashtray on the table. "There are things I must attend to." He stood and looked down at her. "I want you to go to bed."

His tone, though gentle, was firm. She nodded in weary compliance. She didn't have the strength or desire to argue.

He smiled and reached out to lift her chin. "By the

214

way . . . tonight we will be having guests for dinner. Wear something . . . suitable."

She stared at his departing back in confusion. What had he meant by "suitable"? Did he want her veiled and robed, like the women she had seen in Ghardaïa? Or did he want her preened and primped in order to show her off like a prized horse? Neither was a pleasant prospect. Her benevolent feelings of just moments ago vanished in a whirlpool of indignation.

She knew the man he'd been referring to was Montar, and he had said "guests." Did that mean Saleena would be in attendance as well? If so, just what did a Reguibat sheik's current mistress wear when being presented to his former lover? Thinking suddenly of what she'd seen an hour ago at the small tent, she wondered if she might not have the roles reversed.

That afternoon when Dahr-la arrived to help her dress, the girl insisted upon choosing her gown. The one she pulled from the armoire was the most elegant one Eudora owned.

Eudora had the answer to her first question.

It was past sundown when Khamed returned to his tent to wash and change for dinner. He entered the bedroom and found Eudora already dressed. His eyes swept the length of her, noting every detail of the peacock–blue gown he had chosen.

The smooth satin clung to every curve and line. Cut in a deep vee, the bodice possessed not a scrap of fabric from her slender ivory shoulders to the lush separation of her breasts. Even her upper arms were bare, the gown's puffed sleeves being unattached and worn just above the elbow.

To heighten the effect she had arranged her hair in an upswept style with a small knot at the crown. Long teardrop pearls hung from her ears, but no jewelry adorned her throat.

215

Khamed smiled. She had chosen wisely. The bare, flawless skin was far more dramatic unadorned. With the absence of ornament, the eye was free to follow the flat plane beneath her collarbone to the swell of the twin curves below.

He felt his passion surge, and ground his teeth. Though inclined to take her where she stood, he forced himself to settle for a far lesser pleasure. Walking to the armoire and simultaneously stripping off his shirt, he brushed intentionally against her. "As our guests shall be arriving soon, I shall have to wait to avail myself of what you are displaying, little one."

He was rewarded with a sharp gasp and two bright red spots appearing instantly on her cheeks. She bolted from him like a frightened deer.

The sound of his mocking laughter followed Eudora into the next room. Panting as though she had run a great distance, she fought for breath and control. Suddenly the tent flap parted and she found herself face to face with a tall, bearded Arab.

Nearly as large as Khamed, but with straight black hair, he would have been a menacing prospect were it not for his eyes. Hazel in color, they were soft and warm, and filled with a deep inner peace and wisdom few men ever attain. He smiled and the sudden flash of white teeth gleaming amid the black beard startled her.

She barely noticed the woman who entered behind him.

"Eudora, this is my childhood friend, Montar." Khamed's voice rang out from behind her. "And his sister, Saleena." Stepping beside her, he completed his introductions. "Montar, Saleena, may I present Mademoiselle Eudora Morrel."

Eudora met Saleena's cold stare and curtly nodded.

Saleena offered no acknowledgment at all. Her almond eyes, exotically rimmed in kohl, were filled with scorn.

As though to ease the tension, Montar quickly stepped forward and bowed. "Mademoiselle, it is a pleasure."

His voice was as kind as his eyes, and if he felt any surprise or discomfort at her particularly awkward position, he didn't show it.

Suddenly Eudora felt Khamed's hand at her waist. The obvious gesture of possession filled her with shame and outrage.

Yet Montar seemed amused. "I'll not steal her from you, Khamed, though . . ." he grinned mischievously and turned his eyes to her ". . . if you ever grow tired of him, Mademoiselle, please let me know!" And then he winked.

Eudora felt herself blush furiously at the man's blatant flirtation, but with it he had endeared himself to her. By insinuating she possessed some freedom of choice in the matter, he had restored her pride. She smiled warmly at him, glancing at Khamed from the corner of her eye.

He was clearly not amused by the subtle message, yet the fact that he said nothing gave her cause to wonder. There had to be more between the men than a close friendship. No underling would have dared to make such a comment. His friend had to be a powerful man. "You are a sheik of another clan, *Sidi* Montar?"

Khamed laughed silently. She was astute indeed. "No, little one. Montar is not a sheik. He is a *marabout*—a member of a religious, aristocratic class which claims direct lineal descent from Mohammed. In our society they are regarded as living saints whose function is as advisers and judges. Therefore Montar does, as you have guessed, possess power and influence that rivals my own."

"One could say, Mademoiselle, that we are pacific counterparts to the warrior sheiks." In an utterly unassuming manner Montar bowed.

Eudora turned her gaze to Khamed and smiled innocently. "I would never have guessed *your* best friend to be a holy man."

Khamed grinned. Her barely disguised sarcasm amused him. As he had needled her moments ago in the bedroom, she was now attempting to do the same to him. "Montar was not so holy as a boy," he replied. "To that I can attest. Together we managed to get into more trouble than our fathers could handle."

"Without resorting to a whip," Montar joined in laughing. "Khamed, do you remember the time . . ."

Strangely fascinated, Eudora listened as the man plunged into a memory of the childhood he and Khamed had shared.

Throughout dinner the men reminisced. The tales of their boyhood antics and adventures intrigued her. Yet hearing about the boy Khamed had been was somehow disconcerting. It made the stoic, self-controlled desert warrior she knew far more human. An inner voice warned her that seeing him in this light was dangerous. Such a revelation could have disastrous ramifications. And still she listened, captivated by the past of this man who had become such a powerful force in her life. She was oblivious to the pair of eyes focused solely upon her.

From beneath the screen of her thick lashes Saleena studied her rival. She did not like what she saw. The Frenchwoman was beautiful and poised, beguiling even Montar with her shameless Western ways. Both he and Khamed were actually taking pains to draw her into their conversation, while she herself remained virtually ignored.

Saleena toyed with the silver bracelets around her wrist. She had worked too hard to convince Montar to bring her along to let this white witch spoil her plans.

Even now she bristled, remembering how she'd had to plead—after first having been forced to listen to his admonitions. Khamed's interest in a woman was always short-lived, he'd warned her. Once past, it was never rekindled.

Still, there could be no denying that the passion she'd aroused in him that very morning had been strong and true. Montar was mistaken. What had existed between them a year ago *could* be again. It was just a matter of time and planning. Soon he would tire of the French-woman. His eye would wander. When it did, she would be there waiting. And certainly it couldn't hurt to remind him of her presence now.

At the meal's conclusion Saleena saw her opportunity. As his guests lingered over their coffee, Khamed rose to draw back the flap to allow the night breeze to ventilate the room. She jumped to her feet under the pretense of clearing the table. After depositing a few hastily grabbed dishes on a brass-topped table in a corner, she sauntered over to his side.

Montar followed his sister's movements with more than casual interest. With one eye on the couple at the doorway, he looked at the Frenchwoman. Absent-mindedly shooing a fly from the brim of her coffee cup, she was watching them as well. As Saleena slipped her hand into the crook of Khamed's arm, she stiffened visibly. He smiled in silent amusement. It would appear the spitfire had feelings beyond mere contempt for her captor—feelings that perhaps she had not acknowledged even to herself.

He had to say her name twice to bring her attention back to him.

"I'm sorry . . . what were you saying?"

Quickly he feigned a wave at an imaginary fly. "I was explaining, Mademoiselle, that flies are an annoyance one must endure in this lifetime only. For it is written that in our Moslem paradise all flies shall have perished save one."

Out of the corner of his eye he saw Khamed remove Saleena's hand with barely concealed irritation. His silent suspicions grew stronger.

"*One?*" Eudora raised an eyebrow. "Surely Allah could have done away with them all!"

At that moment Montar made a decision. Since his arrival he had been objectively studying her. Deciding he very much liked this woman of Khamed's, he smiled. In him she now had a friend and ally. *Bisillahi!* Pitting

219

herself against Khamed, she was going to need one.

"That lone fly exists in order that one may derive pleasure from wafting it away," he answered easily.

She looked at him in a mixture of disbelief and amusement. "And *where* did you say this is written?"

"In the *Koran*," Khamed replied evenly.

Eudora looked up in surprise. She hadn't heard his approach.

He sat down beside her and casually ran his hand over the curve of her shoulder.

Trying to ignore the way her heart jolted at his touch, she returned her attention to Montar. "Your version of our *Bible*, yes?"

"Actually, Mademoiselle, 'your' *Bible* is very much a part of *our* religion. Mohammed regarded himself as the last prophet in a line which included Isaiah and Jesus. He therefore saw his faith as a culmination of both Judaism and Christianity."

"It must be a very complicated religion then," Eudora exclaimed, "to have had the influence of so many tenets."

"Not at all. Ours is essentially a very simple religion. '*La Allah illa Allahi*'—'there is no God but the God. Give up idolatry; do not steal; do not lie; do not slander; never become intoxicated. If you follow these teachings, then you follow Islam.'"

Though Montar concluded his soft chant with a serene smile, Eudora had the strangest feeling the man's thoughts were not on the dogma of his faith. Suddenly she felt uncomfortable and painfully aware of her unequivocal position. "What happened to 'Thou shalt not kill' and 'Thou shalt not commit adultery'?" she asked.

Without considering the consequences, she had made her question purposely flippant to mask her embarrassment. She knew she had erred when she saw Khamed's brow furrow. There was more than a suggestion of annoyance hovering in his eyes.

"I told you before, little one," he drawled, his tone heavy with sarcasm, "our Prophet has condoned the sword—and *you* are not married."

"Would it have made a difference?" she spat. Though she had baited him, his callous reference to her situation—especially in front of strangers—enraged her.

"No," he stated with brutal candor. The dark scowl she had been waiting for descended. "We Moslems believe woman was created for the pleasure of man. Mohammed tells us, 'Your women are your fields. Go to your field and plough it as often as you like.'"

Eudora glared at him. His mouth was set in mocking arrogance. With lethal calm he waited for her response.

Realizing the direction the conversation had taken, Montar quickly broke the ringing silence and attempted a change of subject. Despite his efforts the Frenchwoman remained distant. Even Khamed's contribution to the conversation was now minimal. Finally Montar stood.

Upon her brother's silent command, Saleena rose. She was careful to keep her features from revealing the joy abounding in her heart. The tension that had surged between Khamed and his white witch delighted her. She was more confident than ever she would win him back. She needed only to wait patiently.

As soon as Montar left, Eudora retreated into the bedroom. Khamed remained in the main room, extinguishing the lanterns. She was grateful for the brief time she would have alone.

A storm of conflicting emotions and desires raged within her. She had wanted to hurt him and to make him want her all at the same time. When she'd seen Saleena touch him, the same gnawing frustration she had felt that morning resurfaced. Now she had no difficulty identifying it: it was jealousy.

Unbidden, other emotions began to well in her. Memories of the fear that had clutched her as she witnessed the "fight" upon Montar's arrival in camp took on a new significance. That emotion, coupled with

221

the feeling of solace she had found in his arms that morning and the delight she had taken in the stories of his childhood, brought the realization that her feelings for him involved a far deeper emotion than jealousy. And with that realization now came a far more chilling prospect—perhaps she was in love with him!

As senseless as it sounded, and as much as her reason fought to deny it, she knew it. She loved him and had done so for a long time, even when she'd thought she hated him.

She'd felt it the night Kahlil's son had been born, but had refused to admit it. Her defiance of his wishes and her disobedience of his orders that night, and the day of Montar's arrival, had been futile attempts to disclaim the hold he had over her. She had deliberately antagonized him then, as she had again tonight. While her heart ached to reclaim the peace she had felt lying in his arms that morning, reason would not allow her to surrender to her feelings.

To love him was madness! He was a barbaric savage who had taken her only to satisfy his basest needs. When he grew tired of toying with the plaything he had appropriated, he would surely cast her aside without a second thought.

Knowing that, she had instinctively erected a wall of defenses using the anger and tension beween them as mortar to hold it together. By concentrating on his savagery, she had kept the heat of his passion from igniting the flame of her love—a love which had been unwanted and unimaginable until now.

In despair she yanked the sleeves from her arms and threw them toward the drape just as Khamed entered.

The first of the peacock-blue projectiles hit him squarely in the chest. Startled, he caught the second out of pure reflex. Bending to retrieve the one lying at his feet, he shook his head in amusement.

Eudora watched him warily as he neared her, stopping at the vanity to place the satin puffs upon it.

"Such an ugly temper," he chided softly.

Suddenly he lunged at her, halting her escape with a firm grasp on her arm. He spun her around to face him. "And in one so beautiful." Lifting her face with the knuckle of his forefinger, he looked deeply into her eyes, holding them as he could when he so desired—in spite of her efforts to turn away. Slowly he began to pull the pins from her hair. Wrapping a freed curl around his finger, he seemed mesmerized by its color and texture. When he finally spoke his voice was a hoarse whisper, thick with emotion.

"Merciful Allah! Do you know what you do to me? You go to my head like wine, Eudora—and render me a fool!"

She saw the smoldering passion flame in his black eyes as he pulled her to him. His fierce, burning kisses soon had her reeling. Lost in the intoxicating, hypnotic spell of his desire, she closed her eyes. She felt him gather her up into his arms, his lips still clinging to hers. Weakly she lay against him. The scorching touch of his lips and the closeness of his hard body robbed her of all strength and resistance.

He carried her to the bed and laid her upon it. As he kissed the soft flesh of her shoulders, his fingers slipped over the cool satin, and with one swift tug her breasts were laid bare for his touch.

As if there was an invisible current between her nipples and her inner desire, his sensuous teasing of one ignited the other. Centered deep within her she felt a warmth spreading which she was helpless to stop.

Impatient now, he stripped her of the rest of her clothing and then stood to remove his own.

She stared up at him, watching as he unfastened his shirt. Button by button, she felt the heat rise as the unsolicited love threatened to consume her in flames. In one last effort to deny her desire, she rolled on her side away from him, refusing to watch as he finished disrobing.

Lying down next to her, he encircled her waist with

one arm, pulling her into his embrace. Her back was pressed to his muscled chest, her buttocks tight against his unyielding hardness. Bearing his weight on his left arm, his right hand traveled down her belly to caress the silkiness between her thighs. She struggled weakly against him—against herself, trying to force his hand away. Slowly he brought the hand back up the length of her body and slipped it under the side of her face, forcing her to turn her head toward him.

"Give yourself to me, Eudora."

She tried to turn her face away. Her barriers were collapsing, crumbling, leaving her incapable of resistance.

He forced her head back, kissing her gently and caressing her cheek with his lips. "Give yourself to me. Let me make love to you." His hand returned to the moist depths of her desire.

As his fingers tormented her, Eudora sobbed in silent agony. His entreaty had unleashed something within her. She could resist no longer, nor did she have the desire to.

He caressed her gently, until he seemed sure her body would easily accept his entry, and then he mounted her. At first moving slowly within her, and then more urgently and demandingly, he took her from one plateau of pleasure to the next.

Her resistance was gone, and with complete abandon Eudora responded to his passion. She slipped her tongue into his mouth and tasted him hungrily as her fingers traveled down his back, kneading the corded muscles. Meeting his thrusting with that of her own, she rode the waves of his desire, seeking the release which would extinguish the flames consuming her. When the waves began to crest, she clung to him. As the crashing tide swept over her, her heart cried out the words her mind could not accept and her lips could not utter.

Only in the trembling aftermath of her release did Khamed take his own. It was several minutes before his labored breathing returned to normal. During that time he continued to stare down at her. In her eyes he read her final surrender but the knowledge that he had won gave him no sense of exultation. A strange feeling gripped his heart. Somehow she had managed to deny him that gratification. Instead of satisfaction, he felt a sense of frustration. His triumph was lacking, his victory hollow.

Swearing softly in Arabic, he withdrew from her and rolled to his side, lighting one of the French cigarettes from the package he now kept on the night table. He lay back against the pillows and watched as she sat up, tucking her knees to her chin and wrapping her arms around her legs. Her hair streamed down her back to her waist, falling in silken waves over her shoulders, hiding her face from his view. He exhaled slowly, watching as her back rose and fell with her breathing.

With each breath she drew, he felt his anger rise. Moments ago there had been such passion between them! Now there was only cold, defiant silence. No . . . he had not won. Even in her submission she had triumphed and defied him. "Eudora, look at me!" he commanded harshly.

She flinched at the sound of his voice and turned her head. The green eyes were rimmed with tears.

"Still angry?" he asked dryly. The mocking tone he'd forced into his voice could not conceal his anger and frustration.

She shook her head. "No," she whispered, closing her eyes wearily. A single tear escaped and rolled down her cheek.

Khamed sat upright and ran a finger down her face, following the wet path of the teardrop. "Then why the tears?" He tore his eyes from her and dragged on the cigarette. "Is it that you still hate me?" The words were curiously difficult to say and his uneasiness spilled over into his voice, making it harsh and cold.

"I hate what you have done to me—what you have made of me!" Eudora opened her eyes and met his narrowed gaze. His eyes were hard, like his voice, and she shrank from him in fear. She knew she had angered him.

"And what is that? What have I made of you?" Laying his cigarette in the ashtray on the table, he pulled her to him roughly, tilting her head to meet his eyes. They—and his voice—were suddenly gentle. "I have made you my woman—is that so terrible?"

"You have made me your whore!" Confused by the swift transition from ferocity to gentleness, she tried to pull away. His strong hands held her fast as his onyx stare bored into her without mercy.

"It is by your laws and morals that you judge my actions. By *your* standards I have made you a whore—not by mine. You are no whore! You are restricted to only one man's attentions . . . mine! I have taken a woman I desired to my bed, to fulfill my needs, just as I would take food to satisfy my hunger . . . or drink to quench my thirst. There is no disgrace in that—not for me, and not for you."

His words were coming too quickly for her to comprehend their meaning. With her confusion growing, she turned her face away. She felt as if she were drowning.

"Look at me!" he growled. "Have any of my people treated you with anything less than respect and honor?"

He did not wait for an answer. "No! They have not. The shame you feel is self-imposed. *I* have not made you a whore, little one—*you* have!"

Khamed knew the words he spoke were in essence true. But he also knew time and emotion had twisted that truth. With full knowledge of the consequences of his actions, he was indirectly as responsible for her shame as she. He had purposely let her feel like a whore, because to do so had suited his objective—to manipulate her into submission. Had he not brought du Bois and Sabatin into his tent that first evening for that very purpose? Had he not also continued to taunt her with her position in order to arouse her temper, in the hope that one passion might trigger another?

Suddenly Khamed did feel responsible, and that realization confused him. As long as he had found satisfaction, it had not mattered how she felt about herself—or him. But now, for a reason he could not comprehend, it did matter. It mattered a great deal.

"Perhaps . . ." once again his voice was made harsh to mask his pain. ". . . it is not that a man has taken you for his own—but that an infidel has! Is that it, Eudora? When you look at me, do you still see an Arab barbarian?"

Eudora lifted her eyes. She found her lips parting in a slight smile. "You are not an Arab, remember?" she replied softly. "And you are not even a full-blooded barbarian. That is *not* it."

As she spoke her voice became stronger, harder. "Can't you understand what I feel? Perhaps in the eyes of your people I am not a whore. But in the eyes of mine, I am! And when you grow tired of me . . . what then? Will you sell me to another? Or give me as a reward to a loyal follower? Perhaps you will make of me a gift to Montar!"

She turned away, but not in time. Khamed saw the sadness in her eyes her sarcasm had sought so valiantly to mask. He now understood at least part of her fear—and the reason for her continued resistance. She believed he would turn her over to others once his own desire had passed. "You will be returned to Ghardaïa safely," he answered, gently. "I give you my word. I will not sell you nor give you to another. That was *never* my intent." He looked into her eyes and tried to read her emotions. They were a kaleidoscope of confusion.

"Eudora, tonight I asked you again to give yourself to me—to let me make love to you. I have never before asked that of another woman. I have only taken what I wanted, as is my right by my laws. The first time I asked you, you denied me. Tonight you did not. Yet each time the result has been the same. It makes no sense to continue to fight me. You once spoke of a truce between us. I ask you now to accept my terms. Yield to my will and

227

pledge to me your obedience."

Eudora trembled inside. She could fight no longer. To wage war with an enemy from without was possible—she had done so for more than a month. But tonight she had learned too much. To do battle with one's own heart was not possible.

She looked into his eyes, wanting with all her being to see love burning in the black coals. But it was with the fire of desire that they burned—not the flame of love. She lowered her eyes to hide her sorrow and nodded in assent.

He gripped her arm tightly. "Look at me and say it!" he demanded.

"Yes," she whispered softly. "I will yield. I will obey."

Khamed laid her head on his chest and embraced her. In his heart he knew she had not surrendered willingly—or even fully. Her will was like a supple reed. He had forced it to bend, but he had not broken it.

Chapter Fourteen

The truce between Khamed and Eudora held, and with her promise of obedience, Khamed's trust in her seemed to grow. He permitted her greater freedom to wander the encampment, and to see Sabatin on a regular basis. Upon her request he even extended the same privilege of unchaperoned movement to the Frenchman.

Eudora knew Khamed had come to respect the reporter. She had told him about the diary, and the sympathetic yet realistic portrayal of his people had pleased him. Still, given his Arab beliefs which forbade a man's woman any contact with another man, his acceptance of her friendship with Sabatin was a great concession.

Khamed's only condition was that she see Sabatin in her own tent. However, he would not relent in his absolute restriction regarding the French lieutenant. She was not to go anywhere near him.

Eudora agreed. From Sabatin's reports, du Bois had become a shriveled shell of a man, consumed by hatred. He accepted his captivity with a martyr's fervor, and both Khamed and Sabatin had serious doubts as to the man's sanity.

As another month slipped by Eudora developed a peculiar sense of balance with regard to her inner conflicts of reason and emotion.

She hid her love from Khamed, and though she ached to give herself to him completely, she never again responded with the same abandon that had consumed her the night their truce was born. Nevertheless, she had changed as a result of it, and the changes manifested themselves in subtle ways.

Colored by her love for their leader, her opinion of the desert tribesmen softened. As she watched them move about the camp, she found herself admiring the simplicity and freedom of their lives, their primitive ways having ceased to disgust her. She saw even small things differently.

She had once told Sabatin she thought Arabic an ugly language—harsh, like the lives of the people who spoke it. But now its sounds were melodious to her ear, softened, it seemed, by the desert people's lilting intonation.

One afternoon, while Khamed was out on patrol and as she sat with Sabatin over tea, she heard a mother call to her children. As the woman's voice floated through the open flap, Eudora casually repeated her observation. "Have you noticed how different Arabic sounds when the Reguibat speak it? It's almost musical."

"Eudora, you have been out in the sun too long." Laughing, Sabatin patted her hand.

Immediately on guard, afraid her true feelings were showing, she masked her expression. "What do you mean?"

"Listen to yourself. Is this the same woman who hated all things Arab? As I recall, unbearable and unendurable were two words you used quite often and passionately."

The spoon she had picked up to stir her tea slipped from her fingers and clattered to the table. She frowned as she retrieved it.

"Perhaps some of your philosophy has finally rubbed off on me," she replied sarcastically. "After all, weren't *you* the one who said I should accept and love them for what they are?"

Sabatin crinkled his forehead. "Actually . . . I believe the word *I* used was 'respect,' not 'love.' But that aside . . . do you?"

"Do I what?"

"Do you love them?"

"Don't be ridiculous, Pierre! Of course I don't love them."

He looked at her with the strangest of expressions and she realized she might be protesting too much. "I have merely come to respect them." In support of her words she offered a nonchalant shrug.

His expression of disbelieving indulgence remained. She felt more uneasy and laughed nervously. "Honestly! I feel as if I'm being interrogated."

"I'm not interrogating you, Eudora." His features and his voice softened. "You've changed, that's all."

"Well, who wouldn't, under the circumstances?"

The tone Sabatin heard in her voice had a familiar ring. It was the same one that always surfaced whenever they discussed Khamed. He couldn't identify it, but he was certain it had to do with the feelings she harbored for the Reguibat sheik. Over the past few weeks he had become increasingly convinced the defiant emotions she displayed outwardly were forced.

"Besides, I'm not the only one who's changed," she continued. "Have you looked at yourself recently?"

He grinned sheepishly and ran his fingers through his hair. It had grown long—nearly as long as the tribesmen's. He had also taken to wearing their clothing . . . not just their robes, but the long, loose shirts which came to the knees, and their short, baggy trousers. Most of the time a half-wrapped, bright orange *shesh* was worn carelessly about his head and shoulders.

Silently he wondered what Eudora would say if she knew of all the changes in his life. Unknown to her he had been sleeping regularly with one of Dahr-la's cousins. He smiled as he thought of the girl, Salwa. Her name was Arabic for "comfort," and it suited the quiet, slightly

231

plump girl perfectly.

"Sometimes I wonder if you even *want* to be ransomed!" Eudora's voice cut into his thoughts.

"I might say the same about you!" he retorted, deciding to play with fire—emerald fire, to be exact.

The metaphor became reality instantly. She rose, green eyes blazing, flashing with the same anger, hurt, and confusion he had seen once before in the outdoor café of the hotel in Ghardaïa. She hadn't wanted to hear the truth then either.

"What you are insinuating, Monsieur Sabatin, is an outrage!"

"Is it?" He rose as well and grabbed her arm, forcing her to face him. She would not run away this time. "You think about it, Mademoiselle Morrel." He, too, reverted to the cool, polite form of address. "Think honestly about the life you have to return to. You are young and beautiful, yet that life is empty. The normal joys that fulfill a woman do not exist for you. Home, family, children, a man to give your love to—you have none of them."

He saw the pain his words wrought, yet continued. "Now . . . I want you to think about this life you have supposedly resigned yourself to here. You tell me you cannot struggle and fight Khamed—that you have no choice but to surrender to him. But you seem to have forgotten that *I* was with you after Cheval's attack. You would have died rather than endure at his hands that which you have *resigned* yourself to at Khamed's."

He took a deep breath to deliver the final blow. "The only struggle I see, Mademoiselle, is the one you are waging with yourself!"

Furiously she yanked her arm from his grasp. "You had better leave, Monsieur."

Sabatin recaptured her wrist. "No. I'm not leaving until I have said all I have to say. I saw how the two of you deliberately goaded and antagonized one another the night Kahlil's son was born. Why? Is it because the only passion you will allow yourself is the passion of anger—and *he* knows that? Are you afraid, or ashamed to admit that you are attracted to him? You once told me you were confused by your feelings. You said you didn't know what you felt, or why. Well, I think it is love that you feel, Mademoiselle. And not for these people—but for their leader!"

Sabatin heard her quick, sharp intake of breath. This time he let her go. With a choked cry she turned and fled into the next room.

"Damn it, Eudora!" he shouted at her back. "You can't continue to run from the truth!"

Eudora remained in the back room until the late afternoon heat transformed the closed space into an oven. Khamed was still out on patrol, but she knew he could return at any moment. She didn't want to be there when he did. She needed time away from him to sort out her jumbled thoughts. Sabatin's accusations had hit too close to home.

She decided to go for a walk. The sun would be setting soon, and a cool breeze would then sweep over the oasis. Perhaps it would blow away her fears and confusion as well.

The sound of childish laughter drew her toward the edge of camp. Among the spiky trunks of the date palms she found a small group of children chasing one another in a game of hide-and-seek.

They spotted her almost at once, ending their game to approach her in cautious curiosity.

"Don't let me interrupt your game." Eudora smiled at one of the girls—a tiny, dark child with huge brown eyes.

She darted behind a tall, curly-headed boy who protectively put his arm around her.

"I didn't mean to frighten her." Eudora looked at the boy. From the resemblance between the children she guessed him to be the girl's brother. "Please, go back to your game." She waved her hands. "Go."

"Please, go back to your game." With flawless mimicry several of the older children imitated her. They even copied her gestures. Their actions brought gales of laughter from their playmates.

"Please, go back to your game," they all repeated.

Eudora realized they had no idea what they were saying, but were merely repeating the sounds she made. She looked among them, searching for a way to communicate. She spied the dark girl still standing by her brother. He took a piece of flat bread from his pocket and handed it to his sister. Apparently pacified with the treat, she eased away from him.

Eudora had an idea. She pointed to the bread. "*Le pain,*" she said firmly.

"*Le pain,*" the children repeated. Then, seeing the object she was referring to, they shouted in unison. "*Hobsa.*"

One of the boys ran to the spring which bubbled up from deep beneath the sand just a few feet from them. He returned with his cupped hands full of water. "*Elma,*" he proclaimed proudly.

"*L'eau,*" she responded.

A new game was born.

As Eudora settled herself down upon the sand, the children took turns pointing to objects and identifying them in Arabic. To shrieks of delight and amusement at her sometimes clumsy pronunciation, she then repeated the word in Arabic before providing its French translation. This the children echoed in a screaming chorus.

The game continued for nearly half an hour. The tall, curly-headed boy stepped forward to take his turn. He looked about and seemed unable to find a word not already used. Finally his gaze fell upon something in the distance. "*Zmal,*" he stated, pointing toward the open desert.

Eudora wasn't sure what it was he was gesturing to. It was the first word the children had used that they hadn't been able to touch or clearly indicate. She offered a few guesses. "Desert, mountain?"

234

Somehow he seemed to know none of the French words she gave were accurate. "*Zmal*," he repeated.

Eudora shook her head helplessly. "I'm sorry. I don't know what it is you are pointing at."

The boy looked to his playmates for aid, and found none. They seemed to be telling him to either choose another word or to forfeit his turn. Stubbornly he jabbed at whatever it was he wanted her to see. "*Zmal!*" he repeated again.

Eudora winced at the look of frustration on his face. She tried another word. "Horizon?"

The boy threw up his hands in frustration.

"Camel."

Eudora jerked her head around at the sound of the deep masculine voice at her back. She didn't have to look upward to know whose voice it was. "What?" she stammered, completely unnerved by his sudden appearance.

"Camel," Khamed repeated. "*Zmal* is Arabic for camel."

She felt a warm flush ascend. True enough, there had been several couched camels in the distance. She quickly returned her attention to the children. "*Le chameau.*" She smiled apologetically at the boy.

But Khamed's presence had brought an end to the game. Without bothering to repeat the French word, they scampered off like mice—each in a different direction.

"We saw your yellow gown through the trees as we were returning to camp. I apologize that our appearance has put an untimely end to your game." The man mounted beside Khamed smiled and inclined his head in greeting. "Were you teaching them French, Mademoiselle, or were they teaching you Arabic?"

Eudora returned Montar's smile warmly. Over the past month she had grown very fond of him. As now, he always seemed to know what to say. She'd been embarrassed to have been found playing with the children. His question

235

had given the foolish game merit. "A little of both, I think." As she watched the children run back to the tents, she stood and brushed the sand from her skirts.

Khamed leaned from his saddle, extending his hand to her.

She hesitated only a second before giving him her arm. He clasped it firmly, lifting her up to sit in front of him. The black stallion tossed his head and snorted in annoyance at the added weight.

Khamed scolded him lightly.

"That isn't Arabic, is it?" Eudora turned to look at him over her shoulder. When he arched an eyebrow she hastened to explain her comment. "I mean . . . it doesn't sound like Arabic."

"You are quite right. It is Berbish. You must have learned a great deal from the children today." He kicked at the stallion's flanks to urge him forward. "In another month, little one, you will return to your world speaking our tongue like an Arab."

Eudora knew he was pleased, for his eyes were soft and golden. And the smile he gave her sent her pulse racing. But the possibility that his words had been designed to convey more than affectionate teasing jabbed at her heart like a needle.

Another month. Was that as long as he intended to keep her? Was he planning then to release her?

A mixture of joy and sorrow welled within her. Dear God . . . had Sabatin been right? *Did* she want to return to the life she had had?

That evening not even Montar's presence at dinner— sans Saleena—could bring her out of her strange and silent mood. She excused herself almost immediately at the meal's conclusion and went into the bedroom.

Montar watched her disappear into the next room. Ever since Khamed's comment that afternoon, the woman had not been herself. She'd barely spoken at dinner and had hardly touched her food. But he, too, had wondered at a hidden meaning in his friend's earlier words.

He looked at the man sitting across from him and decided to broach the subject Khamed had been avoiding ever since his arrival. "How long are you going to keep her here?"

For a brief moment a strange expression crossed Khamed's face. Then it was gone. He shrugged and flicked the ash from his cigarette in a gesture of impatience. "For as long as I find her company enjoyable." Suddenly his eyes narrowed in suspicion. "Why the curiosity, Montar? You have seen women in my camp before and never shown any interest. Why is this time different?"

"Because this woman is different, my friend. *You* are different. She lights a fire in your eyes that has nothing to do with the desire that burns in your loins. She has been here for two months—longer than you have ever kept a woman. Yet your need for her does not diminish. If anything, it has grown stronger. But have you stopped to consider that once the Frenchmen are released you will have to let her go as well? The French government will not stand idly by once they learn a white woman is being held captive in a Reguibat camp."

"Their release is months away," Khamed answered curtly. "The wheels of their bureaucracy turn very slowly. It will take them months to locate Gerard, and by the time they have contacted the proper officials in Paris—"

"What you are telling me is that when the men are released you are going to release her as well?"

Khamed did not answer. His taking of her had not been planned in detail and little thought had been given to the consequences of her captivity. He had simply assumed he would grow bored with her before a decision needed to be made.

"You have not answered, Khamed." Montar's soft voice sliced through his thoughts like a knife.

"She will be released when I am tired of her and when I

no longer want her!" Furiously he stabbed out his cigarette in the ashtray on the table before him.

Montar studied Khamed intently. His friend had never been easy to read. "Khamed . . . are you in love with her?"

Khamed's head snapped up, his eyes blazing in fury. "Have I ever been in love with a woman?" he answered sarcastically. "She intrigues me, and it pleases me to have her here—in my camp, in my tent, and in my bed. There is nothing more to it!" he stated with icy finality.

The deadly silence that settled over the room was suddenly shattered by a woman's scream.

Khamed leaped to his feet. The look Montar saw in his eyes negated every word of denial he had just spoken. Khamed raced to the bedroom and shoved the drape aside.

Montar was only steps behind. He stood hesitantly at the entrance and watched as Khamed crossed the room to the bed. He had apparently realized she'd only had a nightmare. He called out her name softly so as not to frighten her further.

"Eudora?"

She was sitting upright, her face ghostly gray in the low light. Silver streaks of tears shone on her cheeks, and though her eyes were wide open, she continued to stare blankly, unseeingly, straight ahead. Her fingers clawed at the silken sheets which shimmered eerily, reflecting the lamp light from the main room.

Khamed sat down on the edge of the bed. "Eudora," he repeated softly, "wake up." He placed his hands over hers to still the frantic clawing.

At the sound of his voice she had blinked. At his touch she now turned her head to look at him. "My father!" she cried, "my father is dead!"

"No," he assured her gently. He released one of her hands in order to sweep aside the long hair that had fallen across her face. "You were dreaming."

Her hand now free, she clutched at his shirt. "No! I

saw him! I saw him lying in the desert! He was all alone and he wasn't moving!" Her eyes closed and a great sob wracked her body as she seemed to return in her mind to the visions terrifying her. "Papa! Get up, Papa. Don't you see the jackals! They're coming closer! Papa!"

Khamed gathered her into his arms, hoping to still her trembling. Her arms went around him and she clung to him.

Slowly her crying subsided and he felt the tension flow from her body. For a moment she relaxed against him, and then she pulled away.

"I'm all right," she insisted. Fiercely she brushed the tears from her face and sat up straighter.

Khamed drew back in bitter annoyance that she had so quickly and readily forsaken his embrace. Must she always be overcome with sorrow before seeking his arms?

Knowing she now had no further need for his presence, he started to rise.

"Khamed!"

In the same instant he heard her tear-smothered whisper, her hand darted out to touch his arm.

"Please . . . don't go."

Khamed felt his heart tighten. It was the first time he had ever heard her speak his name. Instincts which had protected him for more than twenty-five years cried out a course of action. Walk away, he told himself . . . but his body would not respond.

Suddenly, as if to seal his fate, the heavy folds of the drape fell closed.

Montar walked away from the curtain and moved to extinguish the lamps. His thoughts were full of what he had just witnessed. At the tent's exit he paused to cast a final glance toward the small room. "Khamed, my friend," he whispered, "you are a fool . . . for only a fool denies his own heart."

Slowly Eudora opened her eyes. She knew the hard

warmth beneath her cheek was no dream. Neither was the weight of the brown muscled arm draped across her. Easing her body from the sleeping man at her side, she cautiously lifted her head from his chest.

He moaned at the sudden loss of warmth, and she stiffened. Instinctively he drew her back to him, arching his back to settle more deeply into the bed.

Confident Khamed had not woken, Eudora allowed herself the luxury of his embrace. In his arms the horrifying visions lurking in the recesses of her mind were not so terrifying. Still, she shivered in vivid recollection of the nightmare. The dream had not been the first she'd had of her father. Over the past two months she'd had several. But none had been of his death—and none had been so terrifyingly real.

After her capture she had purposely banished all thoughts of her father from her mind. She knew he was in no position to help her—or she to help him. Louis Morrel was somewhere between Ouargla and Lake Chad, living out his dream. She had forced herself to believe he was safe. If she hadn't, she'd have gone out of her mind.

Why, then, after all this time, had the fears she'd had in France returned to haunt her?

Khamed began to stir, and she quickly pulled away and sat up. Self-consciously she pulled the sheets to her bare shoulders. Though she had been with Khamed for over two months, she was still not accustomed to waking with him still beside her. He slept in the nude, and early on had insisted she do the same. He'd told her he wanted to be able to reach out and feel her next to him—not a swatch of fabric. At night it hadn't mattered much in the darkness. But on those few occasions when he had not already left by dawn, she'd been as she was now—mortified.

"Good morning."

His low voice sent an instantaneous spasm through her body. She stiffened and wrapped her arms tightly about her. She would have to explain her actions from the night before. She couldn't let him know the truth—that she had reached out for him in need, a need fostered and nourished by love.

"I'm sorry about last night," she began quietly, making herself turn to look at him. In spite of herself, she shuddered as the memory of the nightmare flashed through her mind. She forced herself to ignore the vision and continued. "When I was talking to Pierre yesterday, he happened to mention my father . . ." That wasn't exactly the truth, but it wasn't a lie either. "I started thinking about him, wondering where he was, if he were safe. . . . It was just a silly dream!"

Eudora closed her eyes and waited for his response. If her actions the night before had not given the truth away, surely the loud pounding of her heart would now; it beat like a drum in her ears.

She felt his hand sweep the hair from her back. He began to trace the line of her spine with his fingertips, sending fire through every nerve of her being. "It is not silly to fear for a loved one's safety, Eudora. But a dream is only that—a dream and not reality."

His touch and his gentle words were stripping away the remnants of her control. She wanted to throw herself into his arms.

"I told Montar I would go riding with him this morning. Would you like to come along?"

His voice, soft and even, hurtled her back to earth. Eudora opened her eyes and sighed in silent relief. His face was devoid of any sign of recognition. He had not guessed at her feelings, and his deliberate attempt at kindness touched her.

"Could we invite Pierre?" she asked hesitantly. "I was rather . . . unkind to him yesterday. I would like to set things right."

He raised an eyebrow in curiosity but did not question her further. "If you wish."

An hour later Eudora paced the outer room. Khamed and Montar were due to return at any moment. If Sabatin didn't arrive soon, her chance to talk to him in private would be lost.

She heard the tent flap lift and whirled to face the door.

Sabatin stood stiffly in the entrance. As she opened her mouth to speak, he bowed. "Mademoiselle."

She groaned in exasperation at his formal address and cool demeanor. Still, she had been the one to initiate it. "Very well, Pierre, I deserved that." She smiled weakly and gestured for him to enter. "I owe you an apology. My behavior yesterday was—"

"Childish and immature." Sabatin struggled to keep his expression stern and his voice harsh. But the sight of Eudora nervously twisting a scarf in her hands as she looked at him from across the room gave him no pleasure. "I do, however, forgive you," he whispered, allowing a slight grin, followed by a wink.

"Argh!" she shrieked. "You are impossible!"

"I know," he grinned widely, "but that's part of my charm!"

She shook her head and laughed softly. "How *do* you tolerate me?"

Sabatin permitted himself a smile of unabashed affection. Eudora had become very dear to him. What he'd seen her endure would have destroyed most women. Yet she had opened her mind and learned acceptance. If she now could only open her heart. . . .

"It's because I know you, Eudora. I know what really lies beneath that beautiful, icy exterior of yours. What I don't know is what you're planning to do about it."

She glanced down and stared at the length of silk in her hands. "I don't know what you mean."

"Let's not start this again, Eudora. You know what I mean. You have two choices. Either you fight what you feel—as you have been doing—or you accept it."

"And do what then?" she cried helplessly. The eyes she lifted were filled with pain.

"Follow your heart. Admit to yourself that you

242

love him.''

She gasped instantly. "I can't! Don't you see that is impossible? How can I be in love with an uncivilized desert . . . warlord who has taken me for his amusement only until he grows bored with me?"

Sabatin sensed that she was really directing the question to herself. She was fighting valiantly to deny what both he and her heart were telling her. "Eudora, you are not a naive ingénue. Were you never in love with a man who did just that? Flowers and gifts, and whispered words of passion may have made the act 'civilized,' but when the affair ended, was the pain any less than what you are feeling now?"

She did not answer him, and somehow he knew he had struck a nerve. When he'd mentioned "affair," a tinge of pink had risen to her cheeks. There had to be something in her past she was hiding from. "Eudora . . . who was Christian?"

All the color faded from her face. "Where . . . where did you hear that name?"

"The night after Cheval's attack, you cried it out in your sleep," Sabatin answered gently. "Is he the man who hurt you, Eudora? Is he the reason you are afraid to love?"

Eudora fought the flood of unwelcome memories surfacing, memories she had buried long ago. But she couldn't hold them back, nor could she hold in the emotions Sabatin's questions had triggered. She had never spoken to anyone about Christian. Suddenly she needed to.

"Yes. He was older than I was," she began slowly. "He was everything to me: father figure, teacher, lover. But he was married. I didn't know that at first, and when I found out I wanted to stop seeing him, but I couldn't. I believed in his promises. He said he would divorce his wife. He asked me to give him a year because of financial considerations."

"Eudora, you don't have to tell me this."

243

"Yes, yes I do. I want to. I gave him the year he asked for. Then he asked for another. God, I was so naïve! I finally learned the truth—from, of all people, his wife. She contacted me anonymously, and when we met she introduced herself. She was quite understanding, actually. She even offered to provide me with a list of the women who had preceded me in Christian's affections during the course of their fourteen-year marriage. It seemed he was very adept at choosing his mistresses . . . lonely, unloved women, who believed in his empty promises. When I confronted him, he didn't even try to deny it." Her voice caught in her throat. "I swore I would never be hurt like that again."

"That was a long time ago, Eudora. You were hurt, yes. But it's in the past. You can't let it affect the rest of your life. You can't decide not to ever love again because you are afraid of being hurt. There are never guarantees that the person to whom we give our heart will feel the same. And even if that person does return those feelings, there are no guarantees they will last. But it is better to love— even for a short time—than never to love. Eudora, don't be afraid to love Khamed because you are afraid of love itself."

"Are you telling me to love an Arab barbarian who cares nothing for me?" she asked in disbelief.

"You *already* do—so that point is moot. What I'm trying to tell you is to stop battling your heart!"

At that moment Sabatin heard Khamed's voice outside the tent. Eudora heard it, too. He watched in amazement as she squared her shoulders. Glancing down at the twisted scarf in her hands, she quickly unwound it. She smoothed out the wrinkles and tied the silk around her head. A curtain of composure dropped across her face. Not a trace of the emotions he knew were churning within her was evident.

244

Chapter Fifteen

Was Sabatin right?

Eudora glanced at the man beside her.

Sabatin's attention was fixed on the swooping desert larks in the sky. Since leaving camp he had been silent, as though purposely to give her time to mull over his words.

In her heart she knew he had been right. In many ways Khamed's brutal honesty was kinder than Christian's betrayal. There had never been false promises or lies, and no deception. From the beginning she had known his intentions. But if she did give in to her feelings, what would the consequences be? And how would Khamed react if he learned the truth?

She looked at the black-*sheshed* man riding with Montar several yards ahead, and her heart tightened in her chest. After all this time what did she really know of him? Would Khamed be cruel and scorn her love? Perhaps he derived some perverse pleasure from making his women fall in love with him before he cast them aside. Or if he took his pleasure in the pursuit, would his interest wane once he knew she loved him?

She bowed her head and rubbed her fingers across her brow. Either way, she could be putting a merciful end to her misery. Glancing up, she noticed that Montar had slowed his horse. He seemed to be waiting for her.

"What do you think, Mademoiselle?" he asked,

reining in his horse to ride beside her. "Khamed says that his black devil, Hasaad, can outdistance this magnificent beast." He patted his horse's neck proudly.

Eudora smiled cryptically. From what she had seen, Montar appeared to be every bit as skilled a horseman as Khamed. And the two stallions, like the men who rode them, were both strong and powerful. Yet she had a feeling Montar's horse lacked the battlefield experience and training of Hasaad. Of the two, the white also seemed to possess a far gentler disposition. Like its master, a man of peace, Montar's horse reflected tranquil serenity. Khamed's was akin to a raging storm—ridden by a man of war.

"There is only one way to find out," she finally replied, diplomatically. Thinking of the competition that apparently had existed between the men since childhood, she arched a brow. "Perhaps a contest?"

Montar's face split into a wide grin. "And to the victor, what prize?" He studied her carefully for a moment. "Perhaps the favor of a beautiful woman?"

Eudora lowered her eyes at his less than subtle flirtation. "I don't think that would be proper," she replied uneasily.

"Khamed!" Montar shouted to the man now riding some distance ahead of them. "It would appear your woman has no faith in your black *shaitan* either!"

Khamed wheeled Hasaad and rode back toward them. He looked at Eudora in feigned outrage. "Is this true?"

Before she could reply, Montar spoke up. "She is unwilling to grant her favor to the victor in a contest to determine the better horse." He cast Khamed an innocent look. "What else can that mean, old friend, but that she is afraid *you* would lose?"

"That's not what I said!" Eudora turned to glare at the marabout, but in doing so her gaze fell upon Khamed. With a start, she realized that he seemed to know he was being goaded. His dark eyes were flashing with the love of a challenge.

"Very well, *old friend*. Shall we settle this once and for all with a race to the well?" He pointed toward a small oasis in the distance.

Montar nodded and maneuvered his horse into position alongside Khamed.

"Monsieur, would you do the honors?"

Eudora had forgotten Sabatin's presence. As Khamed leaned from his saddle to hand his revolver to the stunned Frenchman, she watched for his reaction. He took the gun hesitantly, his eyes darting to Khamed's face as though he were attempting to read the man's thoughts.

"I trust you," Khamed said softly. He raised a hand to still the protest he seemed to know would come from Montar.

Montar dropped his eyes in mute acknowledgment, but not before Eudora saw the look of surprise which momentarily crossed his face.

Sabatin grinned. He cocked the revolver and raised it into the air. *"Un, deux, trois!"*

At the thunderous crack of the single gunshot, both horses bolted ahead, the men on their backs leaning low over their necks.

Sabatin tucked the gun into his waistband. "Let's go!" he shouted.

Eudora felt a strange sense of exhilaration. As she raced after Sabatin her heart seemed to take flight. For the first time in months she felt free and at peace with herself. She caught up to Sabatin's chestnut mare and together they followed the trail of dust left in the wake of the horses galloping shoulder to shoulder.

It was impossible to tell which one was winning.

By the time they reached the oasis the race was over. Khamed had already dismounted. Kneeling before the well, he was clearing the sand from its surface to allow the horses to drink. Still seated upon his horse, Montar dismounted at their approach.

Eudora searched each man's face for an indication of

the outcome. There was no gloating smile nor begrudging loser's frown from either man. "Who won?" she asked Montar as he walked over to help her dismount.

His large hands encircled her waist and he grinned. "It was very close." He plucked her from the saddle, setting her gently upon the ground.

"But who won?" She took her hands from Montar's shoulders and nervously straightened her riding skirt. All the while she kept her eyes trained on Khamed.

He rose and walked over to Hasaad. Taking the stallion's reins he led the animal to where she and Montar stood. Without looking at Montar, he handed him the reins. "I did."

Eudora looked to Montar for confirmation.

He nodded his head. "By a nose."

Khamed took a step toward her and reached for her arm. "And now, little one," he whispered sinisterly, "I intend to claim what I have won."

Montar smiled as Khamed led the woman to the oasis' edge. His view partially blocked by Hasaad's ebony flanks, he saw him take her into his arms and kiss her passionately.

"You seem surprised."

Montar looked at the man at his side.

Sabatin jerked his head toward the couple as he handed him Khamed's revolver.

Montar tucked the weapon beneath his waistcloth and studied the younger man carefully. Intuitively he knew Khamed's earlier trust in the Frenchman had not been ill placed. "I have known Khamed for a very long time, Monsieur," he stated slowly, deciding he liked the man. "I have never seen him react to a woman as he does to her. As hardened as he is, she is the soft vein that runs up his backbone."

"What are you saying?"

"I am saying that in as much as Khamed is capable of love, I believe he loves her."

"I had wondered as much." Sabatin sighed and passed

his hand wearily across his brow. "She is in love with him, you know."

"Yet your words are weighted with sadness, Monsieur. Why?"

Sabatin stuck out his jaw. His mind was crowded with doubts and fears he had not revealed to Eudora. How could he express them to this man who was a stranger? "Because it cannot possibly work," he stated coolly.

"Because he is of another race?"

In the man's question Sabatin heard his own coolness deflected back to him. Bristling at the allusion to racial prejudice, he glared at him in denial. "Because he is of another world! They have nothing in common—not culture, language, religion . . ."

"They have love," Montar interrupted softly.

"A love neither one of them wants to admit to!"

"Then they have two things in common—love, and a fear of being hurt."

Sabatin found the marabout's words disturbing. He had described Eudora perfectly, yet it was of Khamed he had spoken. What in the proud Reguibat's past had made him unable or afraid to love?

"There is also a third—their *qisma*," Montar continued. "For I believe their meeting was willed by Allah. You see, Monsieur, our God not only guides the world at large, but also predestines the fate of each and every man individually. Whatever man is or does and whatever happens to him is directly willed by Allah. Man has no choice but to go through the course of events which have been written down for him. *Mektoub*—it is written: 'Naught befalleth us save that which Allah hath decreed for us. He is our Protecting Friend. In Allah let believers put their trust.'"

A hot wind rose suddenly, sweeping a cloud of blowing sand across the small oasis. Sabatin turned his attention from Montar to the horses, working with the man to tether the animals.

At the oasis' edge, engulfed by Khamed's embrace,

249

Eudora was protected from the stinging wind. She didn't hear the horses' snorts and whinnying protests. The only sound she heard was Khamed's whisper against her ear.

"You are fortunate, little one, that we are not alone." His tone was half teasing, half threat. "Else you would soon find yourself lying in the sand beneath me."

"I can't imagine it would be very comfortable." She retorted with flippancy, hoping to conceal her rising desire.

"Oh, I assure you . . . it would *not* be discomfort that you felt." Khamed laughed and lowered his head to kiss her again.

Her heart swelled with love and she rose on her tiptoes to meet his lips.

"Khamed!"

Montar's shout shattered the spell.

Khamed turned to look at the marabout. He gestured toward a cloud of dust in the distance. Khamed could see a lone man on horseback racing across the sand toward them. He released Eudora immediately and led her back to where Montar and Sabatin stood. Their eyes were also fixed on the approaching rider.

He entered the oasis and barely bothered to rein in his horse before dismounting. With an obvious urgency in his step, he approached Khamed and bowed. "*Sidi*, a courier has just arrived from one of the outlying camps. He is waiting to deliver a message."

Khamed felt a scowl descend across his face. A courier could be bringing news only of Gerard and the prisoner exchange. He uttered a few words of apology to Eudora and quickly mounted his horse.

As he rode back to camp with his man, his thoughts and emotions warred with one another like enemies on a field of battle. Torn between duty and responsbility to his people, and his own needs and desires, he had been struggling with a decision upon which the courier's news could have a profound effect.

Montar had been right. For him to keep Eudora against her will once the Frenchmen were ransomed would be an irresponsible endangerment to his people. If, as he feared, the courier did bring news of Gerard or the negotiations, he would soon be compelled to release her. The decision weighed heavily on his mind and heart, for he was painfully aware of how important she had become to him.

Eudora was necessary to him as no woman had ever been, filling a void in his life he had not known existed. For two months she had fought and defied him, obstinately refusing to succumb to his will, bending instead in a partial condescension which had only fueled his obsession. His need for her was like a hunger that mere physical possession could not sate. His soul yearned still for that which he could not take—that which only she could give.

He arrived at the camp to find the courier waiting outside his tent. Pulling a soiled piece of parchment from beneath his waistcloth, the man handed it to him and withdrew.

Khamed ripped open the sealed document and scanned the sheet quickly. It was merely an accounting of the booty seized in a raid upon a Tuareg caravan several days earlier. Relief flowed through him. He entered his tent and walked over to the desk, tossing the paper upon it in disinterest. He stripped off his heavy robes and laid them across the back of the chair. The sight of Eudora's shawl carelessly draped there drove home the painful realization that his decision had not been changed by the message, but merely delayed.

He fingered the black fringe of her garment in silent frustration.

The sound of the tent flap falling into place brought his head up. He turned, expecting to see Eudora. Instead he saw Saleena.

Her long lashes dropped and lifted in a coy visual

251

caress. "Khamed, I was looking for Montar." Her eyes swept the room in innocence. "Did he not return with you?"

Khamed turned his back to her and lit a cigarette. "I expect him soon."

"Would it be all right if I waited for him here?"

Khamed shrugged. Saleena was as transparent as glass. He had no doubt she had been watching from the doorway of her tent and had come running the moment she'd seen he was alone. Ignoring her, he sat down at the desk, took up the discarded message, and opened the ledger to transcribe the figures. "Saleena?"

"Yes?" Her voice jumped in anticipation.

"Do not enter my tent unannounced again."

Saleena glared at the broad back turned toward her. Khamed's harsh reprimand was like a slap in the face. And he had not even raised his eyes from the ledger to deliver it! Still, she knew her place too well to dare utter a word of protest.

For several minutes she flounced about the room. Periodically she cast a hopeful look in Khamed's direction. He never moved or gave any indiction he even knew she was in the same room. She found herself awash in memories of a year past, remembering the first time she had entered his tent. Although the room looked exactly as it had then, there seemed to be something very different about it now.

She dropped to the sofa and tried to identify the change which hung in the air like a subtle perfume. Suddenly and furiously she realized it was a perfume—*her* perfume! Once more her eyes scanned the room. This time she saw several details that had escaped her initially. Though minute, they were details that screamed of the Frenchwoman's presence.

Her heart ached as her gaze went to each one. A pair of women's gloves on top of the bookcase, two cups on the silver tray already laid out for tea on the brass table in the corner, a flowered shawl intimately draped with Khamed's own robes across the back of the chair where he sat. . . . They all seemed to mock her with their silent presence.

Yet the most glaring evidence of the woman's existence was the change in Khamed himself. With the exception of the day of her arrival, he had avoided and ignored her the entire month she had been in his camp. The few times he had been forced to speak to her, his words had been curt, his manner brusque. Even now, with the woman miles away in the desert with Montar, his back was purposely turned toward her.

Abandoning all pride, Saleena rose and went to him. She had always been able to arouse his desire. She bargained now on the powers of her seductiveness and his own lust. She encircled his neck with her arms and flicked her tongue at his ear.

"Let's go into the bedroom, my love." She slipped her hands beneath his shirt to snake down the muscled chest. "I am hungry for you," she purred.

He turned immediately and removed her hands from him. "I am not interested, Saleena."

"You used to be." Undaunted, she raked her fingers through his thick hair. "Have you forgotten how good it was between us?" She pouted seductively.

He stood, roughly putting her from him. "Between us there is nothing."

"Why? Because of *her?*" She threw herself at him and clutched the front of his shirt. "I know you, Khamed! Your passion burns as our desert sun. You need a woman who responds with equal fire. Your French whore is ice! She cannot possibly satisfy you as I can!"

Wanting desperately to prove her words, she stood on tiptoe and wrapped her arms around his neck. Pressing her body to his, she kissed him deeply. But unlike that afternoon a month ago, she sensed no response. This time she felt no arousal of his desire.

In defeat she backed away from him. "She has bewitched you!" she spat, her voice full of contempt.

"Your white whore has turned you into something less than a man!"

Khamed began to laugh softly.

His mocking arrogance unleashed within her the unequaled fury of a woman scorned and she plunged on recklessly. "Take heed, Khamed. Or you may soon find yourself guarding a harem—your manhood having disappeared along with your desire!"

His laughter died instantly, and his eyes narrowed. He grabbed her at the nape of her neck and dragged her back hard against him. "You are desperate, Saleena, to risk awakening the devil within me. Or did you hope," he hissed, his dark fury now matching hers, "that by comparing me to a eunuch I would be compelled to bed you in order to prove you wrong?"

Taking her right hand, he suddenly thrust it between their bodies, forcing her fingers to close around the bulge between his legs. "As you can feel, my manhood survives intact, Saleena. All that has disappeared is my desire for you!" Without warning he lowered his head. He kissed her savagely and cruelly, thrusting his tongue into her mouth to punish her, to humiliate her. Without passion, the intimate act was but a taunting gesture of his contempt.

Bright sunlight suddenly penetrated the room. Khamed raised his head and saw a slight figure framed in the doorway. Too late he pushed Saleena from him.

Eudora stood in stunned silence. Pain and anger flashed in her green eyes. He knew she had seen the kiss. She turned blindly and flung the flap aside.

A tall white-robed man standing in the doorway blocked her exit.

His own eyes wide in surprise and confusion, Montar caught her as she ran into him and stumbled backward. He held her arm firmly, thwarting her escape, and looked to Khamed for instructions.

Khamed shook his head. There was no need for words to pass between them. Montar escorted Eudora to the center of the room.

"Let me go!" Eudora gasped angrily, yanking her arm from Montar's grasp. She whirled to face Khamed. Though she held her tongue, her eyes glinted at him like green ice.

Khamed knew her too well not to know an outburst would soon follow. He had no desire that others should witness their private exchange. "Eudora, go into the bedroom."

Forced by her vow to obey him, Eudora walked stiffly to the dividing curtain. She tried to keep her back straight, her head high, but the fingers that untied the scarf knotted behind her neck trembled. She entered the bedroom and sat down on the bed. She felt lightheaded, and told herself the reaction came from the rush of anger and humiliation she had felt upon discovering Saleena in Khamed's arms.

Her eyes filled with tears. The love she felt for him could not temper her rage. It only magnified her pain. She had been a fool to listen to Sabatin. She meant nothing to Khamed. She was merely a plaything he could take or ignore at whim—or easily substitute with another.

Eudora wanted to cry or scream, but she was helpless to do anything other than suffer his rejection. She stood and looked around the small room that had been her prison—and her home—for more than two months. Even if she were to leave tomorrow no details of the room's appearance would ever be forgotten. They were etched forever in memory.

Suddenly the room began to swim before her. The heat and stifling air seemed to be choking the very breath from her. She felt herself falling, spiraling into a black abyss.

"Eudora!"

From far away she heard her name just as two strong hands wrenched her from the darkness. Focusing on the sharp cry which was like a bright light at the end of a dark tunnel, she opened her eyes and saw Khamed's face

255

before her. Instantly the humiliation, pain, and anger came flooding back.

"Are you finished?" she whispered weakly. She pulled away from his hold and staggered to the vanity. "Or did you want the bedroom?"

She felt another wave of dizziness sweep over her, and she swayed. Every breath was a shuddering effort as she fought for strength.

Instinctively Khamed reached out for her.

"No! Don't touch me!" She swayed again and feared she would yield to the nausea that racked her body.

He backed away from her slowly, cautiously staying within arm's reach. "Eudora, you need to sit down."

"I don't need anything . . . *you* need! You need a larger tent—one with a room for your harem. Of course, you would also then need a eunuch to guard it. That is how it's done, isn't it?"

She felt her strength return, and her attack became stronger and more vicious. She wanted to hurt him as he had hurt her. "Just out of curiosity, where do I go the next time you are amusing yourself with another? Am I supposed to watch? Or do you intend to send me to Montar, that he might bed me while you sleep with his sister?"

Her words, hurled like rocks, were unerring in their aim, and Khamed flinched as they found their intended target. Only his concern for her pallor and the glassy look still in her eyes kept his temper in check. "Eudora, stop it," he ordered between teeth clenched in restraint.

"Stop it? Stop what? I am only trying to work out the details. Now, tell me . . . is this to be an arrangement that alternates nightly—or do you prefer the same women in your bed for several nights in a row? Perhaps you simply toss a coin?" Lifting her chin, she met his icy gaze and plunged on carelessly. "Would I be overstepping my position if I insisted upon clean sheets—?"

"That is enough!" he thundered. His fingers gripped her arms violently until she winced from pain. "I owe you no explanations!"

Eudora shrank from him in fear.

Suddenly, understanding leaped across his face. His anger vanished. "You are jealous," he stated softly. Mockery danced in his eyes.

"Damn you!" she cried. She was helpless to stop the tears that began to spill down her cheeks. "I'll not be made part of your harem! I demand you release me!"

Smiling tightly, Khamed dropped his hands to his sides. "You forget yourself, little one. You are in no position to demand anything."

"I demand that you honor your word. You told me when you were tired of me I would be released."

He ran a thumb down the side of her face, tracing a course parallel to her tears. His touch was now so gentle and tender, she quivered.

"Eudora." He sighed wearily, as if in pain. "Do you still know so little of me?"

Hooking his thumb under her chin, he forced her to look at him. His dark eyes stared into hers as if he were trying to bridge their souls, that each could know what existed in the other. "I have taken no other woman," he said softly.

Eudora looked into his eyes and for a brief moment she thought she saw love—and then it was gone.

She could not know that in that moment her own soul was stripped naked. Khamed suddenly saw what she had kept hidden for so long. His own soul recognized it as what her surrender to him a month ago had lacked. It was that which he had been unable to take—that for which he ached. "Say it!" he demanded. He needed to hear the words.

Eudora felt herself slipping back into the abyss. His voice, his words—half plea, half command—were as a lifeline. Desperately she reached for it. "Yes. I love you!"

His mouth lowered to claim hers and she felt herself being lifted up out of the darkness. Clinging to him, she returned his kiss with a passion as fierce and intense as his own.

"God help me!" she cried softly, surrendering her heart to him. "I love you. I love you."

Khamed cupped her face in his large hands. The reed had broken, snapped in two. She now belonged to him completely.

Eudora tilted her head back to meet his gaze. His black eyes burned with hypnotic intensity. As if he were branding her his own, she felt the fire of his passion sear her very soul. Unable to look away, she mutely lowered and then lifted her lashes. In an unspoken, unquestioned understanding he had accepted her love. She now accepted his need, knowing the acceptance bonded them for time eternal.

In the weeks that followed Eudora lived only for the present. She shut her mind to logic and listened only to her heart. In Khamed's company, in his arms and in his bed, she found joy great enough to assuage her fears and doubts. She had a place in his life. She did not question why, nor did she delude herself with schoolgirl dreams of the future. To her mind's need to question, her heart replied: it is what it is. And what it was, she would savor.

All that marred her contentment was a continued uneasy feeling about her father she could not shake. Each night worry and uncertainty returned to haunt her. Often, as Khamed lay sleeping beside her, her dreams would suddenly and inexplicably turn to nightmares. She would wake and go out of the tent to stare up at the night sky. If her father was looking up at the same stars, she hoped she could somehow feel his presence across the vast sands and know he was well.

One night when she had done just that, Khamed awoke and instinctively reached for her. He found the bed beside him empty. He bolted upright, his eyes sweeping the room. As he pulled on a robe, he called out her name.

He heard no answer, and a fearful suspicion began to hammer in his chest. Had she broken her word to him and gone to see the Frenchman, or tried to escape?

He left the bedroom in a rage. He tore aside the flap and stopped. She was there under the awning, staring up at the indigo sky.

"Eudora?" He stepped noiselessly behind her, his hands coming to rest upon her shoulders. "What are you doing out here?"

Eudora leaned back against him. Even before she had heard his voice she had sensed his approach. Reveling in the warm security she experienced as his arms wrapped around her, she laid her head back against his chest. "I couldn't sleep. I was thinking about my father."

"Come inside," he ordered gently. With a hand at her waist he led her back into the tent and to the sofa.

She sat down, tucking her legs beneath her and watched as he went to the desk to light a cigarette. With a pang she realized how well she knew his habits. The peculiar way he always struck a match toward himself rather than away, the manner in which he cupped his hands around the flame as he brought it up to the cigarette between his lips . . . Each move was predictable, familiar, and dear. A wild desire seized her to tell him that she loved him. But as he approached her, she quickly fought back the words. His expression had changed. He was annoyed with her.

Inhaling deeply, he took up a stance before her. "Tell me about your father. Explain to me the reason for these fears you have for his safety which haunt your dreams." He exhaled, waiting for her reply.

Eudora lowered her gaze. How could she explain to him what she could not understand herself?

"I am wondering, little one, if it is not guilt which haunts you—guilt that you failed in your mission to stop him."

Her eyes flew up to stare at him. "How long have you known?"

259

"Almost from the beginning." He dropped down beside her. "I was curious as to your reason for traveling with the caravan. And . . ." He smiled and touched her cheek. "I needed to know if your absence would be noted."

Suddenly overwhelmed by the torment of the past months, she released a sobbing cry. "Then you understand as much as I! If something happens to him, it will be my fault." And yours, she wanted to add, but did not. A dark, unfathomable look had descended across his face. She knew he had guessed at her unspoken words. Her pulse began to beat erratically.

"If something happens to him it is the will of Allah! *Ah allé therkhél kâhl*—that is the way it is! You cannot feel responsible for his fate. It was his choice and his decision." He ground his cigarette out in the ashtray on the table. "Had you remained obedient and stayed in France, would he not be exactly where he is now?"

He rose to his feet and stared down at her. There had been no vestige of sympathy in his voice and his eyes were now cold. "You must learn, little one, to live your own life. And to let your father live his."

His words were nearly identical to those spoken by Sabatin in the hotel months before. Shaken by them, she sat in momentary silence. But her shock quickly yielded to anger. *"My life?"* she cried. "What life have you allowed me to live? I am a prisoner!"

He grabbed her arm and jerked her to her feet. A strange expression entered his eyes. "Do you want your freedom?"

Eudora stared up at him unable to answer.

"Do you want your freedom?" he repeated.

She felt the lean fingers which were gripping her arms tighten. His eyes bored into her demanding a response. She dropped her head in confusion. Would he indeed release her if she said "yes"? Or was he merely testing her? The question hardest to form in her mind was the one which was tearing at her heart. Was he finally offering her her freedom because he had grown tired of her?

"Decide, Eudora."

His steely voice cut through her frantic thoughts.

"Choose now! Do you stay with me of your own free will or shall I have you taken to Ghardaïa, where you can await your father's return?"

Tears welled in her eyes. Had her admission of love not been enough? Must she now prove it? Didn't he know that by forcing her to decide to stay with him willingly he was stripping away her last bit of pride?

Suddenly it didn't matter. It didn't matter whether she remained of his will or her own, so complete was his mastery of her heart.

"I want to stay," she answered softly. "For as long as you will have me."

Khamed released her and turned to hide the relief and joy he feared she would see in his eyes. As he began to walk away her soft whisper floated across the room to him.

"Why?"

Khamed froze.

"Why did you let me choose?"

He whirled to face her. He could not tear the answer from his throat. "How can you not know the answer?"

Suddenly he was standing before her.

"I want you, Eudora. I want you as I have never wanted a woman. But I must know that you are now with me because you choose to be." His arms encircled her, drawing her close in a tender embrace. "I need you," he murmured softly against her ear. "Let that be enough."

She leaned against him in aching confusion. No words of love nor vow of commitment had passed his lips, yet she was sure she had seen a look in his eyes which went beyond passion and physical desire. She was equally as sure it had to be only her own heart's longing she'd seen reflected. She buried her face against his chest.

It wasn't enough. But what choice did she have?

When Eudora awoke the next morning, Khamed was

already gone, leaving a message with Dahr-la that he would not return until evening. He left the message, too, that she should rest.

But in spite of having been awake most of the night, she wasn't tired. She sent Dahr-la to invite Sabatin to join her for breakfast. When he arrived she was already dressed and waiting for him. As he entered, she jumped to her feet to greet him. Suddenly the strength drained from her legs, and she swayed unsteadily.

Sabatin rushed to her side to catch her as she fell. "Eudora! Are you all right?" He set her gently upon the sofa.

"Yes, yes. I'm fine," she insisted weakly. She shook her head to bring the spinning room into focus. "I just became dizzy all of a sudden." She smiled in nervous embarrassment. She had been feeling lightheaded a lot lately. "I must have stood too quickly. It's this damned heat. It makes me feel so faint and weak sometimes."

She raised her head and laughed softly. Sabatin was studying her intently, a worried look on his face. "I'm sorry, Pierre, really I am! I didn't mean to frighten you so. You should see your face! You look as though *you're* about to faint!"

Sabatin felt his stomach twist into a knot of suspicion. He could think of only one reason why a healthy woman would suddenly grow faint.

"Have you eaten anything this morning?" He strove to keep his voice even.

"No, I was waiting for you." She gestured toward the tray before her laden with sweet cakes and fruit. "But frankly, I don't think I shall. My appetite seems to have left me." She smiled almost sheepishly. "It's probably just as well. My clothes are beginning to fit tightly, and I'm afraid Dahr-la's honey-and-date cakes and my own sweet tooth are to blame."

Sabatin fixed her with a penetrating gaze. "Your clothes are too tight?"

"Well, only a little. Around the waist," she hastened

to explain. "Really, Pierre! You are acting very strangely!"

"Eudora . . ." Sabatin considered his words carefully as he took her hand into his own. "Are you nauseated in the mornings?"

"No. Not at all," she replied. She pulled her hand from his clasp in annoyance. "What *is* wrong with you?"

Sabatin ignored her question and ran his fingers nervously through his hair. She still did not understand. Was it possible without a mother or sisters she did *not* know? If she was indeed so ignorant there was no way he could tactfully ask her his next question . . . but he had to ask it. "Eudora, when was the last time you had your monthly time?"

Eudora jumped to her feet, her eyes wide in shock. "That is none of your business!"

She was aghast at his question, and rightly so. Men did not ask women such things. Even a husband would not question his wife on such a delicate, private matter. He stood and grabbed her arm. "Eudora, please. I have seven sisters. I know the signs as well as any woman."

"Signs? What signs? What are you talking about?" Her voice was almost a shriek. She yanked her arm from his grasp. "I think maybe you had better leave."

"Eudora, listen to me. You're pregnant!"

Her face drained instantly of all color. "No. No!" She shook her head furiously. "That isn't possible!"

Sabatin pushed her down upon the sofa and moved aside the tea tray. Sitting on the inlaid table, he took both of her hands, leaned forward, and looked her squarely in the eye. "Think rationally for a moment. You have been with a healthy, obviously virile man for nearly three months."

He paused, noting the color returning to her face as she blushed at the blatant meaning of his words. "You are inexplicably faint, your waist is thickening, and your silence tells me that you have not menstruated recently. Eudora, you must know what all of this means.

You *are* pregnant!"

Eudora felt as if a cold blade had been run through her. Suddenly all the funny, queasy sensations she felt when she first rose in the morning made sense—the odd feeling she had been experiencing for several weeks now which she had simply attributed to the heat.

A mixture of joy and sorrow engulfed her. She was carrying Khamed's child! "Oh, my God!" she whispered. "Pierre, what am I going to do?"

"The first thing you must do is tell Khamed. You have to convince him to let you return to Ghardaïa, where there are doctors and a hospital. You can't carry a baby to term and deliver out here in the desert."

She listened to his words with half an ear. "Reguibat women have been having babies in the desert, without doctors and hospitals, for two thousand years," she replied matter-of-factly.

"My God, Eudora! Think about what you are saying!" Sabatin jumped to his feet. "Being a Reguibat's woman does not *make* you a Reguibat woman!" He began to pace in front of her. "You are not used to the heat, the hardships of desert life. What if there are complications? You could die!"

Sabatin saw the steadfast determination in her eyes and realized he was wasting his words.

"I still have time," she said quietly.

"Time for what? For him to grow tired of you?"

An expression of pure agony flashed in her eyes, and he instantly regretted his rash outburst. "Don't you understand?" he asked gently, wanting desperately to erase the pain his thoughtless words had wrought. "*This* may force him to release you!"

"Pierre, it is *you* who does not understand," she whispered. "Last night he offered me my freedom . . . and I chose to stay."

Sabatin felt as if she had struck him. "For God's sake, why?"

"Because I love him!" she cried helplessly. "Why are

264

you so shocked? A few weeks ago you told me to follow my heart!"

"A few weeks ago you didn't have a choice! A few weeks ago your life wasn't in danger! You told me yourself his own mother almost died in childbirth." He sat down once more and captured her small hand in his. "Eudora, I am only trying to save you from further heartache. This is your chance to make a clean break, to go back to your own world, to your own life."

"A clean break?" She cried out in despair. "Carrying his baby? An illegitimate child of mixed blood who would be ridiculed and outcast in 'my world' just as he was in his mother's! That is what you call saving me from heartache? You who once told me I had no life to return to. You now want me to return to it . . . to nothing? With a child who will remind me of what I once had until the day I die?"

"*Damn it!*" He swore helplessly and rose. He was angry at her, at himself, at Khamed—even at Allah—if, as Montar believed, *He* was responsible for the complicated course their lives had all taken.

As he thought of Montar, the words the marabout had spoken at the oasis came crowding back. Montar believed Khamed loved her. Was it possible? Was it possible she and the Reguibat sheik could have a life together?

"Pierre . . ." Eudora stood and touched his arm. "Please, try to understand."

Sabatin wrapped his arms around her in a comforting embrace. "I'm sorry. I had no right . . ." He felt her melt against him and he buried his face in her hair. "*Le coeur a ses raisons que la raison ne connâit point, ma belle.*"

The words he murmured were as much to comfort himself as they were to comfort her. He repeated them silently. *The heart has its reasons that reason knows nothing of.*

With one unanswered question remaining, he put her gently from him. "There's one thing I don't understand . . . if you love him enough to stay with him, why are you afraid to tell him about the baby?"

Eudora pulled away. "I'm not afraid. I'm just not ready yet."

She was lying. She was afraid, very afraid. A man who refused to live other than in a day-to-day acquiescence to his own passing fancies and changing moods would not want the ties and obligations a child would entail. Khamed would be bound to a woman he had taken in a moment of passion—a passion that by his own admission could be played out at any time.

"Eudora?" Sabatin's voice, now a hushed whisper, startled her out of her thoughts. "Is it because you are hoping he will return your love?"

Eudora's body was racked by a silent cry. Not even to Sabatin could she admit her heart's yearning.

"Eudora, if he loves you, a baby will not change that. You have to tell him."

"I know." She looked at him and forced a weak smile. "I promise I will tell him. But *after* I have sorted things out in my own mind."

Chapter Sixteen

Now painfully aware of her condition, Eudora went to great lengths to conceal it, afraid that each time Khamed looked at her he would notice her thickening figure and guess the truth.

But he didn't. For the past several days he'd seemed preoccupied . . . as did Dahr-la. In fact, the entire camp seemed gripped by the same air of excitement and anticipation.

Unable to contain her curiosity, Eudora finally questioned Dahr-la about it.

"We are preparing for Ramadan," the girl explained as she bustled about the bedroom. "The ninth month of the Moslem year is held sacred by us as the month in which the first revelation of the *Koran* was made to Mohammed. It is a time of feasting as well as fasting, of celebration and prayer."

"I didn't think the Reguibat set much store by religious rituals."

Dahr-la smiled. "We don't, usually. But the observance of Ramadan is one of the five pillars of Islam. Even the least devout among us keeps this ritual. Even my lord." She laughed as if she had suddenly thought of something amusing.

At the mention of Khamed's name, Eudora's pulse quickened. "Why do you laugh, Dahr-la?"

The girl cast a hurried look to the drape. "Because it is not my lord's favorite time of the year, my lady. You see, Ramadan lasts for twenty-nine days, and it is marked by daytime abstinence from food and drink, including water and tobacco." As she spoke her smile widened. "As well as other indulgences of the flesh."

Eudora fought to keep her expression from revealing the embarrassment she instantly felt at the reference to her intimate relationship with the girl's lord.

"This fasting lasts from sunrise to sundown," Dahr-la continued. "And though it is followed by nighttime indulgences, it is always a period of strain. Tempers are short, for work must be performed on empty stomachs, accompanied by great thirst."

Suddenly from outside the tent the sound of Khamed's voice could be heard. Raised in anger, it clearly signified a great displeasure with something or someone.

Dahr-la grimaced. "I think my lord is already dreading the minor incidents which will become major ones once Ramadan begins." She looked at Eudora as though to issue a gentle warning. "I fear his mood will not be improving."

In the week that followed, Dahr-la's words proved to be accurate. Khamed's mood did not improve. Riding with the hunting parties that would supply the fresh meat for the impending festivities, he was gone for days at a time. Even when he was in camp he often did not return to his tent until late into the night. He would fall into bed exhausted without so much as a word to Eudora.

On one hand, she relished the privacy. She did not have to hide her morning queasiness, or worry about her appearance. But the continual solitude was oppressive. Even Dahr-la stayed away now, involved with the other women in food preparation for the month-long feast. Finally, out of sheer loneliness, Eudora sent a message to Sabatin, asking that he join her for tea.

The minute he entered the tent, she regretted the invitation. She could tell by the look of determination gleaming in his eyes that he intended to broach the very subject she did not want to discuss.

"When are you going to tell him?" he demanded almost at once.

She ignored his question and settled down on the sofa, carefully arranging her skirts. "Good afternoon to you, too, Pierre."

"Eudora . . ."

She lifted her gaze and sighed. "I told you before, Pierre—I intend to tell him after I have sorted things out in my mind."

Sabatin glared at her. Her voice was steady, calm and detached. Too detached, he thought. "You are *not* dealing with this, Eudora!" In vexation he began to pace the room.

"I *am* dealing with it—in my own way."

Her protest caused him to whirl to face her. A layer of ice seemed to have glazed over her eyes. "No! No, you're not. Damn it, I know you too well. You are refusing to talk about it—to even think about it. You are simply pretending it does not exist!"

He crossed the room in heated strides and yanked her to her feet, forcing her hand to her belly. "There is a life growing here, Eudora! A child! Yours *and* Khamed's! You cannot continue to deny that knowledge to yourself any more than you can continue to withhold it from him. I will give you one more week. If you have not told him by then, *I shall!*"

Immediately Eudora's fragile veneer of control cracked. "No! You can't!" She clutched his arm, her eyes wide with fright—like those of a trapped animal. "Pierre, please, I beg you! Grant me a little more time. You don't understand."

"Eudora, it would only be until the baby is born. If you wanted to, you could come back."

"No." Eudora sank back down onto the sofa. "I can't ever come back. It's the only way I can keep my child."

"I don't understand, Eudora."

269

"Pierre, if the child I carry is a boy . . ." she placed her hand on her stomach ". . . and in my heart I know it is, we are talking about Khamed's heir and his people's future sheik. Do you really think if he knew I was pregnant, he would permit me to leave?"

She shook her head, the answer to her own question a pain-filled whisper. "No. Whether in my womb or in my arms, my child is his son. If I wanted to leave this desert I would have to do so alone—and I couldn't do that. I couldn't leave my child. I would have to stay."

Sabatin's mind reeled with confusion. "But I thought you had already decided to stay." He sat down weakly beside her.

"Yes!" she cried. "So long as he desired me, I would stay! Don't you see? I have been living without a future, trying to be content with what exists only now. But all this time I have known that when the day came that I was no longer necessary to him, I could leave. But now when that day comes, if I leave, I leave my child. And if I stay, do you know the kind of life I will have? Not only will I be discarded at his pleasure as I was once taken, I will be forced to watch as he turns his attentions to another."

Sabatin saw her eyes darken with pain. But when he reached out to comfort her, she pulled away.

"Do you know what that would do to me? To see the passion that now burns in his eyes for me burn for another? To know another sleeps in his arms while I sleep alone? As his son's mother I would never be allowed to pass from his possession. As long as I stayed I would be kept as in a harem, for no man's bed other than his own."

This time when he moved to comfort her, she yielded. He wrapped his arms around her and pressed her close. He could feel her pain as if it were his own. He knew that all she'd said was true.

"Do you understand now?" she asked, lifting her head from his chest. "Before Khamed learns the truth I must leave—but not yet. Please . . ." The tears she could hold back no longer began to fall. "I want just a little more

270

time with him."

Sabatin nodded mutely.

"And will you swear to me that you will not tell him?"

Again he nodded. With no words to offer her, he remained silent, holding her tightly and letting her weep freely.

After sundown he finally left her, curled on the sofa and asleep.

The soothing hum of whispering voices eased Eudora to consciousness. She opened her eyes to the soft light of a single lantern.

"Did we wake you?"

She sat up instantly at the sound of Khamed's low voice. His eyes, warm and golden in the dim light, swept over her with an almost gentle affection.

In her heart the agony of the decision she had made twisted like a knife. Forcing herself to return his gaze, she shook her head and smiled faintly. A sudden movement drew her attention to the man seated at his side.

Montar lumbered to his feet and looked down at Khamed. "Ramadan begins tomorrow," he decreed solemnly.

Belying his somber tone, Eudora noted a gleam of devilry flashing in his eyes. A second later a wide grin split the bearded face.

"Be sure, therefore, my friend, that you make love to your woman *before* the sun rises."

The teasing remark, which would normally have embarrassed Eudora, filled her with anguish. She pressed a hand to her aching heart and lowered her head as the man walked past. Khamed's response, a muttered oath in Berbish, mixed with the departing marabout's laughter to ring in her ears.

"Eudora."

She raised her head to meet Khamed's eyes. Smoldering with passion, they beckoned her. He held out his hand, and she wordlessly accepted it. The time had come; she had to tell him. But she couldn't force the words to form. Her steps as leaden as her heart, she allowed him to lead her into the bedroom.

Once inside the smaller room Khamed drew her close. With one hand at the nape of her neck his mouth lowered to hers. He tasted her hungrily, exploring the moist orifice as if for the first time. His other hand began a slow journey down her back, leaving a trail of opened buttons in its wake.

Weak and trembling, Eudora fought to regain her senses, to stave off the arousal of desire his touch was igniting. *Now!* her mind shouted. *Tell him now!*

But like an opiate, his desire had numbed her. She stood as in a trance unable to resist—until his fingers deftly slid the bodice of her gown to her waist.

"No!" She pushed herself from him and saw his eyes harden in response to her rebuff—a rebuff she knew he couldn't understand. "Please, I want to talk with you."

Khamed stared at her in silence. He was unable to tear his gaze from her. Her chest was heaving, straining the gossamer fabric of her chemise. Was it his imagination, or did her breasts not seem fuller, the valley between the lush curves deeper? Feeling his need surge like liquid fire in his loins, he reached for her, ignoring her entreaty.

"Khamed, please . . ."

"There will be time enough to talk later." He pulled her close. "Right now it is *not* conversation that I desire."

"Please," she implored softly.

Khamed dropped his hands to his sides and stepped back. "Talk." He made no effort to hide his displeasure, managing with the tone of his voice to make his concession sound like a command.

Eudora drew a shallow breath. The words she had practiced so often in her mind came slowly. "Several weeks ago you asked me if I wanted my freedom. I have been thinking about it, and I have decided it would be better if I *did* leave."

She squeezed her eyes shut to brace herself for his response. Thus she did not see the look of pain which flashed in his.

A heaviness centered in Khamed's chest. He hardened his heart, desperate to hide the hurt her words had induced. "*You* have decided?"

With a low, thunderous growl he lashed out with his words to inflict upon her a pain such as he was now feeling. "Your position does not grant you the right of decision. It is *I* who am master . . . *I* who decides if and when you leave—and I have decided *you stay!*"

He grabbed her and dragged her to him, wincing as he saw the pain in her eyes—the pain he had wanted to put there. Swearing in Arabic, he shoved her from him and wheeled toward the drape.

"Damn you." Eudora staggered after him. She took hold of his arm, forcing him to stop. But he would not turn to face her. "Are you really so cruel and unfeeling? You more than anyone should understand why I want to leave. I don't belong here! This is your world—not mine!"

Suddenly Khamed whirled. "And what of your declaration of love?"

His words seared her with agony. "Loving you is not enough," she whispered. It was the one truth in the web of lies she was clinging to, yet to say it tore her heart with guilt. "I need to be with my own kind. Please understand. Please let me go."

Khamed's hand shot out and he captured her chin. His cold, merciless stare wrapped around her like an icy embrace. "No, you understand, little one. What I have I keep!"

"Until you grow tired of it!"

"Until I no longer want it," he countered. He dropped his hand and turned to the curtain, then stopped. "There will be no food prepared after sunrise. If you are hungry, go to Kiri. She will see that you are fed. Pregnant and

273

nursing women are exempt from the fast."

Eudora froze, gasping in terror. Dear God, did he already know?

Khamed heard her sharp intake of breath. But he mistook it for confusion. "As well as nonbelievers." A heavy tone of sarcasm, his defense against emotion, rose in his voice. "While your 'cruel and unfeeling' captor does intend to keep you, he does not intend to starve you." Flinging aside the drape, he stormed from the room.

Eudora stumbled to the bed, collapsing upon it with a moan of anguish. Her fate was sealed. Soon Khamed would know she was carrying his child. But worse, he would know she had tried to deceive him.

She turned her face into the pillows and sobbed. In her attempt to avoid what she most feared, she had instead guaranteed it. Khamed's inexorable pride would never forgive her attempted deception. He would despise her for it and discard her in contempt, taking her baby and leaving her with nothing.

Yet against the waves of despair assailing her, one fragile hope remained: she still had time, she could still find a way to leave.

For hours she tossed and turned, her mind frantically searching for that escape. Just before dawn she fell into an exhausted sleep. When she awoke, the bedroom was warm with the heat of midday.

She opened her eyes with effort and sat up. The movement wrenched a cry from her lips. She pressed her palms to her throbbing temples and waited for the spinning sensation to pass. What she wouldn't give for a cup of tea! She started to call for Dahr-la, then remembered: the fast of Ramadan had begun. If she wanted anything to eat or drink, she would have to go to Kiri. She crawled from the bed and staggered to the vanity, stripping off the dressing gown she had tossed on over her chemise and petticoat the night before.

The sudden sight of her reflection brought a gasp of

horror. Staring at her from the looking glass was a woman she'd never seen. Pale and drawn, with dark smudges under eyes sunken and hollow, and framed by a mass of matted hair, the face was that of a stranger.

Damn him! And damn me for allowing him to do this to me! Her silent words roused her to action. Furiously she pulled a brush through the tangles and snarls, twisting the tamed waves into a loose chignon. Paints and powders erased the shadows and colored her cheeks and lips. Finally satisfied she had done the best she could, she stood and moved to the armoire to finish dressing. When she left the tent minutes later, the woman in the mirror was gone.

Standing in the doorway of her own tent, Saleena watched as Eudora crossed the compound. Hatred for the woman welled within her. Because of her she had fallen from Khamed's favor—shamelessly humbling herself only to be degraded by his rejection.

"But do not think you have won, white witch," she hissed through bared teeth. "As I have known humiliation, so shall you! Soon Khamed will see you for what you are, and after he casts you aside he will come back to me. It will be again as it was, and as it was meant to be!"

In spite of their vehemence Saleena's words gave her no comfort. A strategy to discredit her rival in Khamed's eyes had eluded her. She knew only that it had to be a plan which involved betrayal—for it was of that which Khamed was most intolerant.

From his men as well as from his women, he demanded absolute obedience, fidelity, and truth. An act of treachery would surely break the spell the Frenchwoman had cast upon him.

But despite weeks of watching Eudora's every movement, Saleena had seen nothing in her behavior that had the potential of being viewed as disloyal—with the possible exception of her occasional visits with the

Frenchman Sabatin.

Indeed, it would have been ideal were the woman to betray Khamed with her countryman. It was, however, well known in the camp that the reporter sought and obtained his physical pleasures from Dahr-la's cousin.

Thinking of the plump girl, Saleena sniffed in disdain. What the man could see in Salwa was a mystery! Still, that he was quite taken with her was evident to all, and it eliminated him from consideration. The only other man Eudora had any contact with was Montar. Concocted gossip of an affair between them would never be believed. Even if she were foolish enough to seek his attentions, Montar would never touch her.

No, Saleena reasoned silently, the Frenchwoman's betrayal had to be of a different sort. But what? She balled her fists in frustration. With each day that passed, the witch's hold on Khamed strengthened. If she did not soon think of a plausible plan, he would be lost to her forever. She looked across the compound to locate Eudora. Realizing she was headed for Kahlil's tent, Saleena turned to reenter her own.

As she did so, she caught sight of a man staring at her from beneath the awning of a small tent along the camp's rim. She tilted her head and squinted into the bright sunlight. Though she had heard the stories of Khamed's mad captive she had never seen him. But even at a distance it was obvious the rumors were not unfounded. The man was filthy and clad in rags. She watched in morbid fascination as he stepped from beneath the awning and proceeded to urinate against the tent wall.

His guard appeared to be watching him as well. Warily he shifted the rifle slung from his shoulder to his hands.

Saleena shuddered in a mixture of disgust and fear. It was no wonder that within the last few days the captive's own countryman had requested and received separate quarters! And while she hardly agreed with Khamed's lenient treatment of Sabatin, she had to admit that his orders concerning du Bois were at least wise. The man

276

was kept under constant armed guard.

She was about to forget the mad Frenchman when a thought crossed her mind, quickly followed by another, and yet another. Saleena laughed aloud. At long last it had come to her. The plan formulating in her mind was flawless!

As she watched du Bois disappear into his tent, her lips curved in a complacent and wicked grin. "And you, my dear mad lieutenant, shall be the principal player!"

At the opposite end of the camp, unaware that she was being watched, Eudora hesitantly entered Kahlil's tent. Though custom dictated the seclusion of both mother and newborn for forty days, with visits permitted by family members only, she had been allowed to visit Kiri on several occasions since Mohmet's birth. Still, she had always been accompanied by Dahr-la. She wasn't sure now if she would be welcomed alone.

The young woman's warm smile swept away her uneasiness at once. *"Imr'ati!* How wonderful! Enter, please. You have arrived just in time to share our midday meal." She gestured to a small form lying on a mat in the corner of the tent. "Come." She patted the cushion beside her. "While my son sleeps we will eat."

Eudora knew an exchange of food and drink was essential to Arab hospitality, still she had a gnawing suspicion that Kiri had been warned to expect her. She shook her head. Khamed's behavior made no sense. Why should he care if she ate or not?

"My lady, please . . ." Kiri smiled and patted the cushion again. As Eudora settled beside her, she moved the bowl on the low wooden table before her closer.

Eudora glanced at its contents and smiled weakly. At the smell of the rich meat dish her stomach had begun to stir. Now that she could actually see the pieces of greasy mutton swimming in the thick sauce, it churned. Though refusal of offered food was considered an insult, she couldn't bring herself to dip her fingers into the bowl. "Perhaps a cup of tea first?"

"Of course." Kiri jumped to her feet. Quickly she disappeared into the room's small annex, which was open to the sky to permit cooking.

Anxious to distance herself from the smells emanating from the bowl, Eudora rose and went to the corner where the baby slept. She knelt by the infant and touched his tiny foot, marveling at the perfectly formed miniature. Her heart gave a sudden tug. She pushed the surging emotions aside and shifted her attention to the swarm of flies that seemed to be engulfing the small child.

Her stomach lurched at the sight. Futilely she tried to wave the black mass off the baby. Hearing Kiri re-enter, she looked at her over her shoulder. "Kiri, perhaps I could find you a basket for Mohmet to sleep in. Then netting could be placed over it."

"Whatever for, my lady?" Though her tone was polite, it was quite clear that she found Eudora's suggestion to be strange indeed. "A baby sleeps on a mat at its mother's side."

"Yes . . . but what of the flies?" Eudora left the sleeping infant, returning to the low table as she continued her explanation. "Netting draped over a basket would keep them away."

Kiri shrugged. Sitting down in front of the table, she began to prepare the tea. "Flies are a way of life in the desert, my lady. As infants we learn to accept their presence. As you can see, he sleeps peacefully."

"Yes, of course," Eudora murmured. She realized that with the characteristic stoicism of her people, Kiri accepted the harshness of her life—and her son's—with a resultant belief in survival of the fittest. If a child were to succumb to a few flies, what chance could he have in the face of greater dangers?

With a fierceness that amazed her, she silently resolved that the child growing within her would not be subjected to such an existence.

"Is Kahlil still delighted with his son?" she asked, striving to change the subject. "Or has some of the excitement of new fatherhood passed?"

Kiri's smile brightened the small, dim space like the desert sun. "His delight grows each day, for my husband now looks forward to the future, anticipating all that he will teach his son. He has always believed that a man who has failed to sire an heir is a man who has failed to be a man."

She glanced quickly toward the doorway and cautiously lowered her voice. "Why, he *even* told our lord as much!"

Eudora's breath caught in her throat, and she had to concentrate to keep her voice steady. "And what was his—Khamed's—reaction to such a statement?"

"My husband did not share his reply with me." Kiri giggled. "But I am sure he was not pleased to hear such a disparagement of his manhood. Our lord obviously has no desire to beget an heir. By choice he has taken no wife, preferring instead to satisfy his needs with—"

At once her voice died. Kiri looked at Eudora in open-mouthed horror. Two circles of red stained her plump cheeks. "I'm sorry, my lady! I did not mean to say—to imply—*Hamdullah!* Forgive me!"

Eudora kept her expression devoid of any emotion. "It's all right, Kiri. I understand my position very well."

At that moment Mohmet awoke, loudly proclaiming his desire to be fed.

"My son possesses his father's patience!" Kiri laughed nervously. Clearly grateful for the interruption, she scrambled to her feet and dashed to the corner. She returned almost at once with the squalling infant cradled in her arms. Cooing softly to him, she sat down, loosening and rearranging her clothing to bare a breast.

Fascinated, Eudora watched the baby turn his head to his mother, instinctively rooting for her nipple. Kiri eased the dark circle and its protruding nub into his mouth. Immediately his jaws began to move, his eyes closing in contentment.

To Eudora's amazement he then smiled, all the while

holding the nipple in his mouth. Again she felt a tug at her heart.

Eudora spent the better part of the afternoon with Kiri. Cautious not to arouse suspicion, she questioned her about the baby and its care. She desperately wanted to confide in the young mother, to ask her the many questions she had concerning the changes occurring within her own body. But she did not. The risk that Khamed would learn of her condition was just too great.

Finally, as sunset approached, she left Kiri and returned to her tent. She selected a book and settled down on the sofa. In spite of the afternoon heat, she read but a few pages before falling asleep.

When she awoke, it was to darkness and a wild throbbing in her head. Confused and disoriented, she found it took a few moments to realize the throbbing was actually the sound of beating drums outside the tent. The celebration of Ramadan had begun.

Eudora stood and slowly walked to the doorway. The drumbeats became louder and more frenzied. As if to answer them, the blood began to pound in her ears. Suddenly, like the savage cry of a wild beast, a chorus of voices joined in. With no beginning and no end, the half-human, half-animal cry set her flesh crawling. Each nerve felt as if it were on fire.

She clasped her hands over her ears to muffle the sound. Bespeaking a life of sorrow, of a people who had lived too long with pain, the wailing was an unbearable embodiment of utter misery and grief. It triggered her own anguish, and in tears she retreated to the room's center.

It seemed like only seconds later that Dahr-la burst into the tent. Her face was flushed, her eyes bright with excitement.

"My lady, are you not going to join the celebration?"

"No, thank you, Dahr-la."

"But why not? The dancing will start soon, and the food is already being served. There is lamb—roasted whole, head and all—and gazelle. Hunted only hours ago, it was skinned and cleaned and put upon the fire before its flesh even cooled. It is so tender it pulls apart in one's fingers, and it has a flavor such as you have never tasted!"

Eudora felt her stomach rise at the girl's description of the meat's preparation. "No . . . I don't think so, Dahr-la." She gasped for a desperately needed breath. "I would feel out of place. But you go. Enjoy yourself."

Dahr-la gave her a puzzled look, but pressed her no further. Shrugging, she left the tent to rejoin the festivities.

The sounds of the desert people's unbridled pursuit of pleasure—in the name of praising their God—continued until late into the night. Just before dawn, as the last meal was being served, Eudora heard Khamed return to the tent.

She tensed, waiting for him to enter the bedroom. She heard him pacing, the occasional strike of a match and the swish of the tent flap at least a dozen times. But he remained in the outer room.

She wept in silent agony. His cold indifference was far more brutal and frightening than his fiery rage. That he could—and would—keep her against her will without even wanting her, reinforced in her mind and heart all that she had told Sabatin.

For the next three days their routine remained unchanged.

Eudora visited Kiri daily, taking her meals with her. But once the sun had set, she remained in self-imposed seclusion in the tent.

Khamed continued to avoid her, returning to his tent in the early hours of the morning. Only once did he lie beside her. He didn't touch her or make any effort to speak to her. Before dawn he was gone.

By the fourth day Eudora felt as if she were going mad. The sanctuary of the tent had become a stifling confinement.

281

That evening, when the drums began their nightly ritual of frenzied beating, she ventured out of the tent to stand under the awning. She listened to the double-headed instruments Kiri had told her were called *tobra*, and the *ardeen*—small upright harps with ten strings.

Suddenly a tall white figure materialized out of the darkness.

"Your absence has been most conspicuous, Mademoiselle." Montar bowed deeply and stepped forward.

"I have not been feeling well." Her feeble excuse was no lie. In recent days she'd been plagued with bouts of morning sickness which had left her so weak she could barely stand.

Montar raised an eyebrow, but if he intended any further expression of curiosity he quickly suppressed it. "No matter." He smiled warmly. "It only makes your presence tonight more welcome."

Eudora returned his smile and took the arm he gallantly offered. Weary of her self-imposed isolation, she welcomed his company and allowed him to lead her to a large fire at the center of the compound. All around her she saw men, women, and children feasting on delicacies designed to delight the palate. Their other senses were equally indulged by the sights, sounds, and smells of the celebration.

"Tell me what the songs are about," she said suddenly, again moved by the savage music and haunting cries.

"They are songs of life and death, Mademoiselle. And of the acceptance of Allah's will. As Islamic tradition and belief do not allow for the making of graven images, we worship our God with words—with these simple and primal poems."

He paused as an old man's plaintive voice rose above the chorus.

Eudora pointed to the man, a dark silhouette in the firelight. "Can you translate his words for me?"

Reluctant to break the spell he was creating, she still felt an urgent need to understand his song.

"He sings of losses suffered," Montar replied. "Of drought, famine, and death. Yet as a follower of Islam, he will accept the destruction as sent by Allah, to rise to sing again—this time of His mercy. For with each sorrow comes joy, with every failure, success. He knows that the increases of his flocks, the births of his children, the beauty he sees around him are all given to him by Allah as constant reminders of His benevolence."

He paused to allow her to hear the old man's words without interruption, and then continued. "First he will sing of the brutal force of the Saharan *ghibli*—the sandstorm. Then he will laud the grace of Allah who sends the cooling wind from the north. It is a wind which 'draws up from the earth the shrubs upon which his flocks feed, a life-giving wind which makes him virile, his woman fertile—his child to grow within her womb.'"

Unconsciously, Eudora's hand slipped to her belly. "His child to grow within her womb," she repeated softly, unaware of the tears that slowly rolled down her cheeks.

"Mademoiselle?" Montar looked at her questioningly.

At that moment Khamed stepped from the shadows.

Eudora watched his approach. The anger in his stride was unmistakable. She shrank against Montar.

"Come with me," he ordered sharply. Ignoring Montar's presence, he grabbed her arm and unceremoniously yanked her from his side.

The blood pounded in Eudora's ears, drowning out all sounds of the celebration.

Roughly Khamed guided her through the crowds to the doorway of his tent. Tearing the flap open he then stepped aside to allow her to enter before him. Only when they were both inside did he speak.

"This deception ends now!"

Chapter Seventeen

Eudora's mind exploded with panic. "What deception?" she gasped.

"This deception of denial—yours *and* mind!" He seized her wrist, his fingers closing like talons around it as he pulled her to him. "You may be able to deny the love you have professed, but *I* will deny my need no longer. If that means I must again take that which should be given, I will do so!"

Eudora looked up into his face. Like a mask of bronze, it was cold and hard, set with determination. She trembled with conflicting emotions. Her heart ached with love, her body with need, and her mind with fear and confusion.

Suddenly she saw the fury rise in his eyes and knew he had taken her silence as disavowal.

"So be it!" he growled. Kissing her savagely, he swept her up into his arms and carried her into the bedroom.

The small room spun around her as she felt herself being lowered onto the bed. His mouth recaptured hers. And though she was sure it was done more to still any protest than to initiate desire, his kiss set off a maelstrom of sensations. For pride's sake she wanted to struggle. But the swirling heat deep within her compelled her to yield.

Before she could decide, Khamed made the decision

for her. She felt his hands beneath her skirts an instant before his entry, swift and complete. She cried out at that particular pairing of pain and pleasure.

Her cry was lost in his own moan of desperation. Driven by instinct and emotion, Khamed plunged into her again.

Driven by the same forces, Eudora responded. She clasped her arms around his neck and lifted her hips, her need to have him as great as his to take her.

Her outcry of fulfillment was followed a moment later by Khamed's.

That he did not immediately withdraw confused Eudora. She opened her eyes to find him staring down at her.

"There is more than what you have told me," he stated quietly. As if to find the truth he knew her lips would not speak, his eyes bored into her. "Can you feel me inside you?"

She nodded, not trusting her voice.

"As can I you. Shall I tell you how you feel? You are warm and moist, swollen to hold me . . . wanting me."

He moved just an inch, and she instinctively rose up to keep him imprisoned.

He smiled tightly. "As I told you once before, little one . . . your body does not lie. It still molds to mine in hunger."

Eudora closed her eyes to shut out the sight of his face. Would that she could shut out the sound of his voice! Soft and gentle, it was merciless in its persistence, in its veracity.

"Eudora, what are you withholding from me? Why do you *really* want to leave?"

"It is as I told you," she whispered. She opened her eyes and blinked back her tears. "I do not belong here with you. I belong with my own kind in my own world—a world to which I will return when your desire for me has passed. Don't you understand that the longer I stay, the harder that will be? I *must* think of the future, and with

286

you I have none!"

For a moment he stared at her in silence. "This is what it is about?" he finally asked in disbelief. "That I have made no commitment, spoken no words of promise—which once formed will cease to exist?" He moved off her abruptly and sat on the edge of the bed. "It is actions you should heed, little one. Not promises that are broken and forgotten, freely tossed away as easily as the wind blows the desert sands."

The bitter anger creeping into his voice was unmistakable. "A month ago I made no such pledge, yet then you were content in the knowledge of my need. Why does that same need not satisfy you now?"

Eudora knew her feeble half-truths had awakened his displeasure. She so feared the return of his cold indifference she considered telling him the entire truth. But the image looming in her mind of a lifetime lived as the past few days had been swept away her indecision.

She shook her head weakly. "I cannot explain it. It is simply how I feel."

Suddenly Khamed gripped her arms tightly, pulling her to a sitting position. "Do you love me?" he demanded.

Lost in his relentless black stare, which accorded her no escape, she reaffirmed the one truth she could neither deny nor disguise.

"Yes."

"Then we will speak no more of this!"

Eudora nodded in silent assent. Yes . . . tonight she would agree to anything he demanded. She had to end the conversation before Khamed's floundering suspicions found a footing. But tomorrow . . . tomorrow she would talk to Sabatin and ask for his help.

The next morning she rose immediately after Khamed left. She dressed quickly and headed for the horse corrals, where she knew Sabatin spent almost every morning, watching as the Reguibat worked their magnificent animals during the cool hours of early day.

287

This morning was no exception. As she neared the corrals, she spotted his orange *shesh* among those of the men gathered there.

Leaning on a crossbar, he pushed away from it at her approach. "Eudora! What are you doing up and about so early?"

"I need to talk to you, Pierre." She cast a cautious glance about her, and the tribesmen who had been standing within listening distance respectfully withdrew.

Her actions were not lost on Sabatin. He raised an eyebrow. "About what?"

"Several nights ago I asked Khamed to release me, and he refused."

"Does that surprise you?"

"No." Eudora dropped her head. It hadn't, really. She'd known deep inside what his answer would be. "But I had hoped," she whispered more in answer to herself than to the man standing at her side. She lifted her chin. "Pierre, I must devise a plan to leave here. Will you help me?"

"Eudora, you know I would do anything I could. But frankly, I don't believe a way exists—"

"There has to be!"

"To be what, Mademoiselle?"

Eudora whirled, her vision blurring with panic.

Montar stood behind her, his head cocked in curiosity. "There has to be what?" he repeated.

Eudora's mind froze. What and how much had the marabout overheard?

"A way to deal with this infernal heat!" Sabatin grinned and brought the end of his *shesh* up to his brow. "With the hottest part of the year approaching, I keep telling her she should shed a few layers of modesty in favor of comfort."

Eudora watched as an amused smile appeared on Montar's face. She cast Sabatin a look of gratitude and quickly joined the ruse. "Really Pierre, you can't expect me to run about half-clothed!"

288

Montar laughed. *"That* would not be necessary!" Skeptically, he eyed the form-fitting gown the woman wore. Clinging to every curve, its only looseness came below the knee as it flared to the ground. He returned his gaze to her face. "Monsieur Sabatin is not entirely wrong, Mademoiselle. Clothing should be worn loose and in layers to allow for free circulation of air. If it is comfort that you seek, perhaps you should consider adopting our women's manner of dress."

"There, see! I told you, Eudora! I told you you should follow my example." Sabatin flung out his arms and turned, proudly modeling his own attire.

Eudora broke into a smile. "Very well, gentlemen. I concede. When next you see me, I may very well be dressed as a native! Now, if you both will excuse me . . . I did promise to visit Kiri this morning."

Montar kept his eyes on her as she walked away. The light note upon which their conversation had ended did not mesh with the anxious, serious tones of the one he had interrupted. He turned his attention and his suspicions to the Frenchman. "Is she all right?"

Unwaveringly Sabatin returned his stare. "She's fine," he replied. "Just bothered by the heat." With a languid shrug he focused his gaze on the horses in the corral.

Eudora walked swiftly across the compound. In spite of the warming temperature she shivered. Thank God for Sabatin's quick thinking! His lie about the heat had apparently satisfied Montar's curiosity.

She sighed in relief and slowed her pace. Suddenly she had the distinct feeling she was being watched. She looked from side to side, but could see no one. The episode with Montar had rattled her more than she'd thought. In spite of her rationalization, the feeling did not subside. She wrapped her shawl tighter about her shoulders and quickened her step.

Eyes narrowed, Saleena dropped the tent flap. As she turned, her gaze fell upon a darkened corner of the room.

She brightened instantly.

Concealed there were the waterskins and foodstuffs she'd collected over the past days. Pilfered in small amounts from tents neighboring Khamed's, the supplies were a small but integral component of her plan—a plan she would soon set into motion.

And it had been so easy! With Ramadan's nightly celebrations attracting every man, woman, and child in the camp, she had been able to search the tents with ease. She'd found everything she'd needed—even a gun.

Initially, she had feared its acquisition would be difficult. Simply taking one of Montar's guns would have provided an all-too-obvious link to herself. Besides, for her plan to succeed, it was imperative that the weapon come from a source reasonably accessible to the Frenchwoman. One of Khamed's would have been ideal. Yet that was impossible. Saleena knew he kept his firearms locked in the chest in the main room, and the only key was always kept on his person.

But last night while searching the tent next to Khamed's she'd happened upon a loaded revolver carelessly left in a bedroll. Convinced her good fortune was a sign of Allah's approval, she'd taken the gun, which now lay concealed with the other supplies.

Resisting the urge to go to the corner, she forced herself to lie down. Montar would be returning soon from his morning prayers. He knew she rarely rose before midday, and she must not let anything in her behavior appear out of the ordinary. Not now, when she was so close. . . .

More than an hour passed before Saleena finally heard Montar's return. Grumbling to himself, he swept into the tent.

"Must you make so much noise?" She rose up on an elbow and feigned a yawn.

"It is time you woke."

His voice carried an uncharacteristic sharpness, and she immediately assumed a wounded pout.

"I'm sorry. I did not mean to snap." Montar threw off his robes and dropped down beside her. Smiling with brotherly affection, he reached out to tweak her braid. "His black mood must be contagious!"

Saleena forced a blank expression. "Whose?"

"Khamed's." Montar shook his head. "Ramadan has but started, yet already his patience is nearly exhausted. Every day some minor skirmish or petty problem seems to set him off. Just now he was ranting about a report of thefts."

Saleena felt as if her heart would jump from her chest. "What kind of thefts?"

Montar shrugged. "Foodstuffs. A *guerba* or two."

"But that is not unusual—not during Ramadan." Fervently Saleena prayed her voice reflected none of the alarm she was feeling.

"As I tried to tell him. The culprit is likely some poor soul unable to endure the fourteen-hour fast. But what has Khamed especially concerned is the theft of a revolver—at least, its owner claims it has been stolen. I think the fool merely misplaced it or lost it gambling and is now too embarrassed to admit it."

"I'm sure it will be found." Saleena smiled. Beneath her outward calm her thoughts were racing. She'd wanted to wait before implementing her plan, to choose a night when Khamed's mood was especially foul. From what Montar had just told her, that night had come. Tonight, when the camp was lost in the throes of celebration, she would set her plan into action.

Amazingly, the day passed quickly. But once the sun set, the hours dragged. With a heart-pounding nervousness that only grew stronger, Saleena forced herself to wait.

Finally, when it was quite dark, when she knew spirits were most high and others' vigilance most lax, she brought the stolen supplies and waterskins from her tent to the edge of the oasis. She concealed them between several large rocks and then walked to the horse corrals.

291

For the past two nights she had made the same trek and had found the fringes of the camp deserted. This night was no different.

She quickly rounded up three mares and led them to the belt of palms. The superbly trained animals uttered no sound as she loaded them with the supplies.

With the first phase completed and the horses safely tethered, Saleena returned to the center of the compound. She knew Khamed was with Montar and Kahlil, involved in a heated game of chance. Before she began the second stage, she had to make certain Eudora was also engaged and not in Khamed's tent.

From the shadows she searched the crowd gathered around the huge fires and spotted Eudora talking with Dahr-la and her mother. Confident the woman was sufficiently preoccupied, she made her way to Khamed's tent, slipped inside, and headed for the armoire in the bedroom.

She pushed several garments to one side. She had to find just the right one—one bright enough in color to attract attention. A yellow gown caught her eye and she reached for it. At the same time her gaze swept the room for a head covering. Draped across the top of the dresser she spied the black and red shawl which had graced Khamed's chair on her last visit.

The pain of his rejection that afternoon flooded back, and she shut her eyes with a whimper . . . yet she did not blame him. The disgust and contempt that had bathed her in shame had not been of his doing. As surely as if he'd drunk poison, he'd been envenomed by his white whore. Once she was exposed he would see everything in a new light.

With that belief firm in her heart, Saleena snatched up the shawl and rolled it with the dress into a tight ball. Hugging the bundle to her breast, she bolted from the tent. Though her pulse raced with fear that she had been seen, the revelers paid her no heed as she passed through their ranks.

Heady with anticipation, she burst into her own tent. Going to the corner to retrieve the gun still hidden there gave her a much needed moment to catch her breath and collect her thoughts. In her mind she had planned and performed each movement until it was rote.

Mindful of the long earrings she wore, which often caught and tangled when she dressed, she gingerly pulled the gown over her head. The added bulk of her own clothing beneath the snug-fitting gown hampered her movements, causing her to don the shawl clumsily. Feeling a painful tug on her earlobe, she swore in annoyance. Impatiently she freed the earring twisted in the shawl's fringe and tossed her head. The familiar clinking sound and feel of cold silver caressing her neck assured her the earring was still in place. She carefully redraped the shawl and then picked up the revolver.

With the gun concealed beneath the wrap, she stepped to the doorway and cautiously pulled aside the flap. Across the compound she saw Eudora disappear into Khamed's tent.

At once a wave of elation enveloped her. Surely Allah was smiling down upon her, for it was just as she had planned! Following her usual routine, the Frenchwoman was retiring for the night—alone.

Saleena lifted her eyes in thanksgiving. With His blessing she could not fail! She wrapped the shawl across her face and exited, making her way quickly to a group of children playing in the flickering light of a small fire. Staying in the shadows she gestured to a tall, curly-headed boy.

Wide-eyed with curiosity, he approached her.

"Do you know the Frenchman Sabatin?"

Her carefully phrased question elicited a look of confusion. She was sure her French was good enough to fool the youngster. Then she realized—he did not understand French! Swallowing back her anxiety, she repeated the question in Arabic, taking care to speak slowly and haltingly as might one who did not know the language.

This time he smiled and nodded.

"Can you find him and tell him Eudora wants to talk to him by the lieutenant's tent?"

The boy's face lit with pleasure, and Saleena sighed in relief. With his child's logic all he had heard in her request was cause for delight—delight that he had been singled out by his lord's woman for what he viewed as an honor. Anxious to serve, he scampered off to deliver the message, and she withdrew.

A few minutes later a lone figure left the camp's center. Sabatin crossed the compound, a single thought on his mind: why would Eudora want to meet him by du Bois's tent? To his knowledge she'd had no contact with the man since the day he had attacked her. There had to be a mistake. Yet Salwa had been adamant about the details of the boy's message, insisting she'd translated it correctly.

Sabatin shook his head. If the boy had misunderstood Eudora, he would know soon enough. Du Bois's tent lay just ahead. With two torches illuminating its front, he could see a man and a woman standing and talking just beyond the awning. The man was obviously du Bois, and even from this distance Sabatin recognized the black and red patterned shawl the woman wore. Out of habit he looked about to locate the guard.

Sitting on the ground and flirting with a young girl who had apparently brought him food and drink, the man only occasionally glanced over his shoulder in the direction of the couple.

Sabatin's confusion mounted. He had truly believed the boy's message was in error. Why would Eudora reestablish contact with du Bois? As he approached, he saw her suddenly hand something to him.

Sabatin recognized the object, and a feeling of unreality instantly descended. As if what was happening were a dream, he then saw her take du Bois's arm. Together she and the man began to run from the tent.

Without realizing it was his, Sabatin heard a shout. In the next instant he, too, was running, following the couple toward the trees.

He watched in horror as du Bois stopped and wheeled, raising his arm. He saw the muzzle flash and heard the gun discharge. Then the ground heaved under his feet.

He tried to rise and felt the unmistakable cold steel of a rifle barrel pressed to the base of his skull, forcing his face into the sand. He lay there helpless. From all directions he heard shots and shouting, the sound of men running.

Suddenly he was grasped by the arms and abruptly jerked to his feet. As two men held him fast, a third bound him. His eyes frantically searched the darkness. In the distance he could see du Bois struggling in the grasp of his own captors. But the woman who had been with him only a moment earlier had vanished.

Now a spectator, Sabatin watched as more men appeared, Khamed and Montar among them. A rapid exchange of Arabic ensued. Khamed knelt by the still form of the guard. Lighted by the torches, his face contorted with rage and he stood. He ordered several of his men back to the center of the camp. Gesturing for the others to follow, he then headed toward the oasis' edge. In seconds the palms were alive with white-robed figures.

Responding to some signal, the men on either side of Sabatin shoved him forward. Within minutes he was lying on his face again, thrown onto the sand floor of his own tent. He could only assume du Bois was receiving the same treatment.

He struggled to sit up, and for the first time he became aware of pain. His head pounded from the crashing blow, which had knocked him to the ground. He forced himself to fight the dizziness waiting to engulf him in darkness.

After what seemed like an eternity, he heard the tent flap lift. He raised his head and saw Montar enter. In the marabout's eyes there burned a rage which

295

rivaled Khamed's.

"You are in a great deal of trouble, Monsieur."

Sabatin had to swallow before he could answer. Even so, his voice cracked. "I don't know what you are talking about."

"There is very little point in denial," Montar replied coldly. He stepped into his view. "Your friends have been captured and your horses found. Would you propose to tell me that the three of you were merely planning a midnight ride?" Angrily he stepped closer. "This escape attempt of yours—"

"Escape attempt? I know nothing of an escape attempt!" Even as his lips shouted the words of denial, his mind filled with the terrible truth. Dear God, he *was* responsible. Eudora had come to him for help. When he had offered her none, she had turned to du Bois!

"I don't believe you, Monsieur." Montar's voice cut into his frantic thoughts. "But at the moment, that doesn't really matter. Luckily for you, before the guard died he identified the man who shot him as du Bois. He also identified Eudora. Right now Khamed is questioning du Bois. If the gun he used was in fact given to him by her . . ." Montar's eyes softened with sorrow. "Monsieur, it is bad enough Khamed knows she has betrayed him. But do you know what he will do to her if he learns she is responsible for the death of one of his men? If there is anything at all that you can tell me about tonight, I suggest you do so."

Sabatin shook his head. "I knew nothing of their plans. But I did know she wanted to leave. She was desperate to get away before Khamed found out—" Suddenly he remembered the promise he had made to her.

"Before Khamed found *what* out?" Montar demanded.

Sabatin shut his eyes in anguish. No matter what he said, she would suffer. How could he decide her fate? Montar's words rose in his mind. *Do you know what he will do to her?* His hesitancy vanished. He opened his eyes, meeting Montar's gaze without wavering.

"She's pregnant."

Henri du Bois lifted his head. His hands tightly bound behind, he was powerless to do anything but glare at the white-robed figure towering above him.

With deadly calm the Arab pulled a package of cigarettes from his waistcloth.

Du Bois followed his every move, flinching as the match he struck burst into flame. Frantically, his fevered mind strove to grasp an understanding of the past, and what would perhaps be the last twenty minutes of his life. . . .

It had been the woman's appearance that had first attracted his attention. Looming suddenly from out of the darkness, mysteriously shrouded in the brightly patterned shawl, he had thought at first it *was* Eudora.

Intrigued by her gesture to come out from under the awning, he had approached, fully expecting to hear Eudora's voice. But when she spoke, it was not Eudora's voice he heard, nor were her words any he could possibly have anticipated.

She said she was a friend—there to help him escape. Taught by his two years in Algeria to trust no Arab, du Bois had been convinced it was a trap of some sort. Spitting contemptuously at her feet, he had turned to go back to his tent. Her hand on his arm stopped him.

Swearing by the grace of Allah that there was a horse loaded with food and water waiting just beyond the first row of palms, she begged him to trust her. As if sensing his hesitation, she had then pressed the gun hidden beneath her shawl into his hands. His hesitation vanished—along with all caution and reason.

Blindly, he had followed her toward the trees. He might have even succeeded, too, had it not been for that fool Sabatin. Coming along when he had, shouting and drawing the guard's attention . . . God, he almost wished

297

he had aimed at the stupid bastard instead of the Arab guard.

Khamed tossed his cigarette to the ground. Crouching down in front of his prisoner, he stared at him coldly. Noting how du Bois's eyes glazed over with fear, he felt a savage sense of satisfaction.

"Was the woman with you Eudora?"

Understanding exploded instantly in du Bois's brain. The Reguibat sheik did not want to know about the details of the escape or the possible existence of other accomplices. He wanted only verification of the woman's identity! Suddenly everything made sense. . . . Why the woman had been dressed in Eudora's clothes. Why Sabatin had appeared at that precise, inopportune moment. Engineered for the express purpose of failure and discovery, the entire escape attempt had been but an ingenious ruse designed by someone to cast doubt on Eudora's loyalty to the very man who now faced him!

As he realized the power he held, du Bois grew lightheaded. By his failure to expose the deception, he could actually administer the most perfect of justices! Eudora had chosen the Arab barbarian—now let her suffer the consequences! A mad plan of twisted revenge began to form in his mind—not only against Eudora, but against the man who had made her his.

"Of course it was." Du Bois noted the disbelief that sparked for a moment in Khamed's eyes. "You don't believe me, do you, Arab?" he sneered. "Because you thought she was happy with you. Fool! You can't possibly have believed that she—a Frenchwoman—would have *willingly* taken an Arab lover? For months she has been deceiving you! Performing in your bed like the whore you made her, waiting and praying for the opportunity to escape. And tonight she saw it!"

He paused and struggled against his bonds to sit up straighter, thereby buying time to put his frenzied thoughts into words.

"She *was* wonderful, wasn't she?" he jeered. "Why, I

was even fooled myself, at first. Especially after she defended you to me. But then, days later, she came back and told me of her plan. She said she was willing to prostitute herself completely in order to win your trust. Do you want to know what her exact words were?"

He squeezed his eyes shut as if to search his memory. "The bastard has made me his whore, and if that is to be the price of my freedom, I will gladly play the part."

Du Bois opened one eye slightly to judge the effect of his performance and found himself alone. Eyes flying open, he began to laugh, lost in the intoxicating euphoria of his vengeance. As his body rocked back and forth, his mind swayed, lurching between sanity and insanity. Suddenly the fine line was crossed—irrevocably and forever.

With the lieutenant's words still ringing in his ears, Khamed stormed across the compound. His heart could not accept du Bois's taunts as truth, and in an instinctive reaction of denial he struggled to find another possible explanation for Eudora's actions.

But by the time he reached his tent he had been able to think of nothing. His denial had become rage. Curtly he dismissed the two men standing guard at his tent. Brushing past them, he entered and went to the bedroom, where he found her seated at the vanity.

Looking at her, he again heard du Bois's words. But this time there was no mental struggle of denial. There was only pain, and with that pain came acceptance. She had lied and deceived him for months—in order to betray him tonight!

"Khamed, what's wrong?" She turned from the vanity to face him.

Her question, brimming with innocence, snapped the slim thread of his control. For the second time in his life, a woman he believed to love him had proved faithless. The agony he had buried more than twenty-five years earlier exploded to life in a violent surge. Like a wounded beast cornered and caught in a trap, he reacted instinctively to the pain twisting in his heart by lashing out at its source. He jerked her to her feet.

"I should kill you for your betrayal!" he thundered. Yet as he lifted his hand to strike her, the look of terror he saw in her eyes pierced through the madness to reveal a small remnant of reason. In disgust he dropped his hand, released her, and turned.

Eudora fell back against the vanity, beholding the violent stranger before her in shock. "I have not betrayed you!" she gasped.

Something deep inside her overrode her fear and compelled her to act. Hesitantly she stepped toward him and reached out to touch the back of his arm. She could feel his muscles tense beneath her fingertips. "Khamed," she whispered, "I swear to you . . . I have not betrayed you. Please look at me. Tell me what you think I have done!"

Her light touch seared his flesh like a white-hot iron. He whirled to face her. "No longer will I listen to your lies, woman, nor respond to your touch! It is but a whore's touch—as much a lie as your words!"

Suddenly his heated anger died. As though his heart had turned to stone, he felt nothing. He pulled her again to him. "I must, however, commend you. For a woman who once professed to be incapable of performing what she did not feel, you have learned the art well. And before I sell you to the lowest sort of brothel I can find, I think it only fitting you have the opportunity to demonstrate this finely tuned talent for my men!"

Clasping her wrist firmly, he began to drag her from the room.

"No!" she screamed, comprehension of his intent dawning. Furiously she fought to free herself. Suddenly, as if realizing her struggle was futile, she began to sob. "Please, no! I beg you. Don't do this!"

"Think of it as another performance," he taunted

cruelly, deaf to her pleas. "Now you will experience all facets of the role you have been playing with such consummate skill!"

Twisting her wrist behind her back, he then pushed her ahead of him and out of the tent. He forced her to the center of the camp, where all music and conversation died as his people watched in stunned silence.

Saleena reveled in the sight. Only moments ago she had been troubled, doubting the success of her scheme. The men who had pursued her at the oasis' edge had been more difficult to evade than she had anticipated. To avoid capture she'd been forced to strip off the yellow dress and shawl and abandon them in the desert. Her original plan had been to return to camp with the clothing and to drop it, during the ensuing confusion, into the fire outside Khamed's tent.

She stepped from the doorway of her tent to get a clearer view. Seeing the woman's dress, she groaned. The disposal of the stolen articles was not the only aspect of her plan which had gone awry! The woman was supposed to have retired for the night. Yet she was not wearing night clothes. Neither was she wearing the yellow gown that would have placed her with du Bois!

But by Khamed's actions it was quite obvious he had noticed neither the green dress she did wear, nor the inconsistency it represented. Saleena shrugged off the disturbing thoughts. She had succeeded! By the time the clothing was discovered, if it was, it would be too late. She stepped closer to the scene, watching as Khamed dragged the Frenchwoman to a large fire, where several of his men stood in shocked bewilderment.

Khamed threw Eudora to the ground at their feet. "I have brought you a gift. When you have finished with her, take her to the others." He then raised his voice to permit his proclamation to ring out across the compound. "Tonight your lord's whore shall service every man in this camp!"

But instead of moving toward the crumpled form on

the ground, his men stood still. Furiously he jerked her to her feet and thrust her into the arms of the nearest man. "Take her!" he ordered, his words an animalistic growl of pain and fury torn from his throat.

The startled man dropped his arms and stepped back, lowering his eyes in fear. "I cannot, my lord," he murmured helplessly. "In my heart I would be betraying you."

Khamed glared at the man. He could not have seen more than eighteen summers. His cheeks, wet with tears, were as smooth as a girl's. For an instant Khamed's anger waned. It had taken a great deal of courage for the boy to stand up to him.

With a curt nod, Khamed acknowledged the youth's mettle. His eyes carefully scanned the remaining four men. His gaze came to rest on one whose eyes gleamed with the anticipation of a man about to savor a long-forbidden fruit. With no doubt that his order would be followed this time, Khamed started to call the man forward, then stopped.

He felt his determination falter and clenched his teeth. He could not let the fury flee or allow mercy to weaken his rage. He had to finish what he had begun and exorcise her from his soul. The only way to ensure that he would never again desire her was to give her over to his men. His pride would never permit him to take back what scores of others had shared.

Still, there was no need to watch it happen. Merely knowing it would—and by his command—brought a taste of bile to his mouth. Unable to swallow it, he spat. Gesturing to his man, he singled him out by name. "You, Habib! Take her!" As the heavyset man bolted forward, Khamed turned to walk away. He heard Eudora cry out and knew Habib had moved to claim her. He forced himself to keep walking, to close his ears and his heart to the sounds of her struggle.

Suddenly from behind him a roarlike command shattered the silence he'd willed into existence.

"Release her!"

Khamed whirled and saw Habib's instant compliance. The man dropped his hand from Eudora's arm, bowing his head in fearful reverence to the disembodied voice.

The crowd fell into a deadly hush, parting to allow a solitary figure to pass through.

Eyes flashing, Montar stepped into view.

"This is not your concern," Khamed warned icily.

"Then I will make it my concern. You have relinquished the woman, Khamed. As your equal I possess the right of first refusal. I am claiming that right. She is now mine, and under my protection." To reinforce his words he reached out, pulled Eudora to him and folded her into his embrace.

In his mind Montar silently, fervently prayed Khamed would, out of trust and faith in their friendship, accept his intercession. But in his heart he knew the man's pride was too strong and his ability to reason now too weak. He braced himself and issued his challenge. "Any man who wants to take her will have to fight me first. That includes you."

"Damn you, Montar! Do not force me to fight a friend!"

Montar felt Eudora shudder in his arms. He knew she had not understood their words, but the savage knell of finality in Khamed's voice needed no translation. "Do not force *me*, Khamed, to make a choice between our friendship and what I know to be right."

Then, because he refused to be the first to draw his weapon, he turned and began to lead Eudora away. He heard a low snarl at his back and pushed her aside just as Khamed lunged, knife drawn. Sidestepping the attack, he spun and pulled his own blade.

The crowd, which had grown even larger, now separated into two distinct groups—those loyal to Khamed, and those to Montar. Each waited for a signal from its lord to act.

Khamed threw off his robes and crouched in an attack

303

position. "You will regret this," he warned, his voice a barely audible whisper.

"No, my friend." Montar shook his head sadly. "It is *you* who will regret it. If I do not stop you, by your own orders every man in this camp will sow his seed where yours already bears fruit."

Chapter Eighteen

Montar had hoped the shock of his words would be enough to rob Khamed of his focus and to allay his need for combat.

But instead of dropping, the hand that held the knife whitened. Like a wild beast crazed with agony, Khamed was beyond rational thought, lost in a nether world.

Montar nodded to one of his men who stood behind Khamed, nervously balancing a rifle in his hands.

At the signal from his lord, he raised the weapon, lunging forward in a single, sudden movement to bring the butt of it down upon the back of Khamed's head.

Almost simultaneously with the dull thud of wood on bone, Montar heard Eudora cry out.

She had not moved from the spot where he had pushed her. Her face ashen, she stood, watching in horror as Khamed collapsed on the ground. Suddenly, as if to seize the only avenue of escape available, she too crumpled into a heap upon the desert floor.

Montar knew that without a direct order from their lord, Khamed's men would not attack. The marabout's rank was too high, and with Khamed unconscious, they were, in fact, obligated to follow his command.

He ordered Khamed's limp body carried to Kahlil's tent, and Eudora's to her own. After seeing that she was resting comfortably, he joined Kahlil in his vigilance at

Khamed's side.

"The Frenchwoman . . . she is all right?" Kahlil asked, as Montar sat down beside him.

"Yes. Given her condition, the fainting was not so unusual."

"It is true, then? She is carrying his child?" Kahlil gestured to the still-unconscious form of the man lying a few feet away.

Montar nodded. "Kahlil, when you and your men found her, did you notice what she was wearing?"

Kahlil looked at him blankly. "No."

"Just now she was wearing a green gown. Didn't your men say the woman with du Bois was wearing a yellow dress, with a shawl wrapped around her head?"

"A black and red shawl," Kahlil confirmed. Slowly, understanding appeared in his eyes. "Yet when we found her, she was wearing none. Still, she could have easily thrown it off."

"Perhaps . . . and then changed her dress after she returned to her tent. That would explain the discrepancy."

"It was not the Frenchwoman."

Kiri's soft voice at the dividing drape caused both men to whirl.

"What are you saying, woman?" Kahlil glared at his young wife. "What do you know of this?"

"Only that the woman with du Bois could not have been our lord's lady." Kiri stepped forward hesitantly. She seemed to know she was treading on dangerous ground. Not only had she interrupted the conversation of men; she was contradicting them. Avoiding her husband's furious stare, she turned to Montar. Her hands joined at her breast in a respectful clasp. "May I speak, my lord?"

Montar was more than intrigued. He nodded.

What Kiri then revealed sent his head swirling.

He was still trying to piece together the puzzle minutes later when he heard Khamed begin to stir. He moved

306

immediately to his side, knowing Khamed's would not be a gradual awakening from a deep sleep, but rather a violent escape across the threshold of darkness into light.

True to his instincts, Khamed bolted upright in a burst of instant recall and rage. Held in check only by the knife Montar had drawn and was holding at this throat, he lay back upon the grass mat.

"I should kill you," he stated flatly.

Montar smiled and sheathed his knife. Khamed was still furious, but his eyes were clear. "For what reason? The only blow struck was to your pride. You know as well as I, you were like a madman. Clear thought was impossible."

Khamed grunted. "I did not know a rifle butt to the head aided the process."

"It is effective. Now . . . are you ready to listen to reason, to what I have to say?"

"I want no lectures."

"It is not a lecture," Montar replied softly. "It is the truth."

"I know the truth!"

"No, my friend. You know only the words told to you by a man whose mind has been poisoned with hatred. Khamed, I don't know what du Bois said, but I do know your woman did not betray you. She couldn't have. When du Bois fired the shot that killed your man, Eudora was here with Kiri."

"That is impossible!" Khamed hissed. He sat up, wincing from the pain caused by the sudden movement.

Montar sat back on his heels and nodded to Kahlil, who was standing at the drape. He disappeared behind the curtain, returning an instant later with Kiri.

Montar waved her closer. "Kiri, tell your lord what you have told me."

She shifted the sleeping infant cradled in her arms to her shoulder and stepped forward, lowering her eyes nervously. "It is true, *ya sidi. Imr'ati* had arrived perhaps a half hour earlier. We were talking when we heard the gunshot. After the shouting and confusion began, she left. On the life of my son, I swear it to be so."

"How can this be?" Khamed turned a steely gaze to Kahlil. "You headed the search party for her. You told me she had been found and escorted back to my tent."

"She was, my lord." Kahlil hung his head. "But she was found in camp. I assumed she had managed to make her way back from the palms."

Quickly Montar came to Kahlil's defense. "The blame does not lie only with Kahlil. He was ordered to find Eudora, which he did. But in the passion of the moment, not one of us stopped to consider the possibility that it may *not* have been Eudora who was with du Bois. No one saw her face. Yet because of the description of her clothing, we all assumed it was she. Kahlil's error was perhaps in not noticing that what she wore did not match the guard's description. But then, neither did *you*, my friend!"

The impact of his words was immediate. Beneath the tanned skin Khamed's face blanched. But Montar did not soften his words. "While that detail would not have exonerated her from guilt, it may have tempered your fury long enough to give you cause to think. And *that* might have provided the opportunity for Kiri to come forth."

At the sound of her name Kiri coughed softly.

Montar turned toward her, dismissing her with a smile before returning his attention to Khamed. "There is no point in assigning blame. A grave mistake has been made."

"Where is she now?"

Khamed's question was emotionless, his expression blank. Still, Montar knew he was suffering. His black eyes were filled with agony. "She fainted after you were struck unconscious. I had her taken to your tent and left instructions with Dahr-la to give her something to help her sleep."

He paused and stared intently at Khamed. "I thought

it best . . . under the circumstances. Regardless of Eudora's guilt or innocence, our actions must now take into account her condition."

Khamed's expression did not change. The only indication of his inner turmoil was the hand he raised to run through his hair. "How long have you known she is carrying my child?" he finally asked.

"Only since tonight. Though I did have suspicions, they were not confirmed until I questioned the Frenchman Sabatin about his presence at du Bois's tent. I believe he told me only that I might stop you from harming her and, unknowingly, the child as well."

Montar paused as Khamed winced. He was not sure if his friend's response stemmed from the physical pain of the earlier blow to his head or whether it was rooted in the deep emotional aching only the heart could feel.

"*Sidi?*"

A man's voice outside the tent interrupted his silent speculation.

Immediately Kahlil moved to the doorway. He brushed aside the flap and stepped out, returning a moment later. "My lord, there is a child here who insists he must speak with you. Shall I send him away?"

Montar was not surprised when Khamed shook his head. Above all else he was these people's lord. Their needs had to come before his own.

Kahlil drew aside the flap and ushered in a tall, curly-headed boy.

The youth dipped his head. Burying a bare toe nervously in the sand floor, he waited for his lord to acknowledge him.

Khamed motioned him closer. "What can be so urgent that it has kept you from your bed at this late hour?"

The boy made a gulping sound and raised his head. "I could not sleep, my lord. I have been thinking about something that happened tonight . . . something I don't understand."

Montar smiled to himself sadly. The boy was not the

309

only one troubled by an event of this night.

"Yes?" Khamed nodded for him to continue.

"Tonight, *imr'ati* asked me to find the Frenchman Sabatin and to tell him that she wanted to talk to him by the lieutenant's tent."

Montar saw Khamed's body stiffen instantly. He knew he had to be thinking the same as he—had Kiri lied? Quickly he reaced out and placed a calming, restraining hand on his friend's shoulder. "Let him finish, Khamed," he murmured softly.

Having apparently seen Khamed's reaction as well, the boy hastened to explain further. "At least, at first, I thought it was *imr'ati*. It was dark and I couldn't see her face. She had it all covered." He mimed a headcovering drawn across his nose and mouth. "I did as she asked. But then I started to think about it and I remembered she spoke our language. That's the part I don't understand! Not long ago she couldn't even understand *zmal!*"

"Are you sure?" Khamed demanded, his voice rising.

"Oh, yes, *ya sidi!* Don't you remember? You were the one who told her what it was."

Montar felt his heart begin to beat faster. He fought to keep his own voice level. "What your lord means, is are you *sure* she spoke to you in Arabic?"

"Very sure!" The boy nodded adamantly first to Khamed and then to him.

"He has to be telling the truth." Kahlil spoke up from his position by the door. "Other than a few words and phrases, none of our children speak French. For this boy to have understood her request the woman—whoever she was—would have had to have made it in Arabic."

"And for Eudora that would have been impossible!" Khamed whirled to face him. "Her Arabic is no better than the children's French!"

Seeing the fierce expression which now burned in Khamed's eyes, Montar knew his attention was no longer on the boy, but on the implications of his information. He stepped forward and clasped the small shoulder. "You

310

have done well. Go to your bed now. Let your dreams be peaceful ones."

Beaming at the praise, the boy scampered joyously from the tent.

Khamed never noticed his departure. He had turned his full attention to Kahlil. "I want to know who it was who spoke to the boy. And I want to know why she took such painstaking care to make it appear as though Eudora and the Frenchmen were planning to escape."

Kahlil cast Montar a nervous glance. "I don't know who this mystery woman was," he replied hesitantly, "but I do think her motive is quite obvious. She intended the blame for her actions to fall upon the Frenchwoman."

Montar watched as Khamed's eyes darkened with rage once the meaning of Kahlil's statement became clear.

"What I don't understand . . ." Kahlil continued softly, as though speaking to himself, "is how she evaded capture. How could she have returned to camp without being seen? There were dozens of men looking for her."

"Men looking for a woman in European dress." Montar could not ignore the sinking, sickening feeling which had begun to gnaw at him. Still, he was not yet ready to voice his suspicions. "Perhaps my earlier speculation was correct. Perhaps she did change her clothing."

"I want the area searched immediately!" Khamed ordered furiously. "If the clothing is found, it may very well provide a clue as to who wore it."

Kahlil set off to dispatch the search parties, leaving Montar alone with Khamed.

He studied his friend carefully. As he withdrew a package of cigarettes from his waistcloth, his thoughts were obviously on what his men might discover near the oasis' edge. Montar decided they needed to be on the woman in his tent. Eventually Khamed would have to face Eudora. Before he could do so, he would have to face himself.

311

"Khamed."

Ignoring him, Khamed struck a match.

Montar continued, undaunted. "Even if we do discover who the woman was, it will not change what has happened. Within Eudora's womb your child now grows. You must come to terms with that, and with the true reason for your fury tonight."

Angrily Khamed tossed the spent match to the floor and moved to the doorway.

"Damn it, Khamed!" Montar grabbed his arm, forcing him to stop and face him. "What you almost did to her tonight was not the action of a rational man. You were not administering a punishment for a crime committed, but exacting retribution for a pain inflicted! *Bismillahi*— in the name of God, what *did* du Bois tell you?"

Khamed shook his head. He could not bring himself to meet Montar's eyes. Though he now knew du Bois had lied about Eudora's participation, the possibility that the remainder of the man's taunts may have been based in some truth haunted him. *Had* she surrendered just to win his trust? Certainly her request to leave had come on the very heels of her declaration of love. He tossed down the cigarette, grinding it into the sand beneath his boot. Not even to Montar could he reveal his private fear.

"Let it be," he answered curtly. He pulled his arm free and exited, crossing the compound to the area where the escapees' horses had been tethered. From the dozens of torch lights in evidence, he knew his men were already searching the site. He crouched down, sitting on his heels to await word of their progress.

Just before dawn Montar joined him. "Have they found anything yet?" He sat beside him and gestured toward the men still combing the area.

"No."

Suddenly a jubilant cry shattered the early morning stillness.

Khamed jumped to his feet, his eyes darting in the direction from which the shout had originated.

Montar rose as well. He watched a single figure break free from the group of searchers near du Bois's tent. Tucking something under his arm, the man raced toward them.

"*Sidi*, this was found there." He handed Khamed an object, turned and pointed to a cluster of large rocks a short distance from the small prison tent.

In the low light the color of the item Khamed now held was indiscernible. That it was a roll of clothing, however, was clear.

Without emotion, Khamed unwound the bundle, pulling out a darker cloth from its center.

A sudden glint caught Montar's eye. He reached out, his thumb and forefinger skimming the silken threads of the garment's fringed hem. He located a small round disc, pulled it free, and handed it to Khamed. "A clue to your mystery woman," he stated softly.

Khamed turned the disc over in his fingers. "It is a coin . . . with a hole bored through it and few links of chain." He held it out. "Do you recognize it?"

Montar took back the coin and walked over to a torch driven into the sand several yards away. He felt his heart tighten. Gleaming in his palm, reflecting the fire's light, the small silver coin was indeed familiar. Imprinted with the palm of Fatima, the daughter of Mohammed, it was just like—"

"Do you recognize it?" Khamed repeated. He had followed him over to the torch and now stood at his back.

"It is a popular design." Montar turned slowly to face him. "Many women have pieces of jewelry made with such coins—believing in the luck they represent."

"Do you recognize *that* coin?" Khamed made a stabbing gesture to the disc of silver.

Reluctantly, Montar nodded. As much as he abhorred the possibility, he could see no other explanation, nor could he lie. "Saleena possesses earrings made of such coins."

Khamed looked at him stonily. "Do you know what

313

you are saying, Montar?"

Again he nodded. Yes, he knew. And the knowledge weighted his heart. "I believe Kahlil was right. What happened last night was a deliberate, calculated deception. And other than my sister, no woman in this camp has reason to want to bring harm to Eudora. You see, my friend . . . in Saleena's mind your rejection of her is due solely to Eudora's presence."

He paused to look at Khamed. Only by the hard line of the man's jaw did he know he had heard his words. "Jealously and the pain of rejection are powerful catalysts, Khamed. They can force the most rational person to desperate acts."

In apprehension, Montar noted how the hard line became instantly harder.

Snatching the coin from him, Khamed clenched it in his fist. Without a word he turned and headed back toward camp.

Montar saw him stop only long enough to throw the clothing to Kahlil. His loyalties torn, he hesitated to follow. But regardless of what Saleena had done, she was still his sister. And if his suspicions did prove true, Khamed's fury would know no bounds.

Khamed entered the small tent without warning.

Saleena sat upon a saffron-yellow cushion, blissfully braiding a length of scarlet cloth into her hair. Hearing him enter, she raised her head. Her kohl-rimmed eyes, wide with anticipation, radiated warmth and passion. She rose and smiled—a lover's smile of welcome.

Khamed stared at her coldly. The woman before him aroused only feelings of callous disgust. "Where were you last night, Saleena?"

Her smile died instantly. "Why . . . what . . . what do you mean?"

Behind him Khamed heard the tent flap fall.

Saleena's eyes darted to the doorway. "Montar!" she

cried, her relief evident.

But before she could run to her brother's protecting arms, Khamed jerked her cruelly to him. Gripping her arm tightly, he turned. He understood Montar's need to be present and accepted it. What he would not accept was any interference.

Montar nodded in silent understanding.

Saleena glared at her brother. "Do you propose to simply stand there and let him treat me like this?" In spite of its scathing tone, her voice wavered.

"I propose to stand here and listen," he replied calmly. "I, too, would like to know where you were last night. Now answer his question."

"I was here!" she cried angrily, defensively, attempting to extricate herself from Khamed's grasp.

Khamed tightened his hold. "You are lying, Saleena. You were seen by du Bois's tent."

"That's a lie! I told you I was here!"

"Then explain this." He unclenched his fist and held the open palm before her.

Saleena glanced at the disc lying in his hand and shrugged. "What's to explain? It's a coin. I've seen a hundred like it!"

Her flippant sarcasm enraged him. "You may have seen a hundred like it," he growled, "but only *this* one was found near du Bois's tent!"

"I don't care where it was found! It has nothing to do with me, and I resent this inquisition!" She tossed her head in indignation.

The motion sent the earrings she wore dancing. The one on her right ear, a cresent-shaped bar clearly bearing seven coins—exact duplicates of the one he now held in his hand—hung freely. But the left one lay tangled, encumbered by the bulk of the thick plait nestled across her shoulder.

Keeping his hold on her arm, Khamed lifted the braid. The broken link on an empty chain precluded any need to count the coins. He now almost enjoyed the game. Like

315

a hunter stalking his prey, he laid his trap. "Did you know this earring is broken?" he asked softly.

Her eyes flew open and he could see the panic ascending. Her hand rose hesitantly to the earring. Tracing the cascade of coins, her trembling fingertips lingered on the broken chain. "I . . . I did go to the lieutenant's tent last night—but it was early!" Her gaze flitted from him to Montar, then back to him. "I was curious about him. I had heard the rumors that he was mad, and I wanted to see for myself. It must have been then that I lost the coin in the sand."

Khamed looked at Montar. Her pathetic lies had fueled his rage, and he no longer trusted his ability to control it. "Put an end to this!" he demanded.

Saleena looked to her brother, her eyes clouding with fear.

"The coin was not found in the sand, Saleena." Montar's voice was hardly above a whisper, yet his words resounded in the small tent like a clap of thunder. "It was found caught in the fringe of the shawl you wore last night while you were masquerading as Eudora."

The color drained from her face. As if realizing there was no further point in denial, she sank to her knees. "Please, Khamed! Please!" She threw her arms around his leg and pressed her head to his thigh. "I had to do it— for you! Don't you see? She was destroying you! She is evil—like a sickness that had to be purged from your heart! Please understand!"

She raised her head. Filled with tears, her frightened eyes beseeched his mercy. Then, as if knowing she would receive none, she released her hold. Her voice melted into sobs. "I did it for us!"

Khamed looked at the huddled form at his feet. A part of him wanted to choke the very life from her body. But a voice echoing hauntingly in his brain stopped him. "The pain of rejection . . . can force . . . desperate acts." Teeth clenching so tightly his jaws ached, he stepped away. In the intense desperation of Saleena's actions he suddenly saw a painful parallel.

He grabbed her arm and jerked her to her feet. "Were it not for the love I have for your brother, and the debt I now owe him, her intended punishment would be yours. *You* would suffer the fate she would have endured because of your deception!"

In disgust he flung her into Montar's arms. At the doorway he paused to address him. "I want her out of this camp within the hour."

He shoved aside the flap and stalked out. His savage pride was embroiled in a fierce battle with his raging emotions. By virtue of the utter despotic power he possessed, explanations and apologies had always been to him an embodiment of impotence. Yet a guilt he could not suppress or ignore was driving him to confront Eudora, to do that which he had never before done.

He stopped at Kahlil's tent to retrieve the bundle of clothing and then headed for his own.

At the entrance to the bedroom he hesitated. The memory of the previous night's confrontation flashed through his mind. He swept it—and the curtain—aside, and entered.

As she had been the night before, Eudora was again seated at the vanity. Her only acknowledgment of his presence was a tensing of her body. She continued to stare into the mirror before her.

"Eudora, look at me," he commanded softly.

She stood slowly and turned, clutching the thin robe she wore tightly to her breasts. The eyes she lifted to meet his were dead and vacant, reflecting a pain no physical blow could inflict.

Silently he stood and waited for her to speak, to break the dead silence. Finally, he breached the cold, empty distance between them by thrusting the bundle of clothing into her hands. "These were found early this morning hidden among some rocks near the edge of camp. Do you recognize them?"

Eudora's gaze lingered but for a second on the clothing

317

she now held. "Of course I do. They are mine."

Her voice was as lifeless as her eyes. Neither carried even a spark of curiosity as to how her clothing had come to be found in the desert.

Khamed clenched his fists and forced himself to speak calmly. "Last night a woman tried to help du Bois escape. She brought him a gun, which he used to kill his guard. But before they could reach the horses she had loaded with supplies and tethered at the oasis' edge, du Bois was recaptured. She managed to escape, however, disappearing into the darkness.

He paused and stared at her. His next words would explain everything. Eudora would know why he had thought her involved. But would she understand? Would she forgive? He drew a deep breath. "She was wearing those clothes."

In immediate understanding her eyes came alive. She looked first at the bundle in her hands and then at him. "You thought it was *I?*" she cried. "*Why?* Why would I have helped him? What possible reason could I have had?"

"I thought you were planning to escape with him, both you *and* Sabatin."

"Pierre?" she gasped. "How could you have thought such a thing?"

"Because you wanted to leave! You had asked and I had refused. Why would I have not thought you had taken matters into your own hands? Given that there were *three* horses saddled and waiting, and with Sabatin's presence, it was a logical assumption!" As he spoke he knew he was attempting to justify his reasoning and his actions not only to her, but to himself.

"Pierre was there? That . . . that isn't possible!" The confusion on her lovely face was mirrored in her eyes. She stared at him blankly. "I don't understand," she whispered, her voice breaking. "But I would have never betrayed you. *I loved you!*"

At her words Khamed felt his heart wrench in pain and

318

guilt. "Eudora, I questioned du Bois. He told me that you had been planning the escape for months, that you had—"

"And you believed *him?*" she spat, not giving him time to finish. Her eyes hardened. The pain and confusion were gone. "You had so little faith and trust in me, in my words of commitment—of *love*—that you could not have first come to me and asked for the truth?" She hurled the bundle back into his face. "Damn you!"

With her accusation his guilt vanished, and along with it the rest of his explanation. In one stride he was beside her. Savagely he grabbed her arm and pulled her to him. "*You* are hardly one to talk about faith and trust and truth, little one! Just when was it you were planning to tell me you carry my child?"

Eudora's face went white. Gasping in horror, she tried to pull away.

"Look at me!" Khamed roared. He twisted her to face him. "Is it true?"

She stared up at him. "Yes," she finally whispered.

Her answer tore at his heart. "And when were you planning to tell me?" he repeated. "Or were you?"

Suddenly it was he who was on the attack. "Is that why you suddenly wanted to leave? Knowing you were pregnant, you would have disappeared from my life without bothering to inform me of that minor detail? As the father I have the right—"

"*Right?*" she screamed. "How dare you speak to me of rights! Where were *my* rights last night? Without giving me a chance to defend myself—my God! Without even telling me what I had done, you judged me guilty. Not of aiding your enemy—but of betraying you! And for that crime had it not been for Montar, I would have been offered to your men like so much carrion to birds of prey!"

She glared at him. "Yes, I would have left without telling you! You have made it absolutely clear I am nothing to you other than a means of relieving your

319

needs. Why would I have thought that a child I carry would matter?"

"You do not carry *a* child!" Khamed thundered. "The child you carry is *mine!*"

"How well I know it!" Eudora shrieked. The hurt within her was unendurable. She had to release it and the only way was an infliction of equal pain. She struck out blindly. Without thinking or hearing the words her anger, pain, and heartache spewed forth. "It sickens me to know a part of you grows within me!" She fought to escape, flailing at his chest with her fists. "I hate it—as I hate you!"

Khamed endured the rain of blows in passive silence. He hardly felt her small fists pounding his chest. What he felt were the venomous words accompanying the attack. They slashed at the very core of his being like a knife.

"Damn you! If I could cut it from my body I would!"

Khamed's control shattered. He pinned her arms to her sides and shook her violently. "Enough! Are you made of ice? What kind of woman feels no love for her own child?"

"*Love?*" she screamed. "This child was not conceived of love—but of lust. How can you have the audacity to expect me to love it? I hate it! I hate it *because* it is yours! I pray I lose it! I hope I fall off a horse, am kicked by a camel. Anything! Anything that will spare me from having to bring into this world the product of your savagery and an eternal reminder of what I have suffered at your hands!"

Breaking free, she tried to flee the small room.

Khamed caught her wrist. "How you feel about me is immaterial. But you will do *nothing* to harm my child! If I have to tie you to that bed for six months, I will do so."

He glared at her, and his voice became a murderous, animalistic growl. "And you need not worry about *it* being any eternal reminder. Once you are delivered of *it*, you will be gone from this camp!" He flung her aside and stormed from the room.

Outside the tent he ran blindly into a tall figure.

Montar seized his arm. "Khamed, have you lost your mind?"

Khamed realized the man had heard every word of the heated exchange. He raised his arm and violently jerked it free. "I am warning you, Montar. Let it be! If you interfere in this, our friendship is over!"

He met and held the marabout's eyes with deadly determination, then turned and walked away.

Chapter Nineteen

Eudora stared at the curtain still swaying from Khamed's exit. Fiercely she held back the tears she'd thought had all been shed. For the moment she had regained consciousness after fainting until just a few hours ago, she had wept. But then her heart had hardened like a stone in her breast, and she had ceased to feel anything. There had been no more pain—only a cold, numbing emptiness.

But now that pain was back. Her dormant heart had wakened. With a strangled cry she stumbled to the bed and sank down. Dear God, what had she done?

"My lady?"

At the sound of Dahr-la's voice Eudora scrambled to her feet. "Come in, Dahr-la."

Eyes lowered, the girl entered. "My lord is moving into a supply *kaima* at the edge of the compound," she explained quietly. "I've been sent to gather his things." She lifted her gaze to look at Eudora, as if she expected some reaction from her.

Eudora rubbed her throbbing temples. She didn't care where Khamed went as long he was away from her. However, the idea of his forsaking the comforts and luxuries to which he was accustomed in favor of a supply tent seemed uncharacteristically melodramatic. Did he think his sacrifice on her behalf might arouse some feeling of guilt or sympathy? "That seems a little Spartan for his tastes, don't you think?" she offered sarcastically.

The venom still present in her voice took her aback. It also elicited a strange look from the girl standing before her. "What you see . . ." she waved her hand at the room's elegant furnishings "are my lord's by right of his station. But make no mistake, my lady. They are only the trappings of his rank and of no importance."

Eudora's eyes widened in surprise at the sharpness of Dahr-la's reply. That her maid could continue to defend Khamed was incomprehensible! "Dahr-la! *I* am the one who has been wronged!"

Dahr-la dropped her gaze. Without another word she set about her task, quickly gathering an armful of Khamed's clothing and personal effects, then moving to the room's doorway. At the drape she paused, turning. "You, though, are not the only one who suffers."

If the girl had reached out and slapped her, Eudora could not have been more shocked. The remark stung. She turned to hide the tears now welling anew, and only moments after she heard the swish of the drape did she let out the sob burning her throat. She felt betrayed—and abandoned.

She looked about the small room. Suddenly it seemed so different. Yet she knew the few things Dahr-la had taken had not effected the change. On the surface everything looked the same, down to the package of French cigarettes on the bedside table. Khamed had taken to leaving them there for her, knowing that sometimes when she was restless, smoking calmed her nerves.

Eudora reached for the package. Suddenly the image of Khamed's face lying beside her, illuminated by the orange glow of a cigarette as he brought it to his lips, flashed before her. With a sharp cry she recoiled from the table.

"Damn you!" she screamed to the vision. "I hate you!" She slumped down to the floor, sobbing the words over and over in helpless despair. But the vacated room could not answer, and the silence mocked her.

She didn't know how long she lay there, weeping, before she finally fell asleep. But when she awoke, the room had warmed and brightened. She rose stiffly and went to the washbasin in the corner. The cool water soothed her puffy eyes, relieving some of the swelling. She returned to the bedside table and reached for a cigarette. This time there was no vision to haunt her, nor were there matches. Knowing there was a tin in the desk in the outer room she walked to the drape and pulled it aside.

"Eudora!"

Sabatin's voice from across the room caused her head to snap up.

The desire to run to him died almost before it was formed. "How dare you!" she hissed.

"What?" He rose from the sofa, confused and embarrassed. "I was told it would be all right if I waited."

"How dare you come here at all!" she qualified, her temper flaring. "You told him—after you swore to me you would not!"

"Eudora, please!" He held out his hands helplessly. "You have to understand." Hesitantly he stepped toward her. "I had no choice."

"*Choice?*" Eudora cast him an icy glare that instantly halted his movement. "*You* had no choice? Do you realize the choice your action has left *me?*"

She watched as he shrank from her, his face pale.

"If there had been any other way, I swear, I would never have betrayed you! But when Montar told me that Khamed believed it was you who was with du Bois, all I could think of was your safety—and the baby's. Eudora, Khamed was like a madman, crazed with rage. Montar was the only one who could have stopped him. And my telling him you were pregnant was the only way I could be sure he would."

Eudora felt her anger begin to waver. She tore her gaze

325

from the man before her and stared at the floor. She had wondered what Montar had said to stop Khamed's attack upon her, the words which had caused the look of horror she'd seen in his eyes just before he'd been struck unconscious.

"I wanted to come to you last night, to explain," Sabatin continued. "But until Saleena's guilt was proven this morning—"

"Saleena?" Eudora gasped, her head raising in shock.

Sabatin's eyes reflected his astonishment. "You didn't know? It was she who engineered the entire escape attempt. Du Bois was just a pawn. The poor mad bastard never knew what was happening. I think he actually thought he was going to get away."

Desperately, Eudora tried to make sense out of what she was hearing. Saleena had been the one, the one to bring du Bois the gun, to betray Khamed. . . .

"She's been banished, Eudora." Sabatin's voice cut into her thoughts. "Khamed ordered her from the camp as soon as he learned the truth. She left hours ago, along with half of Montar's entourage and an escort patrol led by Kahlil."

The realization of what Sabatin had just said suddenly hit her. "She was the guilty one—yet she is now free? While I, who did nothing, am still his prisoner?" Her voice broke, and she brought up a hand to her mouth to stifle a sob.

"Eudora . . ." Sabatin took a tentative step forward.

"No. Don't, Pierre. I can't . . . not now. I just want to be left alone. Please! Leave me."

Sabatin knew it was a mistake not to try to talk to her. The camp was buzzing with the news of a horrible fight that morning between her and Khamed. That he had moved out of his tent as a result of it had fueled rumors of the most disturbing sort. Yet it was clear Eudora was not ready to confide in him. "As you wish," Sabatin answered slowly.

He was still debating the wisdom of his decision when

she abruptly turned and walked from the room. "But I'll be back!" he shouted after her departing form.

True to his word, Sabatin returned the next day.

Eudora refused to see him. She refused to see him the following day as well, and the day after that.

For an entire week Sabatin came to the tent. Each time he was turned away by Dahr-la. As he'd feared, Eudora had shut herself off. Dahr-la's was the only presence she accepted. Yet from the gossip now circulating, *tolerated* was actually a better word. Though no one knew why, Khamed had ordered Eudora never to be left alone. It seemed that if anyone really did know what had passed between their lord and his Frenchwoman, they weren't talking.

Frustrated and afraid for her emotional state, Sabatin finally sent a message to the one person he had a feeling knew the truth.

That evening he responded.

"You requested to see me, Monsieur?" Montar entered the small tent, his curiosity as to the reason for his invitation evident.

Sabatin nodded. "I need to talk to you. You are the only one who may be able to help me."

Montar raised a brow. "All things are with Allah," he stated softly. "Perhaps it is to Him you should be addressing your needs."

"Allah did not overhear- the argument between Khamed and Eudora," Sabatin replied bluntly. "You did. And I need to know what was said."

Montar smiled easily. "I am curious, Monsieur . . . what leads you to think I overheard anything?"

"People talk. Even these fiercely loyal subjects of Khamed's are not above gossip and speculation. I know you know what transpired."

"What was said, Monsieur . . ." Montar looked at him, his eyes suddenly growing cold. "Was said in private."

"My God, man!" Sabatin cried in exasperation. "Do you think I would pry without reason? Have you seen

327

Eudora since that night?" Without giving him a chance to answer, he continued. "Of course you haven't. Except for Dahr-la, no one has. She has exiled herself inside that tent, and I want to know why! What is she hiding from, Montar?"

Montar studied the irate Frenchman in silence. When he had overheard the hateful words that had passed between Khamed and Eudora, he had wondered if Eudora's spate of venom had not been more a catharsis of pain than a proclamation of truth. Perhaps Sabatin could supply the answer. It was obvious his concern for Eudora was real. Certainly something needed to be done. Since that morning Khamed had been like a lit fuse, his temper smoldering, waiting to erupt. . . .

"Very well, Monsieur," he answered slowly. Not without reservations he repeated what he had overheard of the heated exchange. He did not, however, mention Khamed's vow to take Eudora's child. Revealing Khamed's intent would only incense her countryman further.

Sabatin's response was immediate. "She's lying!" he cried, shaking his head insistently. "I know she still loves him."

"Can you be sure?" Montar felt his heart jump at the Frenchman's words. So he *had* been right! Despite her insistence to the contrary, Eudora did still love Khamed.

"As sure as one person can be of another's fears and emotions," Sabatin replied. "I don't believe there is anything Khamed could do to kill the love he has inspired within her. His actions have hurt her—yes! Hurt her deeply. But hate him . . . no! She does not hate him. Inasmuch as she might want to, she cannot. She loves him too deeply. And that love encompasses and embraces their child as well. It was *because* she loves the child that she wanted to leave—before he learned of the pregnancy."

"I don't understand. If she loves him why would she not want him to know?"

"Because of the theory she has to what her future would be should she stay once his desire for her was passed. She believes her status as his son's mother would sentence her to a life of sequestration here. She would be forced to live as in a harem while he was free to take other women."

"Such is our way, Monsieur," Montar replied softly.

"I understand that. But you must understand her position as well. It would hardly be a life she could willingly accept. Loving him as she does, it would destroy her to see others take her place."

"She may not have to." Montar moved to leave. He saw the look of bewilderment his comment had produced on Sabatin's face and clasped the man's shoulder comfortingly. "Let me talk to Khamed. There are factors of which you are unaware. They may change everything."

"Factors? What factors?"

Montar shook his head and smiled. "Patience, Monsieur. Remember what I once told you. All things are with Allah. Man must believe in His wisdom."

Armed with the truth, Montar left the Frenchman. As much as he wanted to confront Khamed immediately, to tell him Eudora's declaration of hatred had been a lie, he knew he had to wait. Nothing he said would make a difference until Khamed was ready to face and admit his own feelings for the woman. And only suffering would bring that about.

Montar would have to follow the advice he had just given Sabatin. He would have to be patient. After all, he reasoned with a private smile, was he not a man of near boundless patience?

It was not long, however, before Montar found that infinite patience almost exhausted. One morning, while waiting at Khamed's side for their horses to be saddled, he thought of the week which had passed since his conversation with Sabatin.

Even with the end of Ramadan, Khamed's mood had

not lightened. To Montar's knowledge he had had no contact with Eudora since that morning. Yet it seemed the mere knowledge of her presence was an open wound. Unable to be healed, it only festered within his mind. He continued to stalk the camp in sullen silence, refusing Montar's repeated offers to share his tent. The reason given was that he preferred the removed location of the supply *kaima*.

Montar was certain it was not the location which he preferred, but the solitude. As long as he remained alone, Khamed was able to keep his anger and bitterness alive— and his true feelings at bay.

A voice, risen in anger, suddenly intruded upon his thoughts.

In scathing tones Khamed was berating the young boy who had apparently not saddled Hasaad to his liking.

"Khamed!" Montar turned to him quickly, but in doing so he caught sight of the child's face. It was filled with terror. His patience came to an abrupt end. "In the name of God, I implore you . . . release her! Her continued presence in this camp is tearing you apart. You refuse to see her, to speak with her. *Bismillahi!* The very mention of her name has been forbidden in your presence! What possible reason can you have for still keeping her?"

'Have you forgotten she carries my child?" Khamed snarled. "Or is that not reason enough?"

Montar saw the onyx eyes ignite. Recognizing the telltale sign of a blinding rage to come, he nevertheless ignored it. If Khamed were to admit the unborn child was more than a bastard born of his mistress, it would be tantamount to an admission that Eudora, too, was more . . . more than a woman merely taken for his pleasure, as so many had been before her.

He struggled to keep the tone of his voice even. "Then you plan to acknowledge the child as your heir?"

"No. The child is a bastard—entitled to no more than

330

any other child I would have sired by mistake."

Montar felt his heart grow heavy, his hopes dashed by the bitter words.

"But he *will* be raised within the tribe, with love and acceptance," Khamed continued. "Neither of which would he receive from his mother or from her world!"

"I don't believe that, Khamed. I don't believe she has no feelings for her own child."

"*My* child!" he corrected. "And by virtue of that fact, by her own admission, she loathes it—as she now loathes me." Turning to mount Hasaad, he shot him a threatening stare. "This discussion has ended! She remains until the child is born. Then, and only then, will I release her."

Montar looked up at Khamed now seated upon the black stallion. Instinctively he braced himself for an attack. "I hear your words, Khamed, but they ring empty. I believe there is more to it."

He paused. While the expression on Khamed's face was inscrutable to him, the black scowl he expected to see was strangely absent. He continued cautiously. "There has always been more to your interest in her than you've been willing to admit—even to yourself."

Khamed glared at him. "What would you have me say, Montar? Do you want me to say I love her?"

Without answering, Montar entwined his horse's reins between his fingers and swung his body up into the saddle. He then turned his head and faced Khamed. It was time for the truth. "Look me in the eye, old friend, and tell me you *do not!*"

Khamed stared at him, and for the first time Montar saw the black eyes soften. An emptiness came over his face which could come only from battling a deep and private war, a war his demons were perhaps winning.

Suddenly Khamed broke the stare and looked away.

With an almost parental understanding Montar smiled. "It's been a long time since I've seen fear in your

331

eyes, Khamed. Not since you were a boy. At least then, though, you faced your fears. Now you run from them and make war on a woman. Tell me, what kind of a man plays with a woman's emotions for fear of his own? What kind of man is afraid to face love? These are not the acts of a man of courage. A man of courage and of strength does not deny love."

Seeing Khamed stiffen, he paused. To challenge the man's actions was one thing. To challenge his manhood and courage was quite another, and for a brief instant he was sure Khamed would strike. But the hand that had gone to the knife at his waist slowly withdrew. It was as if the truth of Montar's words had drained the fight from him.

The sorrow and regret he could see in Khamed's eyes told Montar that he had said enough. "It is possible that your cowardice might have killed a lesser woman's love . . . but not this one's. Hers is a love that can still be saved through courage—if you can face your demons. You see, my friend, in spite of your actions, I do not believe she hates you. Sabatin does not believe so either."

"Sabatin?" His iron control finally unleashed, Khamed's voice was a roar of rage. "Do you now entertain yourself by discussing my private life with a man who is my prisoner?"

Montar flinched. He had finally said too much. "He is a good man, Khamed, a friend. He knows Eudora better than she knows herself—in much the same way as I know you. Surrender your pride and go to her! Tell her what you feel, fight for your love!"

He was almost able to see the wall Khamed now retreated behind.

Erected between himself and his own emotions, it would not allow him to accept the truth. It was as if he believed acceptance would bring further pain. Kicking Hasaad brutally in the side, he rode off.

Montar shook his head in silent frustration. If Khamed's wall were to be breached, indeed, if it could be breached, it would have to be by another. He had done all he could.

Eudora moved under the cold sheets. Still asleep, she instinctively sought the warmth of the man whose bed she had shared. But her hand reached out to find the space beside her empty.

She awoke, shivering. Reality as cold as the desert night enveloped her. Khamed was gone, had been gone for over a month.

She rolled onto her back and pulled the covers to her chin. Their heavy weight did little to stave off the chill. Tears sprang to her eyes. In her heart she knew it was not the night air that caused her discomfort—it was the cold hopelessness of her fate.

Sentenced to remain in the Reguibat camp until she was delivered of the child now growing within her, she would obtain her freedom only with the forfeiture of that child. Automatically her hands went to her belly, now rounded and firm.

At first it had been so easy! She had felt little of the baby's physical existence and had been able to force herself to feel nothing emotionally as well. Not love and not the hatred she had professed to Khamed—but simply nothing. Yet in the past few days something had changed. She'd sensed the life within her womb and try as she would to deaden those feelings, she couldn't.

Suddenly, beneath her fingertips she felt a sensation from deep within. She lay still, not breathing. A moment later she felt it again. It was like a single heartbeat or the faint flutter of butterfly wings. She threw off the covers and opened her gown. Oblivious to the chill, she pressed her palms flat to the cold sheets and stared at her bare stomach. Almost at once she saw the faint rise and fall which had not come from anything she had done. Her breath escaped in a mingled cry of joy and discovery. The tiny being within her womb was moving!

333

Warmth flowed through her, swelling her heart with such intensity she gasped. "Dahr-la! Dahr-la!"

Without realizing she had done so, she called out to the girl asleep in the next room.

"My lady, what's wrong?" White-faced, Dahr-la burst through the drape.

"He's moving!" Eudora cried.

"Who is moving, my lady?" Stepping to the bed, Dahr-la looked at her in wide-eyed bewilderment.

"My baby! Come here, give me your hand! Feel for yourself!" Eudora took the girl's small brown hand and laid it upon her stomach. "Here. Wait now . . . there! Did you feel it? Did you feel him move?"

Dahr-la lifted her eyes, bright with tears, to meet Eudora's. "*Hamdullah!* My lord's heir."

Though her exclamation had been but a reverent whisper of awe, the meaning of the words slammed into Eudora. "No!" she cried. She threw off the girl's hand and clutched her gown closed. "This child is mine alone!"

Suddenly she felt her stomach lurch as if the plethora of emotions she had refused to acknowledge were heaving up within her. The love for her child that she had denied feeling, the heartache she had suffered at Khamed's inability to believe in her, the agony of his condemnation, they were all rising, choking her. Her hand went to her mouth. Dear God, she was going to be sick!

Dahr-la dashed for the wash basin.

As the contents of her stomach rose, Eudora leaned over the edge of the bed. She felt Dahr-la's hand stroke back her hair.

"It's all right, my lady. I'm here. Once your stomach is empty it will stop." The girl continued to murmur in Arabic, comforting her until the heaving did stop.

Eudora sank back weakly and closed her eyes. She could hear Dahr-la bustling about. A moment later a cool, wet cloth was pressed to her forehead.

"There, you see? It's all over. It's all right now."

Eudora turned from the soft voice. Sobbing, she buried her face in the pillow. It wasn't all right. Nothing would ever be right again! Dahr-la's words had shattered the shell of denial she had hidden behind so long. The tiny life within her was not her baby, but Khamed's heir. Once born, he would be taken from her. Never would she know the feel of him in her arms or at her breast.

As if in response to her anguish, the baby inside her moved. It was almost as though he were reassuring her of his presence.

In that instant Eudora knew that as long as the child remained in her womb he was hers. She still had time to leave this place. Hope dried her tears. She had only to find the way.

"My lady? Are you all right?"

With a start, Eudora realized Dahr-la was still in the room. She forced herself to turn and face her. "Yes . . . thank you."

Dahr-la smiled in gentle understanding. "There is nothing to be embarrassed about. Why, when Kiri was carrying Mohmet, she was thus every morning!" Laughing softly, she moved closer. "Perhaps when you are feeling stronger you might take a little walk? The fresh air would do you good."

Eudora declined at once, shaking her head. "No . . . I . . . I can't."

"My lady . . ." Dahr-la reached out to take her hand. "Khamed left with Montar to intercept Kahlil's returning escort party. You need not worry about seeing him . . . or he you."

"Is it so obvious?" Eudora looked at the girl in surprise.

She nodded. "It is often easier to avoid contact than to bear the pain of separation."

Eudora started to protest, to explain that her actions had not been born of love but loathing. Something stopped her.

335

"Perhaps you could pay Monsieur Sabatin a visit. He has been very worried about you." Dahr-la looked at her hopefully. "This afternoon, yes? After you have rested?"

Eudora nodded silently. Talking to Sabatin was not a bad idea. Certainly he was the only one she had to turn to.

That afternoon she ventured outside the tent for the first time in more than a month. She looked about cautiously. In a way it was as if she were seeing the camp for the first time. Yet in another it was as if she had no need. She knew every bit of it by heart.

Stepping out from under the awning, she met the eyes of a man who had been lingering near the tent.

At once he lowered his head.

His embarrassment was so clear that Eudora immediately knew his purpose. He had been stationed at the tent by Khamed as insurance she would do nothing to harm the baby. Shaking with outrage, she forced herself to ignore his presence. She turned in the direction of Sabatin's tent.

Suddenly her attention was drawn to a large party of mounted men in the distance. Swiftly approaching the camp, they rode in close formation, making it impossible to determine their number.

She stepped back under the shade to watch. She knew once the riders neared the oasis' encircling belt of trees, the group would split apart, lengthening into a line of two men riding abreast.

As the solid mass broke, her curiosity grew. She was able to count more than forty riders. Saleena's escort patrol would not have numbered more than a dozen or so men.

Suddenly Eudora froze. "Oh, no!" she gasped. "It can't be!

But even through the thick cloud of dust kicked up by the horses' hooves, there was no mistaking the magnificent black beast at the head of the column—or the man who rode it.

Her eyes riveted to the lead rider, she watched as the

336

horses and men streamed into the camp. Snaking their way through the tents, they reined in abruptly but a few yards from where she stood.

In spite of the heat, an icy perspiration chilled her, and she shrank toward the doorway. But before she could flee into the tent, Khamed's eyes met hers.

Already weakened by the surge of conflicting emotions and desires deluging her, she was robbed of her remaining strength by the relentless dark stare.

Unable to move and unable to tear her gaze from his, Eudora stood and trembled.

Finally Khamed broke the spell, turning to the man at his side.

She fled into the cool sanctuary of the tent. Safely inside, she stumbled to the sofa and sank down into its softness. Her breath was labored, coming in short gasps. She pulled one of the tufted pillows into her lap, hugging it to her tightly. She swallowed, and then swallowed again. Still, her breathing was ragged.

How could merely seeing him cause the familiar feeling gnawing at her heart?

Fighting to be heard against reason's denial, the answer screamed in her brain.

She still loved him!

Chapter Twenty

"Who is the woman, Khamed?"

Khamed dragged his attention from the form silhouetted in the doorway of his tent to the man mounted beside him. He had the distinct feeling Doctor René Gerard already knew the answer to his own question. Certainly there was more than casual interest shining in the man's bright, blue eyes—eyes which had been able to read Khamed's soul since childhood.

Khamed swore silently. He'd received no advance warning of Gerard's arrival, no word that the hostage negotiations had even been completed. Finding the Belgian missionary and his hired guard riding with Kahlil and the men who had escorted Saleena to the borders of Montar's territory had been a shock.

His mind quickly went back to the moment only an hour earlier when he and Montar had met up with Kahlil's advance scout.

Gesturing back to the party behind him, the man had explained that they had intercepted Gerard's contingent only that morning.

"This will change everything." Montar had cocked his head toward the portly figure on horseback breaking away from the main body. "Doctor Gerard is not likely to turn a blind eye to your holding Eudora against her will. You are going to have to release her."

Khamed had dismissed the scout before responding. He'd then snapped his head around to glare at his friend. "Her release is out of the question! She stays until the child is born. Whatever negotiations Gerard has made final do not include her."

"He will never agree to it," Montar had insisted firmly. "The moment he learns of her presence he will insist upon her release as well."

"Then he will not learn of her presence!"

"And how do you propose to accomplish that feat? Your camp is not so large, my friend. And people talk."

"Not if they have been ordered not to!"

"And what of Sabatin and du Bois? Do you propose to order their silence as well?"

"I will take care of the Frenchmen. And as long as I remain in camp, she will not leave the tent." He was powerless to keep the bitterness from his voice. "Surely you have noticed how she hides within its walls to avoid even the sight of me. There is no way Gerard can learn of her presence if I so command it."

Montar shook his head. "Khamed, what you speak is insanity! I want—"

"No! *I* want! I want your word, Montar. Your word that *you* will say nothing of her."

"Khamed, it is impossible to keep such knowledge from Gerard!"

Khamed glared at him, ignoring his protests. "Your word, Montar!"

"Very well. You have it."

Confident he could indeed accomplish what he had just vowed he could, Khamed had then spurred his horse forward to greet Gerard. His confidence had not wavered until they'd entered the camp—and seen Eudora.

Now what was he going to do? he thought furiously. Perhaps he could convince Gerard she was one of his willing guests . . .

"Khamed?"

Gerard's voice broke into his thoughts.

340

"I asked who the woman was."

Khamed clenched his teeth. It was impossible for him to lie to this man whom he loved like a father. He swung his leg over Hasaad's back and dropped to the ground. "Her name is Eudora Morrel."

"Louis Morrel's daughter!" Gerard pressed his lips into a tight line and nodded, as if to himself. "So they were right! This *is* where she's been."

Khamed felt a chilled shock race through him. Still, he permitted himself no outward sign of emotion. "What do you know of her?"

"More than I wished I did." Gerard moaned as he lifted his leg across the saddle to ease his ample, and obviously stiff, form to the ground. "Louis Morrel died a month ago en route with the Lemy/Foureau expedition. When the authorities tried to contact her in France to inform her of his death, they learned that she had booked passage from Marseilles to Algiers shortly after her father's departure. Through a check of the railroad records they were able to track her to Ghardaïa. They know she was registered at the hotel there for several days. Then the trail went cold and she simply vanished. There was no record of her returning to Algiers. Yet at about that same time rumors had circulated of a white woman departing the city with a military supply caravan. Strangely enough, the very caravan *you* attacked, my friend!"

"However . . ." Gerard paused and sighed wearily. He removed his sweat-stained straw hat to reveal a shiny pate, pink and beaded with perspiration. "Without definite proof there had been a woman with the caravan, the French have been reluctant to launch search parties into your territory. Instead, I've been instructed to find out if indeed a woman was captured, and if so, I am to effect her release, along with that of du Bois and Sabatin."

Khamed felt his insides begin to twist and churn. "Her release was not part of the terms *I* agreed to! She was not taken to be used as a bargaining chip against the French!"

341

Gerard lifted a brow. "I realize that, Khamed. I don't have to ask *why* she was taken." A strange tension entered his voice. "I have spent enough of my life in this desert to know your customs. While I can't say I've always understood or agreed with them, I *have* always tried to respect them. This is one instance I cannot. You've obtained your demands from the French. They've agreed to your terms and will honor your sovereignty. Don't jeopardize what you have won for some transient desire burning in your loins!"

"You do not understand, Doctor."

"No, Khamed! It is you who does not understand!" Gerard's voice rose and his face grew red. "I am trying very hard to keep at bay the revulsion I am feeling at your act of barbarism. But my personal feelings aside . . . if I return without her, the French are prepared to void not only this treaty," he gestured to the rolled document he'd withdrawn from his breast pocket, "but all the others they've signed in the past with you and your father. They are prepared to launch a major offensive against you."

"They have neither the resources nor the men," Khamed replied, his words heavy with arrogance, sarcasm, and confidence.

Gerard returned his look with equal confidence. "This is a point of honor, Khamed. The kidnapping and violation of a white woman is an abhorrent crime they will not let go unpunished. They plan to hang you—and that announcement is making them powerful allies. Your enemies would like nothing better. To that end the Chaamba are prepared to put three thousand men under French military authority. Even the Tuareg are talking of a temporary truce. If those two tribes ally themselves with the French, there won't be a Reguibat male of fighting age left alive within this territory you now call your own!"

Khamed forced a blank expression and glanced over his shoulder in the direction of his tent. His mind raced. He could avoid the scenario the doctor had just detailed only if the French believed Eudora was not a prisoner. He returned his gaze to Gerard. "Though it is an interesting tale you tell, Doctor, it is only that—a tale, based upon supposition and not truth. The woman was offered her freedom. She chose to stay. There has been no crime committed—unless, of course, you define passion as a crime."

He could feel his heart hammering in his chest, belying his calm tone. His steel nerves, which had been able to endure combat without so much as a strain, were unraveling into threads. He reached beneath his waist-cloth to withdraw a package of cigarettes. Staring at Gerard through the match flame, he sucked the acrid smoke deep into his lungs, then exhaled. "In fact, her belly now swells with my child."

Gerard's eyes flew open. "*Mon Dieu!* This changes everything!"

"Indeed." Khamed smiled tightly and glanced at Montar.

Standing mutely at Gerard's side, his friend had kept his word and said nothing.

Khamed communicated his gratitude with a curt nod before gesturing to one of his men. He issued an order and returned his attention to Gerard. "We can discuss this later. Right now, she must be informed of her father's death. I have sent for the reporter, Sabatin. He should be the one to tell her."

Khamed saw a flicker of confusion cross Gerard's face and realized his mistake at once. René Gerard was too astute a man not to wonder why he would choose not to tell her himself. He quickly looked to Montar for aid.

Calmly, the marabout turned to Gerard. "Doctor, how did Mademoiselle's father die?"

"Morrel? Uh . . . his . . . his party was attacked . . . by the Tuareg." Clearly startled by Montar's question, Gerard blinked. Then, whatever thoughts had been forming in his mind seemed to vanish as he continued with his answer. "According to the reports, for all its grandiose preparations, the expedition was a disaster from the very beginning."

Carelessly, Gerard pulled a handkerchief from his back pocket and mopped his forehead. His voice remained a disgusted monotone.

"Losses of supplies and ammunition, stolen, abandoned, and lost in sandstorms, resulted in a catastrophic loss of morale. Many of the native soldiers so believed that an attack by hostile tribes was imminent that they chose death by their own hand rather than face capture. The suicides triggered a mutiny by their comrades. Though unsuccessful, it resulted in the loss of more lives. The risk of attack became even greater. A month before the expedition was to reach Lake Chad, they were indeed attacked. According to the survivors' accounts, Louis Morrel was murdered, his throat cut while he lay unconscious in the sand."

"She will not be told any of this!" Khamed leveled an icy stare at both Montar and Gerard. "It would serve no purpose to provide her with these details. Nor are you to relay them to the Frenchman. If he asks, simply tell him the cause of Morrel's death is not known."

"Of course," Gerard nodded in immediate understanding. "In her condition, she must be shielded from as much emotional stress as possible."

"She seems to have taken the news well."

Khamed looked at Montar coolly and offered no reply. Three days had passed since Sabatin had informed Eudora of her father's death. According to Dahr-la she still had shed no tears. To say she was taking it well was an understatement.

"Sabatin said it was as if she had known. It would seem that nightmare of hers was prophetic," Montar continued. "Still, she has to be hurting inside. Why don't you go to her, Khamed? She is not made of ice."

Khamed fought to maintain control. Montar's choice

of words had been no accident. He was purposely reminding him of the cruel accusation he had made to her that morning. But his friend was wrong. She *was* made of ice.

Instead of voicing the thought aloud, he moved to light a cigarette. He had no desire to reopen any discussion of his feelings for her with the man seated across from him. For if the truth be told, he did want to go to her. But his savage pride would not allow him. He too remembered her nightmare—and a discussion he'd once had with her over her father's fate.

It was her unvoiced accusation he'd felt then, which haunted him now. Positive she blamed him for her failure to save her father's life, he would not humble himself only to be castigated by another of her poisonous declarations of loathing. Too vividly did he remember the hatred in her eyes and the venom in her voice to subject himself to them again.

No, he decided fiercely. He would continue to stay away. "I will send her a note," he stated in harsh, clipped tones, flicking away the spent match in his fingers. "Will that satisfy you, Montar?"

His friend jumped to his feet, his eyes blazing. "Your actions are those of a stubborn fool, Khamed!"

"And yours are of a meddlesome old woman!" Khamed stood as well, glaring at him with a vengeance. "Twice already I have warned you not to interfere. I will not warn you a third time."

He saw a strange look cross Montar's face. But before he could identify it, it was gone. The marabout turned to the door.

"Then I leave you to your private rage, my friend. You are welcome to stay, but I will not be returning while you are here. Frankly, to occupy the same space as you has become distasteful." With an angry jerk he opened the flap and walked out.

Khamed paced the small space. Before leaving Montar's tent he would force himself to finish the cigarette he had lit.

But even upon his return to the supply *kaima*, Khamed found he could not put the marabout's words from his mind. Finally he sat down upon a crate, and the note of condolence he had offered to write by way of a sarcastic response to his friend materialized.

Refusing to admit that he might be trying to reach out to Eudora, he told himself it was merely a gesture of respect, and acknowlegment of her loss. The note was purposely short—a concession to his pride which told him he was a fool for writing it at all. To be delivered by Dahr-la the following morning, it would put an end to the matter freeing his mind to turn to others. Matters which, he told himself, were far more pressing than his emotions.

For several weeks Khamed had been receiving reports of sporadic raids by the Tuareg along the fringes of his lands. As yet no lives had been lost, the only booty taken being a dozen camels and a handful of sheep and goats. Still, he knew that without reprisal, the attacks would continue, increasing in frequency and severity.

The next morning Khamed met with his lieutenants, and they concurred with his decision. The Reguibat would retaliate, but not in kind. Theirs would be no half-hearted raid conducted for a few head of livestock. Khamed intended to lead a full-scale attack upon a camp deep within Tuareg territory. Only with bloodshed would his own borders then be safe.

Riders were dispatched to the outlying camps to summon the men he had chosen to accompany him. Preoccupied with the planning of the raid, he was finally able to fill his mind with thoughts other than those of Eudora.

Eudora stood in the center of the main room, staring at the folded paper Dahr-la had wordlessly handed her only seconds ago.

The girl had seemed to be relieved to be free of it, as though she had relinquished into her mistresses care a thing of great value or utmost importance. Before Eudora could question her, she had turned and darted from the tent.

Slowly, Eudora opened the single sheet. Bold black lines cut across the white page.

My condolences

Though she had never seen Khamed's handwriting, other than the scrawling scrolls, dots, and dashes of Arabic that filled his ledger on the desk, she knew it was his.

Her eyes filled with stinging tears. She had hoped he would come to her, to indicate in some way that he cared. But the words blurring before her said nothing of the kind! After all that had passed between them, after all they had shared . . . two words, cold, curt, and unsigned!

Eudora crumpled the paper into a tight ball and threw it blindly across the room. She was no longer able to stop her tears, and they spilled down her face. They were tears of loss, not only for her father, but of her heart. Given in love to the cruel desert lord who had made her his, it could never be reclaimed, for in defiance of all reason, she knew she still loved him, she would always love him. But to him she was nothing, nothing but an inconvenient responsibility rendered because of the life he had planted within her.

Great, choking sobs shook her body as she finally accepted and acknowledged the truth. Like his note now lying wadded in a ball before the carved chest, she had been discarded.

Montar shaded his eyes and watched as a dozen men on horseback entered the compound. Like the men who had

347

been descending upon the camp for days, this group, too, was fully armed and battle ready. Handpicked by Khamed, Montar knew they were the flower of his tribe—men who embodied the very essence of the reckless courage, unwavering obedience, and inborn love of fighting for which the Reguibat had been known and feared for generations.

Once the cloud of dust kicked up by the horses had dissipated, Montar left the shade of the palm trees at the oasis' edge. The decision he'd struggled with for nearly a week had been made. It was time for him to return to his home in Rio de Oro.

He headed across the encampment toward the supply *kaima,* which had become Khamed's residence. With the passing of Ramadan, Montar was confident he could now depart the Reguibat camp without raising his friend's suspicions. Though travelers were exempt from the observance of the fast, for as long as Montar had been making his annual visits, he had kept the same schedule. He arrived before the onset of the holy month and left at its conclusion. There would be nothing in his announcement of departure that would point to the true reason he was leaving. But after the episode days earlier it had become clear.

The tension that existed between him and Khamed because of Eudora had become so great it threatened their friendship. He had to leave before either of them said or did anything which would drive them yet further and perhaps irreconcilably apart.

He found Khamed outside the small tent, seated upon a wooden crate of ammunition. Another box lay open at his feet. Across his lap were two bandoliers he was loading with bullets taken from the open crate.

"Khamed, I've decided it is time that my men and I left."

Khamed raised an eyebrow, yet continued to load the belts. "If that is what you desire, Montar."

"I think it is best. Ramadan has passed, and I have

been gone too long from my home."

Khamed nodded.

Other than a distinct hardening of his chiseled features, Montar could detect no indication as to what his friend's thoughts might be. Frustrated, he watched as Khamed tossed the filled belts of ammunition across his shoulder.

"Wait a few more days and leave with me. You and your escort can accompany the raiding party to the northern *oued*."

Montar nodded. The dry waterbed thirty miles from the camp served as a crossroads of sorts. From there he would be headed west, Khamed and his band east. He could only hope the days he had agreed to would pass without incident.

Slowly Eudora untangled her legs from the folds of her dress. She sat up and wearily brushed a tangled wave of hair from her eyes. Spending the night on the sofa had been foolish and fruitless. Khamed had not returned to collect his rifle and revolver as she'd thought he would.

Rising to her feet, she glanced toward the tent's entrance. If only wishing and wanting could make him appear! She hesitated, then walked to the doorway and swept aside the flap.

Though dawn's light had yet to crest the horizon, a flurry of activity greeted her gaze. The compound was filled with horses and men. In less than an hour's time Khamed and the raiding party would be gone, and with them Montar and his men.

She let the flap fall, turned, and began to pace. One by one she was losing the people she loved and held most dear—first Khamed, then her father, now Montar, and soon Sabatin. Once he was gone, she would have no one. She would be alone in the world except for the tiny life growing within her.

To reassure herself of her child's presence, she pressed

her hands to her belly and was promptly rewarded with movement beneath her fingertips. The sensation brought bittersweet tears to her eyes.

How could she relinquish the only thing she had to live for? The only love fate had not taken or denied her?

Suddenly she heard a noise behind her. She whirled, and in the same instant her heart both skipped a beat and swelled with hope. Khamed had entered the tent and was standing but a few feet from her. She fought the urge to run to him as his eyes raked over her.

Without a word he swept past her, crossing the room to the far wall.

Eudora watched as he knelt before the carved chest to unlock its lid. Still, without acknowledging her presence, he withdrew his rifle and the saddlebag of medical supplies, slinging both over his shoulder.

Like a leaf buffeted by an icy wind, she was set to shaking by his frigid, emotionless response. Her hope shriveled and died.

Khamed removed his revolver and tucked it beneath his waistcloth. He could feel her eyes on him, willing him to turn to speak. Knowing if he looked into those emerald pools he would drown, he forced himself to think of the conversation he'd just had with Kahlil.

Earlier, Gerard had expressed a desire to travel to the outlying camps to renew old friendships. As it would provide the means to keep the doctor and Eudora apart, Khamed had ordered his lieutenant to comply with the man's wishes. It was imperative Gerard not speak with her . . . at least until her condition had progressed to a point where travel would no longer be safe, he thought bitterly.

Slamming the lid shut, he relocked the chest and rocked back on his heels to stand. As he did so, his gaze fell upon a crumpled ball of paper lying at his feet. A flood of turbulent emotions deluged him and he rose unsteadily. She wanted nothing from him—not even a polite expression of his condolences! He whirled and bolted from the room.

Outside the tent his men were already mounted and waiting.

Khamed walked to Hasaad.

Nervously stomping and prancing, the huge black horse quivered with anticipation.

"You are no more anxious to be gone from this place than I," Khamed muttered. As he slung the saddlebag across the animal's neck, Hasaad tossed his magnificent head and nickered, seemingly in response. Without bothering to step into the stirrup, Khamed grabbed a handful of the stallion's mane and threw himself into the saddle.

Montar stood beside his own horse and watched as Khamed wrapped the loose end of his *shesh* across his nose and mouth. The face he covered was hard and set, as if made not of flesh and bone, but of stone.

Slowly the onyx gaze traveled down the row of mounted riders, coming to rest upon him. Wordlessly, Khamed ordered him to mount.

Montar hesitated, and the eyes boring into him from the slit of black narrowed. Unwaveringly he met the cold stare straight on. He'd thought all night about what he was about to do. He would be forfeiting that which he held most dear, but if he obtained the desired result, the price he'd be paying would be worth it.

Montar turned and walked to Khamed's tent. Sweeping aside the flap, he entered.

Eudora stood in the center of the room. As soon as she saw him, she ran to him, throwing herself into his arms.

He held her tightly, his own heart aching with the pain he felt emanating from the delicate form. There was no doubt in his mind as to what he had to do. He forced her head from his chest.

"He will be back, *ma belle*. In my heart I know he loves you. When he holds his son in his arms he will know it as well."

She shook her head frantically. "No . . . no! You don't

know! He cares nothing!" Her voice broke into sobs.

"You must give him time. He has never loved a woman before. He does not know how to respond to what he is feeling for the first time." Putting her gently from him, he took her hand. "Come."

As he began to lead her to the door, she cried out. "No! I cannot! I cannot go out and watch him leave!"

"You must." He drew aside the flap and released her hand. "Eudora, listen to me. Only you can make him face what he will not see." Waiting, he watched the play of emotions on her face.

Finally she squared her shoulders and drew a deep breath. She took a hesitant step, looking to him for reassurance.

He placed a hand at her waist and guided her out into the gray light. But once outside the doorway her courage seemed to falter. Montar could feel the muscles of her back tensing. She began to draw back. He pushed her forward to stand in clear view of the men assembled.

A strangled hush fell over the crowd. Voices died instantly as all heads turned to see Khamed's reaction. His eyes blazed in fury as they shifted from Eudora to Montar and then back to Eudora.

Montar held his breath. Khamed would know this was no accident. By bringing Eudora outside, he was forcing his friend either to acknowledge her or to publicly humiliate her.

According to the custom of his tribe, only wives were permitted to see their men off to battle. Of the women now gathered, many with children in their arms and clinging to their skirts, none were idle spectators. All were the wives of the men accompanying the raiding party. For as long as Reguibat men had been going to battle, it had been so. A man's wife, the instrument of his procreation, stood proudly at his side. His mistress, the instrument only of his pleasure remained hidden inside his tent.

Khamed forced himself to tear his gaze from Eudora

and return it to Montar. The man stared back defiantly. Khamed felt anger mount. Montar knew exactly what he was doing. He was daring him to deny her before witnesses, challenging him to commit himself, if not to her, then to their child.

Throwing a leg over the saddle, he slid from Hasaad's back to the ground. Slowly, he walked toward the couple, stopping directly in front of Eudora. Towering above her, he could see the fear rising in her eyes. She, too, knew what it would mean if he led her back inside the tent. He would be declaring her his mistress and the child she carried a bastard . . . a bastard he refused to acknowledge as his heir.

He took a single step forward, fully intending to take hold of her arm. But the hand he raised felt like lead. He couldn't do it. He couldn't deny her—not to his people, and not to himself. Helplessly he found his hand moving instead to his waist. For a brief second his fingers grasped the hilt of the knife tucked beneath his waistcloth before they then touched his chest above his heart. Finally, the fingers lightly brushed his lips and he bowed. The words of an ancient vow tumbled through his mind: *With these humble gestures I pledge to thee my life.*

Lifting his head, he saw only Eudora's eyes, brimming with tears. Beneath the black cloth, his face twisted in response to the agonizing mixture of emotions tearing at his heart. He turned and walked back to his horse. Mounting, he watched as Montar moved to embrace her, touching her cheek in a farewell caress.

As he walked to his own horse, Montar looked at Khamed.

Sitting rigidly in the saddle, he turned only his eyes to him. The message in their cold depths was unmistakable.

With his actions Montar had won a great victory, but its price had been dear: his friendship with Khamed was ended.

Eudora brushed back her tears and watched as Khamed raised his arm. With a single word of command the column of riders began to move forward, passing before her in a seemingly endless blur. A maelstrom of emotions defying interpretation and control besieged her. Why had he not led her back into the tent?

In desperation her beleagured heart clung to Montar's words. *I know he loves you. When he holds his son in his arms he will know it as well.*

The words reverberated through her mind . . . *when he holds his son . . . holds his son . . . his son . . . his son . . .*

Suddenly, like naked steel, reason and reality plunged through her. She clutched at the bodice of her dress, her fingers clawing at the charmeuse fabric.

But the pain beneath would not be stilled. Hot tears spilled down her cheeks.

Khamed had not acknowledged her. He had acknowledged his son!

Chapter Twenty-One

Eudora walked to the doorway of her tent and swept open the flap. She kept her gaze lowered, refusing to look at the glorious melange of hues still visible in the darkening sky. Their beauty would only trigger memories, memories of sunsets she had viewed while in Khamed's embrace. Tears sprang to her eyes, and though she willed herself not to think about him, his image formed in her mind.

Evening had been his favorite time. With the day's responsibilities finally met, he could relax. How she'd loved the change that occurred within him! His face would lose much of its hardness, his voice becoming gentle and affectionate. Cigarette in hand, he would guide her outside. Then, taking her into his arms, he'd recount his day's events—like a husband to his wife. . . .

Eudora placed her hand over her mouth, trying to stifle a sob. With every breath she drew, she ached for him! He had become a part of her, and without him she could never be whole.

As it had ever since his departure three weeks ago, her heart whispered a prayer for his safe return. Suddenly her inner voice rose above the entreaty.

And when he does return, what then? Will your emptiness and loneliness abate? Fool! the voice screamed. *You must get away, away from these sights and sounds that only serve to remind you of that which is eternally lost!*

Twisting her head from side to side, Eudora tried to silence the voice. But it, and the truths it carried, would not be silenced.

She turned to go back inside the tent, and from the corner of her eye she noticed a pair of men crossing the compound on horseback. In spite of the distance and low light she recognized Kahlil's hawklike profile instantly. Her gaze shifted to the man at his side. Short and plump, he appeared to be dressed in Western clothing, with a straw hat perched atop his head. She was certain he was the same man who had entered the camp with Khamed and Montar a month ago.

She watched the men rein in their horses in front of a small tent across the compound and dismount. With something to focus on other than her sorrow, her mind began to fill with thoughts.

Sabatin had told her of a Belgian missionary's arrival just before he'd informed her of her father's death. At the time she'd been overcome with shock and grief. To inquire further about the man who had negotiated the Frenchmen's release had never entered her mind. Certainly she'd had no interest in making the acquaintance of a man from her own world, one who would no doubt view her position as Khamed's mistress with outrage and revulsion.

It had been many days later, after the questions she'd posed to Sabatin about her father's death had received no answers, that she'd finally requested to meet Gerard. Sabatin had informed her that he'd left to visit the outlying camps, explaining that as a friend of Khamed's father, there were old friendships he wanted to renew. With the doctor gone from the camp, Eudora had put all thoughts of him from her mind.

But now, watching as the small man dismounted, then stood to speak to Kahlil, she found an idea forming. Might this René Gerard possess the influence and government connections which could force Khamed to release her and her child?

Shoving aside the flap, she quickly reentered the tent.

"Dahr-la, I should like to invite Dr. Gerard to dinner."

The girl bustling about the large room froze. The look in her eyes was unfathomable. "Dr. Gerard, my lady?" She repeated the words in a hushed whisper.

"Yes. The Belgian missionary."

"I'm afraid that isn't possible."

Eudora stared at her. "What do you mean, 'that isn't possible'?" I just saw him enter the camp with Kahlil. They are just across the compound."

Dahr-la lowered her head. Suddenly the pattern of the plush Persian carpet beneath her feet seemed to fascinate her. "My lord has left orders that you are not to speak with the doctor. I'm sorry, my lady."

A mixture of surprise and anger coursed through Eudora. "I see," she replied tightly. Returning to the doorway, she drew back the flap and watched the two men still engaged in conversation. She struggled to contain her anger. Even in his absence, Khamed had anticipated her thoughts! To ensure her captivity he had made sure the one person who might help her would be kept from her.

In that instant her spirit rebelled. Without a backward glance she stepped from the tent. Ignoring the startled gaze of her bodyguard she headed straight for the pair of men across the compound. Behind her she could hear the guard's footsteps. Let him follow, she thought. He could not stop her from speaking.

Kahlil spotted her first, and his displeasure at her approach was obvious. Eudora saw his brows draw into a single line across his forehead.

"Madame." He bowed, his voice and demeanor cold.

"Kahlil, I should like to be presented to our guest." Eudora turned to face the man at his side. She knew she had left Khamed's lieutenant no choice.

He cleared his throat. "Doctor René Gerard, may I present Mademoiselle Morrel."

Eudora quickly extended her hand. "Doctor, it is a pleasure to finally meet you. Pierre has told me much about you."

As Gerard clasped her hand and bowed, she continued before he could speak. "Perhaps you would join me for tea after you have rested from your journey. Shall we say, in an hour?" She smiled in secret truimph. She had given the man little opportunity to refuse graciously, and Kahlil none at all to protest. From the corner of her eye she could see his bearded face twist into a scowl.

Gerard smiled warmly. "I would be honored, Mademoiselle."

"Doctor, I don't think—"

"Kahlil, please!" Eudora broke in at once. "I would like to talk to the doctor about my father. Surely you won't deny me such a small request." She cast him an innocent smile. "What harm could there be?"

She was almost positive she saw his gaze go to her rounded belly. But as he nodded his consent, she shrugged off the thought. Kahlil knew he had been defeated, she reasoned silently. If he protested again or refused, Gerard would surely become suspicious. She returned her attention to him. "Doctor, shall I see you in an hour, then?"

Again Gerard bowed. "I look forward to it, Mademoiselle."

An hour later he was at her doorway.

In that time Eudora found her conviction weakening. As much as she wanted to leave, a part of her still hoped Khamed would take her back. But once she asked for Gerard's help, her fate would be sealed. Wanting to or not, she would be leaving.

That realization left her weak and nauseated. She remained seated as Dahr-la escorted him in and then respectfully withdrew.

"So at last we meet." Smiling warmly, Gerard settled his ample form beside her. "Khamed told me you were uncomfortable meeting a man of your own world. I'm

358

glad you've seen fit to change your mind, to give me a chance. Let me assure you, Mademoiselle, I make no judgments. Twenty years in this desert has taught me many things, not the least of which is understanding. Live and let live—"

"Doctor Gerard, please!" Eudora buried her face in her hands. The man's words, designed no doubt to put her at ease, were instead only adding to her pain.

When she looked up a moment later she found his blue eyes studying her with confused intensity.

"Mademoiselle, are you all right?"

Eudora released a quivering sigh. "Doctor Gerard, I am being held in this camp against my will. I need your help. I want to leave."

Gerard's eyes widened, first seemingly in confusion, then in shock. "Are you telling me Khamed lied? You did *not* choose to remain with him?"

Eudora felt her cheeks burn. She should have known Khamed would have told him she was his willing mistress. How else could he have explained her presence? "I . . . I did agree to stay," she stammered. "But . . . things . . . circumstances have changed. Now . . . now I want to leave, and he will not permit it."

Mademoiselle, you *are* carrying his child, are you not?"

Feeling her throat tighten, she could only nod in response.

"Perhaps, then, you have misunderstood Khamed's refusal to allow you to leave." Gerard reached out to take her hands into his own.

Though she could hear the gentleness in his voice, she stiffened.

"I'm sure he feels that for you to travel in your condition would be too dangerous. Once the child is born, if you desire to leave, he would not stop you."

"But that will be too late!" Pulling her hands free, Eudora jumped to her feet. "I must leave *before* my baby is born, for Khamed intends to keep the child here!"

Gerard's eyes narrowed, and he rose awkwardly to his feet. "Young woman, I have known Khamed since he was a small boy. He was himself separated from his mother as a child. I do not believe he is capable of such heartless cruelty."

The man's defenses of Khamed unleashed her anger. She jumped up. "I can assure you, Doctor, he is capable of that . . . and more! In a bitter voice which held firm despite the emotions seething within her, she continued. "We are speaking of his heir—"

She stopped abruptly as a pain in her abdomen nearly took her breath. She had never felt the baby kick so before.

"Mademoiselle?" Gerard reach out. With a hand on her arm, he helped her to sit. "Are you all right?"

"Yes. Yes, I'm fine. The baby kicked. That's all."

"Perhaps I should go. You need to rest."

Eudora looked up at him. She could not read the expression on his face. "Doctor, everything I said is true."

"I will speak to Khamed the moment he returns. If what you have told me *is* the truth, I will not rest until you and your child are safely aboard a ship headed for France."

"Thank you. That is all I wanted to hear." She sank back against the cushions, suddenly drained. She closed her eyes and heard Gerard move toward the door. "Doctor, there is one other thing." Wearily she forced her eyes open. "How did my father die?" Watching for a change in his expression, she could detect none, and his gaze held firm. Did the desert endow all men with the ability to show no emotion?

"I told Monsieur Sabatin all I know, Mademoiselle. However, there is something which may give you comfort. There will be no more lives lost. The French government has reevaluated the entire project. There will be no railroad."

"Comfort?" She looked at him in amazement. "He lied for nothing!" Gathering the little strength she had remaining, she rose to her feet. "How can you have spent twenty years in this damned desert, Doctor? What it does not kill, it destroys!" Without waiting for Gerard's departure, she fled toward the bedroom. All that mattered now was that she had won. She would keep her child.

But where joy and elation should have filled her heart, there was only pain and sorrow—and regret.

Khamed forced himself to pull back on the reins. The raiding party had ridden hard to reach home before nightfall. Still, the last mile of their journey need not be a mad gallop across the sand. He cast a look at the men riding at either side of him. He knew beneath their *sheshes* the bronzed faces were etched with fatigue—as was his own. Without question his men had obeyed him, physically exhausting themselves to keep up with the pace he had set. Did they know the cause for his driving need to reach camp?

Approaching the perimeter of palms, Khamed finally allowed himself to acknowledge it—the fear he'd been unable to quell. Would Eudora still be there? Though he had given Kahlil strict orders to keep Gerard from her, he'd been haunted for days by the thought he might return to find them both gone. He turned Hasaad toward his tent and waved his men on.

Within moments he was at the doorway. He dismounted stiffly, feeling his muscles burn with the simple movement.

"My lord." The guard stepped forward to take the reins from him.

"The Frenchwoman?" Khamed inclined his head toward the tent. "She . . . she is well?"

"Yes, my lord. But you will be surprised at the change

361

in her. Your son grows well." Laughing, he extended a hand in front of him to indicate the girth of Eudora's belly.

Khamed felt his own stomach tighten into a knot. When he'd left she had barely shown her pregnancy. What would she look like swollen with child—his child?

"Are you not going in?" The man's voice broke through his thoughts.

"No." Khamed turned from the tent, snatching the reins from the startled guard's hands. There was no need to see her, he told himself. His fears that she had left with Gerard had proved unfounded. He swung his body up to the saddle and set his heels to Hasaad's flanks.

Riding back across the compound he struggled to quell the emotions welling inside him. He had wanted desperately to enter the tent, to take her into his arms, to acknowledge what he had so long denied. But he could not. He could not step past the wall that was his defense against the vulnerability of commitment.

He rode to the small supply *kaima*. Dismounting, he beckoned to a young boy to lead Hasaad to the corrals, then retrieved the package of cigarettes from beneath his waistcloth. Before he could put one to his lips he caught sight of a plump form hurriedly crossing the compound toward him. With a muttered oath, Khamed tossed the cigarette to the ground and stepped forward to meet the man.

"Khamed!" Gerard gasped, winded by the exertion. As he fought to catch his breath, he mopped at the sweat glistening on his smooth forehead with a handkerchief. "You have some explaining to do! What is this insanity I have heard about your forcing the Frenchwoman to relinquish her child once it is born?"

Khamed's insides knotted. "I will not bother to ask you how you learned of this," he replied evenly, with a calm he did not feel.

"Then it is true?"

"Yes, Doctor. It is true—with one minor change of

362

detail: she is relinquishing *my* child."

"You can't be serious!" Gerard's voice rang with outrage. "By your own laws the nationality of a child of mixed blood is that of the mother."

Khamed glared at him. "I am quite serious, Doctor. Ownership of the womb be damned; my son will stay."

Gerard took a step back. As if he'd realized his own anger was only fueling Khamed's, his demeanor changed. Calmer, with a firmer hold on his emotions, he continued. "Khamed, you can't do this. A child needs its mother. You more than anyone should recognize that fact. Having grown up without yours, how can you now deprive your son of his?"

"So you would deprive him of his father?" Unwaveringly Khamed met the probing blue eyes. "With me he will have roots, a sense of belonging, a home, and a people who will love and accept him. With me he will not be one day ripped from all that he has known—thrust into a foreign land, abandoned by his mother into the hands of a stranger."

The look Khamed saw on Gerard's face was one of dismay.

"You still feel that pain?"

"The only thing I now feel is pity . . . pity for the woman who called herself my mother, yet deserted me."

"She did not desert you, Khamed. Since you were six, you have known about the arrangement between her and your father. Before allowing her to leave the desert, Haisim made her promise to return you to your rightful place as his heir."

"Call it what you will, Doctor Gerard—relinquish, desert, abandon . . . they are all words which hold no difference in meaning to a boy of seven! She left me on that dock without so much as a backward glance."

Khamed paused. A sarcastic smile parted his lips. "No, Doctor. I do *not* still feel that pain. I buried it long ago. And when I did so, any chance for me ever to love died and was buried as well. I vowed never again to be betrayed by any woman's promise of love. Their words are empty, their commitments false."

"And so you decided you would never love a woman?"

"Would not *allow* myself to love. There is a difference."

Gerard stepped forward and laid a hand upon Khamed's arm. "Is that the reason you would send this woman away? Are you so terrified of being hurt again that you would rather drive her away than admit you love her? Are you so scarred by the past that you must live in fear of the future?"

Khamed glared down at Gerard. Years of love and respect for the man who had been his father's friend were all that prevented him from physically striking back. "That is enough! Not even from you will I listen to such—"

"Yes, you will listen!" Gerard tightened his hold. "You will listen to me, Khamed, because it is time you learned the reason why your mother brought you back to your father."

Khamed jerked his arm free. "You are wasting your time. Nothing you can tell me can possibly justify what she did. First, she walked out of my father's life, and then five years later she walked out of mine."

"She had to!" Gerard's voice cracked with emotion. "Khamed, she was dying!"

"You are still wasting your time, Doctor. I know that story as well. She never regained her strength after my birth. Yet my father loved her so deeply he agreed to let her return to England—taking his heir with her."

"Yes! For Haisim knew that if she stayed, the desert would kill her—just as surely as separating her from you would have killed her. You were her life!"

Khamed felt his anger surge. The hands hanging at his sides tightened into fists. Slowly, bitterly, he repeated the older man's words. "If I was . . . 'her life' . . . then tell me, Doctor—why did I not receive so much as a single letter from her during that year she lived in

England before her death? Do you know that for twelve months I met every courier who rode into my father's camp? I was sure each time there would be a letter. I continued to hope, to believe—as only a child can."

"*Mon Dieu.*"

Though Gerard's exclamation had been barely audible, its tone of sorrow and regret instantly compelled Khamed to silence. He stared at the man in confusion.

"You never received a letter from your mother, Khamed, because she never returned to England. She died at sea on the voyage home."

"What?" Khamed felt as if a pair of invisible hands had encircled his throat. Fingers lacing tightly, they were choking the breath from him. "What . . . what are you saying?" he gasped.

"When you were six, your mother learned she was dying. The doctors told her she had at most a year to live. I was in Antwerp at the time. She wrote to me and asked that I contact your father to arrange for your future. She knew she couldn't turn to her own family. They had never forgiven her for marrying out of her race and had disowned her. She'd had no contact with them for years."

He paused as if trying to choose his words carefully. "Yet she knew with your father's people you would be loved and accepted. I traveled to Algiers to meet with Haisim. That's when the lie began. Haisim agreed with your mother and me—you didn't need to know the truth. He told the tribe that his heir would be returning, as it had been agreed years before. Your mother told you the same story, to prepare you. Months later, by the time the arrangements had been made, it seemed as though it had always been known that you would be returned to your father."

Struggling to comprehend the full meaning of Gerard's revelations, Khamed had listened in silence. Suddenly a question burst through the wall of confusion. "Why was I not told of her death until a year later?"

Gerard sighed heavily. "That was my doing. Haisin was devastated when he learned she had died, and he forbade any further mention of her name. And you were having such a difficult time adjusting to your new life . . . I didn't feel any purpose would be served by telling you right away. Later . . . later it seemed an insignificant detail."

"*Insignificant?*" A tumultuous explosion of suppressed pain and anger tore through Khamed. "Do you know what her last words to me were? 'I will always love you.' And then never to hear from her again. . . . Without knowing the truth, what conclusion could I have drawn, other than the one I did? That she had lied and stopped loving me—or worse, that she had lied from the beginning and had never loved me!"

"Khamed, I'm sorry!" Gerard's shoulders slumped. He closed his eyes as if in pain, opening them a second later to look at Khamed. "What we did . . . what I did, I did to protect you. I never wanted to hurt you, you must believe that. But perhaps now you will see this situation with your own son in a different light. Do you want someday to have explain to him why *his* mother left him?" Stepping forward, he laid his hands gently upon Khamed's shoulders.

Khamed reacted to the slight touch as if it had been a blow. He pulled back, his muscles tensing.

"Do you, Khamed?" Gerard persisted. "And will you be able to tell him the truth? Will you be able to tell him that you forced her to leave because you were afraid to love her?"

Khamed leveled an icy stare at the man. "I have heard enough. I have made my decision."

Gerard flinched as if struck. "How can it be that nothing I have said has swayed you?"

"How can you ask me to be less of a man than I am, less of a man than my father was—and still honor his name? On the contrary, Doctor Gerard, when mother and child are able to travel, they shall both be escorted

366

Gharadïa."

"Damn it, Khamed! You have not listened to anything have said. Why are you still forcing her to leave? You ove her!"

"Yes. I love her." Khamed felt his heart twist in his hest as he spoke the words aloud for the first time. He rove back the pain to look at Gerard steadily. "And it is ecause I love her—as my father loved my mother—that shall set her free. Like my mother, she is better off in er own world. To that end my father would have acrificed his son. I can do no less." He moved toward his ent.

"Your father had no choice. The desert was killing er!"

Khamed's head whipped around. "Very ironic, is it ot? A woman who wanted to stay could not. And one who can does not want to. You see, Doctor, you have verlooked one factor in all of this—Eudora's feelings. At one time perhaps she did love me, but no longer."

Turning, he faced Gerard squarely. "When she asked or your help, what did she ask for? Did she ask you to try o convince me to let her stay? Or did she beg you to help er leave with our child?"

When Gerard did not answer, Khamed smiled a bitter smile of triumph. "Your silence answers my question, Doctor. After the child is born, they will be released."

"Is that your final answer?"

Khamed turned and walked toward the tent. As he reached out his hand to draw aside the flap, he finally responded. "It is my only answer."

Chapter Twenty-Two

I have spoken with Khamed. After the birth he has agreed to release both you and your child. Mademoiselle, you don't seem pleased. . . .

Gerard's words echoed hauntingly in Eudora's mind. Three weeks had passed since he had come to her with the news.

No, she thought, picking her way through a flurry of dogs and children scurrying about the camp's center, she hadn't been pleased . . . she'd been devastated.

"Couldn't I leave next month, with you and Pierre?" she had asked, biting back her tears. The thought of being left behind was almost more than she could bear.

The man had nearly choked. "That is out of the question, young woman! Khamed was quite adamant of that point. He will not permit you to travel in your advanced condition, and as a medical doctor I most heartily concur with his decision. In fact, I'm afraid you are going to have to remain here at least another five or six months."

"But you said he has agreed to release me!"

"Indeed . . . after the birth. Surely you realize, for the sake of your health and that of the infant's, you must delay your departure for several months thereafter?"

Several children laughing and running in front of her startled Eudora back to the present. As one of the boys

369

cut across her path, her hand went protectively to her belly.

She was in her sixth month. How could she possibly endure the three months until the birth and another three after that—when each day passed was an eternity filled with memories and pain, longing and despair?

She had not seen Khamed since his departure with the raiding party. The evening of its return she'd heard the excitement and celebration, but had not ventured from behind her tent's walls. Neither had he come to her.

Sabatin had told her Khamed had been in the fields, overseeing the harvest. Yet as soon as the crop had been brought in, he'd left for one of the out camps. That he intended to avoid her was clear. And why not? The only interest he had had in her was the heir she would bear him. Now that Gerard had convinced him to relinquish his claim to their child, that interest was gone as well. He had apparently even rescinded his order regarding her bodyguard. It had been days since Eudora had last seen the man who had once been posted constantly at her tent's entrance.

The baby within her moved, and she winced as a foot or elbow lodged under a rib. She pressed her palm flat against her side and gently pushed the errant body part to a more comfortable position. At least she would have her child. When she returned to France the child would be her reason for living. And with the passage of time she would come to forget this place and the life she'd once led. She would go back to her own world and make in it a new life—one for herself and her son.

Lost in that thought which had become as a cant, mentally recited until it numbed her brain blocking out all else, she paid little heed to a gathering of men some distance away.

Yet at the opposite end of the compound a red-*sheshed* man could concentrate on nothing else.

Kahlil stood, his attention riveted not on the crowd of men, but on the creature in their midst—a magnificent white stallion. Two days ago, when the horses had been brought in by Khamed's order from the out camp, Kahlil had been struck with a sense of fear—as if the animal represented danger. Watching him now, the feeling became stronger.

Kicking and biting, the stallion fought frantically to evade the numerous ropes being tossed at it. With each noose that found its target to slip down his lathered neck, his frenzy increased, fueled, it seemed, by the spectators' shouts of approval and encouragement.

Kahlil stepped forward, then stopped. With a start, he realized his hand was on the revolver beneath his waistcloth. He swore silently. Khamed had ordered the horse broken, scoffing at the stories which proclaimed the stallion to be untamable. How could Kahlil explain overriding his orders, destroying the beast because of a personal sense of fear—an intangible feeling that the animal was endowed with an evil spirit?

Still, he knew. And from the depths of his being something beyond conscious thought warned him to act.

Kahlil shouted to the several men on horseback stationed to prevent the stallion's escape to the open desert, and gestured for them to move in. Until Khamed's return, he would have the beast removed from the camp.

As the mounted men approached it, the stallion reared. Its forelegs slashed the air. Teeth bared, ears laid back, it strove to drive back its new attackers.

Kahlil's anxiety grew. Watching as the men attempted to corner the horse, he felt as if he had already experienced what he was viewing. A feeling of helpless surrender to *quisma* overcame him. He tried to move, but could not.

Suddenly the stallion seemed to catch the scent of the open desert. Its nostrils flared. Hooves flailing at the men and horses in its way, it wheeled and bolted through an opening in the crowd.

In its path stood a lone figure, a woman bent clumsily in the sand, fastening a loose sandal strap.

371

Kahlil bounded forward, a cry of terror rising in his throat. But he was too late. He could not run fast enough, nor shout loud enough. He could only watch in horror what was about to happen.

Eudora heard a man's shout and stood. Turning, she saw a flash of white. There was an explosion of pain—and then nothing.

Khamed pulled back on the reins to slow Hasaad's pace.

Sensing they were near home, the stallion fought his control.

Khamed tightened his grip, and the animal reared in protest. Having anticipated the action, Khamed leaned into the horse, stroking the powerful neck as his gaze swept down the dunes.

Rising like an emerald island above the steaming sea of sand, the oasis both beckoned and repelled him.

His teeth clenched. As real as the stinging wind against his face and the hot sun at his back, he could feel her presence there. Nothing, not his desertion to the fields nor his retreat to the out camp, had been able to drive her from his thoughts.

He still awoke each night drenched in his own sweat, aching for the woman he'd once taken without deliberation. Like eating and drinking, burying himself within her had been but a response to a physical need.

But at some point he had fallen in love with her. How easy that admission was now—now that she was lost to him . . . and with her his child as well!

He kicked Hasaad angrily and the stallion leaped forward, plunging down the dunes.

Khamed rode through the bordering palms, his body tensing. Kahlil's message had requested his immediate return, but no mention had been made of trouble. Yet Hasaad was tossing his huge head nervously, his ears jerking in response to some intangible stimulus.

Khamed gave the horse free rein, and the black galloped across the oasis—straight toward his master's tent. In a rush of adrenaline released from instincts alerted, Khamed's heart began to beat faster.

Sabatin heard the sound of an approaching rider and rose from his haunches. There was no mistaking the black horse bearing down on him. Khamed had returned.

Leaving the cool shade of the tent's awning, he stepped forward and waited for the man to bring his horse to a stop. Gerard had asked him to say nothing. It would not be a difficult request to honor. Nervously he raked his fingers through his hair.

In one sweeping gaze Khamed took in the Frenchman's appearance. Even for Sabatin, his state was disheveled. The man looked as though he hadn't slept for days. The beating of his heart quickened. This was no rush of adrenaline—but fear. "What has happened?" he demanded, dismounting.

Sabatin felt as if Khamed's probing stare had stripped away every ounce of the control he had battled for two days to maintain. Unable to meet the commanding dark eyes, he stared at the reins Khamed still held in his fist. The knuckles were white. "Doctor Gerard is inside," he finally managed to murmur.

Khamed flung the reins in Sabatin's direction. In three strides he was at the tent's entrance, ripping aside the flap. Inside, his eyes squinted automatically to adjust to the room's dim light.

"*Ya sidi.*"

Dahr-la's hushed greeting caused them to fly open. At some unconscious level he noted the girl's red and swollen eyes. The fear which had welled within him at Sabatin's statement rose up like a stranglehold around his throat. He started to push past her, his goal the small room beyond.

"Please, my lord." Her small hand darted out to grasp

373

his arm. "Doctor Gerard is with her now. He asked that you wait."

Khamed stepped back numbly. "It is too early for the child to come." For an instant the thought stunned him. Then, furiously, he shook off the girl's hold. Something was seriously wrong. "What has happened?"

The girl drew back, lowering her head.

Khamed's senses returned fully. He grabbed her arms. "I asked you what happened."

A blubbering, sobbing cry tumbled forth. "She was trampled by a horse," she gasped, lifting her gaze. Her eyes were filled with terror.

Without knowing he was doing so, Khamed dug his fingers into the soft flesh of the girl's arms. The sound of Eudora's voice seemed to be exploding inside his head. *I hope I am thrown by a horse, kicked by a camel—anything! Anything which will prevent me from bringing into this world the product of—* "The child?" he growled, reeling with the realization leaping in his mind. "What of the child?"

Dahr-la emitted a strangled cry.

"Khamed, let her go! What happened was not her fault."

The male voice from the doorway hurtled him back to reality. Releasing Dahr-la, he spun to face the intruder.

Sabatin stepped into the tent. The sight of Khamed's brutal treatment of the girl swept away all fear, all hesitation, and all logic. The frustration and helplessness he had sought to contain were finally beyond control. He lashed out. "Eudora was trampled when that devil horse of yours bolted from its handlers. If there is blame to assign, it is yours. The damned beast should have been destroyed!"

Sabatin almost reveled in the look of agony that came to Khamed's face. Eudora had suffered so at this man's hands. That he should now suffer seemed somehow just.

Suddenly the curtain leading into the bedroom parted and Doctor Gerard appeared. Holding open the panel, he gestured for Dahr-la to enter.

Only after the girl had disappeared into the smaller room did he seem aware of the men's presence.

"Khamed. Monsieur." He looked from one to the other as he pulled his handkerchief from his pocket.

"How is she?" Khamed demanded, stepping forward.

"She is going to be fine. She has suffered a few bruised ribs, and there may be a slight concussion as well. . . ." Gerard's voice drifted into silence as he wiped his forehead.

Sabatin looked at Khamed.

The man was like a statue. Finally he spoke. "And the child?"

As if fearing the response, Gerard looked to the floor. "I'm sorry, Khamed. I did all I could, but the trauma was too great. However, there was no permanent damage. She will be able to have other children."

Khamed did not move. He did not even blink. "What was it?" he asked, his voice dead and hollow.

"Khamed, please . . . there is no point—"

"*What was it?*"

Gerard closed his eyes, sighing. "A boy." He opened his eyes. "It was a boy, Khamed. A son. I'm sorry."

The look Sabatin saw on the bronzed face was no longer human. Raw rage and pain had twisted Khamed's features into something animal-like. Robes whirling, he bolted from the tent.

Sabatin moved instinctively to follow.

"Let him go, Monsieur." Gerard's voice rang out from the drape. "There is nothing you can do. There is nothing any of us can do."

Suddenly the crack of a single gunshot echoed from across the compound.

"Dear God!" Sabatin looked to Gerard in horror.

"Indeed, Monsieur." Gerard shook his head sadly and turned to reenter the bedroom. "God is the only one who can help him now."

*   *   *

Khamed bolted upright. The sound which had awakened him had been no more than a change in the rhythm of Eudora's breathing. Still, he had heard it in spite of three days and nights without sleep. So tuned were his instincts, so powerful his will, a millenium's worth of sleeplessness could not have muted the sound.

He rose from the chair in which he had kept his vigil and stepped to the side of the bed. Eudora had been unconscious since his return. Gerard was at a loss to explain it, insisting her injuries were not so extensive. "Then why does she not wake?" Khamed's question had been a frustrated, curt demand.

"Perhaps she has lost the will to live." Gerard had lifted his hands in a gesture of helplessness. "If the mind so wills it . . ."

Khamed had dismissed the premise with a grunt of disgust. Gerard knew nothing of her. Eudora would live; her spirit was too strong.

But with each passing day his conviction had weakened. He had not left the room to eat, drink, or rest. And his only concession to Gerard's demands that he be granted privacy with his patient had been to turn his head as the Belgian had ministered to her.

Looking down at her now, Khamed felt his certitude waver yet further. She was so still and pale. Like translucent parchment, her skin was drawn tight over sunken cheeks.

He reached out to sweep aside a damp strand of hair, and winced at his fingertips brushed across her forehead. She burned with the fever that had raged since just after his return. But with the fever there had not come the expected delirium. She'd not thrashed about the bed, nor cried out in incoherence. Not one word had she uttered.

He turned away in agony.

"Khamed."

He spun and stared down at her. He saw her lips part. Again he heard his name, and at the sound of it he felt as if his heart had exploded in his chest. His doubts were beaten back, his fears defeated. With her simple utterance his new found love was reaffirmed, his trust rejuvenated, and his conviction reborn. He could not lose her now—he *would* not lose her now! Fate had destined them to be together. He would not let death come.

He took her small hand into his own. Without conscious knowledge he made words of the thoughts in his mind and the emotions in his heart. "I forbid you to leave me. You will live, Eudora. You will live for me. Without you I am no longer whole."

His words echoed in the room. They were not a prayer, nor a request, but a command . . . a command which came not from an arrogance that proposed to override reason, but from a conviction in a destiny that overruled it. There could be only one outcome, for none other was acceptable.

Through the weight of heat upon her body Eudora felt a coolness wash over her. Like a breeze, the merciful chill lifted the heaviness and she felt herself rise. Strangely, she did not fear the journey and surrendered herself to it. Khamed's voice was there to guide her.

"Eudora, I love you. I will not live without you! Please, forgive me. Love me. Love me as I love you."

From a half-sleep of exhaustion Gerard heard the rustle of the drape. He sat upright instantly and stared at the white figure silhouetted in the bedroom's entrance.

"Your vigil has ended. Go back to your tent, Doctor." Khamed looked at him. Slowly, a strange smile touched his lips. "I have seen to it that she will live."

Gerard shook his head and rubbed his eyes. The man before him bore no resemblance to the one of an hour ago who had languished in guilt and pain. This man stood with a regal air that caused Gerard to hesitate in confusion and awe.

As if sensing his feelings, Khamed beckoned to him. "Come. See for yourself."

Gerard rose and walked numbly to the doorway. He passed Khamed to enter and stopped. Somehow the heat in the outer room had not penetrated the bedroom. There was almost a chill in the air—as though a cool breeze had swept through the closed space. His fatigue seemed to abate. Curiously refreshed, he walked to the bed and looked down at the still form upon it.

No more than a brief glance was needed. Without touching her, he knew. She had broken a sweat. "How?" He turned to look at Khamed.

"You said she had lost the will to live. I have given her back that will."

Gerard stared at Khamed in silent bewilderment. The deep lines of fatigue which had etched the bronzed face had vanished. The black eyes so long reflecting a turbulence of the soul were tranquil. The anger within Khamed had been tamed and a void filled.

As he continued to study him, Khamed moved to the chair and sat.

In that instant Gerard realized what he was seeing. Khamed knew it to be so. Eudora would come back to him because he had willed it. He was now patiently awaiting that return.

In a dreamlike state Eudora passed from the darkness of unconsciousness into light. Her journey ended, she slowly opened her eyes to find herself immersed in a brilliant blue stare.

"Mademoiselle?"

"Doctor . . ." Weakly she smiled.

"This is a miracle! Do you know—"

"I know."

Gerard watched as sorrow flashed in her eyes. But

378

then, strangely, it was gone, replaced with complete serenity.

"I know everything, Doctor," she whispered. Though her voice was faint, it carried a curious strength. "While I grieve the life I have lost, I know it is only the physical embodiment which is gone. Its spirit has not been lost, but merely delayed. I know this because I have seen it and felt it. There is no need to grieve further, nor to dwell in the pain of the past. I now understand everything. You see . . . we have been to the place where spirits bond and souls speak."

Gerard stepped closer in alarm. She was talking nonsense—or was she? Her eyes were clear, her speech lucid. And the smile touching her lips was the same smile Khamed had displayed two days earlier when he had proclaimed she would live. No. This was no delirium. "We, Mademoiselle?"

Eudora nodded. "Khamed and I. We have just spent a lifetime together. We will have other children, children who shall know from their conception only love."

At that moment Gerard understood as well. He was a man of faith, and only faith could explain what had passed between Khamed and Eudora. What they had experienced and what they now shared transcended this world.

Suddenly he saw her expression brighten in anticipation. A moment later he heard the curtain part.

Utterly oblivious to his presence, Khamed approached the bed. He took her hand as though to welcome her back from a journey. "I have missed you, my love."

Gerard saw Eudora's eyes mist as she looked up at the man fate had made her captor, and whom love had made her destiny. He moved to the doorway and heard Khamed's voice.

"But this I promise you . . ."

Gerard passed through the drape. Reason told him he could not have possibly heard Khamed's next words. And

379

yet in his soul they sounded, clearly and resonantly.

"We will never be apart again."

Gerard smiled. No. They would not be parted again. Not in this world and most certainly not in the next. For where their love dwelled was in a third world. He left the tent with Eudora's words on his lips.

Where spirits bond and souls speak.

Epilogue

Sabatin made his way through the crowded café to an empty table near the river's bank. The warm July evening had enticed a wealth of patrons to his favorite spot overlooking the Seine. Placing the book he held beside a former customer's abandoned *demitasse,* he settled himself in the wrought-iron chair, watching as a coal-laden barge lazily made its way upriver. He then reached for the letter in his breast pocket.

The crumpled envelope, worn and soiled by the touch of many hands, bore no return address—only his name in care of *L'Étoile,* Paris. His editor told him it had arrived that afternoon, hand-delivered by a man who said that he'd been paid five hundred francs by a sailor in Marseilles to deliver it.

"Did the man happen to mention where the sailor was from?" he had asked.

His editor's answer; *Algiers,* had set his heart pounding.

"Eudora! It has to be!"

Ending the conversation abruptly, he'd raced from the building clutching the letter in his hand. He'd wanted to be alone when he read it.

He now took the spoon from the saucer on the table and used its end to slit open the envelope. His fingers trembled as he withdrew its precious contents. Unfolding them, he began to read.

Dearest Pierre,

I know you will be surprised to receive this, but I wanted to share with you my wonderful news. But first let me tell you of the events of the past ten months.

After you left us I felt as if a part of me had left as well. How terribly I missed you those first weeks—and still do! Your departure has left an empty place in my heart no one shall ever fill.

I cannot describe the agony I felt when we heard that one of Khamed's former prisoners had been bitten by a scorpion and had died en route to Ghardaïa. Khamed sent men to every corner of his territory to find out if it had been you—how I prayed it had not!

When we finally learned it had been du Bois, I was saddened but I could not help but feel the poor man had at last found peace. Khamed scolds me and that black scowl of his descends whenever I speak so! His unforgiving heart will not soften in that regard. I have, however, long ago forgiven du Bois his cruelty. I know it was his madness that created the evil in his soul. But enough of the sadness of the past.

Once my strength returned, Khamed and I planned the honeymoon he had promised—to any place of my choosing. You should have seen his face, Pierre, when I quite adamantly insisted he take me to Rio de Oro to visit Montar! He offered me jewels, but the only treasure I desired was far more precious and rare. I wanted to see the renewal of his friendship with Montar.

Begging forgiveness is something my proud husband has done neither often nor easily. But a part of him died that day Montar rode from our camp, and I believed to have that life reborn was worth the cost of his precious pride. When he agreed, I truly knew the depth of his love for me. When they embraced I wept openly with joy. And though Khamed fiercely denies it—

there were tears in his eyes as well.

And now for the real purpose of this letter—Khamed and I have been blessed with a son! Feburary 18th, Kadar Sabatin el Khamed entered this world in screaming indignation. Even Khamed will not deny he wept as he held his son for the first time. Kadar is his pride and joy. Our tiny baby brings out in him the gentleness and love he has always been capable of—but fought so hard to suppress. I wish you could see this arrogant desert warrior we both know so well tremble as he cradles his son in his arms!

I must confess it was not without difficulty that I convinced him to give his heir a Frenchman's name. But we compromised—for I was hardly thrilled with his choice. You can understand my reluctance to name my son in honor of Abd el Kadar—that celebrated emir of Algeria who led a holy war against the French a half century ago!

Pierre, I am truly happy. My life is rich, my heart fulfilled.

I will never forget you, my dear friend. You shall forever occupy a place in my heart. At night, look up into the sky and search for the star which burns the brightest. Far away beneath the same sky, I will be watching. When I see that star, I will know it shines with your greeting.

Be happy, Pierre. And may the one God—who has so many names—grant you the love and joy I have found.

Salaam al laikum, my friend.

> *All my love,*
> *Eudora*

Sabatin stared at the page and smiled. *Kadar Sabatin.* It had a nice ring, he decided. He lifted the book from the table and opened it. He'd received it only that morning from the printer—one of the first copies of his account of the Reguibat and their struggle for survival and freedom.

He turned to the dedication page. Running his finger lightly across the print, he recited its words by heart.

To Eudora and Khamed
Embodying their different lands, they have illustrated with their love that vast differences can be bridged—not by dwelling in one world to the exclusion of the other, but by dwelling in a third realm—the realm of love.

Closing the book, he smiled and looked up at the darkening sky. The sounds of the café and the river's traffic seemed suddenly to fade. He fixed his focus on the southernmost star just beginning to twinkle and whispered his reply to the woman he knew would be watching the same star.

"*Al laikum el Salaam*, Eudora."